# IF ANYTHING, THEN EVERYTHING

## BROKEN PLANES

### BOOK 1

## CAMERON T. MAY

Paperback ISBN: 979-8-9948542-1-1

Edited By Vivian N. Edits

Proofing & Formatting By Gail Delaney Editing Services

*To my Father: Thank you for being the best example of a man and a father I could have asked for. Your love and guidance has helped me become someone that I can be proud of. I love you, old man.*

*To my wife: You have been my rock since we met. Without you there is no telling where my life would be, but I know it wouldn't be as full of love as it is. I truly can't wait to see where life takes us.*

*To Levi: Son, watching you grow has been one of the greatest joys of my life. The dedication and drive you show in all aspects of life has made you one of my heroes. Love you, boy.*

*To A.J.: You have the most infectious passion and love for life I have ever witnessed. Thank you for being my compass during my storms, whether you realized it or not. Love you, girl.*

*To my kin: We all know there is too many of y'all to name. I want to say thank you all for the love and support. Y'all have done so much for me through all the years and I am forever grateful.*

*To my earliest readers/friends: Thank you all. Without y'all's support and positivity this train never would have reached the station. The positive feedback and occasional kicks in the butt have meant the world to me.*

*To anyone reading this: Thank you for joining this journey. In this book I hope you find a place to be you, whoever that truly is, and I hope this story entertains.*

## CHAPTER ONE

Jayce Torres stared into her reflection in the mirror of her vanity desk and gave a small smile at the piercing blue eyes that returned her gaze. She had always loved how her eyes contrasted with her soft, warm skin that carried just a hint of a golden hue. Other than her eyes and skin, Jayce had never cared much for her looks. Her features, to her, were too sharp and rigid, not rounded and soft like she thought they should be.

Shrugging, she went back to applying the black makeup she had scrounged up enough cash for recently. She had never had the money for anything vanity-related, so this morning was an experiment. Deciding that going intentionally smudged would look better than accidentally doing it, she continued giving light strokes to her eyeshadow with her index finger. Jayce flinched as she raised her arm too high. The sting of an unhealed bruise on her ribs made her breath catch. She rubbed at it through her thick black T-shirt with her clean hand. It wasn't her only bruise, just the newest.

Jayce had been bounced around foster home to foster home since she was born, each new house a fresh, yet familiar, hell. These last six months had been an experience she wouldn't forget if she lived a thousand years. Hector and Belinda, the owners of her current hell, had made life so unbearable that Jayce had nearly quit. But today?



Her phone lit up on her desk. Dreaming of leaving this place for college had always been a pipe dream until she submitted a sculpture to Texas A&M University Corpus Christi. They had seen something in her work that she never had and offered her a partial scholarship. She would have to get a job to pay for housing, but that was something she had planned to do anyway. Her heart began to beat faster. Dreaming of the day of her escape and it actually being here was near crippling.

*What if I fail? What if I have to come back?*

She shook herself. Looking in the mirror one last time, she nodded and stood. She walked to her bed, where a lone bag sat on the brown- and yellow-stained cream sheets. She sighed at her lack of worldly possessions and reached for the peacoat folded on the corner of the bed. She wrapped the coat around herself and let the warm embrace swallow her. Picking up her bag, she scanned the unadorned room one more time, hopefully for the last time, and walked out. The short, musty hallway was covered in photos of Belinda and Hector. Jayce, naturally, was absent from them all.

*Worthless. Stupid. You deserved it.*

The walls seemed to talk as she made her way to the front door. The mixed smell of tequila, stale cigarettes, and rotten laundry assaulted her nostrils. She wrinkled her nose and covered it with a hand as she pushed through the door. Jayce froze as she placed her hand on the doorknob. The warm feel of the fake metal let her know the outside was going to be another hot, sticky day in Texas. Opening the door, she stepped out into the day. The salt-tinted air she breathed in was her first true taste of freedom.

"Cali! Please, for the love of God, eat your breakfast! The bus will be here any minute!" Erin Walker said across the table to her pigtailed blonde thirteen-year-old sister. Cali looked from the burnt bacon to Erin.

"You know bacon isn't supposed to be black, right?" Cali asked, poking the meat skeptically. Okay, so Erin had never really gotten the whole cooking thing down; she could admit that. Though in her own defense, being a mom wasn't supposed to be in her cards. Four years ago, Erin received a call that changed her life.

*Mrs. Walker. This is Dr. Ramirez. There has been an accident.*

Cali saw the faraway look in her sister's eyes. Despite multiple jobs, Erin, who had always been drop-dead gorgeous, had always maintained a look of poise. Her red hair, though slightly frazzled, was always so close to completely put together. Her soft features were always accented by just enough makeup to know she was wearing some.

"Sorry, got distracted," Erin apologized. "Today is the tour." Erin had put off college when she had taken over guardianship of Cali. Now that her sister was old enough to be on her own, she was finally enrolled at TAMUCC for a theatre program.

"Is there any chance you're taking a culinary course?" Cali couldn't help but take a jab. Erin rolled her eyes. Cali loved her sister's emerald eyes; they reminded her of the high-priced gemstones. A loud honk outside made Cali bolt out of her chair. She shoved the bacon in her mouth with a crunch. Cali grabbed her backpack and threw it over her shoulder, kissed Erin on top of the head, and ran.

"Love ya! Proud of ya!" Cali yelled as she slammed the door behind her. Erin snorted. Once the door closed, she strode to her room. On her bed was her favorite light blue sundress.

"College, here I come!" she squealed as she did a little dance.


BEEP. BEEP. BEEP. BEEP. BEEP. BEEP. BEEP. The alarm had been going off for well over an hour, yet the occupant of the bed had barely moved. His large muscles twitched as if trying to wake the brain that refused. Leon Thatcher was a tall, muscular man with tanned skin from years in the outdoors. His right side was covered in tattoos depicting everything from Norse Mythology to 1980s video game characters. His left side was covered in roughly healed scarring and burns.

A veteran of the Army, he had trained himself to sleep through the heaviest mortar barrages. He realized that going to the bunker had become a chore, and if he was going to bite it, it might as well be in his sleep. He reached for his alarm

"Bastard," he muttered. Opening his eyes, he looked at the spot where his left hand should be. It'd been years since he lost that limb, yet every morning he always tried the same futile movement. It still burned in the mornings, a reminder of that abysmal day. Looking at his clock, he sprang out of bed.

"Damn." He was supposed to be guiding a tour for two incoming freshmen fifteen minutes ago.

"Double damn." This was supposed to be for extra credit. And boy, did he need it.

"Come on, Leon," he said, throwing laundry from his basket all over the room. "Stained. Stained. Oh god." He almost gagged as he pulled out week-old gym shorts. The smell was horrendous.

*God. What happened to me? This is pathetic.*

He finally found a pair of jorts, with only a small mustard stain, and a grey long-sleeve shirt that he was pretty sure he bought white. Getting the shorts on, he struggled to one hand his Velcro friction belt.

*Sweatpants and gym shorts from here on out.*

He took a quick look in the mirror, making sure his long blonde hair and beard didn't look like total hell. His bloodshot eyes stared back at him. "Whatever," he said, grabbing his phone and wallet and hustling out the door.


A black combat boot stepped onto the slightly steaming asphalt. Jayce pulled herself from the car, thanked, and paid the driver.

She was already perspiring from the late morning Corpus Christi heat mixed with her coat.

*I'd rather be sweaty than uncomfortable.*

She breathed in the salty air. The campus was adjacent to a beach, which she would love if she could ever force herself into a bathing suit. The water was usually warm this time of year, and she loved the view. But she had never quite had the confidence to go out into it. Just dipping her toes once in a while. She turned her head at some heavy footsteps. Before her stood a mountain of a man, tanned, tattooed with a bushy blonde beard and long hair. He was clearly out of breath.

"S-Sorry. I got a little behind on time." He took a few deep breaths to steady himself. Upon further inspection, she noticed scarring on the left side of his neck and that his arm was gone just below the elbow.

"It's okay. I just got here myself. My cab driver took the scenic route. I'm Jayce," she spoke as she extended her hand.

"Leon. Pleasure to meet you, J." He grasped her hand firmly, but with the gentleness one might pick up a bunny rabbit with. His hand engulfed her, and up close she realized she had to look almost vertically to meet his soft, brown-eyed gaze. "You from around here?" Leon continued, releasing her hand.

"Yeah, more or less. I've lived everywhere within a thirty-mile radius my whole life. What about you?" Jayce asked.

"Nah, Amarillo by birth. Jumped around with the Army a bit, wound up stationed in San Antone for a bit, and decided to come live at the beach. Surf and study, ya know?" He gazed at the low rolling waves. He shook himself to refocus on Jayce.

"Is-is the army where that happened?" She made a subtle nod to his arm. Leon tensed slightly, then relaxed.

"Where what happened?" he replied nonchalantly.

"Where you lost your arm?"

*Why did I even ask that? Stupid girl. Just shut up.*

Leon seemed to notice her internal strife and decided to go easy on her.

"I haven't lost it. It's right here." He pulled back his sleeve, revealing a nub. Looking at it, his eyes went wide in mock-horror. "Oh my god. Where did it go?" He frantically looked around them. Jayce, despite her internal thought, snorted. His smile was the warmest smile she had ever seen, not that she had much to compare it with.

"But yeah, someone thought I was too powerful, so they nerfed me."

*How is he so chill about his situation?*

"Whatcha majoring in, J?" he asked, looking back out to the gulf.

"I'm going to be an art major. I love to draw, paint, and sculpt. My dream is to be a traveling artist. Going from museum to..." She stopped herself and also turned her eyes to the gulf.

*He doesn't care.*

"That's a kick butt dream. Maybe one day I'll get to buy a J original." He winked. Jayce's face reddened; the sweltering heat doing absolutely nothing to help.

"Thank you," she said. "What about you? What are you majoring in, sir?"

"No need to call me sir, I work for a living." He chuckled. "I have no idea, honestly. Kinda just seeing where the GI Bill takes me. Runs out at the end of the year, so I don't know. I've been taking classes since I joined at eighteen. I am a fifth-year senior. Janitor, maybe?" He half-joked, though there was a pang of realness in his eyes.

"Looking like you do, it'd be at least head janitor." Both Leon and Jayce jumped as they saw the speaker was just a few feet from them. A drop-dead gorgeous redhead stood there. Her freckled pale skin almost glowed around a light blue sundress. Jayce looked over her further; her makeup was blended so well that it looked natural, helping to elevate her sharp features. Some of her hair was mussed, but that didn't stop Jayce from thinking,

*Okay. This is the most beautiful human I've ever seen.*

"Erin, I'm assuming." Leon reached out his hand, but Erin

knocked it away, wrapping her arms around him in a friendly hug.

"I am. And you must be Leon." Leon tensed and gave her an awkward pat on the low back. She released him and turned to Jayce, arms up. Jayce, to her credit, only flinched a little as she received the first hug she could remember. Though she did completely forget to return the hug before the taller woman let go.

"Sorry, I'm a hugger. And I'm so excited. I've been waiting for this day for a while now."

Leon flashed his warm smile.

*It doesn't quite reach his eyes. It's not fake, just unnatural.*

"It's okay. I'm just not from a touchy..." She thought of her bruises. Okay, not that kind of touchy. "family. But I one hundred percent understand the excitement! I've been waiting my whole life to get aw...to have my own place."

*Smooth.*

"Are you staying on campus too? Erin, right?" Jayce recovered.

"Yeah, it's Erin, and no. I take care of my baby sister, so we have our own place." She shined a pearly white smile. Erin noticed Jayce's oversized coat; it was adorable, but in the heat, she knew it was there for a reason.

"I absolutely adore your outfit; those leggings are sooo cute!" Erin said. Jayce looked down at her black plaid leggings.

*And here's where the bullying starts.*

Jayce braced herself for whatever insult followed. Only one never came.

"I wish I could pull off black, but on me it just looks forced. You rock it, girl!"

Jayce stared in confusion.

"Th-Thank you. Your dress looks pretty, too." She mumbled. Leon, realizing it was about to get a little awkward, interrupted.

"Sweet, well anyway, before we get started..." He looked around, eyes landing on a Mexican food joint. "Would y'all mind getting some food? Some idiot didn't wake up to my alarm, so I missed breakfast." Jayce and Erin snorted simultaneously.

"Sounds good," they responded in synch.

The steam and glorious smell of three meat fajitas blossomed across the table as the server sat Leon's plate in front of him. Jayce hadn't been able to order at restaurants growing up, so she declined. While Erin had originally not ordered due to "monetary constraints, but Leon had insisted and almost bulldogged her into letting him pay. She was now enjoying a plate of shrimp ceviche. The bitter scent of lime mixing with the fajitas made Jayce regret not ordering.

"So, what do y'all ladies like to do for fun?" Leon asked with his mouth overloaded with shrimp, steak, and chicken.

"I'm lame. Netflix or mall walking with my sister Cali. Oh! And listening to a good murder podcast," Erin replied.

"I guess I'm lame too. I listen to music, sketch, or paint. You said you surf, right?" Jayce added. Leon, apparently realizing his previous faux pas, choked down a bite so large it made Jayce's throat hurt.

"Hell yeah. Surfing is my jam. You don't know true freedom until you hit the perfect wave. The ones here aren't great; you have to have a big ol' long board to even stand most of the time..." His eyes took on a glossy *I'm no longer with you* look.

*I wish I had my sketchbook. Passion is so beautiful.*

Jayce stared at him.

"...but when you do. Pure bliss." He seemed to rejoin them hesitantly.

"That sounds incredible. The way you described it was beautiful. I would love to draw you sur—" Jayce froze.

"Heck yeah. I'm always up to take anyone to the beach. Maybe after the tour we can suit up and hit the shores, if y'all aren't busy?"

Jayce cringed.

"Umm, I have unpacking to do. I'll be really busy. But maybe another time?"

*More like never.*

Leon shrugged and went back to devouring his meal. Erin looked over at Jayce; she looked so hungry. Why didn't she order?

"Hey, Jayce, would you mind helping me finish this? My eyes were bigger than my stomach." She patted her nonexistent belly.

"Are you sure? I'm really not—"

"Oh, pish posh. Just have some. Save me from myself, please." While Erin hadn't eaten out in years and was salivating over the food, she could tell that the little thing hadn't eaten a meal in a while. She had that look that Cali got when money was too tight for any real source of protein. With a slow movement, as though waiting for her hand to get slapped, Jayce got a fork and got a piece of shrimp. Then quickly, before anyone could take it away, shoved it in her mouth.

*Oh my god! This is the most delicious thing I have ever tasted.*

Erin saw the girls' eyes go round as the plate; it brought a warm smile to her face.

"Thank you. It's delicious." Jayce said, not quite meeting the other woman's eyes

"Of course, babe," Erin responded, also digging back into the meal.

*Babe?*

After they finished, Leon settled up on the tab. And they walked outside, the warmth blasting them and immediately bringing Jayce's sweat back. She looked down the road at the archway to the campus...No, *her* campus. They began the walk to the school.

"I will pay you back." Erin almost pleaded. Leon shook his head and waved her off.

"I will legit burn the money if you do. It really was my pleasure, darlin'," he said casually. After a few minutes, they reached the bridge leading to Ward Island, where TAMUCC was located. Leon stopped them.

"Well, y'all... across that bridge starts your new life. What do you think?" he asked. His words put an otherworldly pressure on

Jayce's chest. She looked around and saw Leon and Erin both had a look of discomfort as well.

Leon stumbled forward and vanished.

"What the heck?" Erin asked as she took a step and disappeared. Bewildered, Jayce took a step. As she did, the wind around her stopped blowing and started to pull at her. She was lifted off her feet and pulled into a suffocating torrent of air.

"The plane has been crossed." One.
"So it would seem." Two.
"Shall I intervene?" Three.
"Observe, for now." Four.

# CHAPTER TWO

Jayce stumbled onto all fours alongside Leon and Erin into the white-as-snow, but warm-as-sand dirt.

*What the heck?*

Her head was pounding.

"Professor? Were we expecting more students?" A deep, gravelly yet soothing voice spoke. Erin, the first to look up, screamed in sheer unadulterated horror. Her body shook in sync with her screams as she slammed her eyes shut. Leon was on his feet in an instant, looking at the perceived threat. Jayce, getting some movement back, swiveled her head up and froze. Her hands shook in the pristine dirt.

*Nope. Nope. Nope. Not real. Not possible.*

She found herself unable to move, looking at the literal giant in front of her. An at least nine-foot-tall, shimmering azure troll stood in front of her. Its skin seemed oddly similar to a snake's. He was clad in a black suit, with blues, pinks, and greens seeming to run around it in a constantly random pattern.

"Hello, young ones. I'm afraid we did not have you on the list for this semester. Late entries, I do suppose," the speaker chirped, drawing attention away from the giant.

Perched on its shoulder was the oddest thing she had ever

seen, a human head with very dark facial...feathers? Where a body should have been was the body of an eagle-sized raven.

*What in the actual—*

Jayce's thought finished without her.

"Who the hell are y'all and where the hell are we?" Leon growled, fist clenched and jaw working.

"My dear boy, I am Professor Noctharim." He laid a wing around the giant's neck. "This is my good friend and colleague Jotun. And this." His wing flourished behind him. "This is Aetherion Academy."

Behind the otherworldly pair lay something Jayce in 10,000 years could never forget. A gigantic castle? City? City of castles? Made of the most flawless glass she had ever seen.

The spires and palisades went on for miles in glittering glamour. Shining in the most fantastic deep lavender she had, or would, ever lay her eyes on. Following up one of the spires, it seemed to touch the sky. The sky itself was impossible to understand. Unlike back home, this sky was small and claustrophobic. No, it was limitless, yet reachable.

*Impossible.*

It was perfectly lit with no true source. No sun, no stars. It carried the same shade as was reflected from the crystalline walls of the castle. But there was so much more. Floating around the glistening castle were pure, almost see-through platforms. They seemed to float aimlessly with purpose. A rainbow flew around one of the platforms. On closer inspection, it wasn't a rainbow; it was millions of fishlike creatures *flying?... swimming?...* through the air.

"What the hell are you?" Leon had spread his feet in a stance a professional boxer would feel comfortable in.

"Rude," grumped Jotun.

"My overly aggressive boy, have you never seen a troll? They truly are quite common around the planes." The bird man hopped back and forth dismissively. "Not knowing my species, corvathis by the way, is completely understandable as there are so few of us. Also, were you never taught that when walking, it is best practice to remain civil? Wouldn't do to start an inter-planer conflict." Professor Noctharim gnawed on his wing.

*Troll? Corvathis? I am definitely dreaming, at best, or at worst, hallucinating.*

Erin was heaving at this point; no doubt the ceviche would make an encore. The air felt wrong. Or not wrong. Perfect? The wind wasn't blowing, but Jayce felt the air moving. Both in perpetual motion and sedentary. It carried a wonderfully sweet aroma, like vanilla bean and gasoline. It shouldn't work, but it did. She noted that while just moments ago she was sweating like crazy, now she was comfortable, eerily so. Finally, Jayce willed herself to stand.

"How are we here?" she asked both the creatures, who, now that she stood, were somehow even more imposing.

Jayce didn't even notice that she was shaking like the last leaf on the tree in a hurricane.

"My dear, again, this is the Aetherion Academy, premier school of plane walkers. Oh my." Noctharim's explanation ended abruptly. He batted his wings a few times before taking flight. He came down eye level with her, floating like the world's most grotesque hummingbird. The corvathis eyed her; his dark pupilless eyes flashed red and black rhythmically.

"Oh, this is intriguing. Yes, very strange indeed." The head did slow three-sixties as he thought. Erin's screams had boiled down to sobs, and Jayce couldn't help but break contact to check on her. She knelt beside the other woman.

*How am I supposed to help her? I can't even comprehend what's happening.*

"It's o—We are fi..." Jayce couldn't finish either thought.

*It's not ok and there is a huge chance we are not fine.*

She rested her hand on Erin's shoulder and looked out into the courtyard. There was a fountain in the center that pulsed laser lights into the air in rhythm with unheard music. Surrounding it were trees so black they almost ceased to exist. Their leaves pulsed in rhythm with the fountain. She noted there was a gigantic sloth-like creature pushing a floating wheelbarrow filled with a pulsating mulch-like substance. It hummed in an altogether unfamiliar tone.

*Totally normal.*

"My dear Jotun, would you please assist the young ladies to their feet? I have noted some peculiar findings while scanning these...'Humans'."

Jotun lumbered forward and stretched out a skillet-sized hand. Despite every burning bit of will and self-preservation, she took his hand. It was slick but very warm, and his light grip belied his size. As he pulled, Jayce was thrown dozens of feet into the air. She let out a scream so loud that she would never bring it up upon retelling this event. Turning midair, she careened back to the snow-white ground. The giants' hands deftly caught her well above impact.

"Sorry, Itsy Bitsy, I forget how much strength I possess, and I overestimated your weight by a ton." Jotun looked bashful as he sat down the small woman.

"I-it's-it's okay, sir. Thank you for c-catching me." She flashed the troll a nervous smile, which he returned with a lopsided smile of his own, revealing a ground-down canine. The smile warmed her for some reason, like he was sorry for almost hurting her...

*No one has ever been sorry for hurting me.*

The giant then stepped towards Erin, who opened her eyes and howled in fear. She kicked the ground to get away, hitting herself on a pillar with a massive LED-like sign stating:

"Aetherion Academy of Plane Walking Excellence. EST. Time Immemorial. Current Headmaster: Professor Noctharim, Weaver."

Distracted by the sign, Jayce almost missed the next step. Jotun stepped toward Erin again, presumably to help her, but she screamed again.

"Get it away from me! Get away!" She kicked at the giant. The next events happened fast, and Jayce was never sure she got them in the correct order. Leon, seeing the troll get too close to the cowering woman, acted by throwing himself in front of the giant and swung his fist as hard as he could into Jotun's gut. Before his hit landed, the giant bellowed.

"Accepted." The hit landed with a very audible crack, but it was not Jotun who cracked.

Leon, falling back, bellowed in pain, eyes going wide and red. He pulled back his now ruined hand.

*Not again...I can't lose...not again.*

Leon's thought nearly paralyzed him.

Confusion and pain danced on his face as he analyzed the situation. With nothing else to do, he tried to kick the troll, but Jotun only grabbed him by his foot and brought the small human overhead. Grunting in the most hesitant growl, he began to swing the human down to the soon-to-be red-painted dirt. Watching the ground grow way too fast and feeling the somehow perfect temperature, unmoving breeze, blowing about his hair, Leon only had his thoughts.

*So, this is it. You didn't deserve any better.*

Jayce hyperventilated. Tears she wanted to shed clogged her eyes; her hands gripped her coat so tightly it verged on ripping. That's when it happened, the non-moving yet always moving wind stopped, yet grew so heavy as to suffocate her. Movement ceased. Smell ceased. Sound was gone except for the beating of Jayce's heart. She looked around. Everything, everyone was frozen. Erin, a look of pure terror on her face. Noctharim, halfway to Jotun, was frozen just before he could speak. Jotun had a look of pure regret at his action. Leon, a quiet calm behind the rage.

*He accepted the outcome?*

"No. no. no. This isn't happening. I don't want this to happen," she sniffled. She didn't know Leon that well, but this would mangle him even more, at best.

"I don't want anyone to get hurt!" she yelled so loudly that her ears popped. She flinched in pain as she felt the power in those words.

*What the hell? What was that?*

The world began moving without unfreezing. Leon was

pulled away from Jotun's grasp, floated away, and sat gingerly on his feet. His hand snapped and cracked back into place as it repaired itself.

*How in the world? This is wrong.*

Jayce felt her strength leaving her. Jotun's hand, now about to impact the ground, was raised and put in his pocket. A single tear burned her cheek in relief.

*What the....*

The world came to life all at once. Sound, smell, touch, taste. All the sensations hit Jayce at once.

"The hell was that?" Leon blurted.

"How did that—" Jotun wondered.

"Did anyone else—" Erin asked.

"No. Not again," Noctharim exclaimed.

All the words seemed to run together as Jayce lost her balance and passed out.

*Was it a dream? Am I still asleep? Did I stop time?*

"What happened?" Leon yelled, looking at his repaired hand. His eyes searched for the cause of the disturbance. He saw two human-sized schnauzers peddling what looked like hover bikes around the courtyard.

*Nope. Not that.*

Then he noticed Jayce was motionless. She looked so fragile; her arms extended wide, a pained yet hopeful look plastered on her face. Her hair was strewn on the snow-white dirt, almost in a circle; her blue streak still somehow perfectly laid across her face. Erin was the first to move. Despite her absolute terror, she crawled to the younger girl and touched her face. Jayce, even unconscious, managed to twitch at the touch.

"Hey, babe, it's okay. You're okay. Please be okay." Erin pleaded as she stroked Jayce's cool face.

Meanwhile, Jotun and Leon eyed each other wearily. Leon, seemingly to finally notice his hand, flexed it in amazement.

*How? This was done for.*

His breath caught in his chest.

*You would've been even more irrelevant.*

He shook his negative thought away, went to Jayce, and knelt by her side.

"She will be okay, after a while, that is," Noctharim chirped, landing on Jayce's stomach. "She has done something that very few have been able to do. It takes time for the body to recharge, so to speak."

*What did I do? Why can I hear but not speak? Why do they care?*

Jayce's thoughts swam around her head. She wasn't unconscious, at least she didn't think so. She could hear and smell the sweet scent around her. But no touch. There was no beating of her heart, no warmth, and no chill. Leon eyed the bird man with the gaze of a brother whose sister just got asked out in front of him. Noctharim, seemingly feeling the stare, turned to him.

"My dear boy, are you by chance someone able and willing to give consent for me to wake her?" Leon paused.

"What? Like her guardian? I was just her tour guide," Leon said.

"Hmm, tour guide. Could technically be considered a position of authority. I give tours, and here I am the highest authority." The corvathis hopped lightly on Jayce's belly in contemplation.

"Yes, that should do in a pinch. Young man, do I have your consent to rouse the young lady?" Leon looked to Erin, who nodded furiously.

"Why do you need consent?" Leon wasn't ready to say yes.

"Consent is required for most actions, whether it be violence, healing, or what have you. Did you hear my giant friend state accepted before you assaulted him?" Leon nodded. "That was him consenting to the fight. *Which he should not have!*" Anger was evident in the corvathis' voice as he ended in a chirpy yell. The giant seemed to shrink a few feet. Leon looked from Erin to Jayce's motionless form.

"Do it," Leon consented.

Noctharim hopped.

"I do very much appreciate it, and I'm fully confident she

will thank you as well. Now step back, you two, and do not be concerned." Hesitantly, very hesitantly, Leon and Erin stood and huddled together to watch.

*What is he going to do to me? He's going to hurt you.*

Jayce shuddered internally at the unwelcome thought. The professor walked his way up to Jayce's chest, placing his mouth at her forehead as his eyes began to glow a deep verdant green, and he chanted in low tones that carried endlessly. The odd wind grew heavy around the fivesome. Leon, without any thought, went to step forward, but was stopped by a massive blue hand on his shoulder.

Looking at the owner, he saw Jotun shake his head ever so slightly, mouthing, "It will be okay, brave one."

Fighting his instincts, he nodded and turned to Erin. She was not quite crying, but there were tears. Despite the tears, she was locked onto Jayce, drinking in every subtle movement Noctharim's head made.

The energy around them pulsed rhythmically. The tempo building with purpose as an ethereal grenade syringe, matching the glow of the professor's eyes, manifested mid-air. Erin watched in amazed horror as the syringe plunged and melted into Jayce's temple. She grabbed for Leon's hand, only gripping his nub. She held on regardless, watching with bated breath. Leon looked at the slender hand on his stump, and he noticed that she held it in a way that she felt connected.

*Why is she touching that? I don't even wanna see it.*

He struggled with his doubt as the events kept unfolding.

*Warm. I can feel warm again. Am I dead? Did I do okay?*

Jayce's head was filled with noise. Not external, but a symphony played inside her, and a synthetic beat pulsed through her. The music grew into a crescendo, beating louder and louder. Jayce shuddered in her mental prison. Her body came to life in convulsions. When the music stopped, her eyes flew open, and she yelped. Noctharim was mere inches from her face. The corvathis jumped in tandem, flying up to hover a foot above her.

"I do apologize, dear girl. I must be close for that particular ability to work. Your body should work now, but I do regret to tell you that a rather unfortunate migraine will hit you soon."

As he chirped, the migraine hit with the physical force of a runaway train. It drove the already supine girl farther to the ground. Her teeth ground as she shut her eyes against the not unpleasant lavender sky, hands digging into the soft white dirt. Noctharim looked between the three humans. Erin, still holding Leon's nub to ground herself, asked, "What was that? What did you do to her?"

"Easy." The professor started doing slow barrel rolls. "I simply jump-started her spirit. It was lost, and I helped find it; that is all. I do believe explanations are in order. May we retire to my office?" He flourished a wing towards the glittering, crystalline main castle. Leon and Erin nodded in hesitant assent.

"My dear young one, may Jotun carry you? While I am most assured that you could stumble your way, this will be much easier."

Jayce, still fighting the migraine, flinched. She didn't want to be touched. She didn't want to be a burden. Through gritted teeth and glued shut eyes, she consented.

"Yes, sir." She felt the giant approach her and kneel down.

"It's okay, Itsy Bitsy. I won't hurt you. No harm will come near you while I am around."

*No harm? His voice sounds sincere. He wants to protect me?*

With those thoughts, she was lifted with such ease and care it caused her yet more tears.

"Another sculptor." One.
"So it would seem." Two
"Shall I intervene?" Three.
"Observe, for now." Four.

# CHAPTER THREE

Jayce felt the low vibrations of the troll's trudging footsteps. She heard a whir of voices around her in odd dialects, yet distinctly English. Noctharim's wings buzzed nearby, and she could make out, barely, Leon and Erin talking.

"How long do you think we have been here? I have to pick Cali up from shop class in the afternoon. Oh god, what if she thinks I abandoned her?" Erin mumbled frantically.

"Professor Corvathis, how long have we been here?"

The buzzing of Noctharim's wings paused momentarily. "Well, boy *human*, until I get your plane connected here, I cannot be certain, and it's Professor Noctharim. Corvathis is my species, thank you very much," the professor grumped.

"Erin, you will be able to...Professor, is there a way to get home?" Jayce heard but could not see Leon question Noctharim.

"But of course, simply walk home." The giant's gravely baritone came to life.

"Professor, I must remind you of their reactions to the Nexus and us."

*Nexus?*

Jayce, despite the skull-splitting pain of the migraine, forced her eyes open. She saw Jotun look down at her, and he gave his very warm, lopsided grin. She smiled nervously back and checked her surroundings. The source of the myriads of voices became clear as she looked towards the strobing fountain with creatures, dozens of them, all milling about like a high school lunch period. There were humanoid goats, pigs, and bovines all in the same cyberpunk suit as Jotun, except theirs only pulsed one of a few different colors. There was pink, blue, green, violet, and somehow a black that pulsed on the black suit, giving it a trippy smoke pattern. Looking farther, she saw...

*No way...*

It appeared to be a disco ball slug; at least its skin was made of thousands of reflective mirrors. The fountain danced off it, causing prisms of light to form in the still, deep lavender sky as it circled it slowly. She wished she could stare forever, but the light, while beautiful, only intensified the pain in her head. Noctharim broke into her observations.

"Ah, yes. My findings. You three are likely from a previously unconnected plane. Oh, planes, also foreign. Planes are different realities. Your world exists on its own reality and timeline, while here in the Nexus, what this plane is called, is its own separate plane."

*Alternate realities? Is that possible?*

Jayce craned her neck uncomfortably to see Leon and Erin. Erin, at some point, had pulled Leon's nub around her shoulder, holding it there with her delicate hands, and leaned into him, whispering.

"Cali, I'm not gone." Her voice nearly shattered. "I have not left you." Leon, for his part, only looked extremely uncomfortable about touching someone with that arm.

*She knows it's gross, right? Why is she touching it?*

The thoughts were as evident on his face as the resolve to leave it there as long as she wanted him to. He flexed all he had left past the elbow in what was a futile attempt to encourage her.

"What is the Nexus, Professor?" Jayce fought the urge to vomit. Her stomach tied in knots as the words came out. So much pain.

"My office. Dear girl, wait for the office."

They made their way up the carved-from-ice looking glass staircase. When they approached the door, subverting expectations, the door slid open like a grocery store door, only vertically. The moving door revealed a void; no, it wasn't nothing, just the absence of anything she had ever known. Without a nanosecond of hesitation, Jotun plunged them into the void. Jayce was assaulted by the unfamiliar; there was moisture on her, but her skin felt like a desert; the loudest silence she ever heard rang in her ears. Her nerve endings burned, yet soothed her. Clearing the...*portal?* ...the sensations ceased, and her step down the rabbit hole began.

The crystalline walls of the hallway had all the colors of the rainbow swirling around them in bright neon shades, taking on a kaleidoscopic feel. The movement of the walls was hypnotic. As if to contrast with the brilliant colors, a low music played. It was—to the best of her ability to describe it as—a dark gothic choir accompanied by an altogether indifferent drum line. She didn't know the genre, but she knew she was a fan. Looking around more, she noticed the ceiling was unable to be seen, as if it forgot that physical structures had rules. As her eyes tracked down from the nonexistent ceiling, she saw doors sporadically placed on the walls with no landings in front of them.

*Now I know what acid feels like.*

She mused as she noticed something else; figures walked to the different doors. Sideways, up a wall. Jayce shook at the unfamiliarity. The figures jumped into the doors on the walls and disappeared.

*I've lost it, I'm officially around the bend.*

"Eww, that was slimy!" Erin shook herself in disgust. "I hate slimy, I hate sticky." She shivered again before looking out.

"Okay, that's it. I'm dreaming, or I'm dead, or I got drugged." Erin panted, her breath growing ragged as she again grabbed Leon's missing arm and draped it over herself, pulling him off balance.

"Hey..." Leon almost protested, but stopped as Erin's head lay on his chest. He laid his hand on her shoulder as he scanned the room.

*Over two hundred doors. If buildings match back home, one exit here and a potential secondary down the big fun house hallway.*

He continued to scan as Jotun moved again. The buzzing Noctharim landed on Leon's shoulder like a macabre parrot. Leon tensed, jaw flexing, but he allowed it, not wanting to release Erin.

"My rash boy, please do follow Jotun as there is plenty to do if we are to get you all enrolled and uniformed." Jayce froze...or would have if she wasn't being carried.

*Enrolled? They want us to stay?*

Jayce's lips twitched. An odd sense of excitement grew over her. This place was terrifying for sure, but it was so wondrous.

"Enrolled? I have to get back. I have to see Cali." She could see that punk's beautiful, freckled face, surrounded by her always in a mess of blonde hair.

Soft sobs accompanied Erin's protests. As they spoke, Jotun turned into a massive, almost empty room. The room's walls and ceiling were still glass, yet they carried the darkest obsidian color she had seen. There was a flawless desk with not even a speck of dirt upon it. Behind that was a shockingly white crystal perch that, upon entering, Noctharim flew to and stood like a sentinel.

"Please, do sit. I am under the assumption this will not be a quick discussion." As he spoke, he flourished a wing, causing glass to melt slowly from the ceiling and begin to puddle. The three humans watched in amazed terror as the puddling glass bubbled and formed. In two ticks of a clock, a pristine three-person couch had formed. Erin recoiled into Leon.

"Yup, I'm with you, Erin. We've been drugged," Leon stated, his eyes round and mouth flopping as if a fish would out of water.

"I'm going to sit you down, Bitsy," Jotun cooed.

She looked at his big, goofy, toothy grin and nodded. Gently, he sat her on both feet before letting go. She stumbled instantly. Jotun, seeing her about to fall, grabbed her shoulder. Jayce winced in pain as he managed to grab her fresh bruise. On instinct she jerked away and spun on the troll, shaking and eyes teary and wide.

"Bitsy, I..." The giants' eyes were as wide as the shivering girl.

"I-I'm okay, sir. Just on edge. You didn't hurt me."

*He didn't hurt me.*

The relief and understated joy in Jotun's eyes that she was okay made her feel a deep warmth in her chest. Erin, watching the whole event, pulled Leon's ear to her mouth.

"She's not okay. That flinch wasn't from his grab." Erin's breath was warm on his ear, causing the hair on his neck to stand at attention.

"I know...I know," was all he replied, fire in his eyes.

"Yes, yes. She is fine, now, if you would please sit. You as well, Jotun." He finished speaking as more glass melted down and formed an oversized recliner.

Leon and Erin walked over and helped guide her to the couch.

*They know how worthless you are. So easily broken.*

Jayce tried to stop the thoughts. She always tried...

The others helped Jayce to a seat on the rock-hard glass couch. Only it wasn't hard. It could've been made from the finest down feathers for how soft it was. Despite herself, Jayce leaned back and took a breath to feel comfortable for the first time in what seemed like ages. The comfort even eased the pain in her skull. The others took their seats, Leon bouncing up and down in curiosity, his intrigue seeming to pique for the first time, while Erin sat straight back, legs crossed.

*She looks so strong. It's not real, but she's trying.*

Jayce thought as Noctharim spoke.

"Very good then. Allow me a moment to welcome you all to the Aetherion Academy. Ah, introductions have not been made for you all." He stared expectantly at the trio. They shared glances. "Come, come, don't be shy."

Leon took a breath. "Leon Thatcher."

Erin shifted and exhaled.

"Erin Walker."

"Walker? How fitting," Noctharim said in an amused chirp. She smiled halfheartedly.

He turned to Jayce.

"Jayce Torres, sir."

"Very good then. Okay, I'll give a brief explanation, then questions, if you please." The three nodded as Jotun lumbered over and took his seat as well.

Hopping back and forth on the perch, Noctharim explained.

"So, as I and the sign outside has said, this is a school for plane walkers. As partially explained earlier, planes are different realities. Plane walkers have the ability to step across this threshold."

Jayce's jaw dropped, and she began fidgeting.

*Different realities. Is that really possible? Bird man head, yup, possible.*

Jayce saw Erin looked beside herself in concentration.

"Yeah, walking across different realities sounds like my typical Thursday." Leon rolled his eyes in disbelief despite what he could clearly see.

"Sarcasm, brave one, does not make for meaningful conversation," Jotun chastised grumpily.

Leon, despite the dressing down, puffed his chest at being called brave.

"Moving right along, this plane, the Nexus, serves as an intermediary connection between most planes. Your plane, however, is or was unconnected. Though I cannot explain why currently." The corvathis swung upside down on his perch, his raven hair and wings flopping towards the floor.

"Perhaps yours is a new plane...no, unlikely. A riddle for later, I suppose." He swung himself back upright, gnawing on his wing. Jayce couldn't help but giggle at the feat of gymnastics. Leon tensed, waiting for Jotun to get onto her as well, but it was in vain. The troll only flashed a warm grin.

*Wow, favoritism already.*

"Professor..." Erin's calmly frantic voice broke in, making

Jayce jump and Leon look over. "I have a question. Why are you able to speak English?"

Noctharim scratched his forehead with a talon, one of his small facial feathers coming loose.

"English? Hmm, by context of speech, I assume that is your verbal language. That is easy. I do not, in fact, speak your language nor you mine." He flew over and landed on Jotun's massive blue head.

"Me and my dear Jotun do not speak anywhere near the same language. Plane walkers possess the innate ability to translate will and intent of the native tongue into coherent speech. So to be technically correct, we are all speaking Jotun words, which, if I remember correctly is grunts and roars, yes?"

He finished by plopping on top of the giant's head sideways, as if to get comfortable. Jayce and the others look at each other, absolutely dumb struck.

*I'm grunting? How does the professor explain this as if it is mundanity we should all know, without being overtly condescending?*

"Yes, Professor." Jotun's voice boomed off the walls. "I hear grunts and roars." His eyes twinkled at Jayce, who couldn't help but return it. "To hear Bitsy roar is quite amusing as it does not fit her minuscule frame." He laughed, the sound felt physical as it pleasantly vibrated her chest. She felt warm. She felt...safe? Jayce tried to think of the last time she felt this way.

Noctharim flew back to his perch and squatted down.

"Along with the plane walking that we help train and amplify, we offer many courses related to engineering, energy work, espionage, etcetera. Any skill that may help keep a student healthy and productive on their extra-planar excursions." He swung a full loop as he finished.

"Any questions?"

Erin looked from Jayce to Leon before nodding to herself.

"Sir, I need to get home. I need to look after Cali, my sister." Her muscles tensed, and her mouth went dry waiting for a response. Noctharim stared at her, allowing a heavy silence to fall over the room. Jayce felt the tension, felt Erin's frustration. Shakily, she rested her hand on the other girl's arm.

*She doesn't want someone like you touching her. She's disgusted.*

Crestfallen, she slowly tried to slide her hand off, only for Erin to grasp her hand firmly, fingers interlaced. Jayce's eyes nearly bulged at the action. Erin's hand was so warm, sweaty, but warm. She could feel the beautiful redhead's heart pound in anticipation. Professor Noctharim let out a chirpy laugh.

"But of course, my dear, naturally we will get you home to pack," the professor agreed.

Erin's grip tightened. "No, sir, I need to stay with my sister. I'm all she has."

Noctharim hopped. "Will she be joining you for schooling? I am going to assume she is younger. We don't normally allow younger chil—"

"No." Erin's voice cracked. "Please, just let me go home."

The professor flew to her lap, landing lightly and peering up at her. "Dear girl, I understand you want to go home, and even though initiate students tend to stay on campus, as their walking is not trained, there are those that travel to study." He looked at the other two humans.

"Oh my, I have indeed stumbled upon a rare faux pas of mine. We, Jotun and I, would much appreciate it if you three would study with us. As we have not had an unconnected appearance in some time. And you..." He eyed Erin. "Should you decide to study here, I can personally walk you to and from the Nexus. And build your personal schedules around your, I'm quite sure, lovely sister." Erin's chest froze mid-breath.

Noctharim added

"We can show you three the true world, where if anything is possible, then everything is possible."

"The headmaster wants them." One.
"So it would seem." Two.
"Shall I intervene?" Three.
"Observer for now." Four.

# CHAPTER FOUR

"How do I enroll?" Jayce's mouth moved a thousand miles faster than her brain. "I want to stay here. To study. This place is so unreal but fantastic."

Leon tightened every muscle he possessed.

*Really kid? Just gonna drink the Kool-Aid.*

He looked from her to Erin, Noctharim and landed on Jotun.

"What do you do here?"

The troll nodded his head. "I am what is referred to as the War Master of the Academy. I help to guide those with a high aptitude for war or military-like abilities."

Erin swiveled on him, and the warmth left her voice.

"So it's a freaking military academy?"

Noctharim flew to Jotun's shoulder. "Not hardly, my dear. We do indeed train those with abilities best suited for the military, but that is one part of the academy. Further explanation: we do offer contracts to students, some military, some engineering, some mysticism. Basically, any need any plane has, there is a student here who may be of assistance. In return for the contract, the student receives credits to spend on special training with seasoned walkers."

Erin nodded as if that made perfect sense.

"Naturally, basic lodging, food, and uniforms are provided."

Jayce froze, her mouth getting wet.

*Free food? My own place?*

"So, I would like to revisit how to enroll, Professor."

Noctharim eyed her.

"It is a very hard, very taxing process...some, they do not survive it." The three humans all stiffened and looked amongst themselves. Leon, straightening his back, gave the professor a long stare down. Jayce felt the palms of her and Erin's hands sweat. The rhythm in her chest got quicker.

"Is it really that bad?" There was an edge to Leon's voice.

Noctharim chirped in laughter.

"Not at all, my gullible three. Simply state you want to study here, and you are enrolled in the initiate program." Jotun's shoulders heaved with silent laughter. Even Leon couldn't help but let out a strained chuckle.

"Professor Noctharim, I am the sole guardian of my sister. This is"—she gestured around the alien room—"all so unreal. None of it should exist. I want to go home...I want to go home, sir."

The professor nodded. "Understood." He looked at the other two. "And you—"

"I want to study here." Jayce almost bounced as she spoke, out of nervousness, but also excitement.

Leon rocked on the couch in contemplation.

"Why are you stayin', J?" Leon turned those red-shot brown eyes on her.

"I don't have anything to go back to. If I'm going to be anywhere, why not here?"

Leon bobbed his head back and forth in agreement.

"Screw it, I had a date with a six pack and bad TV, but I can push that back. I want to study here as well."

The professor flourished his wings in what was obvious amusement.

"Very well. On to the agenda. Brave one, I shall have you do an examination with my dear Jotun."

Leon eyed and hesitantly nodded at the troll, who returned the gesture.

"Erin, I shall take you home to be with this wonderful Cali you are so fond of."

Erin nodded her head vigorously, threatening tears again as she squeezed Jayce's hand lightly.

"And you, my dear..." His black eyes lingered on Jayce, analyzing. "You shall have a tour of sorts of the halls and grounds."

Her eyes went saucer-shaped again. "A tour?" she whispered.

"Of sorts, my dear, of sorts." He hop-flew to Erin's shoulder. "Are you ready?"

Erin nodded firmly as the air began to thicken. There was no noise, no disturbance. Erin and Noctharim were just gone. No trace that they had ever existed here remained. Jayce, who had been sitting closest, jumped, bumping into a flabbergasted Leon. His mouth dropped to his collarbone.

"What in the actual f...heck was that?" He caught himself and glanced at Jayce apologetically.

"The professor said he would walk her home, and so he did. You must be more observant, brave one." Jotun lightly admonished the former soldier. His gaze softened as he looked at the small girl with her peacoat that could fit the muscular male sitting next to her.

*So cute. So fragile. So...sad.*

"You will need to go into the lobby to meet Zynka. She will take you around campus, get your uniforms, and get you settled into you all's room." Jayce cocked her head quizzically.

"Who is 'you all', sir?" She bit her bottom lip hard.

"My mistake. It is not a room, Bitsy." She blushed at the name; it felt truly warm in her chest. "It is more a small castle of its own with four rooms. You and Zynka will stay on the upper floor while Leon here stays on the first." He paused. "There are impassible protections put on each room."

Jayce let up on her lip, a slight taste of iron in her mouth.

"What does Zynka look like?" she asked, standing.

"You will see her. Oh, and if it pleases you, she is a fledgling stealth initiate, so build her confidence as she will more likely than not be trying to hide." Jotun smiled at the girl as the doors were sucked up and she, with nervous optimism, stepped outside.

As the door shut, Leon looked over at the giant who, not an hour ago, had tried to kill him. Jotun looked back and winked as a holographic screen materialized and writing scribbled across it.

"Young man." He stood and extended his hand to Leon. "In the events of today, it seems introductions were not made. I am Jotun, War Master of Aetherion Academy, Head Advisor to Professor Noctharim, and the Infotechnic."

Leon stood, feet shoulder-width apart, shoulders pulled back as he raised his hand to meet the giants.

"I'm Leon Thatcher, fifth year senior, surfer, and...no, that's about it." They grasped hands quickly, but firmly, Leon's tough bronzed skin mingling well with the azure scales.

After the greeting, Jotun returned to his seat and gestured for Leon to follow suit.

"Tell me, Leon, what are your aspirations? What was your goal before all of this?"

Leon flinched at the question.

*Aspirations and goals?*

"I really didn't have any. I was just kinda riding the wave, ya know? Seeing where life took me." The scribbling on the holoscreen was rapid. He gave it a nervous glance. "What is that and how is it writing? Voice record?"

Jotun looked in thought for a moment.

"It is a holoscreen. In simple terms, it is our database. Collective knowledge is stored here, and no, it does not record voice. As I said earlier, I am an infotechnic. My unique ability is to create and maintain the holonet. So what goes into my mind is written in the system." He tapped his thick skull with a thump. Despite all the other weird crap, Leon bit on what he thought was most interesting.

"Unique ability?"

Jotun nodded.

"Most, presumably all, plane walkers hold a unique ability, some grand, some chaotic, some..." He bobbled his hands up and down.

"So what Jayce did out there? Is that something anyone can do, or a unique ability?"

Jotun shifted uncomfortably. "I would prefer Noctharim to explain that, but, as this is an open forum, what Jayce did is called sculpting. And it is exceedingly rare. Most definitely, the reason the professor wanted the three of you to stay. An untrained sculptor can destroy whole planes by accident."

Leon looked on without an ounce of understanding.

"Hmm, what it technically boils down to is that sculptors can rewrite the current plane, its logic, its physics, and its events, but it comes with a heavy toll, as you saw."

Leon's gut rolled over, his skin getting gooseflesh at the implications. A hopeful glimmer hit his eye as he stared at his stump. Jotun regretted his choice of words, or lack thereof, immediately.

"Young Leon, I should explain deeper. By changing events, I only mean in the moments she has perceived..." His eyes took a look that only those who have been to the darkest corners can. "What has happened has always happened. I am sorry for the confusion, young warrior."

The glimmer of hope shattered. He slammed his back against the couch, head drooping to his chest.

"Whatever wasn't possible ten minutes ago isn't possible now. Nothing changed." The room grew full of depressing silence. Both warriors on their own battlefield.

Jotun cleared his throat.

"So, warrior, what was your career or desired career?"

Leon wiped at his eyes. "Really nothing special, I wanted to design and sell surfboards on the beach. Ya know, just stay away from all the"—he gestured to nothing, muscles relaxing—"everything." He popped his fingers with his thumb, now gazing out deep in the abyss.

*You don't deserve...*

He shook the thought away. The troll, understanding the thousand-yard stare, took a leap to bring the soldier back.

"Surfing. The word is foreign to me. What is that?"

Instinctively, Leon reached into his pocket and pulled out his smartphone.

"Duh, never mind..." He showed the phone to Jotun. "Back home with cell service, I could've brought up a video. Useless now."

*Useless...*

The giant rose from his chair and extended his hand to the device. Shrugging, Leon handed it over, unlocking it on the way. The giant returned to his seat and plopped down.

"It's not quite useless. It has a connection."

He stared at the phone in contemplation before pressing it against his head. The writing on the screen increased to near light speed. It flashed and hummed in odd shades of muted colors before stopping completely after a few moments. Jotun fell forward out of his chair, not catching himself before his head impacted the dark crystalline floor. The shockwave the fall caused knocked Leon over on the couch.

"Crap! The hell was that?" He mused that he was really putting mileage on that phrase as he bolted toward the giant.

Kneeling down, he went to put a hand on the massive bald scaly head, but stopped short. His hand hovered there for a moment before he resolved himself to lay it on the slick dome.

"Uh, hey, big guy. You good? Don't be dead. That'll add to my abysmal track record." He flexed his jaw as he shook the troll's head.

"I'm not dead, squishy man." The troll's gravelly baritone vibrated the floor it spoke into.

He rolled his massive body over. Leon stood and offered a hand. Jotun's engulfed his, as he used absolutely zero of Leon to get upright. Heads above Leon's 6'3", the giant dwarfed him. Jotun released the handhold and straightened his suit. As he touched it, the darting colors seemed to congregate on the spots, like one of those old electro balls. The troll wobbled over to his chair and fell into it.

"What happened? Why did you shut down?" Leon, concern evident, asked while striding to the worse-for-wear giant. Even sitting, he was still heads taller than himself. Jotun waved away the concern dismissively.

"I synced the database from your plane to ours. Powers have a cost, and I paid mine. I was not under the impression your world would have that much data."

Leon flinched, and his eyes grew wide as his face reddened.

"The whole internet? You took the whole of Earth's internet into your head?" Jotun nodded.

"Two things, young warrior. One, how has your species survived? Two, what in the actual hell is wrong with your species?"

Leon looked everywhere but at the troll, realizing how much messed-up stuff he had just absorbed in mere seconds.

"So, the Earth's internet is available here? I can show you surfing." Leon smiled with more cheese than a proper pizza.

The giant saw the deflection and allowed it. With a twist of his whole sausage-link fingers, the holoscreen doubled its size, and he pointed to it.

"I have made it like one of your touch screens. It should work similar to what you are used to."

Leon dug in and pulled up the best surf spots around the world, delving into rating them and critiquing the surfers' form. Jotun watched the boy more than the screen after a few videos. The passion in his face as he watched people tubing, surfing the barrel of the wave. After the surfing videos came gaming, automotive, and weaponry videos. Around thirty minutes later, the new shiny wore off, and Jotun waved the other man to the couch. Leon sat, muscles relaxed and calm. Jotun truly wished the next question to be asked wasn't as necessary as it was. It was going to crack this brave young man, more than his hand breaking ever could.

He asked quietly, "How were you maimed?"

Every muscle that Leon possessed clinched so tight that it could be used to dam Niagara Falls. The clenching and grinding of teeth echoed through the room, though Leon did his best to answer calmly.

"Wrong place, wrong time."

Jotun let out a low growl.

"It is normal for warriors to hide from actions taken in the dance of blades. We are taught to take orders, take lives, but not how to live when the song ends. But I need to know. I need to know your mental state so I can properly assess you."

Leon wrestled with his thoughts, flexing his hand tight. His left nub twitched as the owner tried in vain to flex it as well. He took a few deep breaths to steady himself; his body took the command and went limp.

"I was...We were on mission in a downtown area..." *Breathe.* "We were there to get the latest big bad or whatever crap they peddled that day." *Clenched fist.* "We were going down an alley, me and my platoon." *Heavy blink.* "It was supposed to be an in-and-out. Home in time for dinner style gig." He chuckled darkly. The target got tipped off by a turned interpreter." *Teeth gnashed.* "When we got there, he was ready." The sounds of gunfire lit up in Leon's head, causing twitches. "They were set up. Had fixed defenses. We were on foot. The gunfire..." A small shadow of a tear blossomed. "It lit up the night sky; the burnt powder, body odor, and fear were the only scents." The tear grew. "I was ordered to find cover in one of the buildings..."

He tried to take a deep breath but choked on a sob instead. His voice was so quiet that Jotun had to strain to hear.

"I always...and I mean *always* checked for door traps. Always." The sole tear slowly made its way into his thick beard.

"The firefight, the yells, the explosions...I got...I got scared... I shouldered into the first door I found...I was met by a flash of light and a searing, burning pain, I can still feel." The tears came in earnest now.

"It knocked me out, and when I woke up...there was nothing. Smoke, ash, and stale gunpowder. My platoon...They didn't...

make it." He broke down in deep, heaving sobs. "They didn't even bother killing me..." Leon wiped hard at his pained face, he tried to blink, to stop the tears.

*I always told you that we were weak. It shouldn't have been you who made it.*

His sobs deepened at his own internal voice. Leon twitched hard as a slick, scaly hand lay on his stained jorts.

"No warrior from any battlefield need hide nor be ashamed of one's tears." Jotun made eye contact with Leon, staring hard. The pair of warriors mentally returned to their own battles, and the silence became comforting.

"They have linked data with Earth." One.
"So it would seem." Two.
"Shall I intervene?" Three.
"Observe for now." Four.

# CHAPTER FIVE

The smell of burnt bacon and iron filled Erin's nose, and a wave of nausea doubled her over. She waddled to the trash can and made use of the liquid resistant bag. Noctharim, meanwhile, had jumped to the table and pecked at the bacon and toast Cali had left that morning.

"Hmm, this protein has quite an odd taste. Sodium and ash. Not entirely unpleasant, I suppose. This grain, though." He ate the two slices of toast rapidly. "That was rather enjoyable."

He looked at Erin, who had finished her...expulsions and had headed to the sink to wash the ick from her hair.

"I do apologize, my dear. I have been walking for many, many eras, so I seem to have forgotten the toll it takes in the beginning. Silly of me, really, as when we walk, we tear through the literal wall of one existence into another. So again, I apologize."

Erin bent over and drank from the running faucet and rinsed out her mouth.

"It's...many eras? How long is that? How old are you?" She popped a hip on the counter, folding her arms.

"How to tell in your time...Do you have a time piece? Or know how your days' work?"

Erin frowned.

*Do I know how our days work? Is he serious?*

"Our planet rotates itself and then rotates as a whole around a sun."

Noctharim gnawed the tip of his wing. He pointed at a window.

"Would you be a dear?" Erin hesitated, then walked to the window and opened it. As the corvathis flew out, she mused.

*Close the window, call a therapist, and lie down.*

She repeated the mantra with her hand on the window as she heard the front door open. Cali came into the kitchen and froze, eyes round.

"Uh, hey, Erin, I was...I thought you were gonna be at school," Cali squeaked.

Erin's blood ran like lava. *Skipping school!*

"What in the world are you doing here? I thought *you* were supposed to be at school."

The younger girl winced.

"I..." There was a loud, shrill scream from out the window, as Noctharim flew in quickly, hitting the table hard enough to rock it.

"Well, I dare say your neighbor has never seen a corvathis before either. And around four billion of your years."

Erin stared blankly at the professor. The professor sniffed as he saw Cali. The smaller girl was in jeans and a T-shirt with a rhinestone skull and wearing flip-flops. Her freckled face and wild blonde hair were a sight for the old bird.

"My dear, I believe introductions are in order." He spoke to Erin, still eyeing the younger sister. Cali returned the stare, studying the soft feathers of the bird man's face, his raven-like hair, and wings that blew slightly from the open window.

"Oh, uh, hmm..." Erin was trying to think of how to explain when Cali acted. She ran to the table, scooping the professor up like a baby, stroking his nose with her finger.

"He's sooo cute! Can I keep him?"

Noctharim almost purred. He made eye contact with Erin,

who looked apologetic at the slight annoyance the professor showed.

"See, young Erin, this! This is how a venerable corvathis is to be greeted." He nuzzled into Cali's neck. She giggled at the tickle.

"Cali, I, uh...He's...I'm not su..." Erin couldn't fathom the imagery of her baby sister just babying a, she assumed, extremely powerful multiversal being. Her jaw was loose, yet with some resolve, she kept it shut. The young girl sat down, putting the professor on her lap towards her.

"What's your name? I'm Cali. Erin over there is my sister, and we live together. Where are you from? How did you get here? And why do you look like a human head bird? Not being mean. You're cute, but different. Different isn't bad, it just—"

"My dear Cali, when in conversation it is widely accepted practice to ask a question, accept an answer, and then ask another question." Noctharim cut her off.

Cali's eyes started to fall. Quickly, he added,

"However, given the exceptional greeting you gave me, I shall answer in turn. I am Professor Noctharim, Headmaster of the Aetherion Academy, School of Plane Walking Excellence. Me and Erin..." He looked over to Erin, who was rubbing her shoulders, not sure how the next bit would play out.

"We walked here together. I am a corvathis, it's my species, as yours is human." He exhaled.

"What is the ae-aet-the Academy?" She scratched behind his wing as she spoke. Noctharim leaned into it as he responded.

"It is an academy that teaches plane walkers, well, how to plane-walk. Walk across planes of existence; that is. We also teach other useful skills and abilities. I was actually trying to convince your sister to join as a student. I even offered room and board at the Academy, though it is standard, I suppose."

Cali snapped her eyes to Erin.

"Convince?"

Erin put her hands up, stalling the girl.

"I was gonna say no, you know I wouldn't let..." Cali trampled over the words.

"He had to convince you?!" The small girl yelled so loud that Noctharim took flight in shock.

"My girl, was that entirely necessary? This room is not that large." While hovering, he picked with his talon at a formerly unnoticed earhole below his wing.

Erin, having also jumped, flattened her hair as if no one saw it.

"I'm sorry, bird-o, but I can't. Someone related to me would join a magical academy and bring her favorite sister without a thought. Are we really related?" Cali stared at her big sister; nostrils flared.

Erin, in shock, swiveled her head between her sister, a corvathis, and back again.

"What the hell? I am still in shock at what I have seen today. I do not need you yelling at me! And I wouldn't leave you! So, of course, I said no." She not quite yelled back; she knew her composure was about to shatter completely.

*You will not break. You will survive.*

"Well, my dear, Cali could always join us. I cannot allow her to join courses; however, she could stay with you at the dorm. Maybe even learn from this old weaver."

Cali bounced.

"Yes, yes, yes. I wanna go. What is a weaver? What should I pack?" she asked.

Noctharim grinned widely at the enthusiasm.

"A weaver, my exuberant child, is an individual who can stitch together the planes. That was one priority of mine upon landing here was to connect the Nexus, my world, to yours. And to pack you—"

Erin glared so hard it broke the professor's train of thought. He slammed his mouth shut.

"You will not be packing." She swung her withering gaze. "We will not be going to the Academy." Swivel back to

Noctharim. "Thank you for the ride, walk, whatever back. Now please get out and leave us the hell alone," Erin sputtered.

*This is too much. It's not real. It's not.*

Her eyes watered yet again, threatening tears. Cali, seeing her sister on the verge of finally breaking down, was oddly cathartic. She knew her sister was human, and this proved it. She slowly walked to her sister and wrapped her so tight she heard Erin's breathing slow down.

At first stiff, Erin leaned her head down and breathed in her sister's familiar, normal scent. The threatening tears became a wave into Cali's hair.

"Erin, with everything we've been through: Mom, Dad... What you had to do...everything you had to do." Cali tightened her grip at a violent sob from her sister. "I love you so much, you have been a mom for long enough. There is a magical place offering us food and shelter...for *school*. No job. Erin, you can take a break."

Erin slid to her knees, bringing Cali with her. Her cries, for the first time in a long time, were not silent.

"Noctharim has re-established connection." One.
"So it would seem." Two.
"Shall I intervene?" Three.
"Observe, for now." Four.

# CHAPTER SIX

Jayce heard the office door slide closed behind her. The kaleidoscopic walls were still just as hypnotic. The low choir was taking away on melodic waves the remaining sting of the migraine.

"Okay, Zynka should be here. Hiding, possibly." Her neck muscles tensed with the thought of a jump scare.

She rubbed her hands together aggressively beneath her coat's sleeves. Slowly, she scanned the surrounding hallway. More humanoid creatures milled about, just like an in-between period back in school. An eight-foot statue-like creature, made of what looked to be marble, cracked and popped as it moved in one of the Academy's cyber suits, electric green pulsing through it. A small, almost rabbit-like being, wearing a minuscule black-on-black uniform, hopped quietly beside the statue.

Jayce gripped her coat tightly. It was amazing, but so alien she still had to wonder if it was real. She shook violently as she looked up the seemingly infinite height of the hall, and saw...a whale?

Floating about forty feet up was an alabaster whale, with an uncountable number of fins guiding it on its way. Its creamy skin played with the neon of the walls in an entirely soothing cascade. Shaking her head, Jayce returned to looking around the immediate area. Goat drinking from a water bottle. Wolf howling at a massive iguana. Neon pink elephant hiding behind a see-through desk. Gargoyles playing a chess-like game on a virtual board.

She stopped. Looking back at the elephant across the hall, she giggled. The Leon-sized elephant was extremely vibrant even when compared to the other worldly walls. She had her trunk under the desk, which had her eyes, a bulbous head, and just gigantic ears all above the desk as she gazed directly at Jayce. Jayce, forgetting Jotun's words, walked to the desk and asked.

"Are you Zynka? Professor Jotun asked me to meet you for a tour."

A low, sad trumpet rang out as the elephant's ears audibly thumped upon the desk in sheer defeat.

"Yeah, I am." The elephant rose to full height, around 6'8", and wore a skintight black cat suit, like a spy would wear in a bad movie.

Zynka stepped forward, surprisingly making no sound as she moved. She looked over the small creature, her emerald eyes shining brightly.

"You must be Jayce. Nice to meet you! Be honest, how was my hide?"

Jayce contemplated the answer.

"I am, and I had to do a double-take, so it was good enough. I guess."

The elephant went rouge on the cheeks. "You know, the unique-abilities-thing can really get stupid. Look at me." Zynka used her trunk to point at herself, showing her bright skin and overly muscled frame. "This, I'm born like this, and my ability is to walk silently. Why? Just why?"

The frustration stemmed from an apparently ongoing internal argument. Jayce still regarded her with wonder.

"Your skin is very beautiful, though. It reminds me of a stuffed elephant I really wanted when I was younger."

Zykna's eyes narrowed. "Stuffed? A stuffed elephant?"

"Yes, it was so cool—Oh, oh no—" Jayce cringed. *Okay*

*translation was not perfect.* "It was a toy made of cloth, not a stuffed—"

Zynka's trunk trumpeted lightly in amusement.

"I'm only kidding, girlie. I knew what you meant. Jotun's message let me know your plane was only recently connected, just teasing you." She wrapped her trunk around Jayce, who tried and failed to suppress a flinch, and pulled her close.

"So bestie, where to first? Room, uniforms, or food?"

*Bestie? There is an insult in there.*

Jayce shook the thoughts away. She realized she was slightly dancing.

"Umm, could we find a restroom, please?" Jayce asked, a little too pleadingly.

"Of course! I remember my tour. I was sooo nervous that I held it for a while. See that symbol?" She pointed her massive elephant-sized hand towards a glowing, half-moon-shaped symbol above one of the doors on the ground, not one randomly thrown on the wall.

Jayce nodded.

"That denotes the bathroom. And that..." She pointed to an orange disc on the otherwise crystal white floor. "That is what's called a scanner. It scans your physiology and, most of the time, builds a bathroom for the user." As she spoke, she guided Jayce to the disk.

Jayce hesitantly stood on the circle. She felt a warm electric wave sweep through her that was quite pleasant. The feeling pulsed through her before an androgynous robotic voice exclaimed.

"Scanning. Processing. Completed. Do enjoy your stay."

The door in front of the girls slid up, revealing one of the void-like entrances. Jayce looked at Zynka, a question evident on her face.

"Duh, those void portals are security devices. Only the one scanned can enter the restroom. The one at the entrance can only be accessed by those Noctharim allows. And our rooms have the same security set to who you allow. Now go." Zynka ended by giving Jayce a light shove into the void.

The wet/dry sensation hit and faded faster, as did the deafening silence. Oddly, as she had gone through with her mouth open, she knew what blue tasted like now. When she cleared the portal, she was met with a from top to bottom orange, claustrophobic room. The only thing making it resemble anything like a restroom was a six-by-six square cutout on the floor. Jayce eyed it bewildered.

"Okay, hole, you can make this work. Just be careful," she told herself. She was, surprisingly, able to do her business rather easily. She froze, realizing there was no toilet paper. Her eyes grew wide in thought and shame.

The androgynous voice chimed, "Cleansing."


Zynka was waiting on the outside when the door slid up. The void rippled as a now soaking wet Jayce emerged. Her coat was soaked, her hair matted down, and her makeup—already pre-smudged—just streaked up and down her face. The large elephant's ears covered her eyes; she tried to suppress a humored trumpet but failed, hard.

"Not quite right?" Zynka almost sputtered the words. Jayce, seeing the humor in the other girl's face, grimaced.

*She's laughing at you. She knows you're a joke.*

She swallowed the thoughts.

"Not at all." Jayce strained a chuckle while wringing out her hair.

"Well, that settles it, uniforms next. Do you want to walk or warp?"

Jayce abruptly stopped wringing. Her eyes grew wide, and she shuddered.

"W-Warp? What does that mean?"

Zynka face-palmed with her trunk. "New, Z, she's new. Sorry, warping is basically plane walking inside the same plane. It's the best way to travel, given this place has a massive expanse."

Jayce shifted uncomfortably. "I don't know how. I'm sorry," she replied quietly, her eyes not meeting the elephant's.

Zynka gave her a little nudge with her trunk. "Duh, if you knew how I wouldn't be here. I'll teach you."

"Really?"

"Damn, bestie, of course. I, the outstanding and drop-dead gorgeous Zynka, will be your guide." She finished in what could loosely be described as a superhero pose, chest out, hand on hips, and head turned facing the bright, fluctuating walls.

Jayce giggled at the sight, eliciting a broad smile from the neon elephant woman.

"Okay, warping is relatively easy. You just have to think of where you want to go and take a step. Like for us, we want to go to the uniform dispensary, so think uniform dispensary and take a step." Putting actions to words, Zynka took a step, the air grew thick, and she vanished without a noise. Jayce jumped back.

*You will screw it up. Don't even try.*

She looked up and down the hall nervously. There were only a few lingering students, all average height human-shaped animals, and one of the living statues. She took a deep breath, thinking *uniform dispensary*, and took a step as the air thickened.

The air froze in her lungs as her body fought an all-consuming pressure. She saw stars whipping past her head as the step moved her over an impossible distance. Making her way through the pressure, she saw a door coming at her rapidly. A light tug around her waist arrested her momentum inches before she head-butted the structure. She immediately yelped and swung her fist at the tugging presence. A light enveloped Zynka's trunk and Jayce's fist stopped an inch away from the trunk. Jayce turned on the assailing savior, looking at her hand in amazement. Zynka looked confused.

"Damn, girlie, I bet that would've hurt. You okay?"

Jayce felt the old bruise around her waist sting, as if mocking her. Taking a deep breath, she replied. "Sorry. I'm a little sore, that's all, I-I didn't mean to try and hit you. Thank you for not letting me hit the wall."

Zynka waved her off with her trunk.

"My fault, I should've said think 'hallway outside of the uniform depository'. By the way, kick-ass job for your first time!" She raised a massive hand for what Jayce thought might be a high five, but she only nodded in return.

After an awkward few seconds, Zynka dropped her hand.

"Well, let's get your uniforms." She stepped to the door. Unlike what Jayce expected, a vertical sliding door, this one unzipped from the top, pulling the flaps to the side.

Her eyes went wide. The revealed room looked like, for lack of a better context, a dry-cleaning carousel rack that went on for miles. The clothes whipped by, blowing Jayce's hair and Zynka's ears about like a tornado. The sound of the gusting wind was deafening. Zynka walked to the wall where there was a barely discernible button inlaid in the kaleidoscopic wall. Pressing it, the sound was dampened, but the movement remained.

"Okay, girlie..." Zynka pointed to another orange disk on the ground. "That will read and tailor your uniforms."

Jayce eyed the circle skeptically, fingering her wet coat.

"Don't worry, no water this time. Just measurements. There are a few prompts as well."

Jayce stepped forward and, taking a deep breath, stepped on. She startled at the androgynous voice, but it wasn't external this time; it rang off the inside of her skull.

"Analyzed. Species...Processing...New species...Database designates human...Measuring...Measurements complete. Pants or skirt?" the voice queried.

Her immediate reaction was to say pants. She had always wanted to wear a skirt back home but...But here, she thought of Jotun's gentle touch and vow to do no harm.

"Pants or skirt?" the voice insisted.

"Skirt."

*A skirt will let everyone know how disgusting you are. They will all see...*

Jayce stiffened her jaw against the wave of anxiety.

*My body, my choice.*

"Accepted...Manufacturing...Complete."

The carousel spun even more rapidly for a few seconds before stopping abruptly.

"Please take the skirt."

She looked at the sleek black skirts hanging in front of her. After a long moment, she grabbed them. They felt how she imagined a cloud would. So soft, but obviously durable. Her eyes twitched.

*These are my first new clothes. These are mine.*

The carousel spun again, blowing Jayce's hair and Zynka's ears about. Jayce giggled at the uniforms flying around. They were like passengers on the world's weirdest rollercoaster.

It came to rest with a silky black top right in front of her.

"Please take the shirt."

Jayce did as instructed and smiled at Zynka.

"Let's go get changed and get some food, yeah?" the elephant asked, returning the smile.

Jayce still stared down at her first non-hand-me-downs and nodded.

"You had a decent first warp, but I'll take you this time, if that's okay. I'll have to touch you."

Jayce reddened. She hated when people could see through to her issues, though she guessed she hadn't made it hard to notice.

*New world, crazy monster, superpowers.*

Kinda hard to hide in a time like this. She nodded.

"Okay." Zynka smiled at the small girl as she placed her trunk on her shoulder.

The air thickened, and the stars came flying by again. The frozen air actually made Jayce choke this time. When they arrived, they were in front of a massive crystalline structure, not quite a castle. It was more like the largest *wood* cabin she had ever seen. The walls played the lavender of the sky so perfectly that it was mesmerizing. Each *timber* was laid with the same glass as the castles, formed together at least a hundred feet high.

"It's..." Jayce's breath caught. "It's so beautiful."

Zynka gave her a nudge.

"And it's all ours."

Jayce gaped.

"All of it? The whole thing? For how many people?"

"In order. Yes. Yes. Just us and your friends."

Jayce rebooted.

*Friends? You don't have any friends.*

"Oh, Leon. Okay. Can we go inside?"

"Duh, oh I set this door up to match the rustic vibe." As the elephant approached the door, a clear fire began at the base, causing the glass door to melt from the bottom up.

"That...is...awesome!" Jayce squealed.

"They have been housed." One.
"So it would seem." Two.
"Shall I intervene?" Three.
"Observe for now." Four.

# CHAPTER SEVEN

Jayce walked through the melting door, mouth agape. The inside was mesmerizing; solid white glass walls with neon lines ranging the entirety of the known color spectrum pulsing through them. There was a kitchen with obsidian black appliances; what they were, she didn't know. There was a white circle-shaped couch you had to hop over the back to sit at, four large gray desks with chairs for people way larger than herself, and a massive black screen on the wall. The floor was a deep, reflective black; she was awed at being able to see herself. She cringed when she remembered the skirts in her arms. She was about to ask Zynka if she could exchange when the other girl knowingly answered.

"The skirts, well, all uniforms, have a somewhat modesty blocker...unless you remove it." She winked at the small, now-fidgeting woman.

"Uh, I, no, I will keep that in place. Thank you." Jayce breathed out in relief.

"Your room is upstairs next to mine. As big as this place is, there are only four bedrooms. Mine has the, well..." She pointed to herself. "Elephant on the door."

Jayce cocked her head.

"So, you are an elephant?"

Zynka cocked her head in response. After thinking for a minute, she replied.

"I guess kind of, when I say my species, the translation ability uses elephant as a placeholder, so again, kind of."

Jayce nodded.

"Okay, I'm gonna go put my *new* clothes on!" She let the excitement spill out, warming at the smile from her neon... friend? Looking around, she found the balcony of the upper floor, but no stairs.

"Umm..."

Again, Zynka read her mind.

"To get upstairs, you can either warp or take the port." She ended by pointing to a green disc glowing on the deep black floor.

Jayce weighed the decision before resolving herself to warp.

*No more discs today.*

She readied herself.

*Upstairs, upstairs, upstairs.*

The air thickened, and breath froze as she stepped. The stars sailed by, uncaring of her presence. When her foot landed...it didn't land. As Jayce fell out of the warp, she plummeted the twenty feet, landing on Zynka's lap on the couch. They stared at each other for a moment before she hopped off.

"I am so sorry, I didn't mean to—are you o—I'm sorry."

Jayce backed up, putting her face in her hands.

*Useless.*

"Damn bestie, calm down. My skin is literally thicker than most walls; I am fine. Are *you* okay? What did you think when you stepped?"

Zynka stood and took a step towards Jayce, who stepped back.

"I'm-I'm fine. I thought upstairs."

Zynka threw her ears over her eyes.

"Stupid, Zynka...Yeah, I can totally show the new kid around. I've been here all of a week. Thanks, War Master. I should be sorry, girl. I'm really new myself and really have made the same mistakes you have. Try warping again, but think 'my room'."

Jayce lowered her hands as Zynka moved her ears. She was surprised to see a bashful smile.

"You've been great. Sorry, my plane has nothing like this." She pointed at the room in general.

Zynka smiled wider.

"Mine, either. We are connected, but I just became a plane walker a month or so ago, so all this"—she made a wide arc with her trunk—"might as well be alien. Try again, and later we can both absolutely freak out about how cool this all is."

Jayce smiled.

"O-Okay."

*My room, my room.*

The air froze as she stepped. The stars passed as she hit solid ground and immediately and loudly tripped over an oversized white recliner. She thankfully, after flinging her uniforms across the room, caught herself, landing in an awkward plank, her feet still on the chair.

*Smooth like butter.*

She righted herself and looked around the room. It had unadorned reflective glass walls and no colors. The floor was the reflective black, as was downstairs. Looking up, she saw herself from above.

"I'm in a mirror!" Jayce giggled.

She quietly looked around, ensuring she was alone, then began making faces at the wall and ceiling. She jumped around silently.

"It's my room! It's my room!" she yell/whispered to herself.

For just a moment, she saw the oddest thing she had seen on this very strange day; she saw a smile fading on and off of her face. It didn't linger, but it had been there. Feeling cautiously warm, she scanned the rest of the room. The...bed?...looked like a sleepover mat thrown in the corner, looking like white strips of the uniforms that were scattered on the floor.

*What?*

She stared at the strips for a bare moment before flinging herself onto them. The sheer comfort that hit when she landed would never be able to be replicated; she just knew it. It was what she imagined floating on the gulf would've felt like. The strips wrapped her in a warm embrace, beckoning sleep to come. She smelled a hint of lavender mixing with the normal vanilla and gasoline blend. Jayce hopped out of the makeshift bed.

*Nope. No rest yet.*

"Clothes!"

Her eyes lit up as she slowly took off her drying safety blanket coat.

*Nobody wants to see you. Keep hiding. Damaged.*

She stopped the tear from forming as the jacket hit the ground. Looking down, she saw the yellow and purple down her arms.

*Deserved!*

She shook the bastard thought. She looked to the long-sleeve shirt and could almost hear it scream, "Wear me!" She took off her old top and reached for the new one. When her fingertips touched the new shirt, it sent electricity through her veins. It began to melt, running up her body and across her chest, forming itself perfectly to her frame. It took the shape of a medieval tunic with loose sleeves, which clashed with the whole cyberpunk feel, but she loved it. Walking to get a closer look in the mirror, she noticed deep violet energy lines crackling through it.

"Whoa. Weird."

She touched the shirt, and the lines ran to her fingers. She got lost in drawing patterns, simple and complex, through the shirt; they didn't stay but lingered for a breath. After getting lost in the patterns for a bit, she pulled out the skirt. She stared at it for a long time, breath catching.

"I could just wear my pants."

Kicking around and even mentally wrestling herself, she sat down and tossed the skirt in front of her. She looked at the endless lacing on her boots and sighed, beginning the arduous process of untying them. Pulling the first boot off gingerly, she eyed the fading handprint bruise just above her ankle and shuddered.

"No harm will come near you while I am around." Jotun's voice pushed away her fear and shame.

She took the other boot off and stood. Rapidly, she took off the black leggings and grabbed the skirt. The material again melted around her legs like warm candle wax before forming a floor-length, sleek, and form-fitting skirt. It, too, pulsed with the violet energy. Walking back to the mirror, she almost gasped. Never had she worn anything not baggy, and here she was in a form-fitting tunic and skirt. At least the sleeves were loose. She finger-combed her hair to loosen a tangle and nodded.

"Jayce, it's Jayce. Nice to meet you." She reached out and touched her reflection's hand; it was such a warm sensation. The girl in the mirror was so beautiful.

*Why can't I be like that?*

Scanning the room, she noticed a few items she missed. Near the toppled recliner was a desk protruding from the wall. It was made of clear glass and had a floating black screen. Other than that, the room was bare. Not being able to resist curiosity, she walked over, uprighted the large chair in front of the desk, and hopped up in it. She groaned as her feet swung a foot above the ground.

*Damn it.*

"Oh well," she muttered.

Even in the chair, the desk was at high chest level as she very carefully touched the screen.

"Identity...Jayce...Tooooorres...Human...adjusting  holonet... Scanning Eeeaarrtthhh records...Keyboard or touch screen?" that androgynous voice monotoned.

"Keyboard, please."

The glass desk in front of her burned out a keyboard directly into itself.

"Whoa."

The screen lit up with a very normal web browser. Curiously, she tapped in a music site, and to her surprise, it brought it right up.

"Pop tunes on, on an alien planet. Totally normal!"

Indulging her impulse to finally be able to play music in her own room without someone yelling, she typed in her favorite song and leaned back in her chair as "High School Never Ends" by Bowling For Soup faded in.

The chair, like every other piece of furniture, seemed to want to wrap her in a warm embrace. It was a long while, most of a B.F.S. playlist had gone by, before she hopped out of the chair. She killed the music and walked to the door, which also had a screen. She touched it.

"Jayce, would you like to set permissions for the room entrance?"

The voice had taken on a warmer and more natural tone.

"Just me." She stated maybe a hair too quick. Two words. Just me. A weight visibly lifted from the small woman's shoulders.

*No one can come in here.*

She saw in the mirror that the fleeting smile had returned to tug at the corners of her mouth. The door opened as she stepped to it, just a "normal" vertical slide. She walked to the balcony, looking down with awe at the way the skirt flowed so airily. Looking down, she saw Zynka was eating...something. It resembled a banana that had mixed with a watermelon. The elephant was casually eating it with her trunk as she scrolled away on a small holoscreen.

*Downstairs. Down...*

Jayce froze before her step.

She turned and found the green disc on the floor and promptly stepped on it. Her body lit up in a fiery heat; every nerve screamed expletives at her. She disappeared from the upstairs landing and rematerialized on the disk below. The heat persisted for a moment before it faded.

"What the hell?" Jayce doubled over.

She heard Zynka's trunk facepalm. When she stood up, the

neon elephant was just feet away. Jayce jumped back, making sure to avoid landing on the green hell again.

"Okay, I forgot to tell you about the port having to break down your body composition the first time. It has to do that to learn how to move you." Zynka's face was in a free fall. "I'm-I'm not great at this." Her ears flopped as her trunk pointed to all of the alien "stuff". She perked up quickly. "Oh my god! Look at you, bestie!" She scanned Jayce up and down. "You look beautiful! Also, I didn't know you were a mystic."

Jayce's cheeks warmed.

*She's playing, and you're the toy.*

Her eyes dropped slightly before catching the last part.

"Mystic? What's that?"

Zynka got a confused look before answering.

"Your uniform is violet. That means you have a unique ability in the mysticism specialization. The smoky pattern on mine designates stealth."

Jayce rubbed her temples.

"Mysticism? Specialization? You lost me completely now."

Zynka walked over and hopped over the back of the couch.

"Come, sit, I just remembered there is an intro video. My bad."

*Intro video? Maybe next time we lead with that.*

Jayce started towards the couch when she heard the front door melting. She couldn't help but giggle at the sight beyond the opening. Leon was drenched, shaking like a dog, spraying water over an equally soaked Erin. Both were holding fresh uniforms. That wasn't the oddest part. Professor Noctharim was cradled in a young teen's arms, getting scratches behind the ears. Behind them, Jotun stood hunched over, waving vigorously, with his big lopsided grin.

"Hey, Bitsy."

Jayce let a real smile play on her face.

"Hello, War Master," she replied.

The blue giant looked dejected. She reeled back to Erin.

"I thought you were going to stay home? Are you enrolling?"

Erin side-eyed Cali and Noctharim.

"It seems I was outvoted. And I guess my sister has a cosmic pet that I would 'ruin her life' if I separated them." She gave Jayce an only slightly frayed smile.

"Are these your friends? Is this our house? Where's the food?"

Jayce felt the young lady's excitement as if it were a physical force. Noctharim took flight at the entrance, hovering.

"A, I am no mere pet. B, the food is in the black box over there. Simply tell it what you want, and it shall retrieve it. C, dear Zynka, have you watched the introduction with the lovely Jayce?"

Jayce shot up like a rocket, heart stopping as she heard Zynka reply from right next to her.

"No, Professor-I-" Her ears flopped. "I forgot."

Noctharim did a loop.

"No trouble, my dear, no trouble at all. In fact, that works out well as we have two other initiate students." As he spoke, Cali skipped over to the black fridge-looking appliance.

"Zynka, I am planning on shifting this part of the Nexus to match the humans' time structure. It is similar to yours. Would that be acceptable?" Noctharim queried.

*Shift the Nexus?*

Jayce tensed at the perceived power that would require.

"Not a problem for me, sir."

Noctharim listed back and forth in the air.

"Very good. Now, my initiates, and my dear Cali, Jotun and I must retire to my office and recruit teachers to work your schedules." With that statement, the air hung heavy, and the corvathis disappeared.

"I look forward to seeing you all in my first class. I am personally taking charge of your war course. Rest well." Jotun's gravelly voice echoed in the room as he warped out.

Cali walked to Jayce, an ice cream sandwich in hand.

"You must be Jayce! On the way over here, ol' blue was gushing about you. I'm Cali. That skirt is lovely. Your blue streak is awesome! It matches your eyes perfectly. Are you excited to be here?" Cali reached out her unoccupied hand.

Jayce, slightly overwhelmed at the younger girl's rapid-fire speech, reached out and shook her hand.

"Thank you. Yes, I am Jayce. And I am... I still can't believe this is actually happening."

Leon and Erin had made their way to the rest of the group.

"Hey, Jayce, Cali can get a little enthusiastic. If we stay, you will, and I almost guarantee this, not get used to it," Erin said as Cali stuck her tongue out at her older sister.

Looking back and forth between Leon and Erin, Jayce replied. "I totally get her excitement. This is unreal. By far the coolest thing that has ever happened to me. And did you two get 'cleansed'?"

Leon looked slightly miffed.

"That is exactly what happened. I freaking love water, but not like this." He shook again, water hitting Jayce's shirt. It absorbed and dried it as it hit. "Whoa, that's...that's awesome!"

Jayce, as with the rest of the day, was just baffled.

*Self-drying clothes. Neon shifting walls. Overly aggressive toilets. Wild.*

"Well, seeing that, I'm going to go get changed," Leon spoke as he turned to Zynka. "Howdy, I'm Leon, this is Erin and Cali," he gestured.

"Nice to meet you guys, I'm Zynka. Your rooms are over by the green disc. Once you get changed, we can watch the intro vid.

"Sounds good." Leon and Erin smiled at each other as they answered in tandem.

They both made their way to their rooms. Cali, meanwhile, had finished her ice cream and gone back to the fridge. She walked back with a drumstick of fried chicken. Walking right up to Zynka, who made the short girl look like a toddler, she spoke.

"You are the coolest thing I've seen today. What is your favorite part of the Nexus? Mine is the fridge. It was Jotun; he's funny, but free food is great. How long have you been here?

What are the courses like?" Cali said and asked all this while gnawing on the drumstick like a feral caveman.

"Thank you, I'm with you on the food. I haven't been here long, and I haven't started courses." Zynka looked amused as she answered.

"Okay, Jayce, did your clothes also melt onto you?" Leon asked as he and Erin walked out of their respective rooms.

Leon's top was a sleek black...tank top? The shirt was every bit a tank, but the left side had a sleeve encasing what was left of his arm; his right arm was covered in tattoos, some line work, and symbols, very well done. Jayce couldn't help but giggle as his bottoms were a multi-pocketed kilt.

"What?" he asked. "It's tactic-cool." He winked at her. She giggled.

Shifting focus, Jayce was again in awe of Erin's beauty. She was in the same solid black, but her uniform was a sleeveless sundress that looked like she just dyed the one she wore earlier.

"Wow. Sis, as always, freaking knockout," Cali said, smiling, as she went back for a second drumstick.

"You guys don't have a main ability yet?" Zynka asked, one eyebrow cocked.

"No, how can you tell?" Erin asked.

"No colors on the uniform. Let's eat and watch the vid, it'll explain way better than I could."

Nodding, Erin, Jayce, and Leon made their way to the fridge.

"They have accepted enrollment." One.
"So it would seem." Two.
"Shall I intervene?" Three.
"Observe, for now." Four.

# CHAPTER EIGHT

Jayce and the group sat on the couch waiting for the video to start. They had all decided on popcorn, butter for Jayce and Cali, and sweet for Erin and Leon. Zynka, having never tried either, scooped up a bit of both from each bowl with her trunk, losing her mind at the flavor and grabbing a huge bowl mixed from the fridge. She then turned on the screen and clicked the play button. The sight that greeted them was interesting to say the least. There was a figure, almost human-looking, but with elvish ears and gold flashing lines throughout his body; his eyes were nearly closed but aware. He was shirtless, showing off a chiseled physique, and wearing harem pants in the sleek black, green lines running through.

"Good whatever time of day it is, initiates. I am Professor Automo. I am a sentient artificial intelligence."

The humans looked at each other, wondering if that would happen back home.

"I am the engineering instructor, and as it happens, the intro falls on me." His voice was very static and digital, no emotion, just statements. "To begin, we have the uniforms, as some of you may have figured, they take the form most appealing to the wearer." Jayce looked over at Leon, who winked, kilt on full display. He grabbed an oversized handful of popcorn and jammed it in his mouth.

*Has he ever heard of bite-sized?*

She giggled internally.

"Now, another feature of the uniforms is that they are self-cleaning, self-drying, self-altering, and self-repairing. That means a cut will be stitched, a stain will be removed, the fabric will keep you dry, and they will form to the wearer's needs."

Erin, Jayce, and Leon looked at each other.

"Good to know for the next 'cleansing'," Erin grumbled.

"Also, I am sure you have noticed the uniforms can take on different lines of energy. Those help amplify the specialization you show the greatest aptitude for."

Jayce looked down at the violet lines running through her uniform, not resisting the urge to draw on it.

"Blue is warrior, green"—he pointed to his pants—"is engineering. Pink is glamour/illusion. Black represents stealth. Violet is mysticism."

Everybody turned to Jayce, who shrank, hiding her face with a handful of popcorn. Leon, still looking at her, reached for popcorn, brushing Erin's hand as she went for the bowl as well. They shared a quick glance before hyper-focusing on the vid. Erin blushed slightly.

"Classes for initiates are simple, one specialization class per scheduled time period. As the time periods vary, I cannot give you that information. Please see your administrator."

Jayce looked at Zynka

"Who is our admin?" she asked

"I guess Jotun; I think he took over this cycle."

Jayce nodded, feeling very warm.

"On to the living areas. Most of you are from planes without our tech and altered physics, so I will give a quick demonstration."

As he monotoned, the screen seemed to ripple. The air in the room condensed, and the group was bogged down. Professor Automo simply walked out of the screen and into the middle of the circular couch. The only sound was the bowl Cali had held flying up before it hit the floor. The smooth black floor absorbed the bowl and spilled popcorn instantly, though it went unnoticed by the humans. Leon jumped up, back in his boxer stance.

"What the hell?"

*I have got to get a new line.*

Cali threw her arms around Jayce, who couldn't suppress the flinch, though she did rest her hand on the young girl's knee. Erin didn't react, presumably frozen.

*This. This is why I wanted to stay home.*

Only Zynka didn't react. "Hey, Professor."

Automo nodded at her. "Greeeeeeeeeeeetings, Zynnnnnka." As his voice glitched, he reached up to an unnoticed dial on his neck and turned it. "My circuits never care for the walk-through. Now, I believe you four are the other new students?" His voice, while still robotic, leveled out.

Cali, head still in an uncomfortable Jayce's neck, whispered, "Three, I-I'm not a student."

"Confirmed. Jayce Torres, Leon Thatcher, Erin Walker. New students. Previously unconnected plane. First class in"—his colorless eyes pulsed gold—"thirty-six of your hours. Jotun, warrior course."

Jayce's heart beat faster.

*A course with Jotun? Yes, please.*

"Now, to show how to use the house. Each uniform comes with a holoscreen embedded. Simply, will it to arrive and it will."

Putting actions to words, Automo mentally called his up. It detached from his pants and floated at chest level, measuring approximately 6 by 6 inches. Leon was the first to bring his screen up, followed by Jayce, then Erin.

"From these devices, you may customize your private rooms at will. However, living area changes must be agreed upon by a majority to keep issue of cohabitation from arising." He looked at the three humans with screens. "I would like to have you demonstrate your ability to adjust as a group," he monotoned, looking at each of the three in turn.

"Well, there's no dinner table. Should we try that?" Leon was clearly talking to Erin and Jayce, though his eyes never left Automo. He replaced his boxer stance with a more casual, yet still guarded, stance.

Jayce, watching Leon, felt...she felt safe. Warm. She looked around the living space, just realizing that, indeed, there was no table.

"I think that's a good choice."

Erin, still looking 'frazzled fake-strong', just nodded.

"Great, Leon Thatcher, with the permission of the other two, you may set the table," Automo said, gesturing at the tablet.

Leon turned and hopped over the back of the couch and, finding the biggest open space, brought up his screen. A design suite populated with options to draw or pick a standard design. He thought for a moment, then picked "Draw." After a minute or so of drawing, he hit the "Build" button. Again, glass melted down from the ceiling, this time, though, it was slower.

*I guess custom takes more effort.*

Seeing it like this, it was obvious the glass was molten hot. It gave him the impression of a glassblower's work. The table was finished and solidified into a three-tier ramped table. On the low end was a place perfect for the three human women, a ramp led slightly up where a flat top was for Leon, and a second ramp led up to a Zynka-sized table.

"Very good. My intro is completed. I will see each of you in my plane when it is time." Without another word, the air suppressed them again as Automo walked through the screen, and it went black.

Erin, without the AI's presence, came back to the world of the living.

"Will we ever get used to that?" she asked no one in particular.

"Been here a week and, so far, no. That's not even one of the weirder moments," Zynka said, grabbing a trunk full of popcorn and eating it.

*You're right, a neon pink elephant talking and eating popcorn is way weirder.*

Erin shook internally.

"So, I'm starving. Wanna do a family-style dinner?" Leon asked, already heading to the fridge.

"Can I...play some music during dinner?" Jayce's voice wavered as she asked.

"Of course, babe, some music might make this place feel less alien." Erin gave Jayce that gorgeous smile.

She smiled back cautiously. Jayce brought up her holo, searching for the music site. She struggled between The Pretty Reckless and Bowling For Soup, but decided B.F.S was more appropriate and a chiller vibe. The music started on her holo, somewhat quietly.

"There's a button to cast it in the house," Zynka told her.

Searching through, she found it and cast the pop punk at a reasonable volume. Leon danced around to the beat as he tried to decide what to eat. Cali and Erin chuckled at the swaying of his hips.

"Hmm, duh steak." Leon reached into the fridge and pulled out a steaming steak and a loaded baked potato.

Jayce's mouth liquefied; she had never had a steak, or a loaded baked potato, for that matter.

"Wait a minute!" Leon sounded giddy. He reached back in the fridge and pulled out a red, white, and gold can. He turned to Erin.

"Do you drink Lone Star? First rounds on me." He moved his eyebrows in a wave. Erin laughed.

"Why not?"

He set the plate on the table and handed her the can as he went back for a second. They all took turns grabbing food. Steak for Jayce. Fried fish for Erin. A tub of ice cream for Cali. And a plate that looked very similar to grass for Zynka. Jayce, excited for her steak, was equally excited for her previously untried Big Red. The first sip of the red liquid did more than just quench her thirst; it helped her realize *she* had made a choice.

They sat around the table enjoying small talk. Zynka wowed the group with tales of her endless savannah-style plane. She was equally wowed by surfing, cars, and airplanes. Jayce, during this time, had devoured her meal and gotten a banana split, savoring the sweet, sweet dessert. The conversations started to die down as they all finished their meals. Cali, Jayce, and Zynka yawned near simultaneously. Zynka stood.

"I'm gonna get some sleep, guys. Would you guys want to check out the campus tomorrow? I've been wanting to explore a bit." There were nods of agreement all around the table. The elephant nodded and walked to her room, stopping on the way to pat Jayce on the head with her trunk.

"Night, bestie."

Jayce didn't flinch.

"Night...bestie."

Zynka smiled and left.

"Me too. Too much ice cream. This place is going to make me fat," Cali stated, standing up.

"Goodnight, Cali," Erin said.

"Night, kid," Leon added.

"See you tomorrow," Jayce said her goodnights, walking and stepping on the port with trepidation. No pain this time, just a feeling of weightlessness. She breathed a sigh of relief. She trusted when Zynka said it only hurt the first time, but was happy to confirm it. She walked into her room and shut the door. Her uniform immediately started crawling and shaping. It tickled like a ladybug was crawling all over her. The form stopped in sleep shorts and an oversized T-shirt. She looked in the mirror, seeing the bruises and scars, but she didn't look away. After a moment, she walked to the strip bed, jumped in, and was asleep in an instant.


"You going to bed too?" Leon asked Erin, taking a big swig from the third beer. Erin shook around her empty second.

"Maybe one more. Actually, do you think we can get a white Russian from there?" She pointed at the glorious fridge.

Leon shrugged and went to get her one.

"The dude abides," he said as he set the mixed drink in front of her.

"Look at you, kilt man, knowing classic cinema."

He smiled at the name. "I was laid up for a while after this." He waved his stump. "Watch movies, play video games, and board games is about all there was to do." He took another pull.

Erin, seeing the tension build in his jaw, pivoted.

"What was, or I guess, is your favorite movie? Actor?"

Leon thought for a moment.

"Movie has got to be *Remember the Titans*. But when it comes to an actor? Mel Gibson every day of the week." He smiled at Erin.

*She's hangin' by a thread, but damn, she is beautiful.*

"What about you, Miss Sundress?"

Erin twitched a grin. "Movie is *Grind*. It's an early 2000's skateboard movie."

Leon cocked an eyebrow. "Didn't take you for a skater, great movie though."

Erin took a light sip of the Russian, letting the bittersweet linger in her mouth before swallowing. "Oh yeah, when I was younger, I was an okay skater. I even sent a few 'sponsor me' videos."

Leon looked floored.

"Are you serious?"

"Are you judging me cause I'm a girl or because I'm wearing a dress?" She smiled, but her words were chilly.

"What? No. I'm judging you on how you carry yourself. Proper. Responsible and poised. Doesn't scream skater punk is all."

Erin relaxed.

"I wasn't always like this. I was a little rebel growing up." She took a swig and laughed. "This one time, a friend and I got caught skating in a mall. The security chased us for a good ten minutes. I only got caught because I tried to grind an escalator handrail. A helpful hint, you can't grind on rubber."

Leon choked on his beer at the thought. He hit his chest to clear the airway.

"You biffed it?" Erin just gave him a double eyebrow raise over her drink. "What made you stop skating? Or...did you stop?"

Erin froze, drink still on her lips. She breathed deeply a few times. "I-I had to start taking care of Cali, so I didn't really have time for much else." She finished her drink and went to get another. Bypassing the table, she hopped over the couch, sitting down.

Leon, feeling this might get a bit heavier, grabbed another beer and sat with her.

"What happened? If it's too personal, tell me to mind my dang business."

Erin considered saying just that, but relented.

*Why not share with a stranger in an alien land?*

"My parents died in a car wreck when I was eighteen. Cali was nine. It was either I take her, or she would've gone into the system. I didn't want that, so I became a Sis-Mom." She took a deep pull.

"I'm sorry that happened to you. For whatever that is worth. But Cali seems to be doing well, so you must be doing something right, yeah?"

"She's a good kid on her own, a real pain in the ass sometimes, but a good kid. Really, all I've had to do is keep food on the table and a roof over us." Erin gestured at the fridge and kaleidoscopic walls. "Guess that's not an issue for a while."

Leon took a drink.

"You're a good person for stepping up like that. A lot of people wouldn't."

She eyed him. "Any siblings?"

He shook his head.

"It would've been impossible to say no, even if I wanted to."

Erin took a long drink before continuing.

"It's-It's been rough. I busted my butt doing retail and restaurants." She finished her drink. Leon remained silent. "But that wasn't enough. The prices of food kept going up, and I kept making the same."

Noticing something heavy was coming, Leon gently set his hand on hers. She looked down at it but made no effort to move it.

"Sometimes you've got to do things...things you aren't proud of to make it through." Her eyes began to water.

Leon's heart ached for her.

*What the hell are you gonna say? Useless.*

Leon's thoughts beat him; his shoulders slumped.

"And now, it's like I have this grime that won't wash off." A tear streaked down her cheek.

"We have blood on our hands that won't wash off. That's just a part of who we are now. I don't think it is possible to push past it; hell, I can barely live with it. But you..." He gently turned Erin's head towards him. "What you had to do, you did for somebody. It doesn't make it feel right or make it have not happened..."

Leon lost his train of thought as explosions sounded in his head, his eyes glossing over. Erin saw he wasn't with her anymore.

*Broken, in a different way, but still broken.*

Another tear came at her thoughts.

In a move to save herself and him, she put his arm over her shoulder and rested her head on his chest again. No more words were exchanged. Just two broken humans staring into the abyss.


"That plane was connected before. I am not sure how. I could feel it there," Noctharim said, looking grimly at Jotun.

"What do you think it means?" the gravelly voice replied.

"I do not know, my dear friend. But we must be vigilant," Noctharim ended.

"They have been orientated." One.
"So it would seem." Two.
"Shall I intervene?" Three.
"Observe for now." Four.

<hr>

# CHAPTER NINE

<hr>

Jayce awoke what felt early, with not enough sleep, yet the most peaceful sleep she had ever had. She stretched hard with a yawn so loud she looked around to see if anyone heard. Her mouth twitched up.

*No one is here.*

She rolled the short distance to the floor and stood.

"Guess I'd better get ready," she said as she watched her clothes slide over her scarred legs and arm, returning to the skirt and tunic.

*Disgusting.*

Her eyes went from the mirror to the floor in an instant. Sighing, she walked to her door and headed down the port. When she landed, she saw Cali with her finger over her lips, waving her over. Quiet as she could, she crept over, not sure what was happening. She made it over, and Cali pointed at the couch. There, cradled and still upright, were Erin and Leon.

Cali bounced excitedly and whispered, "She hasn't been on a date in years." She was giddy.

Jayce cracked a smile while simultaneously wondering what it felt like to be held. As if in response to her thoughts, Cali threw her arms around Jayce's midsection. She froze; the pain of the fading bruise hurt like hell under Cali's death grip. Despite the pain and overall uncomfortableness, she did nothing to stop it. This young girl was so joyous for a small cuddle.

*It must be important to her.*

"What's up, bestie?"

Cali and Jayce jumped and screamed together as Zynka's voice sounded right next to them.

*Damn silent footsteps.*

Leon pounced off the couch, still half asleep and only half here. Inadvertently, he knocked Erin over on her side. To her credit, she didn't even try to wake up. He took his boxer's stance.

"Crap, sorry." Zynka blushed, putting her hands up.

"Can we put a bell on her?" Cali half-joked, looking up at the towering elephant.

"Coffee. Coffee is how to wake me up." Leon relaxed and gave a smile at the still sleeping Erin before hopping over the couch and retrieving a steaming coffee from the fridge. He took a long sip. "Breakfast?" he asked over his mug.

They all, minus Erin, got food and sat together.

"She never, I mean never, sleeps in," Cali said, mouth full of bacon and eggs.

"She definitely seems to need it," Leon replied, mouth equally as full.

"She has worked so hard. Having a break is exactly what she needed," Cali said.

"Where are we exploring today...bestie?" Jayce whispered the last word.

"I don't know, I haven't been around much. I figured we would just start walking and see," Zynka replied before stuffing her mouth.

*The elephant has the best manners, really?*

Jayce grinned at her own thought. After they finished breakfast, Cali woke Erin. Once she finished her grapefruit, the group headed outside. The wonder hit Jayce again. The lavender sky, brighter now, and she realized that there was no discernible source of light. It just was. The dozens of glistening castles screamed majesty. Another fish rainbow was chasing the aimless platforms.

"Let's go that way." Zynka's trunk pointed to a forest of the almost-not-there trees.

The group headed that way, Leon and Erin falling behind slightly.

"Thank you for last night," Erin spoke softly.

"No need for thanks. I was just there," he answered just as quietly. She bumped into him gently.

"That's exactly why I thanked you."

They shared a fleeting glance, both reddening as they walked. Cali, meanwhile, listed off everything she saw in excruciating detail. Jayce didn't mind; the girl was only voicing the thoughts she had as well. When they got to the forest, they stopped. The unreal black trunks of the trees contrasted the snow-white ground in a gray beauty. Thinking for a minute, Jayce pulled up her holo and scrolled until she found what she was looking for. Pressing a button, a sketch pad appeared.

"If y'all want to go in, you should. I want to draw this," Jayce said.

The group shared a look and a shrug.

"Just send me a message when you're done, girlie," Zynka said.

Seeing the confused look on Jayce's face, she sighed and walked over. She took a couple of clicks on her holo, showing Jayce the messaging app. With that, the group headed into the forest. Jayce sat cross-legged on the ground and began trying to decide which style to draw in. Her favorite was always realism, but looking around, she decided realism was out the window. She decided on surrealism, sketching the trees in wild directions and drooping limbs upon an ominous sky. She had been sketching for about an hour, lost in it, when she heard a familiar flapping. Jayce turned to see Noctharim flying lazily towards her. She stood up, dismissing her holo.

"Good morning, Professor."

He got within a few feet and stopped to hover; ear wings not seeming to flap fast enough for this feat.

"Good morning, my dear. How was the first night? I do hope the accommodations were acceptable."

Jayce nodded. "It was perfect, sir, thank you."

"Very good. I came to ask... do you have a while to talk? I fear there are some details I missed yesterday in all the excitement." He did a lazy loop.

"Y-Yes, sir." She shivered with anxiety.

*He's going to send you home.*

She shook her head to clear the thought.

"May I walk with you? It truly is, as always, a lovely day."

Jayce nodded in reply. The professor proceeded to fly and land on her shoulder.

"This way, if you please." He pointed his wing to a large expanse of open ground. Jayce started walking.

They got to the middle before Noctharim pointed to a large crystal platform on the ground.

"If you would be so kind."

With the prompt, Jayce stepped on, walking to the center. As she reached it, the platform began to vibrate and crackle with energy. She locked her knees and clung to her tunic's sleeve.

"It is okay, my dear. Simply relax." Despite his attempt to calm her, she shuddered and stumbled as the platform slowly broke free of the ground.

She fell to her hands and knees, Noctharim taking flight.

"My dear girl, these daises are quite safe. If you look to the edge, you will see a shimmer." Following his words, she saw a very faint disturbance against the gorgeous sky. "That is a barrier that you have to consent to go through."

She bit at that word.

"Consent, you have said that before. When you woke me up, and about Leon hitting Professor Jotun. Why?" She shakily stood.

Looking out past the barrier, she gasped. Miles upon miles of glass castles all reflecting the sky. It looked like a shifting lavender lake. Hundreds of other platforms and fish rainbows flew across the horizon.

"Simple answer, really. When I started this Academy, my goal was for walkers to have a place of respite. A place truly safe. So, to do that, when I stitched this plane to mine, I weaved in the consent rule as a safeguard."

Jayce knew in her bones that the corvathis was powerful, but she shivered at writing rules for an entire reality.

"Professor, Leon told me that Jotun called what I did 'sculpting'? And you were worried when it happened. Why?" She made eye contact with him; she actually made eye contact.

Noctharim breathed out slowly.

"For the first question, yes, it is indeed called sculpting. It is a rare ability, even rarer than my own."

Jayce cocked her head. "I thought it was a unique ability."

Noctharim nodded, causing a front flip.

"Yes, unique is what it's considered, however in infinite planes with infinite realities, no ability is truly the only one of its kind."

Jayce nodded.

*Infinite everything?*

The thought gave Jayce a slight feeling of agoraphobia. Her breathing became shallow.

"And, my dear, the reason I was and am concerned is because"—he took a quick breath—"sculptors have the power to reshape the events they perceive. If an event is occurring not to their liking, they change it. With proper training, the sculptor may erase something or someone from reality."

He landed, looking up at Jayce.

"The last sculptor I and Jotun had encountered had to be neutralized by the two of us. He had blinked multiple realities out of existence," he finished.

Jayce, wide-eyed and biting her lip, stared at the professor.

*You have the power to do what you want. You will ruin lives.*

She clamped her lip, causing the iron taste of blood to pool in her mouth. Her hand fidgeted as her tunic grew slightly looser.

"How did you stop them?"

Noctharim pecked lightly at the empty platform.

"To be completely honest, neither I nor Jotun can remember. We were in the midst of battle when everything just ended. The sculptor lay dead; I and my dear azure friend were hailed as the victors. He would have beaten us had it not been for the toll." He gnawed his wing.

Jayce's head throbbed, remembering her migraine.

"Power demands a toll. Only those willing to pay it can defy infinity." He ended with a chirp.

"D-Do you think I have that potential?" The tunic had grown baggier again.

"Indeed, I do, dear Jayce, indeed I do." He looked up to her. "That is why I wanted you in the Academy. Here we can teach you to truly unlock that potential, to harness your power."

Jayce rocked on her heels before squatting down. It felt wrong looking down on someone so powerful.

"So I don't become evil?"

Noctharim scoffed.

"There is no good and evil. Simply choices. To some, the action may be horrendous, while it might be lauded by others. One cannot look at the planes with such binary opinions." His voice was firm, but it wasn't a dressing down. He needed this point to get across.

"But what if—" Jayce started.

"If you were to delete a plane? In the vast infinity, does it really matter? The only reason Jotun and I fought back against Four, was because it was my reality he deleted." The professor slightly snarled. Jayce moved to lay a hand on his ear wing.

"No, it's quite all right, my dear. That was billions of your years ago."

She froze, hand midair.

"H-how is that possible?" Jayce stood and backed a few paces.

"The gift and the curse of plane walkers. We live until we decide not to, or someone else decides for us." He scratched his chin with a talon, returning to his disinterested state.

*He just shrugged off being immortal...*

Her eyes went so wide that they threatened to fall out.

*I-I'm-I'm immortal?*

"Professor, does that mean—"

He waved a wing dismissively.

"Yes, yes. You, too, have the gift...or curse, depending on how you view it. Just know that nothing is as beautiful when you know there isn't a perceivable end." He finished and pointed his wing towards a canyon as the platform continued to aimlessly drift on purpose.

Jayce marveled. Orange water ran through a massive white and grey canyon. She could see more of the trees on top, leaves dancing with the unheard music. Small creatures darted between them, but it was too far away to tell what they were. She was blown away by the sheer beauty of the sight. All of it with the lavender sky and rainbow. Her eye misted. Never did she think she would ever see such grandeur.


Erin walked beside Leon through the forest, watching the colorful leaves dance in the nonexistent breeze. Small golden mouse-like creatures became curious as they approached, stopping and sniffing at them before scampering off. Cali had been going crazy trying to catch one for the past few minutes. Erin smiled; a tear brewing, watching her sister be the kid she was.

"She's sure is a cute kid, ain't she?" Leon smiled at the excitable child.

"She does have her moments. Trust me, the punk will come out eventually," Erin replied.

"You did good." With Leon's short praise, her brewing tear fell, but it didn't sting. It was warm and comforting. She shouldered him gently.

"Hey guys, it looks like a lake is up here! Let's go swim!" Zynka trumpeted as she silently tore through the last bit of foliage to a large orange lake surrounded by the snow-white dirt.

Cali, not to be outdone, tried to get her little legs to keep up with the large elephant. She turned to Leon and cocked an eyebrow.

"Water? You know I'm in." He winked and sprinted to the lake, kilt molding into board shorts while his shirt came off except for a sleeve over his left arm.

*He shouldn't be ashamed.*

Erin slowly walked into the clearing. Nearing the water, she felt the electric static of her dress as it separated into a two-piece bikini. Leon, who had already dove headfirst into the water, surfaced and stared at her, mouth slightly open. He maintained the stare until Cali, who decided to swim in full clothes, swam up and shut his mouth for him.

"You'll catch flies with your mouth like that," Cali croaked in a very old lady's voice.

Leon shook himself.

"Sorry." He turned and dove, swimming a good distance away.

*Still got it.*

Erin walked into the surprisingly warm water.

It wasn't quite a hot tub, but close enough for her. She went just deep enough to sit with water shoulder-high and stared up at the limitless yet reachable sky.

"Hmm." She thought about how that worked. It was like if she tried to reach hard enough, she could grab it. She lost that train as one of the rainbows began looping. Forgetting everything, she just existed. No customers, no stress. Well, other than the fact that she was in a different reality than the one she was native to. Plus, the fact that this entire place was populated by English-speaking monsters. The sound of splashing broke her free from that thought as Leon swam up and sat next to her.

"Hey, uh, that wasn't super chill that I stared at you. I'm sorry."

Compared to a lot of what she had been through, a look seemed innocuous. It still made her feel amazing that he cared enough to say it.

"Yeah, what the hell is wrong with you?" she tried, and failed, to maintain an affronted tone.

Leon smiled.

"You are exceptionally gorgeous, just wanted you to know that shi—dang, sorry." Leon's jaw tensed. She didn't need to hear what he thought of her.

*She needs space. After what she told you, you're hitting on her?*

"It's okay, and thank you. You're not bad looking yourself, kilt man." She blushed as she replied.

Erin saw Leon's eyes catch just a touch of life before it faded. Changing the subject, she pointed to a many-pointed tattoo on his forearm.

"What's this one?"

Leon looked down, rotating his arm to see the tattoos there.

"Which one?"

Erin ran her finger along the one she meant. Gooseflesh formed on him as she did.

"Oh, that one. That's a vegvisir. Honestly, when I got it, I was like 'Sick Viking Stuff'. But after I got it and did some research, yup, did it backwards, it's actually an Icelandic symbol. It's supposed to be a compass or Wayfinder, which helps to protect against getting lost in a storm."

Erin looked at the other shapes and landed on the good old-fashioned anarchy symbol.

"Anarchist soldier, huh?"

Leon chuckled.

"I like what is stands for, but I am also fully away the tat makes me an edgelord." He finished with a self-deprecating laugh.

"You don't think it is a cool tattoo?" Erin eyed him.

"Oh, I love it, I just know how it comes across."

Erin, looking in Leon's eyes, moved her hair back over her ear, revealing the A in the circle. Leon stared at her.

"You weren't kidding. You were a little skate punk." He leaned in closer to get a better look. "Holy crap. That's stick-and-poke. Behind the ear! You're freaking tough," he exclaimed.

Erin laughed.

"Yup. Safety pin when I was fifteen. I don't recommend it. I was crazy worried about infection for days." She stared off, remembering what freedom that allowed that asinine decision.

"Well, it looks tough as hell and actually well done, for a dumb teenager decision."

Erin splashed him.

"Come on." She stood up, took his hand, and led him deeper to actually get a swim in.

They all swam for a while, Zynka squirt-gunning Cali with her trunk and general horseplay. At one point, Leon suggested a chicken fight as Cali had climbed to her shoulders, but Zynka pointed out that she was a literal freaking elephant. She pulled up her holo at one point to return a message to Jayce, letting her know where they were. They continued their play, nothing real lingered on any of them, until one of the floating platforms landed to the side of the lake. Cali, the first to react, swam like a fish, then ran to the platform and snatched up Noctharim. He let out a hoot of joy at the barrage of pets he got. Jayce, meanwhile, walked off the platform and began unlacing her boots. Leon and Erin joined her while Zynka kept turning herself into a fountain.

"So much for sketching, huh, J?"

She looked at Leon. "I got a little bit." Jayce quickly brought up her holo and started searching for it.

*He still doesn't care. Stupid.*

She stopped mid-swipe. Clenching her teeth against herself, she found the picture and turned her holo, fidgeting and counting individual grains of dirt.

"Damn kid, that's amazing. Erin, check it out, she captured the freaking soul of this place."

As Erin looked over it as well, Jayce's chest puffed, though she still eyed the ground.

"Wow, how did you do that? And can I have it for my room's wall?"

Jayce snapped up at Erin's words.

"You-You want it? Why?"

Erin walked to her side and, making sure her arm was seen, put it around Jayce's shoulder. It was very small, but the twitch was there. Erin softly pulled her tighter.

"Because, babe, I want something to look at that isn't a mirror."

*She doesn't mean it.*

Jayce leaned away, and Erin released her.

"I'm serious. Let's figure it out when we get back...Cali! No!" Erin dashed to the water to stop a cackling Cali from dunking Noctharim in the water.

Jayce froze wide-eyed at the sight, trembling slightly.

"That may be one of the most powerful beings. And that kid is trying to dunk him." Her mouth just flopped.

Leon first looked at the commotion, and then back.

"Whatever. Ready to go swimming?"

Jayce chewed her raw lip.

"I don't know how."

Leon looked confused.

"You're from Corpus, and you don't know how to swim? Screw that. We gotta go now, J." Even though Leon saw and knew why she struggled, he persisted.

Jayce rubbed her now baggy tunic, staring longingly at the water.

*Go ahead. Let them see how broken you are.*

"J, we all have scars. I'll show you mine if you show me yours." He gave her a broad smile that she forgot to return.

*Don't do it. You're not ready.*

Shaking off his own thoughts, he mentally directed the sleeve off the nub. It had the suture marks scarred in an altogether unpleasant visage. Jayce looked up into his eyes. There was a deep void where she should be able to see a spark of life. She shivered violently.

*If he can do it, so can I. Everyone will know...*

She cut herself off, willing her uniform into a one-piece. The skirt slowly molded up, revealing the yellow purple on her olive skin. Scars crossed up her thighs. When the bathing suit was formed, Jayce looked into Leon's eyes again. They scanned her completely. Where there had been a void, there was now pure, unbridled anger.

"I'm okay..." Jayce softly whispered.

"You will be..." There was an undeniable promise in Leon's voice. With that, he guided her to the water. She walked in, for once, not just dipping her toes.

"He remembers." One.
"So it would seem." Two.
"Shall I intervene?" Three.
"Observe for now." Four.

# CHAPTER TEN

After the fun at the lake, the group retired to the cabin for some dinner and chill. Erin, true to her word, had dragged Jayce to her room to figure out how to transfer the sketch to the wall. When they were finished, Jayce excused herself in embarrassment at Erin's praise. Back in her room, she pulled up her design suite.

"Okay, room, what are we doing?" Her voice bounced off the mirrored walls.

"That first."

Jayce looked through the holo, deciding to make the walls match the reflective black. All, except one part that she left as a full-sized mirror. Crafting a chair, she sat in front of it and stared at herself.

She hummed as she looked over her image. Her clothes had already become sleepwear. She glanced at her thigh scars only momentarily. She looked at the blue streak in her hair; she didn't like the way it meshed with the violet lines of the uniform.

*You are a sculptor, try it.*

*You'll screw it up.*

Deciding to go with the first voice, she focused hard, trying to will her ability to activate. After a moment of nothing happening, she breathed.

"Okay, overwhelming emotion caused a trigger last time," she mused.

Thinking harder, she decided on something she both thought would work; and would equally suck. If it wanted pain, she knew where to find it.

"It's not about the hair. It's about the power."

She gritted her teeth. Breathing in and out heavily, she began to think of the nights trapped in foster hell. The fear rose steadily through her. Each footstep outside that ran shivers throughout her body. The footsteps were getting closer. She stopped breathing.

*If you don't breathe, they won't find you.*

The doorknob started to rattle; tears formed. The knob turned; tears fell. As the door began to crack, she felt it. The air stopped; the only sound was her hammering heart. She tried to breathe the unmoving air to no avail.

*Quick girl, quick.*

She focused on her blue streak, willing it to change. Slowly, from the root, the streak took on the violet of her uniform. She smelled the iron of blood in her nostrils.

*Not yet; still more.*

She turned her focus on those piercing blue eyes that had shed so many tears. With a burst of will, her irises began to burn. Tears fell as the pain took hold; they came out a murky red. The blue of the irises began to chip and disintegrate, making way for her new violet eyes. She smiled at the look. The streak and eyes matching her uniform were magnificent.

*It costs a toll; I'll gladly pay it for the power.*

The senses hit like a freight train; the vanilla bean and gasoline she was so fond of was tinged with the iron of a bloody nose. Then the headache hit. Not the migraine from the first day, still not a good one. She stumbled over to bed and fell in.


The next morning, Jayce awoke early again, feeling more refreshed than ever. If it hadn't been for the lingering headache, she would've called it the perfect wakeup. Walking over and looking at the mirror, while her uniform molded back to skirt and tunic, she grinned. Her eyes were alien, something not real; something of the Nexus was a part of her now.

"You look bad ass!" She giggled to herself.

*You're still...*

Jayce got ahead of the thought and readied for a warp.

*Downst—kitchen, kitchen.*

She stepped through the nothing. The stars were still careless as they crackled past. She felt the ground, her momentum carrying through the step, guiding her head directly into Cali's.

"Ow!" Both girls yelped as they landed on their butts. Cali had a small cut on her blonde eyebrow where Jayce had head-butted her. She wiped away a trickle of blood.

"Okay, this is obviously gonna be a problem." Cali stood and walked to the fridge. She hummed in front of it as Jayce got to her feet.

"What are you doing?" Jayce questioned.

"Trying to figure out how to get spray paint out of here." She crossed one arm and tapped her lip with a finger. "If it can reach across planes for food. Whatever, that'll give me something to do after I shadow Nocti today."

Jayce cringed at the nickname. The rest of the group awoke for breakfast, stopping at the sight of Jayce.

"Wow. That looks amazing!" Erin exclaimed.

"So that was the feeling last night, looks great, J." Leon added.

"Bestie, that's a killer look!" Zynka marveled.

Jayce shrank at the compliments, though the voices didn't come. She said her thanks, then focused on getting food. Eating quickly, they got up to leave, only to realize no one knew where to go. A quick text exchange between Zynka and Jotun had the giant outside their door in moments.

"Hello, initiates." He smiled and nodded at Jayce. "Bitsy, the new look suits you. So, the mission for today is simple. We are going to go to a plane that is having an invasion of sorts. Once in that plane, you will be given a quick combat tutorial, then push back the invasion. Questions?"

The four students stood dumbstruck. They exchanged glances and looked to see if he was kidding, but his giant azure face was stoic.

"Oh, he's screwing with us. Good one, War Master." Leon laughed, though the laugh didn't even convince himself.

Jotun looked confused. He looked at his holo.

"No, says right here that the instructor took a contract to help repel an invasion on the Crest plane."

"Says the instructor? You are the instructor?" Leon questioned.

Jotun nodded.

"Exactly, let's go," he grumped.

He held out his hands. Very slowly, Erin and Zynka grabbed Jotun's hands, Leon and Jayce grabbing theirs.

"Hang on."

The ground left their feet. They were pulled through a hurricane. Shapes flew. The colors sounded wrong, and the taste of music was non-palatable. Jayce's headache pounded. Her screams went unheard.

*Used to that.*

The hurricane died down as they approached a light. When they landed, the students let forth a chorus of heaves, and the smell of vomit permeated the air. Outside of the smell of sick was a grounded scent of grass; it smelled oddly like the woods on Earth. Jayce, gathering herself, stood and surveyed the area. About half a mile in front of them was a village that looked straight out of a medieval sketch. The buildings were sloppily made of roughhewn wood and straw roofs. Their colors were muted browns and dark greys. There were creatures scurrying around on all fours, all in equally muted robes. Surrounding that was a forest of vaguely pine-looking trees. Colors were just slightly wrong for the Christmas-style trees. Rather than the dark green she would expect on the pines, they were a bright chartreuse. The trunks ran at an almost white. Familiar, yet alien. The rest of the group seemed to recover, wobbly. Jotun stepped in front of the initiates.

"Right then. The invasion is set to occur in around four Earth hours. Plenty of time to train."

Leon looked at the other three students.

"Four hours? To turn noncombatants into soldiers? We used to spend months, only barely, accomplishing that in the Army." His jaw was tight, fist clenched.

Jotun nodded.

"Then it's best we get started." He pulled out what resembled four black pen-shaped objects. "These are Nexus-made reaction armaments, known as eidolons. They take the weapon form it deems most applicable to the user."

He held one out for no one in particular. The students all eyed each other wearily. After a moment and a Jotun growl, Zynka stepped up. Wrapping her trunk around the eidolon, it hummed to life. The exterior broke apart, whizzing and whirring, as it determined its shape. As it started to piece back together, Zynka groaned.

"Stealth, my ability is stealth." She looked dejectedly at the now-formed massive obsidian war hammer. The head was almost as big as her own, yet seemed weightless as she moved it around in a less than excited arc.

"You will notice that the eidolon has minimal weight for the user, but that does not translate to the impact."

Zynka walked back to the group, head down, and mumbled.

"Supposed to be a rogue. Built like a tank."

Jayce fought hard to ignore the urge to laugh at yet more absurdity. Jotun handed one towards Erin, deciding a targeted offering would be a quicker approach. She stepped forward, clutching the eidolon. This time it still made noise but didn't break apart, just extended to meet her height and quieted. Erin cocked an eyebrow at the staff before rejoining the group. Jayce stepped up for her turn. Grabbing the offered weapon, it whirred and broke, reforming into what looked like a slim sword with joints throughout. Swinging it, it extended into a bladed whip. Seeing the whip, Jayce began to sweat and went as white as the Nexus dirt. In her mind, she heard a whip crack and a scream in her own voice, followed by an all too familiar laugh. She dropped the eidolon immediately, shaking and tripping backwards. She landed on her butt.

*You deserved it. Every time. You deserved it.*

The fear in her eyes could be felt throughout the group. Erin stooped next to her, placing her hand on Jayce's shoulder. The younger girl slapped her hand away hard as she pushed herself away. Leon stepped up and gently stopped Erin from encroaching again. She reared on him angrily; he only gave a solemn shake of his head. Jotun's face had a pained expression as he approached the cowering girl.

"Itsy Bitsy, it is hard to confront the past. But it is what must be done to get to the future."

Jayce shivered but slightly warmed at the name.

"I-I don't-I don't think I can use that."

Jotun looked at the whip blade that began to lose shape.

"You need to, though. It took that shape for a reason. You are strong, Bitsy. You can do this."

She slowly looked all the way up to Jotun's face. There was so much confidence in his eyes at his own words that she couldn't help but nod. The big blue troll grabbed the eidolon and handed it back. Hesitantly, she stood and accepted the proffered armament. She walked to the group, looking at Erin, who was rubbing her hand.

"I'm-I'm very sorry. I didn't mean to hit you." Jayce couldn't make eye contact.

"Yes, you did. And that's okay. You're a fighter, babe. Own it," Erin said, flashing that too pretty to be here smile.

Jayce just nodded, reddening slightly.

"Okay, squishy man, now you." Jotun offered the last eidolon.

Leon looked at it and shook his head.

"I think I'm good. Last time I picked up a weapon was almost my last night." The smell of alcohol and flashes of white powder filled his head; he heard the metallic click of a revolver's hammer. He shook himself.

Jotun squatted to look him in the eyes.

"I understand trepidation, but we are here to fight off an invasion." He offered the eidolon again. "It will take the form you need it to."

Leon, again, waved it away.

"That's what I'm afraid of. I'm good."

Seeing the resolve in the face of the broken man, Jotun shrugged.

"Alright, let's get training then."

With that, the group tested out their weapons, or lack thereof. Leon turned out to have been a boxer during his youth, so, one armed combat was, while not comfortable, familiar. Jayce and Erin had never used weapons before, and they struggled to figure out the proper way to wield them. Zynka, despite her growing annoyance with her ability/weapon combo, flourished.

Her movements were precise. Her silent footwork screamed, "I've been here before." She told stories of tribal warfare back on her plane; she had been a quietly formidable opponent. After about two hours of familiarization, Jotun called a halt.

"So now we are all comfortable with our eidolon."

Erin and Jayce immediately disagreed with shakes of their heads. Jotun smiled.

"Very good. Now, we have some time for sparing. Leon and Zynka, if you would." He drew a large circle on the ground, and when he was done, he pointed to the hammer in Zynka's trunk.

"If you would set it to no lasting damage. That way, the pain of the hit will be there. But no lingering effects."

Zynka, following the order, searched over the weapon and found a sliding button. Moving it to the proper setting, she nodded.

"Very good. Step in the ring, the first one knocked out of the ring loses. Good luck."

With his words ending, Leon and Zynka eyed each other, analyzing as they entered the ring. They maintained eye contact as they circled, neither willing to cross their own feet. Zynka was the first to attack, sending a slow sideways hammer blow towards Leon's ribs. He deftly dodged, immediately kicking himself. Having overcommitted to the dodge, Zynka reversed her feint, catching him in the other side of the ribs with a crack. Leon let out a growl as it nearly knocked him from the circle. The pain was intense, but fleeting as promised. Stepping back to the center of the ring, he contemplated how to win this. His mind raced with possibilities and options. He was too caught up to realize he had lost sight of Zynka. She has silently moved behind him. By the time he turned, it was too late. The hammer impacted his face as soon as he saw her. It sent him flying out of the circle to the feet of the other two girls. Blinking away the fleeting pain, he looked up at Jayce and Erin.

"Exactly as I planned." He gave a defeated smile as he one-armed his way back to his feet, returning to Zynka.

"And you were complaining about your stealth?" Leon smiled, offering a fist. Zynka stared quizzically at it for a moment before covering his fist with her hand. He laughed.

"Close enough, silent tank, close enough."

Jotun gruffed. "That was not an ideal fight, squishy man. A Wrembler would have seen that feint from a hundred yards away." His scowl was palpable.

Erin leaned into Jayce's ear. "I don't know what a Wrembler is, but I know that was an insult."

Jayce shivered at the warmth of the words on her skin. She just nodded. Leon shrugged.

"I haven't fought in about this long." He waved his missing arm.

"The planes are not going to care." Jotun shook his head as he spoke. "Bitsy, Erin. You are up."

The two girls looked wide-eyed at each other. They knew they were going to be next, but it just became real. They slowly made their way into the circle as the others left.

"Okay, same rules. And remember, for now at least, pain is temporary. Fight." Jotun's voice boomed on the last word.

Jayce looked at Erin, both equally rooted to the ground. It was a long moment of nothing before Jayce stepped forward, whip sword held more or less in a defensive position.

"Train, fight. Or I will," Jotun growled.

The words cut through the girls' hesitation. They didn't want to fight each other, but they really didn't want to fight the troll. Erin stepped forward, holding the staff like a mop. They met in the middle of the ring. Jayce mouthed "Sorry" before taking a lazy swing. Erin blocked it, kind of, the sword hitting her slender hand. She shook it for a second as the pain faded. When she had her grip back, she began swinging the staff wildly. Jayce fell back, accidentally blocking the blows. One, though, made it through, hitting her freshest shoulder bruise.

Her eyes went feral. Howling, she began swinging her sword like a bat, pushing Erin to the back foot. Jayce, while swinging, thought of how to get past the other woman's guard. Distracted in thought, she missed Erin's low sweep. It hit her on the side of the knee, stinging and causing her to lose her balance. Erin, seeing an opening, stepped forward, sending a poke check into Jayce's chest. The younger girl was knocked off her feet, landing on her back. Jayce felt the old marks and internally heard the whip crack and sadistic laughter.

*Always the punching bag. This is who you are.*

An anger that had never been, now was.

"No!"

Jayce roared, pointing the sword up at Erin. The whip blade launched out, connecting with Erin's chest, knocking/pushing her off the ground and out of the ring. There was a loud thud as the redhead landed a dozen feet away. Jayce, coming back to reality, jumped and ran to Erin's side.

"Freaking ouch," Erin said, slowly moving to a seated position. "That hurt bad."

Jayce's eyes grew misty.

"I-I'm so sorry, Erin, I didn't-I don't know what happened."

Erin gave her an easy wave-off.

"I'm tougher than I look, besides, you fought back, babe.

Sure, it means I got my ass kicked, but you did good." She reached up for a hand. Jayce, fighting her resistance, reached and helped the other woman up. Jotun made his way over.

"Good move, Bitsy. The invasion is going to happen soon; let us go get set up in the village."

"They have begun training." One.
"So it would seem." Two.
"Shall I intervene?" Three.
"Entertain me." Four.

# CHAPTER ELEVEN

The short walk to the village was surprisingly pleasant. Jayce didn't know she could miss a light breeze, but after the moving, not-there-air of the Nexus, the chill was nice. Despite the easy walk, there was a heavy overburden in the group. They weren't fighters; she looked at Leon. Okay, not all of them. The closer they got to the village, the clearer the occupants became. Mastiff-sized, rat-like animals, front teeth way too large for their mouths, and mangy fur matted down with various unspeakables. The smell reminded Jayce of the hamster cage of the class pet back in school. Stale ammonia and wood shavings mixed with rotting fruit and meat. Altogether, highly disgusting. Jotun led the group through the center of the village. The rats sniffed as they passed but seemed uninterested otherwise.

Jotun looked around for a moment before eyeing a bipedal rat with dark grey fur. Making his way over, he crossed his arms in an X.

"Elder Squee. It is an honor to see you still well."

The rat with its arthritic bones and wrongly shaped joints, did his best to return the obvious salute.

"War Master Jotun, we are privileged to have you here, and to have your assistance," the elder squeaked, nose and whiskers twitching.

"What is the situation? Do you have numbers?" Jotun dropped the salute.

Unnoticed, Leon tried the salute, sighing as he made a Y instead of an X.

"Quite dire, I am afraid. The numbers I don't believe are high; however, they are the kingdom's finest."

Jotun cocked his head.

"The kingdom? I thought you were under their protection?"

Squee started bruxing.

"We were, I do not know what occurred to change that." As he finished, a loud, very high-pitched horn sounded. The elder and the rest of the rats scurried off and vanished into various domiciles.

"Courage is strong around here," Leon joked as he stared wonderingly at how quickly they were alone.

"Not every creature is a fighter, brave one," the giant chided.

Without another word, Jotun pressed a point on his suit. Colors rushed to the touched spot and pulsed. His suit swirled, dancing on his skin. It shifted silently until it came to rest. Standing in front of them was no longer the professor in a smart suit. What stood now was a War Master in black plate armor; multicolored lines still coursing through it. He pulled out two eidolons, each whirring into position as an oversized mace and tower shield. The group stared at him in awe.

*What the hell can't this do?*

Jayce stared at her uniform.

"Press the left breast of the uniforms. It activates their armor."

Quickly, as the horn blew again, the initiates followed the order. A moment later, there stood Erin in a flowing robe. Leon, shirtless, his arm cover was gone, in a pleated kilt. Zynka, kicking the ground, was also in heavy plate, and Jayce had become enveloped in what looked like a ring-mail suit with violet sparks throughout.

"Trippy academy, check. Monsters, check. Role-playing video game, why not?" Leon joked but did not seem pleased.

He made sure to look everywhere but at his arm. Jayce shivered and perspired in terror.

*You can't even stand up for yourself.*

She didn't disagree with the voice this time. The horn blew again, so much closer now. She started to lock up, sword quivering in front of her. The group lined up: Jayce, Zynka, Jotun, Leon, and Erin. The footsteps could be heard now, not a lot, but enough. A fragrant smell of perfume accompanied the footsteps, at least the freshly washed scent. After an agonizing eternity of waiting, a group of five bipedal rats rounded a building. Two things stood out. One, these rats were clean, fur unmated and flowing. Two, they had more bulk, not muscle, for the most part. They looked like warriors that had been fed too well with no war to fight. One of them was overlarge, not quite Jotun's size but close. The rest ran in heights between Leon and Zynka. All five carried spears and had a single piece of plate armor covering their chests. They halted about twenty-five paces away.

"We are here for the tribute. Not a fight," the large, obvious leader spoke in a deep squeak.

Jotun responded by slamming his mace into his shield.

"Very well. I did offer," the leader squeaked again.

With that, he and Jotun charged, Jotun blocking a thrust and missing his own swing. Both groups forgot that they were all supposed to fight for a moment. Until one of the subordinate rats charged at Jayce. Her fear nearly paralyzed her, only at the last moment, hitting the spear away with her sword. The metal-on-metal clang vibrated all the way up to her shoulder. And with that, the brawl was on. Leon effortlessly dodged the spear of his rat, landing small jabs when the opportunity arose. Erin and her rat circled each other, neither making a move.

Zynka, however, battered hers senselessly. She had grabbed and held its spear in her massive hands and was walloping the rat with the hammer in her trunk. Jayce, returning to her own issues, saw the rat readying for a charge. As it approached, she missed her attempt to parry, taking the spear square in the ribs. The armor negated a pierce, but it sent a wave of pain. She kicked the large rat, knocking it back as she retreated a few steps.

"You're gonna pay for that."

She was sure the rat said it, but it was in her foster father's voice. Ice crept down her spine. She began hyperventilating as the rat charged again. She was frozen.

The rat got closer; spear leveled at her head. Before he could reach her, a spear flashed through the air, piercing through the rat's soft neck, releasing a green mist as it fell. Looking at the source of the throw, she saw Zynka wink at her and went back to pummeling an already green-misted rat. Leon had his rat's spear held back with all his strength, just inches from his bare chest. Erin was knocked to the ground by the butt of a spear to her temple. She groggily crawled towards Leon. Her rat slowly walked after her, taunting her.

"You aren't even worth the sweat I have shed," he squeaked.

Without realizing, Erin bumped into Leon's leg. Still holding the spear, he looked down and saw blood on the side of her face. His eyes went feral. Erin's rat approached and raised his spear to end the dance.

*You can't help her; you can't help anyone. You're going to let her die. Coward.*

Leon's rage-filled eyes watered at the thought as he reached his nub towards Erin's assailant. The rat's spear descended. Leon's kilt buzzed with blue energy, and he bellowed. Pain, the worst he had ever felt, pulsed at the tip of his nub as it started to crack and pop. The sound made Jayce want to wretch. It slowly, at first, formed into a flesh, bone, and vein-made knife tip. With another roar of pain, it extended so quickly that Jayce barely saw it stab through the skull of the menacing rat. It retracted, cracking, and forming a grotesque sword. He swung it at the neck of the rat he ought, nearly severing its head. Green mist covered Leon as he fell to the ground, screaming in pain. Jayce ran to him and knelt.

"Leon, what can I do?" she asked.

His eyes were glazed over with agony as he continued howling. Jotun, having seen the gruesome scene, took a long upward swing, launching his opponent dozens of feet in the air, and jogged over. He noted the blue in the kilt and nodded.

"You did well, brave one." No one heard him over the pained cries.

Erin crawled over and lay her head on his chest.

"Thank you. Thank you so much, Leon. I-I would've died without you." With her head there, she thought she could see his pain. See under the skin. It was vibrant. Very red, very real. The agony he felt was almost tangible to her. Leaning deeper into the thoughts, she found it. There was the pain. Looking at it, she imagined taking it from him.

*It's your fault it's there.*

Nodding slightly, she mentally reached out and grabbed it. It sent a searing pain down her left; an almost unbearable pain. The more she took, the worse it got; silent tears burned her cheeks. Leon, meanwhile, had slowed his hoarse screams. Erin kept taking it until there was nothing left. Her arm twitched wildly even as she tried to simmer it. Jotun was the first to notice the faint pink lines forming in her robes. Erin stayed in corralling his pain; her arm was in so much pain it went numb. Gritting her teeth, she didn't quit until it was gone. Leon's body went limp.

"What happened? Is he okay?" Zynka kneeled beside him.

"He will be fine, I assure you. Erin, come with me." He gently picked up Erin from the ground.

Silently, they walked a few dozen yards away.

"Where does it hurt?" He looked down on the quivering woman.

"I'm-I'm fine. Just scared is all, you know? Weird shit just went down," she said unconvincingly as she cradled her throbbing arm.

Jotun growled.

"My arm is sore. That's all," she relented.

"Erin, what you just did is extremely dangerous. You can't do that. Well, you can, but it is very hard to release pain of your own, much less others." He thought for a moment. "Unless." He held out his hand. "Give it to me."

She flinched at the gruffness in his command.

"I don't want to hurt you. I'm fine." Erin fidgeted.

The pain was excruciating; there was no way she would put someone through it. Jotun was about to growl again when he heard Jayce shout.

"Something is coming!"

Jotun scanned for the threat and cursed loudly.

"No, that's not supposed to be here. How?"

He and Erin rushed back to the group, and the form in the distance grew. Leon struggled back to his feet, his pain gone, but exhaustion evident.

"What is that thing?" There was a hint of fear in his voice.

Coming towards them was a massive, around two dozen feet in height, bloated and mangy rat tarantula hybrid. Its eight legs had rat feet at the end. Its fur had fallen out in places, revealing scabbed pale green skin. It skittered slowly towards them. Its overly large teeth gnashed between vicious snarls.

"Murdenex, that wasn't a part of this trial. It shouldn't be here." Jotun looked perplexed.

"Trial? I thought this was a contract." Leon tried to side-eye him while focusing on the horror in front of them.

It moved forward, rocking side to side as it did, almost like its bulk was too much for the skeletal legs.

"Later. We must go. Grab my hands."

Without any ceremony, the initiates grabbed on. Jotun breathed in and stepped. There was no sensation; they hadn't walked. A slight trace of fear could be seen on his face. "We are blocked. Damn."

Jayce shivered, her hands gripping her ring mail sleeves.

"Okay, what's the backup plan, 'War Master'? I know there is one," Leon prompted.

"No backup plan. This world is supposed to be a simulation. A mere trial run of a possible contract. This isn't making sense." Jotun finished as he hefted his shield. "Stay here."

With that, he bellowed and charged the Murdenex. The group tensed as the two massive beings collided. Jotun, being much smaller, was temporarily overwhelmed by the sheer mass of the rat thing. He recovered quickly and delivered a shield bash to one of the legs; it connected, but the Murdenex either didn't notice or didn't care. They both exchanged blows, Jotun slowly being pushed back.

"We-We have to do something. We have to help him!" Jayce screamed, eyes gleaming.

She took a step forward but flinched at a neon hand on her shoulder.

"Bestie, there is nothing we can do that Jotun can't," Zynka quietly spoke.

The battle in front of them raged. Jotun gave as good as he got, but it was clear who had the edge.

"That's bullshit, Zynka. We can do a few things," Erin spoke as she walked up. "We can at least distract it so he can get a good hit in."

As she spoke, the Murdenex opened its mouth and blew a large stream of acidic mist onto Jotun's shield, causing him to throw it aside before the corrosion reached him. That momentary loss of focus cost him. The rat swung two of its forelegs, catching Jotun in the midsection, sending him spiraling through one of the small huts. The building collapsed on top of him. Leon instinctively stepped in front of the group. Jayce looked around for somewhere to hide and noticed Zynka was gone.

"What do we do? How?" Jayce asked, her teeth chattering rapidly.

The Murdenex slowly started towards them, swaying lazily. Leon took another step forward; nub starting to twitch and stretch. The sound of bones snapping and teeth gritting drowned out the massive creature's movements. The cracking sound stopped as Leon's arm took the shape of a two-yard-long Dane ax, blade made of sharpened bone. The pain on his face was visible to the two women behind him, yet he still trudged forward.

The combatants were only meters away now. Leon had to look almost straight up at the beast when he charged. The monster took a swipe at his head. He dodged it, bringing the axe up and biting deep into the leg. Jayce watched in horror as the Murdenex raised its leg, Leon still struggling to break free, and opened its mouth, green acid building up. She saw what was happening and knew what would happen. She thought of the smile Leon had given her not even a week ago; the first smile ever directed at her, not in malice. And now it was going to be gone. That smile, that self-deprecating charm, that...friend.

As the last word entered her head, she felt it. The breeze was absent, the hammering of her heart deafening her; the taste in the air of rotten meat was gone. She jogged to the statue-like structure and began to think. She tried to figure out how to blink it out of existence, but nothing came. Her hold on time was slipping.

*Do something! Do anything, big or small, just do it.*

That was it. She focused on the Murdenex and tried to imagine it smaller, just a little bit. The creature began to crackle, and she could hear bones, not breaking, but shrinking. The monster went from twenty feet to eighteen feet to fifteen feet. Jayce felt her nose start to drip. Thick red tears streaked her face. Twelve feet. With a final push of energy, the creature solidified at a height of about ten feet. Still massive but better. The last hammer of her heart popped her ears as sensation came rushing in and then faded just as quickly as she hit the ground; eyes, nose, and ears dripping red.

Leon hit the ground when time returned, looking at the half-sized Murdenex. Its green eyes were wide. Was it fear or anger? It didn't matter. Its eyes were locked on Jayce's unmoving body; its mouth gaped open, green fizzling.

"Not a chance." Leon roared in pain and defiance as his arm

quickly and loudly became a round shield. He dove in front of Jayce as the acidic stream leapt for her. It impacted on his shield arm, and he released the most guttural cry Erin had ever heard.

*You are just going to watch them die?*

Erin snapped up. Not knowing what good she could do, she clutched her staff and ran towards the fight.

*"Give it to me."*

Jotun's words went through her mind as she made it behind Leon. She raised her staff, pointing it at the monster, and imagined her borrowed pain flowing through it. Nothing happened until a pitiful yelp came from Leon. He was fading.

*No! He dies, we all die.*

She clamped her hand on his shoulder, willing with everything she had to take his pain. It hit her with the force of a tsunami. Fire lit up every nerve ending. She tried to focus on channeling it, but her mind wouldn't let her stop thinking of the agony.

The Murdenex stopped its stream and battered Leon's shield, taking chunks with each swipe. He tried to parry a blow, only sending its claw to the side. Its claws gouged through Erin's pale, beautiful cheek. The hit left deep red claw marks. The hit, though, enraged Erin. She gave a war cry a Valkyrie would have trembled at. The staff pulsed pink, faster and faster, until a beam emerged. It hit the monster square in the face. It let out a soul-splitting squeal. It fell to the ground and convulsed in pure, blinding pain. Erin couldn't think as the pain left her. It ripped holes in her insides as it exited her, not in her organs, but in her very soul. She saw a pink blur run and jump off a roof.

"It's Zynka, bitch," the elephant screamed as she brought her war hammer down through its head, imbedding it about a foot deep in the ground.

Leon and Erin collapsed, both in anguish, but safe.

"Did you guys see it! I snuck up on it! I actually did it!" Zynka refrained from a happy dance.

"You sure did, silent tank. Thank you," Leon muttered

through gritted teeth, before finally allowing himself to lose consciousness.

Erin lay there, between a broken girl and a shattered man, and breathed. She reached out and interlaced her fingers with Jayce's, who still managed a flinch. Reaching over to Leon, she did the same, his hand wrapping hers like an anaconda. She stared up at the sky that wasn't hers and drifted off.

Zynka stared at the three unconscious humans. They looked so broken. She looked around for any looming threat, eyeing the Murdenex cautiously. Where its head used to be, now poured the acrid green mist.

*Well, that's dead at least.*

Looking at the ruined building that had collapsed onto Jotun, she jogged over. The troll was buried under the shredded timbers of the house. Two of the peasant rats were crushed under his immense weight. She started pulling the timbers off him. He was more covered than she thought, and it took her more than fifteen minutes to uncover him completely. His arms and face were covered in a white liquid that Zynka determined was his blood. He was unconscious, just like the humans. The rats had started to reemerge. Finding Squee, she approached.

"Elder, do you have any water?"

The old, molted rat creaked as he answered. "Many of the homes have wash basins. I would not recommend drinking it, however." His voice cracked like an old hardwood staircase.

"Not for drinking!" Zynka shouted over her shoulder.

Entering one of the houses, her ears flopped, looking at the basin. The stagnant water was filthy; scum and flies floated on the surface. Steeling herself, she dunked her trunk in and inhaled all she could, gagging repeatedly. She sprinted back to Jotun's limp body and, with the most force she could, blew the water over his face. Zynka jumped backwards as the giant flailed wildly, coming to his feet in an instant. He sputtered and spat violently.

"That taste is horrendous. You couldn't have shaken me?" He wiped his mouth with his armored hand.

The elephant reddened, having not thought of such a simple solution. Jotun's eyes widened.

"The others? Bitsy?" he asked worriedly as he rushed to where they lay.

Kneeling beside them, he checked their pulses, his massive fingers covering their necks. Zynka caught up and relayed what had happened to them and the downfall of the monster. Satisfied, Jotun lay down beside them.

"We rest, then we return," he said, drifting off as well. Zynka shrugged, lay down, and attempted to join them.

"They have slain the beast." One.
"So it would seem." Two.
"Did I entertain?" Three.
"Indeed, you did." Four.

# CHAPTER TWELVE

A few hours after losing consciousness, Jayce began to stir. Her eyes fluttered open and snapped shut against the light. The migraine was back with a vengeance. She tried to move her body to get some feeling back; it was slow and gave the asleep muscle tingle. When feeling returned to her hand, she froze. Fighting her throbbing head, she looked down and opened her eyes. Erin's hand was firmly clasped around her own. It was warm and sweaty, but she cherished the feeling. Laying there, she closed her eyes again and just let Erin's warmth run through her.

*She cares. She doesn—*

She shut out the second thought and clung to the first. Erin started to move shortly after, rolling and gently placing her head on Jayce's shoulder.

"You okay?"

There was so much in that question. Have you recovered? Are you feeling okay? Can I lay my head here? Jayce teared at the thought.

"I'm-I'm okay, thank you." And she meant it. For the first time she could remember, she was okay. Minus the skull-splitting headache, fear of an unknown planet, and general nervousness of all things plane walking, of course.

Erin nuzzled her shoulder before getting to her knees. She

looked at Jayce, so small, so fragile, yet so strong. It was amazing how strong the girl was without even having a clue about it. Erin bent down and pressed her lips onto the younger girl's forehead. Jayce's eyes went wide. The fight in her wanted to scream and fight back, but she lay there, the cracked lips on her forehead like a drink of water in the desert. Erin got up and roused the others. Jayce just lay there, an actual smile fighting for prominence on her face.

The others arose and helped Jayce to her feet.

"What the hell was that 'War Master'?" Leon finally gained his bearing turned on Jotun, not an ounce of fear in his eyes.

"Brave one, I have stated that this plane is supposed to be a simulation. The entire thing, Squee, the village, and the invaders, all simulations. Very realistic but not life-threatening. The Murdenex aren't inhabitants of this plane, or walkers in their own right. Someone had to have manipulated the system. We need to get back so I can speak with Professor Noctharim." He paused. "I would never knowingly endanger my students." He sighed and held out his hands. "Let us go."

With not even a moment of hesitation, they latched on and were gone.


After the normal walking ailments had subsided, Jotun made his exit to Noctharim's office. The students watched as he lumbered off and warped.

"I need some serious munchies." Leon tried to lighten the mood, undercut by the massive stomach growl.

"Yeah, food, shower..." Erin paused, eyes wide. "Has anyone found a shower? And on a lesser note, makeup?"

Jayce reached up and rubbed at the last remnants of black makeup.

"Why don't you just go home and grab some? And you can set up bathing arrangements and a bathroom in your room." Zynka answered.

"Go back?" The three humans chorused.

The elephant cocked her head.

"I mean, you are walkers."

The three looked amongst themselves. Yes, it was true; they were walkers. But this was the first time any of them had even considered that an option. Leon opened his mouth and shut it.

"Food first, then walking tips," the elephant said as the front door started to melt.

Following close behind, the three humans ran smack into Zynka's back. Seeing what stopped the neon tank, Jayce froze. There was thick smoke in the air, mechanical parts scattered around, Professor Automo shaking his head, Noctharim laughing on the table, and Cali, cheeks covered in dirt and grease, hair in dirty pig tails with a chaotic grin on her face, a can of spray paint in her hand. The part that really caught the group's eyes was that Cali had an eyepatch over her left eye, with a small green skull. Her normal pink shirt and jeans combo was replaced with the cyber slick black uniform in the shape of ripped jeans and a sleeveless T-shirt with a pulsing green skull. She looked over at the four, grin widening.

"So...a thing happened."

* * *

Cali walked back to the fridge, arms crossed, finger tapping her lip, and humming.

"Spray paint," she spoke to the machine. Nothing happened. She tried again. Again, no result. Cali thought. "I'm hungry for some spray paint." Nothing.

*So, if it doesn't recognize it as edible, it won't give it to me.*

She mulled over the thought for a bit.

"Ice cream sandwich." And presto, she was enjoying the scrumptious cookies and cream flavored treat. "Well, if the problem can't be fixed from the outside..."

She started scanning the fridge and found what looked like a screw hole set well into the base. She looked in and decided it was something like a flathead screw. "Well, if I had tools, I wouldn't need this to work."

She snapped her fingers and ran to the living room's holoscreen. She found the messaging app and sent Noctharim a request. As if he didn't want to miss a second of pets, he warped into the round couch with Cali. Instead of being startled, she scooped him up, petting him as she went to the fridge.

"I need a thingy to go in that thing, so I can pull off that part and see why it won't give me what I want." She said this with quick hand movements, though Noctharim was still slow to catch.

"You want what, my dear?"

Cali sighed.

"I want to take this apart so I can see how it works, because it doesn't give me anything inedible. And I need spray paint," she grumped, petting his ear wing furiously in frustration. Far from feeling assaulted, he leaned in.

"First, why do you need spray paint?"

"Duh! So, I can put a mark on the floor, so warpers know where to aim. So *this* doesn't happen again!" She pointed to her cut eyebrow.

"Ah, yes, the early days of warping, and walking for that matter, can be quite the uphill battle. How have you been handling it?"

Cali held the flying head at her eye level.

"I. Got. Head. Butted. So. Not. Well." She emphasized every word as though to a child.

"And that was when you warped?"

Cali just looked confused.

"No, Jayce warped into me."

Noctharim took flight, doing his lazy loops.

"Yes, that was Jayce. How. Have. You. Been. Doing. With. The. Warping?" he emphasized back.

They stared at each other for a long moment before Cali pointed to herself.

"Not a walker, remember?"

Noctharim did a slow roll before landing on the table.

"How can I remember something that was never stated?"

Cali just stared at him. She opened her mouth, but only air escaped.

"I never said you were not a walker. I merely stated you were too young to begin classes, though I do admit you are older than Zynka."

Cali didn't know which piece of information to latch onto first. So, she went for both.

"I'm older than a walker?" And failed on both. "I mean, I am a walker? And I am older than Zynka?" she corrected.

Noctharim nodded. "Yes, on both counts. I, however, made my decision about you not being a student based on the fact that her species is born moving, while yours is squishy and incapable of viability solo for many years." He gnawed his wing tip.

Cali thought about that for a moment and bobbed her head.

"So, how do I warp?"

"Think of where you want to go and step; it truly is very simple." He flourished his wing dismissively.

She thought for a moment, looked at the center of the circular couch, and stepped. In a blink, she was standing where she wanted, slight nausea hitting her as she stumbled slightly. Shaking her head, she looked at the professor with a feral grin. She stepped again, appearing before the professor.

"This is awesome!" she screeched with glee. She stepped again, landing on the upstairs balcony. "Come on, Birdo." She stepped again, landing by the front door. The nausea was building up, but the young girl ignored it, having way too much fun to care.

Noctharim shrugged and stepped as well.

A solid fifteen minutes passed of the pair warping all around the large living area. Cali's excitement was so infectious that Noctharim couldn't help but smile. For eras he had warped, and it had become so mundane, but this girl, *this girl*, had reminded him how wondrous the ability was. He found himself giggling along with the young lady.

Finally, the nausea caught up with Cali, and she buckled and vomited on the floor. The ground quickly ate it and released concentrated vanilla bean and gasoline deodorant. She wiped her mouth.

"Thank god for that." Standing up, she went directly back to the fridge.

Noctharim followed, landing on her shoulder.

"You know, we could just walk back to Earth and get what you want."

Cali thought a bit.

"Yeah, but that seems like a lot of effort, when I know we can make this stupid thing do what I want. I need tools." Cali reexamined the screw holes.

Noctharim's eyes glazed over for a moment before refocusing. "Automo is on his way. This could be interesting. He created most of the tech here after all."

Seconds later, a robotic voice sounded behind them.

"I received the request. Tools are on hand. What problem needs my attention?" Automo's voice crackled, and his joints whizzed as he approached.

"This dumb box can give me all the ice cream I want, but can't give me spray paint. I want that fixed." She slapped the door. "Give it to me!"

Automo gently moved the girl aside. He pulled out a long screwdriver-like device and inserted it into the screw holes. Moments later, the fridge was free from the wall. He set it on the floor and opened up a panel on the back, revealing wiring and a very odd-looking circuit board. The board had normal-looking diodes and tracers; what might have been a fuse of sorts; the standout was a large, clear capacitor with gray smoke coursing through it. Cali got close to have a better look.

Pointing to the capacitor, she asked. "This, what is this? It looks important. Why is there smoke? What does it do?"

Automo's head made a sound like dial-up internet restarting.

"That is a planar capacity generator. The 'smoke' as you call it, is walking debris. The debris is what makes your body compressed on a walk. It serves to open a wormhole. So, in total, that generator is what allows this machine to operate."

Cali got closer to it. She stared into it as if it would tell her how to modify it. She scratched her left eye, as it started to itch. Having a burst of an idea, she slapped the generator. The debris kicked around violently before settling down.

"What was that meant to accomplish?" Automo monotoned.

"Well, my dad always said you can fix anything with a big enough hammer. He fixed the alternator on our car by hitting it." She smiled sadly, remembering her dad teaching her about cars and other general handywork.

"It is not broken, my dear. Because something doesn't do what you would prefer it do, doesn't make it inoperable." Noctharim said, landing on Automo's bald head.

She leaned even closer, eying the circuit board.

"Come on, punk, tell me how to do it."

Her eye started to burn. She hit the generator harder. The debris turned into a tornado in the glass container before popping and covering Cali's pink shirt. Where it landed disappeared as it sent those stitches to who knows where.

"Okay, that isn't what I thought would happen." She fingered the holes in her shirt. "I should've brought clothes."

Noctharim shook his head.

"My dear Automo, would you be so kind as to fetch a uniform for young Cali and a replacement generator?" He flew to the table, doing a flip before landing.

"Accepted," Automo said as he disappeared.

"Young Cali, that was not a very safe thing to do. Had it landed on your skin, we would have had to search for pieces of you around the multiverse."

Cali shrugged. "It didn't."

She rubbed her eye furiously as she examined the board again. She followed the traces, mapping out the diodes and trying to figure out what did what. A tear came out of her left eye, but she wiped it away, not noticing it was red. Noctharim didn't miss it, though. He was about to speak but decided to watch instead. The girl was so focused, he didn't want to interrupt. Cali continued scanning, the traces on the board becoming more and more clear. She still had no idea what they did but was able to piece together the layout. Another tear and more burning in her eye. The wiring began to make a bit more sense.

"Okay, that wire." She touched it and received a decent shock for her effort. "Damn. Okay, that should be the incoming voltage." She looked puzzled.

*Incoming voltage. Why do I know that?*

Another tear, and the burning intensified. She went to scratch again. As she touched her eye, she screamed in pain. She hit her knees as the most intense pain she had ever experienced shot through her head. Noctharim moved to help but stopped himself.

*This is her moment. You need not be involved.*

So, he perched on the table and watched. Cali's eye started to harden. All moisture seemed to get boiled away in the heat. Her vision started to transition from normal to green, the circuits becoming more vivid and defined. She fell back, letting out another bloodcurdling howl. As the boiling sensation started to fall off, a new hell began. Her socket felt empty, void of the green eye that had inhabited it for years. A hissing sound sprang from her socket. It felt like molten steel was poured straight into her skull. It filled the emptiness, slowly forming and growing. Cali was out of screams, just writhing in pure agony. Once her socket was full, the burning ceased immediately, leaving Cali sweating on the ground, trying to get motor control back.

She lay there, eyes closed, until she felt a weight land on her chest. Opening her eyes slowly, vertigo hit her instantly. She fought through it as best she could, but her vision was wrong. Through her right eye she saw Noctharim as clear as normal. But through her left eye, through a very green view, she saw through the professor. Well, kind of through him. She closed her right eye to focus. She saw Noctharim's internals, more like a schematic of how his body worked. His brain was connected to many small lines through his body, leading to his muscles. Every time he moved, she saw electric pulses run to the body part in question. She closed that eye and opened the other, returning to normal vision.

"What the hell is going on?" she asked through gritted teeth.

"My young Cali, it would seem that your ability has manifested. What do you see?" Noctharim asked, hopping up to her chest and touching her closed eye with a talon.

She switched eyes. Noctharim looked in awe at the silver metallic eye with a neon green pupil.

"I see you, well, inside of you. I can watch your body move through electric pulses, your nervous system." Closing both eyes, she lay back and just breathed for a while. Noctharim did not interrupt.

A few minutes later, Cali heard Automo return. Opening her normal eye, she saw the professor had gone to sleep on her belly. She smiled and winced. The left side of her face was still extremely sore. Noctharim woke and took flight at her movement.

"My apologies, dear Cali. It has been a while since I have just laid down. Thank you."

She gave him two thumbs up before rolling to her belly and getting to her feet. Looking at Automo, she switched eyes. His internal wiring almost sang to her. She could look at one wire, and it would highlight, showing its entire path. She followed a large wire that went from his "heart" to a box in his mid-back. Instinctually, she knew that if the box was disabled, the professor would shut down. She also knew that shutting him down wouldn't be the end for him, as there was a faint smoke-like substance. The smoke, she could tell, was a wireless feed, more than likely returning to his central hub.

*Interesting. I wonder what that would look like.*

She tapped her lips again.

"Your scan is unpleasant, human child," Automo said without a trace of emotion.

Cali shrugged her shoulders, switching eyes, and took her uniform from him. Without a word, she walked to her room.

"That child has changed."

"Indeed, she has and has not, my old friend," Noctharim concluded.

Noctharim looked to Cali's room as he heard her humming. She came out; her uniform had shaped into ripped skinny jeans and a black sleeveless shirt with the uniform color in the shape of a neon green skull. As the energy pulsed, the skull seemed to laugh. And over her left eye was a black patch with a matching skull. She skipped to Automo and took the generator, walking to the fridge. *Hmm.* The patch melted over to her other eye. The circuit board buzzed as she looked.

"How do I get more than food from you?" she asked the inanimate object. As she spoke, different wires started to pulse. Following one, she came to a diode. "Is that for redundancy?"

It blinked fast, which she knew meant no.

*Hmm.*

She followed another flashing wire to the broken generator.

"Duh." She pulled out the old one and gently put in the new one. It buzzed to life.

*Okay, now we have a circuit. Now, do I up the voltage or swap wiring?*

The pulsing wire grew steady, and she looked elsewhere. The fuse caught her eye; she saw that one trace went to the generator and one to a wire terminal.

"I wonder." She thought about taking out the fuse. And it came out. "Whoa!" She hopped back. Automo cocked his head. Noctharim only hooted loudly.

*Okay, so the fuse is gone. I need more volts to the generator.*

She looked at where the fuse had been and willed her thoughts to work. Slowly, a small square box formed. It came together like building blocks. When it was completed, the traces joined to either side of the newly formed step-up transformer. They connected, and the generator went wild with energy, chaotic, but contained. She reached into the fridge and pulled out a can of pink spray paint. With a feral grin, she turned to the melting door.


"And then you guys got here," Cali said around a huge mouthful of Rocky Road. She immediately grabbed her head. "Brain freeze."

The group sat at the dinner table, slack-jawed.

"You know what? Today has been pretty not-chill. I'm going to bed." Leon shook his head and walked to his room, muttering.

"What up with the big guy?" Cali swallowed before asking this time.

"Today has just not been super chill," Erin also stated, getting up, and she went around the table giving Cali and Zynka forehead kisses. When she got to Jayce, she stopped and took the younger girl's face in her hands. "You saved us all today. Thank you." She laid a soft kiss on a barely flinching Jayce's forehead and walked away. Jayce's red face couldn't win the fight against her smile.

"So, what happened?" Cali asked.

* * *


"Someone blocked off the Nexus," a disheartened Jotun said.

"Indeed, very curious. It appears we may have another weaver," Noctharim said, hanging upside down on his perch.

"What should we do, Professor?"

"My dear War Master, of that I am unsure."

"We have made an impact." One.
"So it would seem." Two.
"Shall I continue to intervene?" Three.
"Observe for now." Four.

## CHAPTER THIRTEEN

The next morning, the group met for a quiet breakfast. At least it would have been if Cali wasn't complaining.

"I'm just saying, you guys got a hardcore boss fight. I got an eye melted out of my skull," Cali said, eliciting a chuckle from Zynka.

Her complaints had been a version of the same for over an hour. She was only interrupted when her holo pinged. Bringing it up, she read the message and smiled.

"Well, y'all have fun at class today. I'm off to show robot head how to fix stuff." With that she stood and took a step, disappearing.

"How is she more comfortable than me doing that? I've been here for a week!" Zynka said, rubbing her temple with her trunk.

Four more holo pings sounded out. Checking them, the group saw that they were to go to a classroom in the main castle on the fifth floor, row six, for Mysticism. Hurrying to finish their assorted breakfasts, they decided to walk as there was no designated time. Jayce, the first one out, couldn't help but marvel again at the reflective castles. The rainbow fish were in a frenzy today; the lavender sky added to the depth of color.

"Hey, it's a bit of a walk, but how about we take a hover bike?" Zynka asked, pulling out her holo and typing away.

Instantly, the white dirt spun like a dust devil. It grew wider, then seemed to condense, fluctuating a few times before taking the form of a bicycle. Only the "tires" were horizontal, rather than vertical. It floated around eight inches off the ground, making a small whirring noise. Zynka threw a leg over and waited as the bike formed to her size. Jayce and the others were dumbstruck.

"Does it ever stop being weird as hell around here?" Leon shook his head as he brought up his holo and summoned a bike as well.

The others followed suit, with Jayce only slightly miffed at hers being tiny.

"How do they work?" Erin asked, playing with the triangle-shaped steering wheel.

"Intent. It will follow what you want to happen. Weird, but if it works, it works," Zynka said, leaning forward and moving the bike at a slow walking speed. Leon looked at the human girls and winked.

"Later," he said as his bike took off at an impossible speed.

"Oh hell no!" Erin hollered as she tore off after him.

Jayce decided to stay with Zynka.

"Hey, bestie, I'm glad you stuck back. I feel like we haven't had just us since the tour." She looked happily at Jayce.

"Yeah. There's not been a shortage of interruptions, for sure. How are you liking everybody?"

Jayce mentally guided her bike close enough so they didn't have to yell. As she did, she saw the sides of the bikes facing each other glimmer with the same barricade from the platform.

*So, you can't wreck, neat.*

"Oh, everyone is awesome! Leon is a real hard softy. Erin is like a cool mom. It's great," Zynka stated happily.

"What about Cali?"

Jayce looked over to see the usually pink elephant go red. She bit a smile away, deciding not to pry into that.

"She's pretty awesome, too. She has this, like, ability to make things fun. Crap, she made me laugh this morning, telling a story about her eye melting. And her style is so laid back in your face, ya know?" Zynka turned redder as she stopped talking.

She half-smiled at Jayce. "What about you? Liking everyone?"

Jayce smiled before replying. "They are really great. I'm not used to having people seem to care for me." She moved her bike slightly back and forth.

"Seems to? Girlie, they lurve you." Zynka smile was huge.

*Love? No. Not for me.*

Almost reading her thoughts, Zynka shifted topics.

"What did you think of your first trip into the planes? Outside of here, I mean."

Jayce thought about the Murdenex and shivered. She contemplated her answer as they cruised along.

"It was cool seeing what my ability could do. Really don't need this migraine, but that's the toll, I guess." She rubbed her temple hard with a knuckle. "And I didn't get to see it, but I heard your awesome finishing line!" Jayce smiled at the large elephant through the pulsing in her head.

"Oh, uh, yeah, so that was something that happened. I guess I am a tank." Zynka drifted off.

"What are you talking about...bestie...if you hadn't of snuck up on it, who knows what would've happened. I was useless."

"Damn, bestie, we have got to work on your self-esteem. Not only did you shrink that freaky rat, but you also looked stunning doing it. Ten out of ten on my scorecard." Zynka nodded, agreeing with herself.

*It's all lies. You were a burden; you got them hurt.*

As Jayce and Zynka approached the main castle, a sound made her look up to one of the massive spires that threatened to scrape the sky.

"Yeehaw!" Leon yelled as he and Erin came racing down the side of the castle.

"Physics be dammed!" Erin hollered in reply.

The two seemed to be racing back to the ground. Leon pulled ahead when Erin pulled back as they reached the base.

Leon just kept barreling down. Jayce tightened as he got closer and closer. But right when he should have hit the ground, the bike changed its gravity and landed perfectly upright on the white dirt, not even disturbing it. Erin followed, shaking her head.

"There was no way you knew that was going to happen, psycho." She shook out her long red hair.

Leon pulled his hair back, and his uniform sent a piece of itself to tie it.

"Are you serious? How did I not think of that?" Erin quickly braided her hair and tied it up.

"And I had a fifty/fifty chance." Leon shrugged as they all rode around the last corner to the main entrance. And saw a scene out of an acid trip.

What lay before them was the same courtyard they had arrived in, the LED fountain playing to unheard music, those so-black-they-weren't-there trees, their LED-like leaves dancing along. The infinite fin whale was speaking with a four-foot-tall squirrel in uniform black leather like armor. There were a few bipedal animals, a warthog, a ram, and one of the schnauzers from the other day, gathered around the fountain. Circling the fountain was the disco ball creature, slithering like a slug, the lights of the fountain playing hypnotically off of it. When the ram noticed them, the others all stopped and looked momentarily before returning to their conversations. The whale, however, float-swam over to them.

"Greetings, initiates. I am Professor Selvoth, one of the instructors of energy work. You are obviously the new humans. What class do you all have next?" Its voice was very ethereal, both loud and sounding far off.

The group introduced themselves.

"We are headed to Mysticism, sir," Jayce answered.

"Understood, I believe that Antoinette is hosting the initiate class today. She is very wise. It would do you well to pay attention. Have you any questions? I know being new is hard for those unaware of this place."

Jayce found herself enthralled by his tones.

"Yeah, do you know why it was only us in class with Jotun yesterday?" Leon spoke up.

Jayce, now hearing it said out loud, was also curious. With how many students were here, having a teacher to themselves seemed strange.

"You are initiates. Until you complete your five introductory courses and placement exams, you are to receive private classes. It lets us be able to properly evaluate the initiates." Selvoth's voice carried a gravitas that bespoke a deep wisdom.

"A placement exam?" Erin asked.

"Yes. It is an evaluation of what you have learned that allows us to place you in proper courses going forward. But I apologize, I must be getting to my own class. Remember to do well and learn what you can." With that, Selvoth simply disappeared.

The group spoke among themselves as they walked up the icy-looking stairs to the main castle. The doors shot up as they approached, revealing the void. They all took a deep breath before entering it. The claustrophobic feeling and loud silence hit hard but fast. Only Erin was left panting.

"No way does that ever become normal," she griped as they walked to row six of the doors and looked up.

Jayce fidgeted nervously. She was about to ask how to get up there when Zynka simply stepped onto the wall and began walking up it. The humans exchanged slack-jawed looks. Leon got his bearings first and easily followed Zynka, followed by Erin. Jayce, with much trepidation, put her foot on the wall. Immediately, it felt like she was being pulled in two separate directions, by two separate gravities. Quickly, she put her other foot up to end the sensation. And just like that, the wall became her floor, her floor becoming her wall. The feeling made her uneasy as she shuddered. She carefully walked towards the rest of the group.

"Okay, this is ridiculous. Just this whole place, utterly ridiculous," Erin said, leaning up against Leon, who looked equally unsteady.

"You're not kidding. This is gnarly," he responded.

Zynka, obviously the least concerned, reached down with her trunk and tapped the door in a light knock. The door turned solid violet before simply disappearing. Looking through the door on the floor, Jayce saw a musty room, much like a cigar lounge. Smoke billowed throughout it. There were two large, overstuffed cloth couches, one violet and one pink. Jayce shivered as she looked at the ceiling and saw massive, intricate spiderwebs.

"You first, bestie," Zynka said before giving her a light trunk push.

Jayce yelled as her feet rocketed to the far side of the classroom. Halfway through the room, her body arrested its momentum and rotated her, setting her on her feet gently. The quick stop and turn made Jayce grab her mouth and gag. Zynka came through next, laughing. Her body was doing the same movements.

"Sorry, girlie, I couldn't help myself," she trumpeted quietly.

Jayce just gave her a small smile and went back to trying not to puke. Looking back at the door, she saw Leon lowering Erin in; her landing was much more subdued.

"Think I can do a flip?" Leon queried before turning his back to the door and doing a back flip into the opening.

As he came in, his spinning momentum carried him through multiple three-sixties before landing him safely on his feet. He threw his arm in the air like a gymnast. Erin clapped sarcastically. Then, Leon doubled over and vomited.

"Oh my god, so gross." Zynka shoved her trunk into her mouth to avoid the smell that never came.

The sick was absorbed instantly, and the room let off a very strong smell of sage to cover it.

"I love this place," Leon said, wiping his mouth.

The group wandered to the couches and sat down. At the end of one of them was a life-sized doll. Its face was white porcelain in the visage of a young adult female, and it wore a black Victorian dress with a white neck ruffle.

"When do you think the teacher will get here?" Jayce asked, continuing to scan the room.

Oddities were scattered about the room. An ivory horse statue with a missing ear. A glass ball wrapped by a lavender serpent. A mirror cracked and splintered completely throughout.

"I'm sure they will make some form of grand entry, to shock and amaze!" Leon said in his best ringleader voice.

When he finished, as if the universe agreed with him, faint tendrils of violet energy began slowly braiding themselves together as they came down from the ceiling to the doll. First one connected to the head, then two to the shoulders, then the elbows. The group jumped up and backed behind Leon, who took his stance. The connecting process continued until each section of its body was connected. Then some of the tendrils grew taught, and the doll, no, marionette, was raised to its feet. The frozen porcelain face slowly turned in their direction. Its eyes had the same violet as the tendrils and Jayce's own eyes.

"Welcome to Introduction of Mysticism. I am Professor Antoinette." The doll's voice was so cold and distant. Her mouth didn't move either; her voice just was. The group visibly relaxed.

"Hello, Professor." Zynka recovered first.

"Would you mind taking your seats? I would much like to get through this," the doll's cold voice demanded while asking a question.

They all sat quickly. Jayce and Erin on one couch, Leon and Zynka on the other.

"Very good. Mysticism is a specialization that focuses on the strange and the weird. It is a broad subject that I neither have the time nor the patience to fully delve into today." Her cold voice made a shiver run down Jayce's spine.

"The basics and abilities are to be covered once classes begin in earnest. Today, my only task is to complete a contract with the help of the initiates." Antoinette spoke as if reading from an invisible note.

"The contract we are doing is on my plane. There have been

some lost pets that must be recovered, so that is what we will do. Questions?" She scanned each of the four.

"How are we going to be of help if we don't know how to do anything?" Jayce's voice was barely a whisper.

"I do not believe that initiates are useful. But Jotun asked me to help, and here I am." The professor's porcelain cheek reddened slightly.

"Moving on. Grab my hands and let us be off." She ended by extending her hands to the group. Skeptically, the group did as they were told and swiftly vanished.

* * *

"Studying their earth made me remember Four. Though he was known as 'Wanderer'. Our memories have been altered." Noctharim hung from his perch as he spoke.

"That does seem to ring true. What does it mean, Professor?" a sitting Jotun asked.

"Of that, my friend, I am unsure."

"Mysticism." One.
"So it would seem." Two.
"Shall I intervene?" Three.
"I shall." Wanderer.

# CHAPTER FOURTEEN

The hurricane between planes ripped at Jayce as she was yanked through to the other side. As her feet hit solid ground, her ankle rolled hard on a cobblestone. She caught herself on Leon's left arm. He grimaced but pulled her upright with his good hand.

"Thank you," she squeaked. But his focus was not on her.

She looked around what was clearly a Victorian city. All the houses looked as if they were haunted mansions. Each one was a different shade of black. They all varied in height and had different gable ends, but the color scheme was a mash of muted dark. Jayce fidgeted as she looked down the streets and noticed there were no streetlights. The only real light on the streets was from fires within the homes themselves. There was nothing in the sky, not a sun or moon, no clouds, or stars. She felt claustrophobic in her assessment of the place. Looking at Erin, she saw that the other girl was equally uneasy.

"Would you mind not being so promiscuous?" a voice came from the face of one of tens of marionettes walking the streets. Each had its own set of strings strung straight to the absent heavens.

Antoinette nodded in agreement.

"It would do well if you all didn't look so provocative. Left breast, please." She ended by pointing to the same spot on the uniform Jotun had shown for the armor.

Jayce was the first to press. As she did, her uniform took shape into a black and violet crinoline-style skirt with a ruffled violet top and a black corset. She couldn't help but twirl slightly, giggling at the rigidity of the skirt. Erin, who had followed suit, was now clad in a very similar fashion, only with pink instead of violet. Leon made her and Jayce awestruck as he took the form of a very form-fitting pair of black knee trousers, a pair of very sleek black riding boots, and a professionally tailored-looking frock coat. Noticing the stares, Leon held up one finger as he concentrated. Slowly, as if pulling from the coat, a tall top hat formed on his head. He removed it and bowed deeply.

"My ladies, had you no faith I had the potential to clean up well?" He laughed at himself as he reseated the hat.

"A dress, that would've been nice. Another catsuit would've been acceptable. Nope, not you, Zynka." Zynka sighed as they looked her way.

She was clad in a black short sleeve covered in what looked like a brass cuirass. Knee trousers, brass greaves, and barefoot. She looked downtrodden.

"I know I can change it, but come on. This is how it sees me?" Zynka actually looked pained.

"I think you look kickass!" Jayce heard herself say. "Cali would love it, too...bestie." She finished with a real smile.

She did look awesome. No matter what, Jayce wanted her to know that. Leon and Erin shared a look and a quiet smile at the mention of Cali.

"Thanks, girlie. Like I know what I look like—" Zynka started, but Antoinette interrupted.

"It doesn't matter how you look, stupid girl. What matters is who you know you are. Now shut up and follow me." She ended and turned with extra drama. Despite being called stupid, Zynka looked... not happy, but slightly at peace.

The group fell into step behind the teacher, trying not to roll an ankle on the dark cobblestone road. As Jayce walked, she heard the melodic twang of the marionette strings as they moved. They passed more dark houses. With nothing to compare them to, it was still obvious that this was a poorer side of town; most of the houses had cracks in the walls and overgrown black grass.

"This is eerie as hell," Leon whispered.

"Yeah, I wish there was more lighting. I'm expecting a jump scare with each step." Erin shivered.

"I don't know, I think it's hauntingly beautiful. Kind of a gothic feel," Jayce replied.

They continued down the narrow street, gazing at the houses that were slowly growing in size and grandeur. The dark houses started to get a touch of color, mainly tarnished silver and faded gold. The cracks in the walls were fewer now, and the lawns were more manicured. The black grass caught the now kerosene lights from the houses. Passing more marionettes, their outfits grew more extravagant with each step. The shabby frocks made way for silver and gold hoop dresses. The smell of acrylic paint filled the air. Jayce realized it was what was used for the makeup on the porcelain faces. The faces had become equally more extravagant. What started as basic blush and muted lipstick gave way to outlandish designs that reminded her of Egyptian styles. The look clashed with the Victorian aesthetic.

The twanging of the strings continued as they approached a market square with vendors of clothes and accessories. Erin got distracted and went to a dark stall with a quiet pink umbrella covering, selling necklaces. She eyed a blue pendant that had a clasp like a locket. Its silver chain flowed like liquid around it.

"This is beautiful," she told the male marionette. "How much is it?" she asked before realizing there was no way she could buy it.

"Two months." His tone was as cold as Antoinette's.

"Two months? I don't get it," Erin questioned.

"Two months in my service gets the necklace."

Erin stood confused before it dawned on her.

*He owns the person that buys it?*

The realization made her stomach drop. She looked around at the strings, seeing them for what they were.

*They are slaves!*

Watching the stiff, jerky movements, she blanched. Leon, having come up behind her, flexed his jaw; pain evident in his eyes. He scanned the square thoroughly. The marionettes ranged from child-size to adults, all with the same pink ethereal strings.

*Even the children?*

His eyes grew heavy with the thought. Zynka, meanwhile, seemed unfazed.

"This type of control, in one way or another, is common. There is always someone in control of someone else," Zynka commented nonchalantly.

Erin and Leon looked at each other grimly.

Jayce had decided to continue following Antoinette. The strings had become obvious tethers.

"Why do people enslave themselves for trinkets?" Jayce asked quietly.

Antoinette either didn't hear or care to answer.

"In your realm, they take out loans for random commodities as well," a voice came from her shoulder. She startled and jumped. Jayce hadn't felt the weight of the raven now standing on her shoulder.

"Who are you?" she asked quietly.

"You may call me Thought. No need to look around, no one can see or hear me but you. But does your realm not have that practice?" Thought questioned.

Jayce paused her walk momentarily, contemplating.

"Well, yes, but that's a choice. And to live, you need a house and a car for the most part."

"This is a choice as well. No one forces these people to purchase luxury items. And you put yourselves on contracts for phones. You all have strings like these marionettes. Theirs are just visible," Thought explained.

Jayce cocked an eyebrow and pursed her lips.

*He has a point, but does that make it right?*

She was slightly torn. This wasn't right, but is this the way universes worked? Footsteps pulled her away from her thoughts. Leon and the others had caught up to her.

"You okay, J?"

Jayce was a little weirded out that they couldn't see Thought on her shoulder, she opened her mouth to tell them about the creature, but decided last minute to pivot.

"This place's feel has such an overwhelming...something to it." Jayce looked around with unease.

"If you people would keep up, we could be there by now! Now hurry up." Antoinette's voice was cold and clipped.

The group sped up to keep pace with the brisk-moving woman. Jayce noticed for the first time that the strings binding the citizens made low, melodic twangs as they moved. There was no tune or cadence, just a quiet cacophony of strings. Her tunic began to get baggier as she gripped the hem of her sleeves.

"This place is unsettling to you?" Thought spoke directly into her head.

"It feels so unnatural, even compared to everything else I have seen recently," she mentally replied.

The houses now looked glamorous. They had brightly polished gold trim and silver window shutters. The houses themselves were still black, but darker, and more evenly coated.

They had continued down the same cobblestone street until it ended in a cul-de-sac. The house in the back was the most ornate by a landslide. Instead of the black walls with gold and silver trim, this one was solid silver with intricate gold designs laid into it. Standing around five stories tall and sprawling wide in all directions, it was a massive, absolutely gorgeous mansion.

"If I had more than one, I'd give an arm and a leg for a place like this," Leon spoke first, amazement screaming loudly. Zynka snorted despite herself.

"I'm sure it only costs a few decades."

"This is how those on top of most societies live. Those with power and resources tend to allow themselves lavish lifestyles. It gives them comfort but makes them weak." Thought spoke into Jayce's mind.

She looked at the glitz of the house and was repulsed. The clear differential was so vibrant it almost hurt.

"Though with an infinite life, does it not make sense to be comfortable?" Thought probed.

"I guess." Jayce softened slightly.

*If I truly am immortal, it does make sense to live in a form of security. Maybe not like this, but I guess.*

"It just seems unfair," she ended.

"Fair is what we make, my friend. What you believe is fair, what I believe is fair, and what my master believes is fair all differ. So, a universal fairness is a dream built on delusion."

Jayce was about to bite onto the master bit, but was cut short.

"We are here. I will talk; you all will shut up unless spoken to," Antoinette said as they approached the door and hit the baroque knocker in the shape of a demon's head.

The knock had a lot more reverberation than it had any right to. It shook Jayce's ribcage and put pressure on her chest.

"That is intense for absolutely no reason," Erin exclaimed while digging at her ear.

Zynka looked in physical pain as she mirrored the action. Leon stood stoic as usual. After a long stretch of moments, the door opened to a marionette dressed as a butler with blue strings rather than violet.

"Good evening, madams and sir. How may I be of assistance?" His voice was at the same level of detachment as the rest of the population. His demeanor was professional, yet bored and tired.

"We are here to see The Baron about his missing pet. We are from Aetherion Academy and have accepted the contract," Antoinette stated.

The butler eyed them wearily before giving a slight bow.

"Very well. Please come in and follow me." He eyed the humans and Zynka. "If it would please you, keep your grubby hands off of anything in The Baron's possession," the butler ended with an edge.

The group eyed each other uncomfortably. Zynka in particular seemed offended, but Jayce could tell it was an offended that meant she absolutely would've touched something. They all nodded at the butler and followed him inside.

The view was beautiful as they entered. The walls were glistening gold, reflecting the light from subtly sweet-smelling beeswax candles. Silk-like tapestries hung on the walls in reds and blues, depicting wars and document signings, treaties by the context. There were silver desks in the foyer and some plush chairs lining the walls. Doors on each side were made of a deep brown wood, and a massive, flared staircase ended the room.

"Please have a seat, and The Baron will be down at some point," the butler ordered more than he had said as he whisked up the staircase.

Antoinette, Leon, and Zynka sat on three chairs on one side, Jayce and Erin on the other.

"It's quite the sight, isn't it?" Erin half-whispered.

Jayce shivered slightly. "It is beautiful, but something about it is off." She shivered again. "Like it's wrong, I don't know what is wrong, but something is."

She jumped as Erin's hand slid into hers and their fingers interlocked. Warmth filled Jayce's chest, and she knew her face went pink. She tried to cover it with her raven hair.

"Hey, it's okay. I get what you mean, though. It's eerie. Oppressive even. But we're all here, and I think it'll be okay." Erin released Jayce's hand and slowly put her arm around the smaller woman's shoulder. Jayce, to her own surprise, leaned her head onto Erin's shoulder. Thought had leapt off and was busy inspecting the tapestries.

"Thank you." Jayce's voice was barely audible.

Erin cocked her head. "For what?"

"You, Leon, Cali, and Zynka have been so nice to me. I just wanted to thank y'all for that. I've felt safe with y'all, and I wasn't sure that was possible." Jayce's voice cracked slightly, a lump in her throat threatening to choke her out. Erin's lips pressed on her forehead again, and drank deep from the much-needed affection.

"Babe, you are great! I'm glad that if we had to be pulled into this acid trip, it was you and Leon to be the ones with me. Even with all the WTF moments, it's been like a reprieve from the stresses of normal life. I love you guys," Erin said.

Jayce hid the tears that formed in her eyes.

*Love. She loves me? Is there a joke...No, she's serious.*

Jayce looked up at Erin's caring face and gave her a quick peck on the cheek before going scarlet and burying her head back on Erin's shoulder. She felt the weight of the taller woman's head lying on hers.

On the other side of the room, Leon watched the two women with a smile. Zynka looked at him.

"It really is beautiful watching her become herself, isn't it?"

Leon nodded.

"I think this plane walking thing is exactly what the kid needed. I've seen her scars; not all of them were externally inflicted. Definitely been through way too much at her age." Leon had a slight glint in his eye.

"What about you? How is all this settling with you?"

All Leon could muster was a shrug.

"Honestly, I was supposed to be dead by twenty, so anything else is just icing. It's all cool, but I can't help but feel it's not real. Like, no offense, but I'm talking to a pink bipedal pachyderm who walks silently while sitting next to a living puppet. Not exactly normal where we come from."

"Marionette, not puppet, boy. Learn some respect," Antoinette snapped.

Leon raised his hands in surrender.

"Sorry, Professor. Misuse of my words, won't happen again."

It looked like he was about to receive another tongue-lashing when the sound of steps came from the staircase. A stringless marionette in a modern slate gray suit walked in front of the butler down the stairs. His face was not porcelain like the rest of the population, but a solid silver. Its mouth was carved into a smile, and blue lights filled the eye sockets. When they reached the bottom of the stairs, Antoinette, followed by the rest of the group, stood and approached The Baron.

"Good evening, my valued visitors from the Academy. It, I'm sure, is my absolute pleasure to make your acquaintance. I am Baron Kingsly. Welcome to my world." He gave an almost imperceptible bow. He whispered something over his shoulder to the butler, who scurried off. "I truly hope you all may be able to help me find my pet. I am distraught without her. Light of my life, she is."

"Yes, Baron. We will be able to fulfill the contract. Once we have a confirmation of description, preferably a copy of a picture, and potential routes of escape, we shall start the hunt and have your pet back in the shortest time we can," Antoinette answered in an overly professional tone.

"Very good. And I have decided just for you, I will throw in a small bonus upon completion," The Baron said. If Antoinette could've cocked an eyebrow, she would have. "I will wipe away three years' worth of your debt to me."

Antoinette fell to her knees, almost groveling.

"Thank you, sir, thank you very much. I will not let you down or forget your generosity."

It looked as though she was about to kiss his feet when the sound of the butler's trotting feet sounded out. She righted herself as he finished his approach and handed the Baron a small, framed picture. The Baron touched his lips and touched the photo.

"Here is my beautiful pet." As he spoke, he turned the picture their way, and Leon saw nothing but red.

"Thought has made contact." One.
"So it would seem." Two.
"How shall you move forward?" Three.
"Observe, she intrigues me." Wanderer.

# CHAPTER FIFTEEN

Jayce felt a lead weight as she stared at the obviously scared young girl in the photograph. The Baron's "pet" was an elvish looking girl around Jayce's age, and it was clear she was not enjoying herself.

"This is your pet?" Leon's voice was quiet, yet held a glacial frost to it. "Your pet is a young woman?"

"Why yes." The Baron looked confused. "She came under my servitude when her parents traded her."

Antoinette took the picture and bowed.

"We will do our best to have it home shortly. Come, initiates," she ordered.

After a final stare down, Leon did an abrupt about-face and marched/stormed out, the rest of the group on his heels. They exited the door which closed as soon as Jayce crossed the threshold. Antoinette spun furiously on Leon.

"What the hell is your problem? The Baron is not one to be crossed. God, if I didn't promise Jotun I would take you all with me, I would send you home in the blink of an eye. Don't you ever embarrass me like that again." She was in a rage.

Leon not only didn't back down, he also stepped body-to-body with her and looked down on her.

"If you don't have a problem with this situation, then my problem is with you. Not only is he calling a sentient being a pet, but he also made her a slave off her parents' debt. There was no choice for her. Just a life of hell under a tyrant. Is that a life you condone, *Professor*?"

No fear showed on her unmoving face, though there was a tremble in her shoulders. She sighed.

"Leon, that's just the way it is here. You know what you are getting into when you go into debt. Does it make it right? Well, if the one in power says it is, then it is. Might makes right, and all that."

The two stared each other down until Erin stepped in.

"Look, one way or another, we need to find this girl before someone else does. She's definitely scared and needs help. Let's do that, then fight one another," she said, laying a soft hand on Leon's chest.

It broke his tension immediately, and he nodded to her.

"Is there an elven district or something?" Zynka asked. "If I was scared and alone, I would try and find my pack as fast as possible."

"Not really, they stay pretty spread out," Antoinette answered. She pulled out the picture and surveyed it. "Her only distinguishing feature is her silver hair. Not natural for this area. I would assume she is from the mountains. But there's no way she would've made it back. Baron Kingsly holds the strings for the entire population; I'm surprised she has been able to evade this long. Maybe she went underground? Sewers would go unchecked, I would bet." She nodded in agreement with herself.

"Sewers, yay, I hate this place," Zynka said and let out a sad trumpet.

They followed the professor to a grated manhole cover. Luckily, there was no horrid smell like Jayce thought there would be. Leon, at a look from Antoinette, lifted out the cover and tossed it aside. Erin and Jayce looked down the hole and then at each other's oversized skirts. With a thought, they both changed their clothes to pants and shirts. Zynka eyed the opening. She could fit, just not comfortably. Antoinette pointed down.

"You four go down and look for the pet." Leon bristled at the word. "I will see if there is any useful information to be found in the square."

With that, the professor turned and briskly walked away. Jayce felt in the chest of her shirt to make sure her pen-sized eidolon was still there and felt her muscles loosen. Leon looked at the group, shrugged, and climbed down the rusty ladder, followed by Erin, then Zynka, and finally Jayce. It was twenty feet down the ladder to the ground, and when Jayce reached the bottom, the smell hit. Bodily waste, damp fur, and rotten eggs assaulted her nostrils, causing a violent gag. Her uniform made a hasty decision to form a half face mask, covering her nose and mouth, and releasing the sweet gas and vanilla smell into her. She breathed in deep a few times before looking around. The walls and ceiling were made of mud-brown brick. The ceiling was vaulted and rounded. Two narrow sidewalks lined a four-foot-wide murky stream. The walls were lined with dim, flickering torches. All in all, it reminded her of every sewer in every medieval movie.

"Left, or right?" Leon asked no one in particular.

Erin looked this way and that before nodding to her thoughts. "No idea."

"Left?" Jayce heard herself suggest.

*Why are you even talking?*

Her thought rammed into her skull. Leon shrugged and started down that way, with Zynka close behind. Jayce's muscles had tensed back up, and her breathing had become labored as she looked down the passageway. Erin took a look and noted the fear; hell, she had the same fear. Refusing to show it, she again slowly inserted her hand into Jayce's and interlaced their fingers. Jayce didn't flinch.

"Come on, babe. Adventure awaits," Erin said in a voice from an infomercial.

Jayce felt the warmth of her touch and allowed a small grin at the goofy voice. With that, they followed the others in step with each other.

After what seemed like an hour, they ended up at a T-intersection. Leon looked either way, flipped an imaginary coin, hopped over the stream, and continued to the right. The others followed suit. Erin and Jayce's hands came apart for the jump, and then came together like magnets again. They walked until they heard voices in the distance.

"Do you think they will come after Azreal?" a deep voice asked.

"I would almost guarantee it," a female voice replied.

Leon held up a fist and got to one knee in a well-practiced cadence. He leaned forward to hear better.

"Tinnitus is killing my hearing," he whispered back to the group. "How do we play this? Do we approach truthfully or try and sneak around?"

"Might as well just talk to them. I mean, we aren't going to actually give her back, right?" Erin said.

Leon nodded and stood. He slowly rounded the corner and made his presence known.

"Excuse me," he said, making the two elves down the passage jump and clutch their shabby wooden spears.

The large male elf had bright red hair tied in intricate braids. The smaller female also had the same style. They both wore light brown articulating leather armor. Without hesitation, the larger male elf lowered his spear and trotted towards them.

"They are from the Academy. They are here to take her back. Not today!" the male elf bellowed as he charged Leon, spear leveled at his chest.

Leon only shook his head and took his boxer's stance. The gap was closed quickly as the elf lunged his spear straight for Leon's heart. Leon grabbed the spear's shaft, dropped to a knee, and booted the elf's leg below the knee, inverting the leg and eliciting a howl of agony as the assailant hit the ground. Leon wrenched the spear free, spun it on end, and placed the tip to the writhing elf's throat.

"This was unnecessary," Leon said, holding the spear in place. "You're right, we are with the Academy, we are looking for the girl, but we have no intention of returning her as a slave."

The elf was still rolling as the female approached.

"I apologize for Orin's hastiness. We are a bit on edge since Azreal's return. If you are from the Academy, doesn't that mean you are here for the contract on her?" the female elf asked.

It was Zynka who stepped up.

"We are initiates, on a tag-along contract. We weren't aware of what was covered. The humans here have a very aggressive stance against the socio-political structure on this plane, and I guess we are going to try and help however we can." The pink elephant shrugged.

Orin continued to roll in pain, though he was mostly silent now. Erin reluctantly let go of Jayce's hand and stepped forward to the elf and laid her hand on him.

"Erin, no!" Leon exclaimed.

"I'm only taking a little. Enough so he might be able to walk," Erin said as she closed her eyes and searched for Orin's pain. She found it, a whole mountain of anguish. Carefully, she began taking small chunks into herself. Her knee started to ache and burn. She hid a grimace as she took more.

*Smile for the crowd, scream backstage.*

The pain grew. Orin finally stilled, the agony on his face softening. When Erin knew she was on the verge of not being able to stand, she released her grip. She wavered, getting to her feet. Jayce quickly put her arm around Erin's waist to steady her.

Erin draped an arm around her shoulder and thanked her. The female elf pulled Orin up and put his arm over her to keep his bad leg off the ground, then looked at Erin.

"Thank you, and my husband thanks you as well. Not many would take the pain of someone who just attacked them. I'm Talia, by the way."

"I'm just awesome like that," Erin joked through gritted teeth.

The group introduced themselves and exchanged some tense pleasantries before Talia offered to show them the way to the elves' bunker.

The walk found Erin and Jayce leaning on each other as Zynka and Leon talked with the elves.

"We aren't really native to this land. We are originally from the snowy mountains to the south, but our parents became enthralled with the idea of luxury items. They ended up in debt, and that usually fell on us. The strings that hold the others are stronger due to them being voluntary. The ones we got as the children of the in debt are far weaker," Talia finished.

"But we all had to find ways of breaking the bonds. Be it physically, mentally, or spiritually," Orin added.

"If y'all have all broken the bonds, why is the contract just for this Azreal?" Leon inquired.

"Kingsly has a...special attraction to her. He sees her as more of his property than anyone else. It's...sick really. He sees her as a daughter...and a lover." Orin spat in the murky stream.

Leon's head jerked back like he just took a jab to the nose. Erin and Jayce shared a disgusted look.

"Honestly, kinda standard," Zynka said, but due to the looks she received, she added. "Doesn't make it right, but that's how it works on my plane. You conquer a kingdom, you take the youngest daughter as your ward, then eventually you marry her." Her addition did nothing to change the looks she received, so she popped the tip of her trunk in her mouth and kept walking.

The walk was silent for the rest of the way until they ran across two more guards. Talia and Orin explained the situation, and they were let through.

"It is curious that they took your words at face value and allowed you into their bunker."

Jayce froze, having completely forgotten that Thought existed.

"We had no reason to lie. I think they could tell that," she said internally.

"Not true at all. From their perspective, you had every reason to lie. They allowed blind faith in 'humanity' to guide their decision. It is just interesting to me is all," he said as he flew off into the tunnel.

*They really did just bite onto us telling the truth. They wanted or needed it to be true.*

"Penny for your thoughts, babe?" Erin's voice was still pained, but stifled.

"They believed us rather quickly, didn't they? I mean, we said we weren't going to take Azreal, and they just go 'yup, makes sense.' I don't know, something feels off," Jayce finished, eyes flicking up and down the passageway.

Erin also scanned the area. She intentionally tripped, loudly falling to her knees. The shock of pain through the knee she took Orin's pain into made her gasp. Leon and Zynka fell back to check on her.

"Are you okay? What happened?" Leon asked, looking her over.

"I'm fine. I needed y'all to come back here so we could talk. They are trusting us too easily. Something is wrong. Right, Jayce?" Erin looked at the smaller woman.

"Uhm. I think so," she said quietly. "Why would they go from you breaking Orin's leg to taking us to the center of their camp unless they had a reason to?" She looked at Leon, who, to her surprise, smiled and nodded.

"Agreed, J. These guys definitely have something planned. Whatever it is, I assume it ain't all that pleasant." He hoisted Erin to her feet and looked at Zynka. "Think you can do your silent tank skedaddle? Find a way to cover us?"

Zynka nodded enthusiastically and disappeared down a side corridor.

"Everything okay back there?" Talia called from up around a bend.

"All good. Knee is bothering Erin, is all. We're coming,"

Leon said, trotting to catch up. Jayce again wrapped her arm around Erin's waist, and they continued forward.

"Where is the elephant?" Orin asked.

"I sent her back to get our professor," Erin replied. "She might be able to take some pain off both of us."

The elves shrugged and kept walking down the passage towards a wrought iron gate. Talia took out a key and unlocked it. She pushed it in and entered, gesturing for them to follow. The humans shared a look and followed. Jayce felt reassured by Leon's intimidating presence and the very light weight of her eidolon, and of course, the warmth of Erin leaning into her. Her closeness brought a glint to Jayce's eye, and a smile threatened to pull her lips apart.

They followed through the gate and were greeted with a sprawling dome-like area. Makeshift houses on small square pieces of concrete were laid out like a chessboard, with the murky brown water running between each square. It was like a disgusting and poor version of Venice, Italy. There were about a dozen or so of the houses. Leon scanned the room.

*Fourteen houses. One large building, possibly a town hall. Ten visible residents plus Talia and Orin. One resident has what looks like a musket. Gate behind us is an exit, and across to the right seems to be another gate.*

His veteran mind ramped up as his sense of danger started to awaken. They continued following the elves until they reached one of the outside houses.

"This is us. Let me get Orin laid down and we will go see the mayor and figure out what to do," Talia said, opening the door and taking her husband in.

"I still can't put a finger on what is going on here. It's wrong for sure, but why?" Leon whispered to the two women. "Also, I think if anything goes down, we are looking at guns." He added, looking at the elf with the rifle.

"God, I hate guns." Erin shook.

"Yeah? Well, I'd kill for one about now," Leon replied, his hand involuntarily reaching where a pistol would be holstered.

Talia came back out and motioned for the group to follow

her to the large building in the center. They walked up four steps to a set of double doors bordered by two blunderbuss-wielding guards. They bowed at Talia as the doors opened. Walking through, the foursome entered a room about the size of a school gymnasium. It was a large open space with a few pillars and a small section of auditorium seating. There was a figure at a desk in the center; a broad and tall elf, even sitting down. Jayce could only describe him as having a commanding presence.

"Father. I have brought outsiders from Aetherion. They are here to help recover Azreal." A smirk crossed Talia's face briefly as she spoke.

Though it was brief, Jayce caught it. She squeezed Erin's hip, who squeezed her shoulder in acknowledgement. The elf stood, his full height putting him at mid-seven feet. The height, plus his bulk, red hair, and beard, reminded Jayce of a picture of a Kodiak bear she saw once.

"Come to lay claim to my bounty, have ye?" His deep voice carried a brogue to it. "I say, I can never have me a simple little trade. Nope, nothing easy for Talio. So, tell me, to whom do ye plan on turning her in? The Baron? Wastelanders? The djinn? Or do ye plan on ransoming her back to her own kind?" The fury in his voice was evident, but so was the curiosity that undercut it.

Leon rolled his shoulders and neck while maintaining eye contact with the potential opponent.

"We are here to figure out what to do. We don't want money or goods. We just want to make sure the girl is safe." Leon's voice was calm but with a definite edge. "Where is she?"

Talio smiled, showing sharp canines. A predator's smile.

"M' dear daughter, go fetch the pet. I want to see how this goes. You a fighter, boy?" His eyes never left Leon's.

Leon's clothes shifted back into the plated kilt, his shirt disappearing into the lower half.

"I can sing the tune and dance a few steps. Why? Care to find out?" His amber eyes were ablaze.

Talio stepped around the desk and raised his hand. As he did, five elves brandishing muskets came from around the pillars and leveled their weapons at the humans. Leon cursed. Erin and Jayce looked wide-eyed at the developing situation.

*Oh my god. Please. Not here. Please.*

Jayce mentally pleaded with whoever would listen.

"I may be big, but I'm also old. My one-on-one days are well behind me." Talio smiled at Leon's sudden trapped deer face.

Talia, meanwhile, made her way back to her father with a chained elf with silver hair. She was barely clad in a slip, and her body was covered in blue marks and scars. She barely looked up, showing off the most beautiful yellow eyes, before snapping her attention back to the ground. Jayce froze, seeing one of the deepest bruises just above Azrael's knee. Her mind went back to her room at the cabin when she first put on her uniform, remembering the same bruise on herself, making her subconsciously rub at the area. The musketeers made a half circle around the group between them and Talia and Talio. The mayor roughly grabbed Azreal's chin and lifted her face to the group.

"Look at that. Someone sent people to save your worthless self," he sneered. Jayce pricked at 'worthless'. "They don't know that we are having a grand time together. Tell them. Tell them how much fun ol' Talio is." His voice was venom. Azreal clutched her elbows tightly.

"Y-yes, sir. A won-wonderful time." The quietly angelic voice stuttered out of her.

The fear did nothing but amplify Talio's joy and deepen Leon's rage. Talio released her chin, and her eyes snapped back to the floor.

"Moon elves are so rare here. Not from this plane originally. Immensely powerful bitties. But no moon to feed on here, is there, girl?" He slapped her thigh, causing a pained squeak.

"Screw it," Leon yelled as he lowered his shoulder and charged through the elfish musketeer standing between him and Talio.

Four muskets shot off in surprise. Jayce's eyes burned as time stopped. The pressure mounted in her chest, and the loud silence was as deafening as always, but she tried to brush it aside.

She surveyed the scene. Four musket balls were inches from Leon's back. He was about to barrel into Talio. Talia had already started pulling Azreal away.

*Okay. Should be easier than shrinking the Murdenex.*

She walked to the musket balls and grabbed one; the searing heat blistered her fingers immediately.

"Dammit!" she screamed.

Her uniform covered her hand in a glove so she could handle the projectiles. She moved each one a foot in front of the different shooters and gave them all a slight push. Her nose filled with the iron tint of an upcoming nosebleed. She walked to Talia and wrapped the leading end of Azreal's chain around her ankles, and gave her a small shove. Her heartbeat was the first thing to come back to life, and at once her work concluded itself. Four heads exploded in blue mist, and Talia was knocked out after landing face-first on the ground. Leon, at the same time, slammed into Talio, tackling him over the table. Jayce grabbed her face as her eyes and nose leaked red. Erin and Jayce pulled their eidolons and waited for them to form. Leon and Talio rolled on the ground, getting swings in where they could. The women stepped to approach but stopped at a look from Leon.

This was his fight.

As the two men rolled around, Jayce grabbed her head and went to her knees.

"Dammit. This doesn't get better," she said through gritted teeth.

She looked at the carnage, realizing that she had just taken four lives. She felt Thought land.

"You did what was necessary for you and them to survive. The first lives are the hardest, by far."

"They didn't have to die. I didn't have to kill them," Jayce stated internally, her breath fighting past a rock in her throat.

Thought lightly pecked her ear in a calming gesture.

"Fight isn't over. Mourn or move on later. For now, survive." With that, he was gone again.

Erin's focus had never left Leon's struggle. There was no clear advantage until Talio landed a dirty knee to Leon's groin. The opening gave him time to wrap both hands tightly around the human's neck. Erin moved to leap forward but was again stopped by a look. Leon never broke eye contact with his assailant. His eyes grew hazy, and his head began to swim.

*This could be it. No more suffering. Just shuffle off and call it a life.*

He half-smiled as his vision faded back in.

The last thing Talio ever heard was the grotesque sound of bones breaking and flesh ripping as a four-foot bone and flesh spear pierced his chest at an upward angle and exited his skull. He dropped off Leon, whose arm was already reforming into his stump. He grimaced as he tried to rub away the pain. Azreal, through all this, had never looked up from the ground. Leon got up and cautiously walked to her. He stopped a double arm's length away and kneeled down to look up at her.

"Ma'am? I'm Leon. I would like to take your chains off if you'd be willing to let me." He conjured up all the gentleness of a man that just killed another man.

She didn't look up or seem to react in any way. He was about to ask again when the most imperceptible nod came from the girl.

"Okay, I'm going to get close, and I'll have to touch your hands and wrists to remove the chains. Is that okay?" he asked, slowly going forward on his knees. He did not want to stand over this poor girl.

She nodded again and moved her hand well away from her body to him. Leon took her hand with every ounce of delicacy he possessed. His eyes grew fiery again as he noted the wrist scars that shown like blue rivers through her snow-white skin.

Erin and Jayce watched the interaction. Erin smiled, seeing the absolute gentleman work. Jayce's tears, still red, now fell out of a sick sense of jealousy.

*Nobody came for you. You weren't worth saving.*

She had nothing to fight the thought off with this time.

Leon found the keyhole in the cuff around Azreal's wrists, but rather than look for the key, he just put his nub up to the hole and allowed his arm to form the key. The cuffs popped with a click, and the heavy chains slammed them into the ground. Azreal looked at her wrists and, for the first time, looked Leon in the eye. She stood about a head higher than him on his knees. Tears streaked her grimy face. Her yellow eyes glowed. She caught Leon off guard by throwing her arms around his neck, crying deeply into his long hair. He gently put his arm around her upper back and leaned into her embrace.

"That was not the expected outcome." One.
"Casual violence." Two.
"What is next?" Three.
"Observe and be entertained." Wanderer.

# CHAPTER SIXTEEN

Leon allowed the embrace for as long as Azreal needed it to last. The small woman practically vibrated in fear, pain, and relief. Her weight was completely on his shoulders.

"Thank you, thank you so much." Her small angelic voice wavered as she spoke.

Leon slightly tightened his grip on the elf's upper back.

"Of course. You are safe now, darlin'. I won't let anyone near you for as long as you need." His voice was heavy-laden with promise and fire.

Erin and Jayce sat together, Erin rubbing Jayce's palms roughly with her thumbs.

"There is a point in your hand that's supposed to help settle headaches. I don't know where, but I hope this is helping," Erin said, looking Jayce in the eyes.

Jayce couldn't feel anything helping her head, but the warmth coming off of Erin was as soothing as a lavender bath.

"Thank you. I think it is helping," she partially lied.

The group was startled at the sound of a pistol's hammer cocking. Talia was on her knees, a revolver pointed at Azreal's back. Leon quickly stood, lifting the small elf and turning his back to the pistol.

"*You*. You ruined everything! She was our ticket out of this hellhole. You killed my father." Talia's finger squeezed the trigger as Leon braced for the impact.

A shot rang out, and Leon felt hot liquid cover his back. He sat Azreal down and felt his shoulder. Bringing his hand around it was covered in hot, sticky blue blood. He turned quickly and saw a giant obsidian war hammer where Talia's head should've been. A smiling pink elephant stared back at him.

"Sorry," Zynka said, flushing red. "I got a little hung up. Bright side is we can just walk out of here," she ended with a bigger smile.

Leon walked to her, eyes wide with an undiscernible emotion. He threw both arms around Zynka's trunk and held tightly.

"You saved my life...again. The debt I'm building with you is going to be unpayable soon." He laughed as he released her.

Zynka awkwardly patted him on the head with her trunk.

"All good, homie. Just doing the damn thing, ya know?" Her smile fell as she saw Azreal's pitiful visage. "How is she?"

"Not great, but I think she can recover." Leon dropped his voice. He noticed Azreal shivered due to the cold and looked around. His eyes landed on Talio and his trousers. They were rough-looking linen pants that should fit him if he could find a belt.

"Could y'all look that way for a minute?" he asked, pointing towards the door.

The group complied, and he went to work removing Talio's pants. Luckily, the big elf had undergarments, otherwise Leon would've seen his junk. Once the pants were removed, he looked and made sure the women were still looking away before willing his kilt off. The uniform melted down his legs and puddled on the floor. He took a fleeting glance at the grafted skin on his left leg before quickly donning the pants. They were a little loose, but would stay up fine. He thought about taking a shirt but shrugged. All of the tops were covered in blood, and hell, he was a surfer, very much used to being topless.

"Okay, thank y'all."

The group turned back to him. Leon picked up the uniform and walked to Azreal and handed it to her.

"This will shape to your will. And it's climate-controlled, so it'll take the bite out of the air."

Azreal grabbed it quickly, and it formed around her. It settled into what looked like a mix of a priest's vestments.

"Thank you. It-it has been a long time since I was able to clothe myself properly. I am Azreal of the Moon Elves. I cannot thank you enough for freeing me from this bondage." Her ethereal voice carried a quiet, scarred strength. The group introduced themselves as well.

"Where will you go after here?" Erin asked after the formalities.

Azreal shook her head. "My clan traded me here for shiny baubles. I do not know where to go," she replied sadly.

Leon cleared his throat. "How about we figure things out with Kingsly and then decide what to do?"

At the name, the elf seemed to shrink a few inches. Normally at the same height as Jayce, the shrinking made her look too small.

"It's okay, darlin'. There ain't no way we are letting him have you back. We just have to figure out what to do. This is all new to us," he finished with a comforting nod in Azreal's direction.

She surveyed him, his long blonde hair and large beard were thick with Talio's blue blood, and his tan, muscled skin was covered in Talia's blood. The carnage seemed to be lost on him. In the whole room filled with death, she knew he only cared for her and the others' safety, his comfort and emotions came in a distant second. The realization made her flush, and her muscles relaxed for the first time in a long time. She nodded at him.

Leon walked to Talia's body and picked up the small revolver. He stared at it for a long moment; many dark nights of booze and bad thoughts flooded his mind. Pushing them away, he put the pistol in the back of his waistband, and they walked out the front of the building.

When the group exited the building, they froze. It was

obvious why Zynka had been tardy. The entire village of elves seemed to be stacked like cord wood at the center of the buildings. Tens of bodies lie broken. Zynka rubbed the back of her head with her trunk.

"There was talk of them converging on the town hall to 'protect the slave and kill the outsiders'. I couldn't have that."

Jayce saw her discomfort.

"Damn...bestie. I will not be upsetting you anytime soon." Jayce offered a small smile to her pink friend. Zynka nudged her with her trunk.

"You better don't," she joked, sticking out her oversized tongue at the small woman.

Jayce smiled and again surveyed the brutality of the scene.

*Why am I not freaking out?*

The newly familiar weight of a raven settled on her shoulder.

"Why am I okay with all of this?" she internalized.

Thought stretched.

"Many reasons, I assume. One, these aren't your species, so you are detached from the reality and gravity. Two, your mind is coming to see life as less valuable due to immortality, less likely yet possible. Three, perhaps your views on the culture here skew your perception of these elves' worthiness. The true answer is somewhere in there. It doesn't matter the why so much, just the result," Thought finished, fluttering his wings, the feathers brushing her ears tickled.

She nodded in agreement that it wasn't relevant currently, though it was something she decided to keep an eye on. Not even a week in, the planes and her viewpoints had shifted.

Leon led the group back the way they entered, avoiding the pile of bodies. Luckily, he remembered the way because Jayce got mentally lost multiple times on the way back to the ladder. They grouped up at the base of the rusty ladder.

"Alright, alright, alright," Leon said with a very recognizable accent. "Next step is to go back to The Baron's house and see what happens. Azreal, if it is okay with you, I'd prefer you stay near me. I don't want that bastard getting any ideas," he said, looking at the elf.

She nodded enthusiastically. He gave her a warm smile and ascended the ladder. Once they were all up, Leon replaced the manhole cover, and they made their way to the mansion.

After the short walk, they found themselves back at The Baron's doors. As Erin reached for the knocker, the door opened creakily on its own. The Baron, the butler, and Antoinette waited in the middle of the foyer when they entered.

"It seems there was more excitement than planned," The Baron stated with a hint of glee in his voice. "You have solved my underground elf problem." The glee was more evident. The group moved forward as he continued talking. "And I see you have retrieved my pet."

Azreal immediately stepped behind Leon with a quiet yelp of fear. The fire in Leon's eyes was rekindled.

"Nope."

That is all he said as he pulled the revolver and put a bullet between the eyes of Baron Kingsly's golden face. Strings of all different colors left the smoking hole as he hit the ground. The strings went through the ceiling and disappeared. Simultaneously, the strings holding Antoinette and the butler vanished, causing them both to hit the ground in a heap. Screams could be heard from outside of the mansion as all the tethers were severed. Antoinette tried to move, but it was like watching a baby deer try and take its first steps.

"What have you done?" she screamed as she tried and failed to stand.

Leon did not look empathetic.

"You are free from your bonds. Isn't that a good thing?" he asked, though the normal gentleness in his voice was gone.

Jayce, Erin, and Zynka were still trying to process the rapid actions, barely just catching up with the situation. Azreal, still behind Leon, had wrapped her arms around the remains of his left arm. Though uncomfortable as hell, he allowed the touch, knowing it was more soothing to her than uncomfortable to him.

"Free? This is how our society works!" Antoinette screamed. "We are meant to be bound. It's how we move, how we live. We don't know how to be without our tethers." She was hyperventilating at this point, still failing to stand.

"Figure it out," Leon scoffed. He looked at Zynka.

"Can you get us back to Aetherion?"

The large elephant nodded and held out her hands.

"Azreal, would you want to come with us back to the Academy? Rest, food, and time to think?"

"I would very much appreciate that, Mr. Leon." Azreal curtsied as she answered.

Leon laughed at being called "Mister." Jayce and Erin took Zynka's hands, Leon and Azreal took theirs, and they were pulled into the void's hurricane.

Jayce felt the whirlwind pulling at her very soul this time; whether it was more hardcore, or Zynka's walk was less coordinated, she couldn't tell. It felt like her skin wanted to separate from her bones. The deafening roar of the wind threatened to blow her eardrums until she felt two feathered wings cover her ears and a voice, not Thought's, but a deeper, wiser one, drowned out the noise.

"You are unexpected. All of you. We look forward to your continued performance."

For a brief moment, she could've sworn she saw a man with a long white beard wearing a wide-brimmed hat. Before she could be sure, she saw their cabin, heaving to catch her breath.

The rest of the group, minus Zynka, were in the same sorry state. Azreal seemed to be hit the hardest as she was on her knees, her hands in the white dirt. If it hadn't been for the blue scars on her hands and wrists, she would have blended in with the ground perfectly. Zynka, not needing to recover, melted the door and entered, followed by a staggering Erin and Jayce. Leon put a hand out to Azreal, who gladly took it, and he led her inside. At the table were Cali and Professor Automo. Cali stared at Leon who, despite it being blue, was obviously covered in blood. He gave the teen a small smile.

"You should see the other guy."

Erin snorted and took a seat at the table.

"No, Cali, no, you should not," she said, settling back in her chair.

Cali looked at the group, lingering on Azreal, then to Automo.

"Seriously? How much cool crap am I gonna miss out on before I can start schooling?" Cali's tone was light yet pointed. "Stay in the room. Help the robot guy. Have your eye melt out. Bull crap," she mumbled before she perked up. "So why are you blue? Who is she? Did y'all have fun? How was the teacher?" Cali's exuberance returned forcefully.

Leon shook his head as he walked to the repaired fridge and summoned a beer. He tossed one to Erin without asking, pulled another out, put it in his pocket, and grabbed a cold bottle of water. He walked back to the table and pulled a chair out for Azreal. She took the seat and the offered drink. Slowly, she sipped from the bottle, feeling the cold water rush through her veins. Jayce and Zynka also grabbed drinks, a Big Red a piece, and found their seats as well. When everyone was seated, the silence hung heavily.

"Okay, Birdo said one at a time helps. Who is the new girl?" Cali asked slowly.

"Azreal. I am Azreal. Your friends...helped me." The elf's angelic voice played uneasily through the air.

"Sweet. Are you staying? Whose room? Your hair is pretty. Are your eyes naturally yellow? Are—" Cali was cut off by Automo's hand softly resting on her mouth.

"Dear. Young. Cali. Assessing the situation, it seems that silence is pertinent at this juncture. Perhaps we enjoy the sounds of nothing." Automo's clipped monotone centered Cali, who nodded apologetically. He removed his hand.

"No, it is quite alright. It has been some time since I have been asked anything. I do not know if I am able to stay. I would hope for my own room if that were accommodatable. Thank you, though my hair has lost its shine since there was no moon on that world. And yes, my eyes are naturally this color," Azreal finished with a deep pull from the water.

Cali smiled wide in thanks but kept quiet.

After a very long, somewhat comfortable stretch, Automo stood. "I have no further business here." And with that he was gone.

"Okay, bye?" Cali was miffed by the lack of a real goodbye.

The room fell quiet again. Everyone focused on their drinks and avoided eye contact. Leon sat internalizing the day.

*Killed one in a struggle and one in cold blood. Justifiable for sure. You're still a murderer.*

His eyes lowered at his thoughts. He forced them up to scan the group. Jayce was obviously dealing with the aftermath headache and the guilt of four deaths on her hands, while Erin was weary from the knee pain she still carried. Azreal still wasn't sure how safe she was, and Zynka...Zynka was Zynka. Cali looked as though not talking might actually kill her.

*Screw it. Make 'em laugh, clown.*

Leon excused himself to his room to get a new uniform. He returned in his signature kilt and tank top combo, though he had no sleeve on his nub. Messing with his holo as he approached the table, and the opening beat of "Narcissist" by Gold Steps played. Erin and Jayce looked quizzically at him. He just shrugged and cranked it to eleven. As the music ramped up, Leon jumped onto the low tier of the table and, very much out of key and rhythm, began singing.

"You're a Fu—" He smiled and winked at Erin and Jayce. Before jumping and hitting the jersey fist pump. "Na Na Na Na Narcissist! Fooled me once..."

He continued singing and dancing, absolutely butchering the song, yet surprisingly nailed every word. Erin smiled at the gesture and effort he was going through to bring them back to reality. Even though she could see the pain of his decisions today in his eyes, he still tried. She mocked making it rain on him as the song ended. He bowed deeply at them and was about to do a flip off the table before thinking better of it and hopped off.

"Didn't take you for a pop punk fan," Erin said over a cocked eyebrow.

Leon grabbed his chest in a mock offense. "I do find myself enjoying a plethora of different music, and let's be honest, Gold Steps gets extra points for being from Texas."

The other humans, all Texans, nodded in agreement. Zynka, meanwhile, had restarted the song and waved her trunk around in a one elephant woman mosh pit. Even Azreal stiffly nodded along.

"Screw it. I want to dance." Erin stood up and extended a hand to Jayce. "Dance with me?"

Jayce, wide-eyed, stared at her hand, not sure if it was a lifeline or a cobra. Hesitation evident, Erin did her best to keep her hand from shaking. Their eyes met, and Jayce slowly placed her hand in Erin's, who slowly pulled her to her feet. Leon put on a 2000s pop punk playlist and sat with Cali, Azreal, and Zynka. Erin led Jayce to an open area between the couch and table, took both her hands, and began swaying back and forth together.

"I-I've never danced before," Jayce said unnecessarily as she continually tripped on her own feet.

"I can tell." Erin gave her a brilliant white smile. "That's okay, though, you kind of just move to this music. Nothing really intricate. Jump, wave, fist pump, horns. All basic as hell. Now, country dancing is a whole other thing. You listen to any country?" She smiled when she realized Jayce was looking at her feet, trying not to fall.

"What? Oh...uhm, not really. Never heard any that caught my ear, I guess." She still stared at her feet and managed to step on Erin's toe, who laughed.

"Kilt man, play some King George," Erin hollered over the loud music.

Leon stood and gave a quick salute.

"Ma'am, yes, ma'am." He played an older song about passing notes.

"Here." Erin placed Jayce's hand on her shoulder, placed her own hand on Jayce's hip, and interlaced their other hands together. "Now just follow my lead," Erin said as she began walking her through the motions.

Leon looked on with such a smile on his face that it confused Cali.

"You ain't jealous?" she asked Leon.

He looked offended. "Two amazing people are finding comfort; only a real d-bag would be jealous of that." His voice was playful and sincere. "Though I wouldn't mind dancing. It has been a good long while."

Cali jumped up immediately and grabbed Leon's tank top and drug him to the open area. "Then let's dance!" Cali squealed as she stood up on Leon's toes, wrapped his arm around her, and took the end of his left arm in her hand. She tutted at him when he protested.

"No, sir. The only one in this entire plane of existence who cares what that"—she nodded to his nub—"looks like is you, and I won't have you thinking less of one of my friends." Her tone was clipped, serious, and carried the weight of a ten-pound hammer.

He looked down at her remaining eye and smiled a real, genuine smile.

"Yes, ma'am. I won't talk or feel any kinda way about your friends. I promise."

And the promise held weight; she knew it wasn't just lip service as she was moved around the dance floor. Try as she might, she couldn't fight a single tear from escaping her eye. Hoping he didn't notice, but knowing he did, she wiped it away.

"What's wrong, kiddo?"

"Me and Dad used to dance like this. He also called me kiddo. Y'all have the same warmth." She looked up at Leon, who smiled.

She yelped as he hoisted her to his hip. She felt like a child and relished every second of it as they danced. Azreal and Zynka watched and relished the moment of respite.

After a few King George songs, some fast, some slow, a slow

buckle-rubbing tune came on. Erin pulled Jayce close as they swayed to the sad tune together.

"Thank you for teaching me how to dance. It's a lot of fun. Exhausting, but fun," Jayce said as she lay her head in the crook of the taller woman's neck.

Erin, in turn, laid her cheek on Jayce's head and silently continued to sway. With much hesitation, Jayce pulled her head away and looked into Erin's light blue eyes. She slid her hand to the redhead's cheeks and leaned forward, kissing her. She felt every bad situation she had ever been in, every unwanted touch, every cross word melt away in her mind. Erin leaned into her; she cradled the back of Jayce's head and returned the kiss with the same intensity. Jayce pulled back, red-faced and wide-eyed.

"I-I'm so sorry." A tear shed as she abruptly warped away.

Erin stood there dumbstruck, both from the kiss and the reaction to it. She turned to the rest of the group, with a dumb smile, all but Cali being just as bewildered. Cali, however, was giving a double thumbs up.

* * *

"Should we go to Antoinette's plane and help?" Jotun's deep voice echoed in Noctharim's barren office.

The corvathis did a few lazy loops on his perch and chirped in contemplation.

"There really is no need to. Something will fill the vacuum as it always does. Though not the outcome I was expecting. They are both more forceful and protective than I would have thought. I believe they will be a good fit after their exam." Noctharim chirped in approval. Jotun only grunted in response.

"They have altered the course of the marionette plane." One.
"So it would seem." Two.
"Next steps?" Three.
"Allow Thought to continue digging." Wanderer.

# CHAPTER SEVENTEEN

Erin stared back at the empty space Jayce had just occupied, confused. She couldn't figure out if she had done something wrong.

"Should I go talk—" She started before Cali cut her off.

"I'll go," She said and warped away, leaving Erin to stare at a new empty space, confused.

"How is that going to help? *I* should talk to her," She said, sitting down with Leon despite her words.

Leon looked amused.

"That kiddo just wants her hand in the cookie jar." He looked at her seriously for a moment. "Are you okay?"

She thought about all that had happened and cringed.

"Leon, I just realized...I-I didn't mean to lead you on."

He only smiled back, perpetually unbothered.

"You didn't lead me on, Erin. We talked. We connected a bit. But that in no way made us anything more than friends. You don't owe me an apology or anything else. Plus, if you could've seen your smile, that was beautiful." His words were sincere and warm as always.

It made her feel safe in a way a man had never let her feel; there was no possession in his tone, just happiness, even if it meant he didn't get what she figured he wanted. His eyes glinted with joy for something that didn't even affect him.

"You care for people, truly?" the ethereal voice of Azreal spoke out.

He looked over to her and smiled.

"Honestly, when other people smile, it makes the world worth being in," he replied, uncharacteristically sheepishly.

They maintained eye contact for a moment before Erin spoke again. "Thank you. I really didn't expect that. She's so sweet and a really awesome person. Do you think she's okay?"

Jayce stared at herself in the mirror.

*What the hell is your problem? Why would you ever think that was the right move?*

She put her forehead on the mirror and sighed deeply. The tears had stopped, though the trails remained. She dropped to her knees and sat down, cradling her legs with her arms. She sat there rocking and thinking about all she had ruined. Erin and Leon were a thing, and she just potentially destroyed that. Her chin dropped to her chest.

*"You ruin everything!"* she heard a feminine voice yell in a heavy Mexican accent.

Another tear fell. Belinda had always told her that everything that went wrong was her fault. And Jayce had started to agree. Every time someone was aggressive with her or their gaze lingered, it could always be traced back to what she did or what she wore. Her thoughts were interrupted, and she jumped at a knock on her door.

*They're here to tell you to leave.*

She struggled to her feet and went to the door.

"Erin, I'm sor—" she started as the door went up, only to reveal Cali instead.

Jayce's heart fell slightly, but Cali smiled wide.

"Nope, just little old me. Can I come in? You have to say I can, otherwise I can't come in. Erin was messing with me and didn't let me in for like ten minutes. It was really weird to see in, but not be able to walk in. I think there is a barrier or something. So can I come in?"

Jayce was confused as to how the younger girl wasn't out of breath with how fast she talked. She nodded and allowed the permissions to let Cali in. The small girl stepped in and hopped on the cloth strip bed. She patted the spot next to her, beckoning Jayce to sit with her. Hesitantly, she walked over and lay on the bed, staring at the mirrored ceiling. Cali quickly laid her head on Jayce's chest and put her arm across to her opposite shoulder. Jayce saw in the mirror how wide her own eyes became.

"So, do you think we will be sisters one day? I like you and think that would be awesome. Do you really like Erin? I don't want her to get hurt. She cares about you. But we all care about you, I guess. Hers is different, though." Cali took a breath, giving Jayce a small amount of time to contemplate an answer.

Her face had become the color of a stop sign at the mention of being sisters.

"I-I do like your sister. Very much. She has been a constant anchor in this place—"

"She is. She has a way of making the most messed-up times feel okay. After our parents died..." Cali blinked rapidly. "She was able to keep me from knowing how bad off we were. I just want to make sure you won't hurt her." She looked at Jayce seriously. "If you hurt her, I'd have to stab you, and that prolly wouldn't be fun." Her tone was playful, but Jayce felt the edge to her voice.

"I wouldn't," is all she replied.

Cali nodded, kissed Jayce on the cheek, and hopped up.

"Good, let's go see your girlfriend." Cali stuck her tongue out at the freshly red Jayce before warping away.

Jayce looked at the empty space the chaos gremlin had just been. She blinked, trying to process the short and rapid conversation. Deciding to just rip the bandage off, she got up, went to the mirror, and tried to lighten the tear streaks. After doing as much as she could, she took a deep breath and warped to the previous dance floor.

The world rematerialized in front of Jayce as she landed in the living room. Leon and Azreal were chatting and giggling. Zynka was gone, likely in bed. Cali was just sitting down as Jayce arrived. Erin, it was hard to determine, but she looked nervous. In the short time they had known each other, minus day one here, she had never let herself show any nerves. Why now?

Erin stood and walked to Jayce.

"Erin, I'm—" Before she could finish, Erin wrapped her in the tightest yet most tender hug she had ever felt, not much frame of reference, but still.

She felt herself leaning in and wrapping Erin in an equally tight embrace. Nothing needed to be said for a time as they stood there, sharing body heat. Jayce buried her face in Erin's neck and chose to just exist. Erin lightly scratched Jayce's back in what was the most soothing gesture she had ever experienced.

"Erin, I didn't—I shouldn't have—" Jayce again started, but Erin gently put Jayce's head back in the crook of her neck.

"You didn't do anything I didn't want. Remember, the Academy has rules on consent. You have no reason to apologize, babe." Erin rubbed Jayce's head. "I was caught off guard, but that was in the best way possible." She gently pulled Jayce's head back and looked deeply into her violet eyes.

If Jayce didn't know any better, she could've sworn there was actual electricity in their stare. Erin began to lower her head to Jayce's, whose heart started racing rapidly. The kiss was cut off before it could start by a loud crash and a chirpy voice.

"Very sorry for the intrusion, my young initiates, but there seems to be a new resident, and that must be addressed," Noctharim stated as he hopped on the table towards Azreal. Erin sighed and gave Jayce a quick peck on the forehead, which Jayce thoroughly enjoyed.

"What a cock block," Erin said as she took a giggling Jayce's hand and led her back to the table and sat down.

Once they were all seated, Noctharim began.

"Well, my young friends, it seems as though neither of the first two contracts have gone as planned." Erin and Leon shared a 'No, duh' look. "I would say that is not typical, but I have never been much into bending the truth. I will say that the partial extermination of a species and disruption of an entire planes economic structure is a new one," Noctharim ended, gnawing his wing.

The group shared a look before finding anywhere to stare but at the professor. He flourished a wing.

"Come now. There is no need to feel any kind of way about it. While the contract was most assuredly not completed as intended, it did have results. And if it ended in one person"—he focused on Azreal— " being freed, then I have no qualms with the journey to get there. And, young elf, I do apologize. I am not able to keep an eye on every goings-on in all the realms. Perhaps that is something I shall work on in the future. Ah, my manners. I am Professor Noctharim, Headmaster of the Aetherion Academy. Are you yourself a walker?" Noctharim took flight and hovered around Azreal.

For her part, Azreal only looked slightly uncomfortable. She had wrapped her arms around herself and subtly scooted her chair towards Leon's. He looked at her and mouthed, "One of the good ones...I think."

She nodded in response.

"I am Azreal, a moon elf of Astrevia. I am a walker, though having spent as much time as I have in bonds, it may take time to reacquaint myself with the action." Her voice carried the angelic regality that could enchant someone not careful.

Noctharim did a loop.

"Shall we return you to your home? Would you rather stay? What outcome is your desired one?" the professor asked.

She looked out the corner of her eye at Leon and the three human women before steeling herself.

"My clan traded me into that hell for baubles. I have no home to return to. I would like to stay with Le—I would like to stay here. It is unfamiliar, but reassuring." She nodded in agreement with her own statement, while blushing a deep blue at her near admission.

Noctharim landed and looked amused at the situation.

"Very well. You may join the humans—yes, Cali, that means you—and Zynka in Professor Selvoth's class tomorrow."

Cali practically vibrated next to Leon.

Noctharim held up a wing to forestall a response.

"Automo let me know that you have helped him in the repair and manufacturing of the upgraded 'fridges' and said you were quite impressive, so I see no reason to hold you out of the classwork. Just be care—"

Noctharim was cut off by a tiny teenager lunging across the table and scooping him up. In an instant, he was cradled and receiving glorious nose scritches; he didn't even judge himself for purring.

"Thanks, birdo. You really are a cool...thing," Cali finished, vigorously scratching behind one of his wings.

She even cooed at him. Though it wasn't the first time they saw it, the humans cringed at the show. Azreal looked highly offended on the powerful being's behalf.

"Stay out of trouble." He nipped Cali's finger lightly to get away and warped.

Cali slapped her face hard enough to make Jayce's own nose hurt.

"Ouch, stupid. Anyway, I totally forgot that while me and Sparky were messing around, he gave me some materials, and I made y'all gifts! Well, technically, Leon has two, but one of them would suck for the rest of y'all. Azreal, I didn't make you a present, but in my defense, I didn't know you existed. I can make you one tomorrow if you like it."

She smiled at the group for a long, awkwardly silent moment. Finally, Erin sighed.

"Cal, if you are going to tell people you have gifts, the next step is to give them." Erin looked tired, as though this wasn't the first walkthrough of decorum.

Cali shot up and ran to her room. Leon blinked at the figurative smoke outline of the wild child.

"Can you remember the excitement of youth? Life always

seemed in bloom back then." Azreal's delicate voice sounded wistful.

Leon nodded solemnly.

"Nothing gold can stay. At least that's what an old poem said, but I would give my other arm to keep that kid exactly how she is." The fact that there was no exaggeration in his voice brought a small tear to Erin's eye and made Jayce smile as they squeezed hands.

*Is this what family is supposed to be?*

Jayce couldn't—and didn't want to—help but lean on that thought.

*Family.*

"Leon! Close your eyes," Cali yelled from her door.

Leon complied.

"Yes, ma'am, they are closed."

Cali came bounding back to the table, carrying a large silver gauntlet with multicolored lines of circuitry running through it. Around the base were six screws, also with traces of circuits. Cali eyed the screws sadly for a moment before shaking her head.

"Do you trust me, Leon?"

"With all my heart, kiddo."

Cali smiled.

"This is going to hurt a lot for a very quick moment, but I promise it's worth it."

Leon, without hesitation, nodded. He flinched when she grabbed his left arm, but steadied fast, and Cali fit the gauntlet over the end of his elbow.

"Are you ready?"

The group looked on in morbid curiosity. Jayce's hand had gone numb from the vice grip of Erin's hand. Leon breathed in, nodded, and exhaled slowly. As Cali pressed a button, the screws drove into Leon's arm agonizingly slowly. He continued releasing his breath slowly as the screws dug deeper. Sweat began to form, but he wouldn't allow himself to flinch. The wounds were being cauterized as they dug, so to Jayce's surprise, there was no blood.

After a minute of agony, the gauntlet's screws stopped. His breathing had steadied.

"May I open my eyes?"

Cali was almost in tears.

*I hurt him so badly.*

"Yes."

Leon opened his eyes and stared at the unfamiliar silver appendage. He didn't blink, as though when he closed his eyes, the arm would go back to its normal self. He felt that nerves, or at least simulated ones, went to the new arm. Even still, he was hesitant to try. He wasn't in shock, but damn near. He finally tried to close the hand, and to his shock and relief, it closed just how his right hand would have. The group jumped when Leon stood quickly, turning to Cali. She looked a foot shorter than usual under his gaze. He took a step towards her; she trembled. Then, in one motion, he grabbed Cali under the arms and tossed her up just to land in a massive bear hug. Leon's shoulders heaved as he squeezed the small girl.

"Thank you, kiddo. Thank you so much. You can't know what this means." He spoke in chokes as the words fought for space in his throat.

Cali giggled with glee and threw her arms around his neck. Azreal looked on, her look warming with the rest of the group. She noted that this man, who had murdered two men in front of her, held more love than anyone she had ever met; a love without possession. It all landed strangely to her, but she looked forward to seeing it grow. Erin leaned on Jayce's shoulder, happily sobbing at the scene. And Jayce...Jayce felt secure.

"Well, this is gonna make the second gift suck. So, I'm just going to give it to y'all tomorrow. Goodnight," Cali said as Leon gently set her back on her feet.

She blew kisses and ran off to her and Erin's room. The group chorused their goodnights back to her as she disappeared.

"I think we can add a room for Azreal. Like the table, it just needs a consensus," Leon said as the two human women nodded.

"Upstairs or downstairs, ma'am?" Leon asked Azreal as the permissions allowed him to create.

"Could it be near your room? I do not mean to come off as over-reliant, but it would help me sleep knowing a warrior slept near me," the elf spoke with elegance.

Leon nodded intently and tapped away on the holo. After a minute, he looked up.

"Okay, it's next to mine. Can I show you the way?" He started to reach out his right hand, but switched to his left mid-motion.

Azreal eyed his prosthetic before taking it gracefully and stood. They too said their good nights and left, leaving Erin and Jayce alone. Erin got up and went to the fridge, returning with two banana splits. She sat across from Jayce and slid one to her.

"Ice cream too cliché for a first date?" she asked, taking a bite.

Jayce went scarlet.

*Date?!?*

Her breathing became labored as her head swam.

"No. Not cliché at all," she squeezed out.

She took a bite of the sweet vanilla ice cream. It melted as soon as it touched her lips.

"It doesn't have to be a date," Erin added quickly. "It doesn't have to be anything. That was dumb."

Jayce was caught off guard by the nervousness of this usual stalwart of steel nerves. She offered the most disarming smile she could.

"I've never been on a date. I mean, coming to this place"— Jayce gestured around the alien room— "was the first time I had ice cream. The first time I had...friends." The word came out cautiously optimistic. "A lot is new. But I do." She reached out and took Erin's hand in her own. "I do want this to be a date." She ended with a squeeze of her hand and a smile.

Erin's eyes lit up. Her perfect smile parted her face as she returned the squeeze.

"Can you even picture being in a normal classroom right now?" Erin asked.

Jayce tried to imagine it, but came up empty.

"Not really. I know it hasn't been that long, but I couldn't imagine being anywhere else. All of this is absolutely bananas, but it just feels right, you know?" Jayce finished and took a big bite of the ice cream with a bit of the fudge and peanuts.

Erin mimicked the bite before speaking.

"It does feel kind of homey. And besides the murderous rats, evil elves, and tyrannical marionette, it feels like a break. One I needed. I loved taking care of Cali and always will, but it got overwhelming at times." Erin took a deep breath. "Full disclosure, I have done a lot I ain't proud of."

Jayce instinctively grasped Erin's trembling hand.

"How about we pretend life started when we got to Aetherion? The 'real world' sucked. We may as well start over, yeah?" Jayce felt a reassuring smile part her lips.

Erin returned it and nodded.

"Sounds good to me, babe."

They finished their desserts with small talk of plans for the next day, and Erin entertained with stories of Cali's shenanigans. When the bowls were thoroughly emptied, Erin tossed hers on the floor and giggled as the bowl was swallowed up. She stood and offered Jayce her arm.

"May I walk you home?" she asked cheekily.

Jayce stood and hooked her arm in Erin's, and they warped to Jayce's door. They stood looking at each other; neither moved. Jayce watched Erin's figure sway slightly and felt the nervous energy.

*Screw it.*

She again took Erin's face in her hands and pressed their lips together. This time Jayce felt no guilt, no shame, just safety. Just bliss.

Erin leaned into the kiss with a fury, as though the moment might end and be gone forever if she let it slip away. The kiss was long and deep; the world, or worlds, disappeared. There was only

Jayce and Erin. Pulling back for a breath, Jayce's chest heaved. They stood, catching their breaths and sharing a gaze. Eventually, Erin straightened.

"I'll see you in the morning?"

"Of course. Good night...babe."

"Good night." Erin gave her a warm peck on the lips and warped away. Jayce put her back against the wall and allowed herself a moment of happiness.

* * *

"The wanderer was in a group," Noctharim said in a serious tone. "The more research I do into the humans' world, the more I remember."

"What does that mean for us? For the students?" Jotun's gravelly voice responded.

"I do not know. And not knowing is causing me to molt, and it is quite unpleasant. Could you see if you can dig out any information from their internet?"

"Already began, Professor."

"They have dug deeper." One.
"So it would seem." Two.
"Shall I intervene?" Three.
"Perhaps it is time we became public again." Wanderer.

# CHAPTER EIGHTEEN

The morning wouldn't come quick enough for Jayce. She had barely slept, contemplating and reliving her time with Erin. It had been the single greatest night of her life. Nothing was even comparable in her mind. The flapping of wings pulled her from her thoughts as she lay on her bed.

"We have been watching your group since your first trip into Aetherion. And last night was the first true smile you have shown. It was good to see, and my master agrees." Thought perched on her desk.

"Who is 'we'? And why have y'all been watching us?" Jayce couldn't help her curiosity.

Thought pecked at nothing on the desk before answering.

"'We' is me, my master, and his associates. The why is simple. After billions of years, life gets boring, and the way to stay entertained is to find something worth watching. We have been confined to Earth for so long; voluntarily, but still." He flapped his wings to emphasize the boredom. "No walkers had spawned from your realm in, well, ever. So, the rise of four was intriguing to say the least. And my master thought it was humorous that there was four of you, given that's the number of his compatriots as well," he ended, looking at Jayce.

She thought for a moment about the appropriate response

and best follow-up. She bit her lip, trying to come to terms with being watched.

"Did they send the Murdenex after us in the crest plane?"

Thought cawed. "Indeed, they did. The way your group handled it was wildly entertaining."

"You tried to kill us! That's entertainment to y'all?" She rose from the bed, staring down the raven.

He flapped his wings in a flippant motion.

"Kill? I guess that would have been a potential outcome. But not the only possible one. On Earth, did you watch movies with violence?"

"Sometimes, I guess."

"There was no more killing intent from my master there than a director has for his actors. The goal was entertainment. If you had died, then what would he watch?" The raven did his best to shrug. "It will not be the last time he intervenes. Just know your death is not his goal, though it is always a possible outcome. I need to return to him for now. Should you need to talk, I will be here. Stay safe, young Jayce." Without waiting for a reply, he was gone.

Leaving Jayce alone with the new information. She sat in her chair, lost in thought.

*Do I tell the others? Would they believe that I can talk to an invisible bird? Would it do anything to make the others aware? Or would it cause stress where none is needed?*

She mulled over these questions, letting herself melt into the comfortable chair.


Leon was the first to the kitchen. He pulled out plates of bacon and eggs for the four humans and set them out; his absolute joy at carrying two at once was palpable. He got a plate of the grass Zynka enjoyed and a small bowl of popcorn for her as well. Pausing, he tried to think of what to get for Azreal. She was human enough, so would that make the bacon and eggs the right call? Or what if she was some kind of vegetarian? Would that offend her?

*So many questions. Navigating multi-planar norms is going to take some getting used to.*

He decided to wait and just ask her when she got down. Luckily, he didn't have to wait long as Azreal was the second to make her way in. She stretched and let out an overly loud yawn before clamping a hand over her mouth.

"I am very sorry, that was very uncouth." Her paper-white skin took a blueish hue.

Leon assumed that was her blushing. He waved away her apology. "Good morning, darlin'. Did you sleep all right?"

Azreal practically glided across the room; her uniform, which had taken the appearance of a night gown, flowed behind her. She took the seat next to him.

"I did, better than I have in years, honestly. That bed wanted to swallow me whole. And I absolutely let it!" Azreal gave another stretch and a silent yawn before looking at Leon's plate.

He had four fried eggs and a pound of bacon piled up. She looked at it curiously before grabbing a piece of the bacon and taking a bite. Her yellow eyes dilated, almost removing the iris completely. She scarfed that piece and four more, plus bare-handed a fried egg into her mouth. Leon couldn't help but let out a hardy chuckle.

The elf seemed to catch back up to the world and went almost completely blue. Even her hair reflected her temporary coloring. She was about to speak when Leon held up a hand. Azreal shut her mouth. Leon smiled at her, then dove face-first into his plate. He made sure to clean the plate with no hands. When he finished, he came up, smiling still. Bacon bits and chunks of egg stuck in his bushy beard.

Azreal's lips quivered. She tried really hard not to laugh, but failed. Her laugh was hypnotic to Leon. It was a twinkling sound, and he could tell it hadn't come out to play in some time. To add to her humor, Leon began picking out and eating the crumbs from his beard. She grabbed her stomach and tried to regain composure.

"Thank you, Mister Leon. I needed to laugh. And also thank you for not judging my ill-mannered eating." Her voice held the humor still, but was reined in by her grace.

"Hey, when we are hungry, we are hungry. Plus, this is one of the greatest foods in our world. It'd have been weird if that wasn't your first reaction, honestly." He gave her his white smile before going and retrieving two more plates.

When he set the plate in front of Azreal, he also placed a fork down. She blushed again, picking up the utensil. They quieted to eat.

A few minutes later, the dining room was full of noise from the chattering group. Cali sat as close to Leon as she could. Jayce and Erin were elbow-to-elbow as well. They all ate their meals happily and spoke of their thoughts of the previous days and guesses as to the next day.

"Y'all remember Professor Selvoth talking about the initiate exam?" Leon asked in a lull.

"Yeah, what do you think it is? I'd go out on a limb and say it won't be a written test," Erin answered.

Jayce nodded in agreement.

"Maybe it's a deathmatch with other initiates. Whoever lives gets to actually start school." There was a hint of humor to Cali's response, though the rest of the group shared a silent look.

"I mean, I'd like to think the War Master would have told us if that's the case," Jayce replied with about as much confidence as she could.

Hell, with what this place was, who knew. Cali tapped away at her holo.

"Nope. No deathmatch," Cali said, only slightly downtrodden. "Personalized deep dives." She pointed to her screen. "At least that's what Professor Sparky said."

The group let out a collective breath. All of their holos dinged simultaneously. Jayce read her message.

*Initiates, please meet me in the courtyard where we first met. Professor Selvoth.*

"Well, shall we?" Leon asked.

They headed out the door. They were about to summon the hover bikes when a noise from Cali stopped them.

"My gifts! Now is the perfect time!" Cali squealed in excitement as she ran up to Leon and held out a ring.

Leon cocked an eyebrow.

"Now, kiddo, I do have an affection for ya. However, I do believe you are quite young to be proposing." Leon's light and playful tone was lost on Cali.

"Just throw it on the ground," she said, miming the motion.

Leon shrugged, took the ring, and threw it at the ground. Before it could hit, it expanded rapidly. In moments, hovering just inches off the ground was an eight-foot-long, three-finned surfboard. Leon stared at it longingly. He looked like a lion about to pounce on a gazelle.

"It flies. It has the fall barrier and should ride like a normal board. See you at the courtyard." Cali read it off like a pamphlet.

Leon swiftly planted a big kiss on Cali's head, jumped on the board, and was gone. The group watched as he faded away in the distance. Cali pulled out four more rings and gave them to the others. Azreal was slow to take hers.

"You said you didn't have one for me. I do not wish to take an item meant for another."

"Oh, shut up and take it. I couldn't sleep last night so I made another. No big deal," Cali said, throwing her ring.

Within a minute, the whole group was surfing the Nexus, trying to catch up to the one real surfer. Jayce's long hair whipped in the wind. It was so freeing to fly through the air, helped a lot by the fact that she couldn't fall. There was a lot of hollering and shouting as the group carved through the lavender sky. They caught up to Leon, who was as at peace as one could be. He gestured for them to follow, and he barreled down to the top of the castles. Flying so close that he reached out and touched a few spires. Eventually, they made their way to the front of the main castle and landed in the courtyard. Leon immediately embraced Cali.

"Kiddo, you are the single most awesome person I have ever met," he told her as he spun her around.

She squirmed out of his grip and straightened her unblemished uniform.

"Yeah, yeah, yeah. Don't get all sappy. I am glad you liked it," Cali said as her board reverted to a ring, and she slipped it on her finger.

"Initiates, welcome. It is my pleasure to have you all today," Selvoth's deep, resonant voice reverberated amongst the group.

They all exchanged hellos and introductions for Cali and Azreal.

"We shall be doing things differently from your first two courses. We have no contract. Just time for me to teach some universal techniques and abilities." The large whale swayed with the nonexistent breeze.

Jayce perked up at the aspect of actual learning and not a life-or-death struggle, though she still checked her eidolon.

"What will we be studying, good professor?" Azreal's angel voice sounded out.

He adjusted his massive frame to face her.

"First will be the basics of walking. I always ask the headmaster to start with this, but he must have his reasons. To truly learn to walk is the most basic, yet most crucial ability you will attain. And that is what we will start with today. Solo walks."

Jayce sucked in a breath as her skin prickled. Erin scooted closer, her presence a reassurance. Zynka looked bored already. Cali was, as usual, vibrating.

"How does it work? How do we know where to go? Is there a way to mess it up so bad you die? How long have you been walking?" Cali's cadence, while rapid, was more reserved than usual.

"Cali, Automo told me of your inquisitive nature. In order. One, when we walk, it is like tearing a hole in the fabric between the planes. Two, when you first walk, it is helpful to use an item of the desired destination." He finished that sentence by floating rusted utensils to each member of the group. "These will help guide your steps towards my plane. Three, the chances of walking into a deadly situation are minimal but not zero. Four, I have been walking for longer than your plane has existed."

He surveyed the group now holding the tokens from his world.

"Now you simply focus on the item you hold and take a step as you would during a warp. Please, execute the task." His voice carried a command that the group accepted.

Leon was the first to steel himself and blink away. Then Zynka, followed by Cali. Azreal looked to the lavender sky before disappearing. Erin leaned over and kissed Jayce on the cheek.

"See you on the other side, babe." Then, she too blinked away.

With a newfound vigor, Jayce took a deep breath and stepped, the castles disappearing.

Like watching babes take their first step." One.
"Shaky, yet steady." Two.
"Shall I intervene?" Three.
"Continue to observe." Wanderer.

# CHAPTER NINETEEN

Jayce felt the ever more familiar sensation of the void hurricane pulling her forward. The sound was muted compared to her last walk. The rusted utensil in her hand glowed and pointed to her right. She turned in the air and leaned in the direction she felt it wanted her to go.

*This is way more involved than I thought it was.*

The hurricane propelled her at a speed that should have scared her. And it did, kind of.

While the speed was faster than anything she could compare it to, it also felt safe. A small rip in the void marked her exit point. She braced against the coming nausea as she closed the distance. The void propelled her through the rip. Water wrapped around and compressed her body with the taste of salt on her tongue. Her eyes shot open as the realization set it.

Jayce was underwater, deep underwater.

She looked all around for the surface but couldn't orient herself. Flailing, she cursed never learning to swim. Her chest grew tight, the pressure and desire for air overwhelming. Just as she thought she would pass out, a familiar whale swam up.

"You may breathe, young one. Walkers adapt to their surroundings. So, your body will filter the oxygen from the water." Selvoth's voice was somehow deeper here in his own world. Its rhythmic pulse relaxing.

Fully expecting her lungs to flood, Jayce took in a small breath through her nose. To her surprise, no water entered. Just the purest burst of oxygen she had ever experienced. Her eyes shot wide as she stared at Selvoth.

"I do apologize. These little things sometimes get lost in our knowledge. We don't know one hundred percent why, but we think walkers are all gifted with this talent in case they step somewhere unexpected. Though I wouldn't walk into a fire, I doubt the same courtesy would be afforded." The giant whale smiled as the rest of the group arrived.

All looked worse for wear except for Cali, who immediately swam off after a school of chartreuse fish. Selvoth explained the breathing to everyone to a huge relief to all. There was a collective deep breath. Though they trusted the professor, they all still held back from speaking. After a few minutes of adjusting and upon Cali's return, Selvoth began.

"Glad we have all arrived and somewhat acclimated. Today, we are starting slow with minor abilities that most are capable of. The first of which is telekinesis. Nothing grand, but we will basically play catch with the items that got you all here."

Putting action to words, Selvoth tugged at Jayce's utensil with his mind. She let it go and watched in amazement as it flew effortlessly through the water. The group watched in silence as Selvoth flourished the item wildly yet with a controlled grace. It finally came to a rest. Then he floated it back to Jayce, who grabbed it.

"Now, how that is possible is that every walker has innate energy." Selvoth waved a fin at Erin's uniform. "Those lines in your uniforms are a part of that energy. What we are going to do first is learn to find that energy inside you. Close your eyes and follow along with my words."

Jayce closed her eyes tightly.

"Okay, feel the rhythm of your heart. Follow the beat."

Jayce did as she was instructed.

*Dum dum-dum, dum dum-dum.*

She sensed something there. Something she had never felt, or something she had overlooked. It was a fluid strength. She knew she could manipulate it.

"Once you find it, try and course it through your veins."

Jayce again focused on the liquid. With a thought, it started to move slowly. Her jaw clenched as the trail the liquid left burned her insides. It was like a mini fire in her veins. Jayce gasped as it passed through her heart.

*So much pain...So much power!*

She instinctively knew that this was a lot of power to hurt this bad. Past the heart, she split the liquid in two, sending the burning energy down each arm.

"Very good. Now feel it in the tips of your fingers."

The energy infiltrated the tips of her fingers. Internally, it felt as though they were swelling enough to pop, though there was no external sign. It began pulsating. Azreal let out a small whimper to her left.

"Alright, open your eyes and try to trickle out a little energy to the utensils. That will be enough to connect it," the professor's deep voice reverberated through the group.

Looking around, Jayce saw Leon connect and move his item almost effortlessly. Erin faltered and pushed hers a dozen feet away. Cali was already swinging hers about and cackling. Azrael couldn't seem to get her energy to reach the fork she worked with. Zynka had given up and was poking hers with her trunk. Focusing back on her spoon, she tried to let out a small amount of energy. It felt like a dam broke as the liquid shot out of her fingers like a rocket. The violet energy melted the spoon as it shot past it, straight towards Cali.

"Cali, move!" Leon yelled, kicking off towards her.

Cali pushed to the side, but the energy caught her on her left pinky and ring finger. The energy melted away flesh and bone. Her eyes went wide as she held up her now-melting finger. The two fingers were burnt off to the first joint. Cali shook her hand rapidly as if she could shake them back to full length. Jayce only stared in disbelief.

*You hurt her.*

One voice said.

*So much power.*

Another replied.

Jayce fought tears as she got motion back in her legs and swam over.

"Cali—I-I'm—" Jayce started before being cut off.

"Seriously? How many body parts can a girl lose in a week?" Cali whined, more annoyed than pained. "So don't stand in front of Jayce during training. Got it," she finished, giving Jayce a weak thumbs up.

"Cali, is it painful? Can I help? Are you okay?" Zynka asked.

Cali squirmed and laid her good hand on the elephant's trunk.

"I'm good. It hurts like hell, but it's fading. Thanks." Cali finished by softly rubbing her forehead against Zynka's ear.

The elephant went from neon to scarlet in an instant. Erin, still in shock, managed to give Leon a look, which he returned with a sly smile and a shrug. She then turned to Jayce.

"What the hell happened?" Erin's tone was pointed, yet tempered.

Jayce still flinched and shrunk.

"Erin, I-I don't know what happened. I tried to trickle, but it all just burst out. I didn't mean to hurt her." Jayce's breath caught.

Erin had a slowly dying fire in her eyes.

"Hey, Sis, chill. I'm not mad, you can't be either. It happens. Well, it happens in these weird places we end up. Plus, I can build new fingers. Oh, maybe I'll put a screwdriver. Screw that! I'm putting a flamethrower!" Cali almost squealed at the thought.

Zynka couldn't suppress a laugh.

"Sorry, not funny. Kind of funny."

"I'd say you get used to a missing body part, but I'm not a liar." Leon ruffled her hair. "You'll be okay, kid."

"I cannot say this was an expected outcome. Jayce, you seem to have an immense energy pool to do that by accident. The rest of you try to play catch while I speak with her," Selvoth said, putting a fin around Jayce and swimming away.

They swam a few hundred yards. Selvoth let her go and turned his body to face her.

"Have you figured out how these powers work? Both this one and your sculpting?"

Jayce couldn't figure out why she couldn't meet his eyes as she nodded.

"Yes, sir. Well, I think so. I think it comes from pain?" It came out as more of a question than she intended.

Selvoth rolled his body back and forth.

"Yes and no. Pain is the toll; the more powerful the magic, the more backlash. But the power itself draws on internal anguish. The more trauma a person has, the more power."

*How am I not a superhero then?*

"I brought you away from them because I do not know how much they know. But I wanted to let you know that if you need to talk about it, I am here. And it is okay to talk about it. There should be no shame. If it makes it easier to do that, just know I am the third most powerful at the Academy." He ended on a somber pulse. Jayce picked up on what he meant; it wasn't a brag.

She thought for a long moment before rolling her shoulders and speaking.

"I-I was raised in foster care. Meaning, my parents abandoned me at a church, and I was raised by strangers. Every one of the houses was screwed up in its own way. So, over the years, stuff kept happening."

She paused, fighting ghosts and demons. The crack of a whip sounded. Deep rumbling laughs played in her mind. And the sound of a slap brought her back to reality. She wanted to continue, to let it all out. Seventeen years' worth of anger wanted to explode out of her harder than the energy had. Though she only shook her head.

"That's about it."

Selvoth's eyes grew weary and narrowed slightly, but he didn't push it. He simply nodded.

"Well, you can always reach me on the holo. Let us return and make sure there are the correct number of limbs left." He winked at her blush and swam them back to the group.


"Dang, Erin, calm down." Leon laughed as the knife whizzed by his head again.

He brought it back to himself and slowly guided it back to Erin.

"I don't get it. I'm doing the trickle, I think." Erin focused hard on the knife, willing it to go to Leon.

"Damn!" Erin exclaimed as Leon had to actually dodge this time.

Cali, Zynka, and Azrael were having about as much luck. While Cali was able to manipulate her energy with surprising efficiency, thanks to her "how it works eye", the other two were having issues.

"We don't use energy on my planet. We never need it. Something's heavy; we lift it. We need to reach something; we are massive. I hate this," Zynka complained as she resolved to just throw the spoon to Azrael, who in turn struggled to make it do more than twitch.

"Ugh, this is unacceptable. Years of my life training for this, all for nothing thanks to that disgusting baron." Azreal's shoulders slumped. "I could barely make the walk and now this."

Cali, using her mechanical eye, stared at the elf. She could see the power lines in her system, but they were clogged. They barely let through a drop of energy at a time. Cali gazed deeper at the blockage, really trying to zero in on the problem.

Suddenly, a scream lit up Cali's mind, not external, but

bouncing around her brain. She saw vague outlines of an elf being dragged down a corridor in chains she knew dampened power. The screams only grew louder when a door closed behind the elf. Thuds and slaps permeated Cali's skull. She quickly had her eyepatch melt to cover the robotic eye, causing the memory to fade. Cali's breathing was labored, her eyes wide as she looked at Azreal. The elf also looked out of breath as she glared at the young girl.

"What did you do? How? What all did you see?" Azreal snapped, the venom in her voice almost palpable.

Cali was thankful for being underwater because she didn't want anyone to see her tears as she flinched at the words. A pink and black blur broke their line of sight.

"Don't talk to her like that, elf!" Zynka nearly roared.

Her chest heaved in indignation. The elephant's aura was almost physical as she closed the distance to Azreal.

"Elephant, you have no idea what just took place. Remove yourself from—"

"What just took place is you scared Cali. Anything outside of that is not my issue."

"It's-It's okay, Zynka. She's right. I saw something I shouldn't have," Cali began quietly. "She is right to be mad; it just caught me off guard. I'm fine."

She floated towards Azreal, stopping only to pat Zynka on the shoulder. Cali swam up to the elf and wrapped her in a tight hug, causing a tremor in Azreal, and whispered in her ear.

"I'm so sorry for what you went through. I know that doesn't mean a lot, but I am. You are safe now. I won't let anything happen to you." Cali squeezed her tighter and let go, only to find herself locked in a death grip.

*She can do nothing to protect me, yet she offers with such fervor.*

"I am sorry as well, young Cali. It was not a mistake you made intentionally. Thank you for your words. Please release me."

Cali did as instructed. As they broke apart, Azreal noted the rage still trying to subside in Zynka's eyes.

"I apologize to you as well. I let my anger and fear dictate my reactions."

Zynka's shoulders tensed as she squinted at the elf before she swam off to join Leon and Erin.

"That Zynka cares very deeply about you, child," Azreal stated when the elephant was out of earshot.

"Duh, I'm awesome! Also, I'm not a child, you old crone!" Cali teased as she grabbed Azrael's wrist and pulled her to the other group.

"I hope the training has gone decent in my absence." The booming voice of Selvoth made even the atoms in the water vibrate.

Jayce, close to the professor, stared silently at Cali's hand. Cali looked back at Jayce and just smiled and mouthed, "All good, homie." Jayce returned the smile as Selvoth continued.

"So, this is a very basic task, yet when first introduced, it can prove most difficult. This is learning to manipulate energy that has remained dormant for years. Circle up and let's walk through it."

Selvoth backed up and had the others spread around. When they got into a circle about fifty yards in diameter, Selvoth floated a knife in front of himself. He looked around, eyes landing on Azreal. With a mental command, the knife went end-over-end until it was about four feet from her.

"Azreal, you are dealing with a block, and I know why. You are shutting out the negative emotions, blocking yourself from feeling them. Remember, magic is pain. We all must learn to live with that pain if we wish to be strong." Selvoth's words were heavy, but the weight was soothing.

Azreal tensed, her whole body fighting the words. She knew how to use her energy; she just didn't know if she wanted to. After a few deep breaths and a silent prayer to the moon goddess, she raised a hand and felt the burn of energy she hadn't felt in years. It stung more than she remembered as the knife went across the circle to Leon. Leon sent it to Cali, who sent it to Jayce. Jayce looked at Erin and took in a lungful of air. She let the breath out slowly as she tried to focus on controlling the power. The knife jerked and jumped for a few feet, causing Erin's eyes to widen, before stabilizing and stopping in front of the red head. Erin looked at Zynka and mouthed "Sorry" as the knife shot like a rocket towards her. Zynka deftly caught the rampaging knife while laughing.

"Ninja elephant," Zynka said triumphantly.

She let out a small trumpet, muffled by the water, as she tossed the knife back to Selvoth.

Over the next few hours, the group played variations on catch, each growing in confidence, though Zynka didn't even attempt energy work.

* * *

"It was a group, my dear Jotun?" Professor Noctharim said, swinging around his crystalline perch.

Jotun nodded.

"Yes, Professor, the more I investigate the humans' universe, the more I am sure of it. There were four, which makes a lot of sense considering we knew the Wanderer as Four." Jotun scratched at the scowl on his face. "I think the humans may have seen them as gods after they cut the plane off from the Nexus."

"Keep me up to date in real time. Something does not sit right here," the professor stated.

* * *

Thought flew through the fabrics of universes as quickly as he could. He stopped when he landed on cool red dirt. He looked up at the four figures standing before him. The Wanderer, in his normal cloak and wide-brimmed hat, held his spear, a dark grey raven with milky eyes on his shoulder. Next to him was an obsidian black man, bipedal with six double-jointed arms in a solid white suit. His eight eyes each focused on a different point in space and time. The lone woman of the group stood tall, her chestnut hair tied in multiple thick braids, clad in hunting leathers. She leaned on a bow, her brilliantly blue eyes fixed on him. The fourth figure was massive, but surrounded by a thick haze. Thought had never fully seen this member of the party.

"Wanderer, I have returned. Spending the little time I have with the Sculptor has been enlightening." Thought bobbed his head and looked at his brother.

The other raven only gave a nearly imperceptible nod in return.

"Yes, my old friend. The way they think is truly intriguing. It has been far too long since we have watched the mortals. Such curious creatures, wouldn't you say, Anansi?" The Wanderer looked over towards the black spider man.

"I tink dey be fun ta watch. Dey have such a way about dem," he answered in a thick Patois.

The woman nodded in agreement. "We have watched so many other worlds that we have missed this one. But this reconnection should be entertaining."

She looked around the sky, not at the sky but through it, like a predator looking for prey. The large shape in the haze merely growled.

"I would like to return, Master. And if it is acceptable, I would like to stay with Jayce. She is young and has adventures ahead. We have become stale here. I wish to continue having stories." Thought directed the question to the Wanderer.

The Wanderer looked at his oldest friend and sighed.

"Of course, Thought, I release you from any bonds. I wish you safe travel, and may we meet again. Do help them stay alive. Watching them is great fun, but we must amplify the show of course," the Wanderer replied.

Thought nodded and took flight. He gave the Wanderer an affectionate nibble on the ear and nuzzled his brother before disappearing.

"They are learning of energy." Huntress.
"So it would seem." Two.
"Shall I intervene?" Anansi.
"I will." Wanderer.

# CHAPTER TWENTY

The group had wrapped on playing catch and sat to eat with the professor.

"I could really go for some sushi," Cali spoke around a bite of overly salty seaweed.

Selvoth had brought along a small snack for the students.

"What is sushi, young one?" the professor asked.

Erin stared daggers at her sister.

*Don't say it, don't say it, don't say it.*

Cali swallowed.

"Oh, it is fantastic, you'd love it. It's raw fish, well, usually raw, wrapped in rice and wrapped in nori, kinda like this stuff but not really. Hey, you're kind of a fish, right? I wonder if you would make for good sushi—Not that I want to eat you, well, unless I was sure you'd taste—"

"Cali, shut up!" Erin's voice was both pointed and shocked.

*This brat just said she'd eat the teacher, freaking sweet.*

Erin's thought brought an unrequested giggle from herself.

"In the years, a few billion mind you, I have never once had a student express interest in eating me. I can say with the utmost certainty I don't know what to say." Selvoth's resonant voice held no mirth. Leon had his head on Azreal's shoulder, laughing hysterically.

"Young one, what would you say if I wondered what you tasted like?" the professor asked.

Cali took another bite and shrugged. Before swallowing, she replied. "Well, I saw in a documentary that cannibals say we are a sweet meat. Cannibals are humans who eat other humans. But yeah, they say it's sweet. It was weird. After watching that, I just wanted ribs with tons of sauce. So yeah, I think I would taste pretty good. I'd offer you a bite, but honestly, I'm running out of body parts," Cali finished with another aggressive bite.

Leon jerked around in the water, trying to calm himself from his laughter fit. Azreal and Erin just blinked at the unaware girl. Zynka had her trunk in her mouth, biting hard to stop a laugh. Jayce watched Selvoth, whose body had begun to vibrate. Soon, a boom erupted from him so forcefully it pushed the group back dozens of feet. They tried to steady themselves, but there was no purchase in the water.

"It would seem offering a piece of yourself is unwise, my young friend." Selvoth tried to maintain decorum, failing miserably. Trying to push through, he continued. "So, we have a new rule. No eating fellow students or faculty."

That got a muted chuckle from the group. He waited a second longer for another laugh, shaking his head when he didn't receive it.

"Alright. Well, now that we have the basics in hand, there are some ruins with energy puzzles. It will be a good bit of practice for the participating students." He shot a slightly snarky look towards Zynka, who barely managed a shrug.

Selvoth, with a touch of indignation, turned downwards and began his descent. The group followed. After a bit of swimming, Erin tugged on Jayce's hand, stopping her. Jayce flinched at the touch but turned to meet the other girl's eyes. Erin had a sadly sweet look on her face.

"I wanted to say sorry for snapping at you with the whole Cali thing. I know you didn't do it on purpose, I just, I don't know," Erin said, her eyes searching for forgiveness.

Jayce shook her head.

"I was surprised by the yell, but you just saw your sister lose another body part. I get that. I should be—"

Jayce was cut off as Erin's lips planted on hers. Jayce, not recoiling, pulled Erin's head in to deepen the kiss. She could feel the energy coalescing in her chest. It was almost overwhelming; her hands began to shake. Erin pulled back, brushing the wet violet streak of hair out of Jayce's face. She smiled.

"How about we don't apologize and just move on? Cali seems fine, and I think it's too early for our first spat as a couple," Erin said as her eyes continued to search.

Jayce's mouth hung open slightly.

*Couple? Like a dating couple?*

Erin, as if reading her mind, said, "Was that too possessive? I'm sorry. Stupid Erin. I thought. I don't know what I thought." Erin's head fell slightly, only to be raised again by Jayce's hand.

"A couple. I like that." Jayce's voice was quiet but confident.

Erin reflexively gave Jayce another quick kiss on the cheek and let out a squeal she was immediately embarrassed by. Jayce could only laugh at the red hue of Erin's porcelain skin. They locked hands and headed in the direction they thought the group had gone.

After fifteen minutes of swimming, the two girls began to get nervous. Looking this way and that, there was only water. No surface, no floor.

"Duh, I'm so dumb," Jayce said as she pulled out her holo. As she went to type a message, the screen froze. "Hey, Erin, is your holo working?"

She looked over to the other girl only to see her frozen as well. Her hair was not even drifting with the tide. Jayce's breath caught, or it would have. No air entered or exited her lungs. Not like she was holding her breath, but like the need and the access were gone. The only time she could think of this happening was...Her eyes grew.

Sculpting.

"I knew you would feel it. I wanted to personally thank you

for the entertainment before the next episode. Stay well, my star," the voice of the man from the void boomed.

As his words faded, a black smoke appeared in the distance. She looked on in pure terror as it went on for hundreds of yards. As it solidified, Jayce prayed and begged to be able to scream. Her body shook so violently that if the water could move, there would have been a whirlpool.

The smoke turned to liquid that concreted into two-yard-long scales; hundreds, if not thousands of them. The body was the first to become corporeal, black, bronze, and fetid green scales writhing as it became comfortable existing. The head formed next, a solid, sickly green snake's head the size of a mansion. Its singular eye opened, revealing an angry, deep red iris. Its jaw opened, showing off semi-trailer-long, sharp, white teeth. Behind the teeth was a black hole of a void. Jayce knew now what absolute nothing looked like.

"You're not dumb, babe."

Erin's words sounded like a cannon as the world and Jayce's senses, snapped back into place. The following shriek from Erin punctuated Jayce's own horror. A death grip clasped around her hand.

*She's holding you for safety. You will let her down.*

Jayce's thoughts froze her.

The massive creature slowly wrapped around them. Lying layer upon layer on top of itself as it encased the girls. Erin and Jayce's mouths were wide in screams that wouldn't come as the creature folded itself over top and bottom, trapping them in a three-hundred-yard diameter dome, its head looking up at the duo from the bottom. Both Erin and Jayce subconsciously reached for their eidolons. The familiar weightlessness was but a very, very small comfort.

"On your plane, it is considered rude to play with your food. Where I am from, it is required."

They weren't words, but Jayce felt the intent bleed off the giant snake.

"What are you?" Jayce managed to whisper, her body not allowing her any more exertion than that.

"Leviathan," was the only response she felt as the said leviathan opened its void-like maw.

The void blinked once as two "smaller" versions of the leviathan slithered out, each around twenty meters long. The red eyes of both snakes locked on either girl. Erin and Jayce were shoulder to shoulder, their eidolons finishing taking form. Jayce's whip sword felt like a child's toy in comparison to the massive, armored void snake approaching her. The main leviathan opened its mouth and sent out a torrent of steaming water, ripping the girls from each other.

Jayce was thrown all the way to the body dome, slamming her back against the scales of the monster. Her arms had small burns from the water, and her tunic was torn, though the tunic at least repaired itself. She rubbed the already swelling bruise on her head. The smaller snake slowly made its way to her. Jayce readied herself as she raised her sword. The snake opened its maw and emitted a dark cloud, which worked to quickly envelop her. She looked across the dome and saw the same fate befall Erin. The cloud surrounded Jayce and quickly cut off her breathing. She lost feeling in her hands and the rest of her body in short order. The last thing she processed was the leviathan's intent.

"Feed me!"


Jayce yawned and rolled over. She opened one eye and saw her blue eyes staring back at her.

*What a dream.*

She quickly scrambled out of bed, threw on her clothes, and looked at her packed bags.

*Finally, out of this hell.*

Jayce had finally been heard and was moved from this "overly loving" family. She waited by her barely hanging bedroom door until she heard Margaret, her social worker. Jayce grabbed her bag and nearly sprinted past Margaret and shot out the door. Margaret followed.

"Surprise, surprise. Jayce had a 'bad' experience again." There were spite and sarcasm dripping from her words.

Jayce's eyes hit the floor in competition with her falling heart.

"I..."

"Oh, save it. 'The bad man did this; oh, the mean woman did that'. It's always a problem with you. And I hope one day these B.S. claims catch up with you. Get in the damn car." Margaret shoved past a teary-eyed Jayce.

Silently sobbing, Jayce made her way and loaded up in the car. They pulled away and headed towards the 35. Her new home was in Rockport, another coastal town in Texas.

"You know, I could be at home with *my* family right now. But no, our special case pops up again. Over twenty homes in ten years? Really? You know, when you make these claims, you ruin the lives of people just looking to help," Margaret berated Jayce, who in turn silently rubbed the bruise on her thigh.

She didn't respond, just stared out the window as the bay passed by. She always loved the bay; looking at it, that is. It was what most of the sketches in her notebook were of. The way the waves danced playfully against the sand. Or the way the mischievous seagulls hunted for open chip bags. She closed her eyes and tried to put herself back on the beach. The feeling of sand made her heart...

"I mean, really. One or two, 'oh, this house doesn't have cool stuff' is normal. But crying abuse every other month, it gets a bit melodramatic, don't you think?" The social worker's tone dared Jayce to rise to it. But instead, she simply hung her head and used her nails to rake at her cuticles.

*So much for today being awesome.*

The rest of the drive was silent. They passed very nice houses, which excited Jayce.

*Maybe it will be nice for a change.*

They kept driving, and the houses looked more and more in disrepair. Margaret stopped in front of a house on 7$^{th}$ Street.

"They've already signed the paperwork. Get the hell out," the social worker said, lighting a cigarette as Jayce unpacked.

The second the trunk closed, her sedan peeled out. Jayce stood on the road looking at the house, a small suitcase in both hands. Her peacoat made her sweat, but she made no move towards the door.

*Run. Don't look back. Just run.*

The voice screamed in her head, physically rebounding off the walls of her skull. She shook her head and took a step forward.

*I gave you a chance. You deserve what life gives you.*

The voice had changed, angrier and more malicious. Brushing it off, she approached the door. She knocked gingerly, hearing a dog lose its mind on the other side. She had always wanted a dog. Jayce smiled as the door cracked open. A little old Mexican woman's face popped out.

"Can I help you, *mi hija*?" Her voice was tough from years of smoking and hard living.

"Yes, ma'am, I'm Jayce. I'm supposed to be moving in here today. I'm in the foster program," Jayce spoke softly.

"No, baby. Not here." Her crooked finger came out and pointed next door.

The house was deplorable, with broken windows, a lawn that hadn't been mowed in who knows how long, and weeds growing through an old Trans Am.

"But this is the address they gave me." Jayce's voice wavered.

"Hey, you Jayce?" a deep voice yelled from the barely-there porch of her new home. The man speaking was a severely overweight Mexican man in a wife-beater. "Get over here, leave *mi abuela* alone."

The old lady gave Jayce a broken look before closing the door. Jayce took a deep breath before walking down the sidewalk to the other house.

"Good morning, sir. I'm Jayce...thank you for having me."
She gave a small head bow in greeting.

Up close, the man smelled like tequila and cheap tobacco.
His head was shaved, and he sported a thin moustache.

"Not at all. I am certain it will be my pleasure. I'm Hector.
My old lady is inside," Hector stated with a look that made Jayce
realize she should have run. Hector got up and guided Jayce in,
hand on her low back.

"Ey, Belinda, the new one is here. Jayce."

Jayce cringed internally at "the new one". A squat woman
came in and scowled at Jayce.

"Cute ones, it's always cute ones." The look Belinda gave her
made Jayce recoil slightly.

It was anger—that was normal—but also a tinge of jealousy.

"Do you know how to do anything? Cook, clean, laundry? Or
are you just one of those useless Gen Z kids?"

"I-I can do all of that, ma'am," Jayce replied with
trepidation.

Hector stepped between them as Belinda seemed to fume.

"Back off, woman. I'm going to show her to her room and
give her the ground rules. Why don't you go shopping?" Hector
asked, but it was more of an order.

Belinda gave Jayce a fatal look as she grabbed a purse and
stormed out of the front door.

"Don't mind her, she's always like this when we get a new
foster. Here, down here on the left is your room." Hector
pointed, and Jayce moved that way. She walked down the small
hallway and turned into her new room. It was beige with a small
vanity and a single bed. Tears formed as she felt two massive
hands on her shoulders.

"I'm gonna make you feel right at home."


Erin looked down the half pipe, judging her angles. Her
skateboard lipped on the edge. The hot Texas summer made her
tank top cling to her uncomfortably. After settling on an

approach, she looked at her friend holding a phone ready to record.

"Eric, you better not screw up this shot. I got something here," Erin said as she took off her cap and wiped her forehead. She put it back on backwards and took a deep breath.

"We got this, bro. This is the one we get noticed on. Ready in three, two, one..." Eric counted down and pointed to Erin.

Erin closed her eyes until the countdown ended, then stared at the camera.

"Mornin', y'all. This is Erin Walker coming to you live from Cole Park in Corpus Christi. Without any ado whatsoever... Sponsor me, bitches!" Erin yelled the last words as she dropped in.

The blow-dryer-like wind blew her hair in any direction it could. Her soaked shirt gave her an uncomfortable chill as she tore down one side of the pipe and up the other. On this first pass, she only looked to gain momentum, so as she got into the air, she did a quick frontside grab and turn, landing back on the concrete pipe with blood pumping speed. She recreated the movement for a few more passes before she steeled herself. When she hit the pipe again, she had gained enough speed to try her trick. She said a small prayer to no one as she lifted off the pipe on the other side. Erin grabbed her board and made herself into a T while turning. The Christ Air felt smooth this time, smoother than it ever had. She quickly passed the board to her other hand while spinning, before getting it back under her feet.

*Two turns, hand swap, gotta be worth something.*

The half pipe rapidly approached her. A smile danced on her lips. A smile that was replaced with horror as her front wheels hit the lip of the pipe. Her board went back the way it came as she tumbled forward. Erin's head was the first thing to contact the burning concrete. Her vision went dark immediately, but she wasn't unconscious, more like her body wanted to remove any sensations.

It unfortunately didn't last. The bright summer sun tore into her vision as quickly as it had left, and it roared into her leaking head. Outside of the overly bright sun, the next thing Erin noticed was that her hair was matted in an alarming amount of viscous red fluid. It wasn't a fast leak, but it was persistent. The third thing she noticed was a lot of feet approaching her.

"Erin, damn, that's a lot of blood. Can you hear me?" Eric's voice sounded like it was miles away from her.

*Another concussion, really?*

Erin rolled to her side and proceeded to vomit aggressively.

After a few minutes of being sick and drinking two of the energy drinks they had brought, Erin was sitting on a bench overlooking the bay.

"Dude, that was gnarly. You couldn't have biffed it better." Eric, while caring and empathetic, had rewatched the video multiple times.

Each time Erin heard the thud, she wanted to vomit again. "I really wish that we had decided not to livestream that. That being said, we did get over two hundred views," he continued. Erin's guts wrenched.

*Damn.*

Most watched live, and it was of herself wiping out in epic fashion. They had tried to clean her up, but her red hair was still matted to the right side of her face, and flaky blood covered most of her upper body. Erin jumped slightly as her phone went off in her pocket. She pulled it out and groaned at the shattered screen.

*Mom and Dad are going to kill me.*

She swiped where she thought the answer button was.

"Hello?" she stumbled out the greeting.

"Erin Walker?" a male voice asked in a serious enough tone to make her sit up.

"Yes, this is her. Who's this?" Erin asked, stomach already turning again.

"This is Dr. Vincent at Spohn South. I need you to come to the hospital. There has been an accident," the voice replied.

Erin already felt tears trying to break through the blood on her face. Her phone fell to the ground as she lost motor function. The voice could still be heard making noise from the ground. Eric grabbed her hand.

"What's up, bro?"

Erin shook her head.

"Can you take me to the hospital? Something happened."

The ride to and the walk through the hospital were a blur for Erin, only snapping back into focus when a tiny pigtailed blonde in a fresh arm cast buried into her. Erin wrapped her arms shakily around her sister.

"Cali...are you okay? What happened?" Erin asked.

The eight-year-old looked up into Erin's red face, not even questioning the state of her face.

"It was my fault...it was all my fault. I had made a picture on my tablet, and I wanted Mom and Dad to see..." Cali sobbed so hard the words were shallow and weak, but the implication came through clear as day.

"Was Dad...was he driving?"

Before Cali could answer, a man in a lab coat walked over to them. Erin couldn't understand what he said as she fainted.


Jayce looked into her mirror and applied concealer to her bruised cheeks. Hector's friends were coming over, and a facial bruise was "unacceptable"; like she had chosen to have it. It had been worse here than she thought. She looked over her arms and legs, fresh and faded marks made for ugly coloring on her skin tone.

*I told you to run. Worthless.*

The voice had gotten more aggressive over the months. She also felt something tugging at her soul during the roughest times. It wasn't tangible, just like something was leeching off of her. She shook her head at the thought. Standing, she put on her "we've got company" uniform. Black denim short shorts and a white mid drift. The mirror mocked her as she checked herself. The yellow and purple bruises the shirt allowed made her cringe.

*This is what you are worth.*

Her eyes teared up. Pushing past, she adjusted her long raven hair and fixed her blue streak. She shrugged her shoulders as she got ready to look at the floor for the next few hours.

"Where's that girl of yours, homie?" Richard, a friend of Hector's, yelled. "I missed her, you know?"

Jayce shuddered. Outside of Hector, there was no one she feared more than that brute. While most of his friends just got what they wanted and left, Richard was different. Her spine tingled as she braced and steeled herself to leave the room. Before she could, she felt a familiar yet foreign weight on her shoulder. Looking in the mirror, she didn't see the cause, which made the disembodied voice cause her to freeze.

"This isn't real, Jayce. Not anymore. You are past this chapter. Fight. He is feeding. Free yourself." Thought tried to push his voice into Jayce's nightmare. "You are powerful. Remember, girl."

Jayce looked on her shoulder and around the room to find any trace of the speaker. Finding nothing, she shook her head.

*And now you are breaking. Pathetic.*

"Whatever," she said as she stepped into the hallway.

Her fear rose as she saw Richard in the living room. His giant frame was wrapped in old military BDUs, already holding a tequila and smoking those disgusting cigars. She rubbed the burn on her rib absentmindedly. Jayce felt it again. Something tugged at her discomfort, her fear. "He is feeding," replayed in her head.

*Who's feeding? On what?*

Jayce brushed away the thought as she took the extremely short walk to the kitchen. Hector and Richard eyed her, but she kept her eyes on the ground as she went to the sink to get a glass of water. When she got the water in a cup, she drank deeply, wishing it had a numbing effect.

"Hey, girl, you miss me?" The smug tone in Richard's voice made her want to vomit.

"Ey, she prolly too excited to talk," Hector responded with a chuckle.

Their voices were like a thousand nails on a chalkboard. She focused every piece of energy she had on the cup of water. The water which had an odd red tint to it. The tugging hit again.

"I said, did you miss me?" Richard's voice was closer.

Jayce stared at the red in the cup. It was moving, slightly, but moving. The weight on her shoulder came back. There was still nothing there, but for a brief moment she thought she saw a black feather. Footsteps got closer. Her heart began to sputter. How many times had she looked into this sink in front of Richard? But the red in the water blinked, drawing her focus back. Tug. There was green wrapped around the red "eye".

*Why is this familiar?*

A black and bronze body materialized in her cup. The footsteps stopped too close behind her. A large hand wrapped around her hip. The tugging reached a crescendo. The creature in her cup swirled around and around as her eyes went wide. The snake being was chasing a beautiful red-haired woman.

"Erin," she whispered.

Snippets of non-existent memories flooded her head. A hug, a smile, a kiss. Aetherion. Jotun. Leon.

She felt wind split as a large hand slapped her hard on the butt. Her body jolted forward from the impact. Tears welling up, she spun on Richard, her blue irises and hair streak burning into violet. The big man took a slow step backwards. His fist came up and struck out towards her before it froze. Again, no sound, no air, no movement. Jayce could feel her veins burning with energy, just wanting an escape.

"Never again!" Jayce screamed as the violet energy exploded from her.

The image of Richard being torn apart was replaced with the smaller leviathan being disintegrated as she was brought back to the dome on the water plane. Her energy didn't stop. It erupted like the night sky on the Fourth of July.

"She shows tremendous power." Huntress.
"So it would seem." Two.
"Success, or no?" Anansi.
"Immense success." Wanderer.

# CHAPTER TWENTY-ONE

L eon smiled as he looked over his shoulder at Erin holding Jayce back.

*Cuties, the both of them.*

He returned his gaze to watch Cali riding Zynka like a seahorse after Selvoth, while Azreal stuck close by.

"You have a joyous aura around you, Mister Thatcher. One that, if it is not too far for me to say, is foreign to you. It wears well, yet uncomfortably, around you." Azreal's angelic voice was only amplified by the underwater setting.

It threatened to lull him to sleep.

"I guess I ain't had much of a reason to be joyous, darlin'. And I just enjoy seeing them happy in all this weirdness. Plus, they've been through the wringer." He snuck a quick look back as he spoke, but the couple was gone from sight.

They continued following Selvoth for a minute before the elf spoke again.

"Mister Thatcher, you also have seen things that would be considered going through the wringer, no?"

She turned her striking golden eyes on him. The intensity of them made Leon falter slightly.

*Voice, eyes, looks. This girl is dangerous.*

He laughed internally.

"I really ain't seen much more than any other military vet, I figure." Leon wanted to shrug the question off and look away, but in his head, he knew it would be painful to do so. As he watched the elf, he saw her uniform start to spark pink lines on the surface.

"You can tell me, Leon. I will keep safe your words." Azreal's voice came out as a purr. The feeling in Leon's chest begged him to tell her anything she wanted to hear.

*Give her your words, your belongings, whatever she wants. What? No.*

His thoughts crashed into his head as he opened his mouth to speak. Before words came out, Azreal interrupted.

"Leon, do not answer that." As she spoke, the feeling in Leon's chest dissipated. He shook himself.

"The heck was that?" he asked, rubbing through his long blonde hair to his scalp.

"I do apologize, Mister Leon. My ability has been locked away for so long. I swear, truly I did not mean to manipulate you." Those beautiful golden eyes held fear more than regret.

Leon, stiff at first, relaxed.

"Hey, when my power manifested, I committed double rat homicide, though it was a simulation. Does that count? Anyway, don't do it again and we're good, okay?" His smile shone in the watery depth in a way that made Azreal feel like telling him all he wanted to know. She nodded.

"So, is it like a truth ability?"

The elf shook her head, then nodded.

"Yes and no, I believe. It is a compulsion ability. Mental manipulation is what it is widely considered to be. That is why when one of us is captured, they put special chains that eliminate energy flow." She subconsciously rubbed her wrists as she spoke.

"Are there many like you?" Leon was starting to realize there was so much he didn't know.

"Yes, all moon elves have this gift in one fashion or another. It is what gives us value for 'trade', unfortunately. The buyers always believe that we will win them the war, or the stock market, or the love of their lives." She flipped her silver hair through the water, and Leon now understood how fishing lures worked. He was mesmerized by the way the silver strands swayed with the tide and reflected the ambient light.

"So, you're like a walking truth serum mixed with a siren? Also, does your ability do that to your hair?" he asked, still watching it sway.

Azreal smirked.

"Yes, that would be an accurate description." She played with a stray strand of hair. "And no. I just have beautiful hair." She smiled, her teeth barely whiter than her skin.

*Leon, she was just released from a god knows how bad captivity. Swim away.*

He heard and agreed with the voice.

"You really are beautiful, Miss Azreal."

*And that's you ignoring me. Got it.*

His own thoughts were exasperated. To her credit, Azreal only widened her smile. Her parting lips revealed fang-like canines, a predator's smile. Her eyes almost shimmered in the depths.

"That I know, Leon. But thank you. It feels good to be told in a...more enjoyable setting. You are also beautiful. Rugged, broken, young. With a wonderful soul." Her smile never faltered with her speech.

Leon's face grew stoic as he mulled over the compliment before catching on to one item.

"Young? I'm almost thirty? That's not that young." He feigned indignance. Azreal laughed. It was a full, from-the-belly laugh.

"You humans have no reference. Where you rescued me, I was there for longer than some of your civilizations. Thirty of your years barely grows hair on the heads of our babes. So yes, you are young."

The revelation hit Leon like a sucker punch. Not the age, he had come to realize that from the view of immortality, a few years may as well be seconds, but that she had been held and...he shuddered again.

"I'm so sorry that we couldn't be there sooner. I—"

"You arrived when you arrived, and of that I am grateful." She ended by swimming up to him and laying her cold lips on his cheek. She pulled back and stared into his eyes. "Forever grateful."

Leon felt himself drawn forward, not against his own judgement. Azreal stopped him.

"Something is wrong."

"We lost two more, fishy," Cali called after Selvoth. She currently sat around the back of Zynka's neck, holding the elephant's ears as it swam gracefully after the whale. Zynka let out a humored trumpet.

"She called him fishy," she chuckled. Selvoth slowed momentarily, shook his head, then resumed mumbling.

"The most uncivilized race I have ever taught, and I have taught goblins. 'I'm gonna eat you', 'I'm gonna exchange saliva with my partner rather than go to class.' Ridiculous." He hit the humans' accents with surprising accuracy, causing both Cali and Zynka to cackle stupidly.

"He's probably right, though. Jayce and Sis are most definitely making out right now. Leon and Azreal, probably. I don't get it. What is the appeal of having someone's tongue in your mouth?" Cali said, then faked a gag. "Food, food goes into your mouth. Yum, food. Seriously, though. Next time we go to class, we should bring the fridge. Oh, oh, I can make a travel fridge. Do you like watches?" Cali leaned her head over Zynka's forehead to look her in the eye.

Zynka let her mind catch up.

"Yeah, tongues are weird. If we are interested in someone, we just hit 'em with our trunk. That would be a great idea! And I've never worn a watch, but I would if you made me one." Zynka reddened slightly as she glimpsed the ring Cali had given her this morning.

Cali chewed on her lip.

"Would you hit me? Like that? Does it hurt?" Her question had the same Cali cadence, but there was a bit of hesitation in there as well.

She stuck her trunk in her mouth and chewed for a moment before removing it, and lightly bopped Cali on the head with it. Cali immediately bopped Zynka on the head with her hand, harder than she intended. Zynka rubbed the spot.

"Hey, what was—" Zynka cut herself off. Her eyes went wide as realization struck. Cali let out an exasperated breath.

"I don't have a trunk, duh. But to be clear, I don't do the kissing thing, or the touchy stuff." Cali made another gag noise. "Also, I've never dated before. And how does dating work? Erin never really dated. Kids in my school just went to Walmart and walked around. That seems fun, but I don't think they have those here. Oh well, I'm sure there's something. So, are we dating now? We did hit each other. But Dad did say never let a man hit me. You're not a man, or a human though, so I guess that's okay." Cali sank into contemplation.

*Not a man equals hitting is okay? Is this what kind of hitting Dad meant? If someone else hits me, am I dating them too?*

Her thoughts carried her for a while before Zynka spoke.

"Where I'm from, new couples attack a neighboring village and steal resources to build a new home. That could be fun. But...if you would like to be dating, we can figure something out." Zynka's words came out unsure, yet hopeful.

Cali smacked the elephant's scalp again and cackled. Zynka's face was split in half with a smile as they approached. Selvoth let out a pulse of energy and shook his head.

"Ridiculous. Two of six students. Fine. Look."

He pointed at a structure with the appearance of a mid-century brick house with no obvious windows or doors. Cali willed her eye patch over her normal eye and scanned the house. The entire structure was like one of those mazes on kids' menus at restaurants. She saw the start, the blockages, and the pitfalls. The pitfalls would absorb the energy if you went down that path, thus weakening the approach. She imagined doing the puzzle with her finger and grinned when she got the right path. Cali infused energy into the puzzle as Selvoth resumed speaking.

"Inside this building, there are more puzzles if you are able to get past the entrance. But do not be ashamed if you cannot breach the first layer, as it is extremely..." Selvoth sighed as the brick twisted and turned behind him, breaking and rejoining itself as it made an opening wide enough for Zynka to swim through.

"Extremely what?" Cali asked genuinely.

Zynka couldn't hold back a loud trumpet. Cali switched back to her normal eye and watched the professor. He shook his head and flexed his many fins.

"Let the professor finish his explanation, no. Let's all just do what we want. Who even needs a professor?" Selvoth tried to mumble, but the resonance in his voice vibrated the two girls' chests. "Maybe I should just..." Selvoth whipped his body around, tail annihilating the brick structure. "Students, stay close."


Azreal's eyes scanned the distant water. She didn't know what to look for, only that there was a disturbance.

"What do you see?" Leon asked while willing his eyes to see farther. He tried to listen, but the "eeeee" from his tinnitus was overwhelming underwater.

"Send energy to your eyes. It will help with distance and clarity," Azreal said as faint pink lines showed in her golden irises.

The power extended her vision tenfold. Her chest froze mid-breath. She could barely see two dots in the distance, Erin and Jayce, but that wasn't what made Azreal stop. Swimming around the two dots was a gigantic, even at this distance, multicolored snake-like creature with a glowing red eye, wrapping itself around the girls.

"What is that thing?" Leon's voice was angry but wavering.

*Fear, but not for himself. He wants to attack now.*

Azreal smiled.

*Brave. Extremely stupid, but brave.*

"Leviathan," she replied stoically.

"Like from the Bible?" Leon asked as he touched his uniform. His kilt began to melt around him, taking the shape of a wetsuit complete with flippers. He kicked off towards the leviathan that was now a dome wrapped around Jayce and Erin. Azreal followed suit and fell in beside him.

"I do not know this word. But this creature feeds on pain, humiliation, any kind of trauma, really."

They made good strides, but the distance would still take time to cross. Leon winced.

"It won't want for food with them."

"We must hope—" She was cut off as Selvoth barreled into her and Leon.

They both ended up on his face like bugs on a windshield as he used every fin to push them along. She looked around and saw Cali and Zynka were gripping each other's hands, Zynka had her eyes closed, and seemed to be mumbling a prayer. Cali, on the other hand, was hooting and hollering. Even a loud "wheeeeee!" escaped her. Azreal wanted to be frightened, but the little chaos gremlin made her chuckle.

With Selvoth's speed, they closed the distance in minutes, coming to rest a quarter mile away from the dome. The black, bronze, and fetid green scales shimmered and writhed unpleasantly.

"Students, stay here," Selvoth bellowed as he rocketed towards the mass of scale and flesh.

His speed was even more impressive without their weight holding him back. His alabaster skin began pulsing with pink energy. It started slow, then picked up in intensity. The pulses sent waves through the water as his body started to split down the middle. The skin ripped audibly under the water. Like wet construction paper being cut with scissors. Once the final fibers tore away from the two halves, both bodies began spewing sinew that formed the missing half of its body. The sinew solidified into a full body again. This process took less than a second. Then both bodies split again and again. When it was said and done, there were thirty full sized Selvoth's slamming into the dome at full speed.

The ramming caused the dome to cave in slightly, but it held fast. The copies fell back and, in unison, opened their mouths and blew pink lasers of energy into the side of the creature. It was as effective as shooting a spit wad in the back of someone's head. While the scales steamed and there was an audible crack, the damage was repaired as quickly as it was caused. The group watched in macabre fascination at the spectacle. Cali had already switched to her mechanical eye, looking through its body. Instead of the lay lines she could normally see, there was only smoke. It was almost as if it wasn't there. Zynka had her eidolon hammer in her trunk and was psyching herself up. Leon made his prosthetic retract over his nub and eyed the area between layers of scales.

"Why not?" Azreal muttered as she shot forward to the leviathan. Leon and Zynka came in hot on her heels.

"What is the plan, elf?" Zynka asked, voice still carrying an edge towards Azreal.

She ignored it.

"I think we must get between where the creature layered on top of itself."

Leon looked and nodded, shooting past and stopping at one of the folds. His eyes went wide as he noticed one of its layers was nearly a dozen times his height. The positive thing about this was that he could easily get a hand in the fold. He eyed the opening and looked at his nub. Without hesitation, bone snapped, and flesh tore as his arm became a wedge that he shoved between two of the layers of the leviathan. He gritted his teeth against the pain coursing through his entire system. He focused on sending power to the wedge, causing the flesh and veins around it to pulse blue. Some of the veins popped from the energy, causing blue leakage.

"Zynka, use that hammer and drive my wedge deeper," he yelled, pain ripping through every syllable.

Zynka hesitated for a mere moment before winding up and slamming her war hammer into the back of Leon's elbow. The snap was deafening. Leon's wedge was driven in by a few feet, the flesh being ripped, torn, and replaced as it went deeper, but his scream was something Azreal, no matter how long eternity was for her, could never forget. Even underwater, she saw the tears on his face as he tried to maintain his grip on his powers.

"Az-Azre-Azreal, I am about to stop. I-I need you to keep me going...to 'inflate' the wedge. I...need you..." Leon's voice was so weak. So much pain behind every word. Azreal's heart broke.

"How do—" she started as realization set in; she was going to confirm what he wanted, but didn't want him to speak.

She quickly looked around. Zynka was uselessly hammering a scale. All the Selvoths were still futilely trying to burn through the creature, and Cali seemed to be doing an analysis. She focused back on Leon, who was in the middle stage of passing out, though he fought to maintain. Sadly, she swam close and turned his face towards hers, his eyelids heavy and eyes pleading. Azreal let her power into her eyes and voice.

"Dear Leon, do not sleep. Be mine. Be who Azreal needs you to be." The sensual words played in Leon's ear. His eyes went wide.

"Tell me what I need to do, darlin'?" His voice was pained, but level.

"I need Cali inside this dome, my dear. Would you kindly grant her entry?" She hated herself, hated doing this to her savior.

Without a thought, Leon's wedge arm began swelling, ripping, and tearing his own flesh. Bones broke and reformed as the two wraps of the leviathan parted, eighth inch by eighth inch. A whimper escaped his lips as the pain overwhelmed him.

Azreal wanted to stop right then, but knew it had to be done. She stroked Leon's cheek.

"Think not of the pain, my dear. Think of my gratitude." As she said this, she felt an odd sensation; she laid a kiss on his lips, a deep, real, and regrettable kiss.

The lines between compulsion and desire tore through Azreal as she pulled Leon's mouth hard against her own. She pushed energy into him. It coursed through him, both adding to his strength and subtly rewiring his internal processes. The gap began spreading rapidly. Inch by inch now. The tearing of flesh reached a crescendo. Leon's arm snapped one final time before even Azreal's ability couldn't keep him conscious. His eyes closed, and his body went limp in the water, the wedge holding an opening just over a foot wide. Azreal felt her body and mind fade, as well as the sound of Selvoth's energy beams crackling the scales. She laid a kiss on Leon's forehead.

"Sleep well, brave prince." Slowly, her eyes faded, and her body began to drift.

Tears streamed down Cali's face as she watched the horrible scene unfold. Leon was left anchored to the leviathan, while Azreal had gone Dutchman.

*There is no energy to mess with. No structure to sabotage.*

She wished her thoughts would give her anything but problems. She rubbed her shoulders and, with her normal eye, looked at the opening.

*I could go in. Then what?*

The thought was still processing when her body launched towards the opening. She did her best to avoid Leon as she flung herself between the two layers of scales.

"Cali, no—" Zynka's words died in Cali's ears as she found herself on the inside of the dome.

Her heart stopped at the scene. Erin was half-constricted by a smaller version of the beast with a black haze working to obscure it. On the other end, Jayce was in much the same situation. In the center of the dome, a video, comprised of different colored smoke, played the two girls' flashbacks. The smoke was being drawn to the bottom of the dome. Cali shook with rage as she saw what was happening in Jayce's mind, only for that feeling to be replaced with a crippling guilt when she heard the words "Was he driving?".

*I'm so sorry, Dad. Mom, I never...Erin, I...*

Cali was near a breakdown. She thought of how *she* had caused her parents' death. How *she* had made Erin a parent. How *she* had caused Erin so much stress, guilt, and shame. The tears felt molten as they floated around her. She shook herself.

*Act now. Cry later...Maybe.*

She looked around the dome for anything until her gaze landed on an unformed eidolon.

"That's something," she said as she took off towards it.

When she got to it, she grabbed it, willing it to form into something useful. It took its time shaping itself into a long black tube. Cali grinned ferally.

"Oh, hell yes!" she screamed as the rocket launcher took shape.

She couldn't help the cackle. She switched to her mechanical eye and scanned for an appropriate target.

*Smoke. Smoke. More smoke.*

The leviathan came off as nearly completely non-corporeal to her vision. Until she found a pulsing light at the bottom of the dome. Switching back to normal vision, she saw it was the creature's main head. She nodded, grinned, and lined up the crosshairs in the center of the red eyes. Without any ado whatsoever, she launched the rocket. A large neon green ball of energy shot forth. As it neared its target, the eye blinked once, twice, then it impacted.

"Ba ba boom, bitch!" Cali screamed as the shockwave launched her near Erin. The entire dome shuddered, causing some scales to shake loose. The smaller versions around Jayce and Erin uncoiled and were pulled towards the center of the dome. Cali grabbed Erin and looked over at Jayce, whose entire body had taken on a violet hue.

"Never again!" Jayce's voice boomed from across the dome as the built-up energy exploded from her.

Cali, wide-eyed and shaking, grabbed Erin and darted to the opening to the outside. As they approached it, she felt the heat and rage from the violet power looking to devour everything. She put Erin's limp body ahead of her and shoved her sister through the opening. As she herself exited, the energy licked her foot. She didn't stop her escape or slow down as she felt her toes start to melt. She pushed to the outside and turned, watching slack-jawed as the energy made it to Leon's wedge, disintegrating it in a violet, red cloud as the two layers of leviathan slammed back together. She took a quick breath.

"Damnit!!!" she screamed.

Looking down, she saw two legs and only one foot. Zynka was on her in an instant.

"Cali, oh my god, Cali! Are you—"

Cali cut her off with a wave.

"I'm fine. Well, I will be. But seriously, after another week here, you are going to be dating a robot," Cali said, shaking her leg to make sure it wasn't still melting.

Every part of Zynka tried to resist laughing, but every part was overridden as she let out a small trumpet. Cali looked up and smiled at the elephant. Then she looked over at the dome. All of Selvoth's clones swam away in different directions, with only one coming towards them, carrying both Azreal and Leon.

"Young lady," his resonant voice boomed, "What happened?"

"Where'd your friends go?" Cali cut him off, watching the last white shape disappear. Selvoth looked around.

"Wherever they please. Copies can only be controlled for so long. Now they will go live out their eternity." He shrugged his many fins. "The part I find odd is that none of us know if we are the original." Selvoth looked as though he wanted to explain further, but the dome began to melt in a violet and green mush.

Cali wrinkled her nose. She wasn't sure what it would smell

like to have a bonfire using hair and dog poo as fuel, but this had to be close. She watched as the dome melted away completely, revealing Jayce's floating body. Switching to her mechanical eye, she looked for signs of life. The energy lines running through her still flowed, but very slow. Cali took off towards her. She had to fight to stay swimming straight, given her recent disability, but she made it to the floating body quickly enough. Cali was dumbstruck at the visage before her. Jayce's skin was blistering to the point of flaking; thin violet lines coursed through her veins; her eyes were swollen and closed over. Jayce's breath was shallow and ragged.

"Jayce. Be okay, please. Professor!"

"They have defeated the leviathan." Huntress.
"So it would seem." Two
"Me tink dey be mor capable dan we tink." Anansi.
"Very impressive. This was a worthy show." Wanderer.

# CHAPTER TWENTY-TWO

Jayce shook awake, staring at a mirrored ceiling. Her body ached in areas she didn't know she had.

"Uughhh."

She saw in the mirror that she was not in a great state. Her skin was peeling, like coming away from the most horrific sunburn. Violet lines painfully ran through her face. Beside her, Erin was asleep between her and Leon. Jayce gagged when she saw his nub. It was raw with a light seepage of white fluid. He was out cold with a machine hooked into his vein. Azreal was draped over his chest, muttering a quiet apology.

"Wha..." Jayce started to speak, but her words were fire in her throat.

The small noise stirred the sleeping redhead. Erin's eyes fluttered open and fell on Jayce, the look on her face unreadable. Erin leaned forward and laid a small kiss on her forehead. As much as Jayce wanted to scream from the touch, she quelled the protest.

"Thank you, babe," Erin started. "I don't know what would have happened if you hadn't, well, exploded. You saved us."

The warmth of Erin's eyes made Jayce's heart stutter.

"Cali? Zynka?" Jayce forced the words out and grimaced.

"Cali is off with Zynka in the engineering area. She's building a new foot and fingers. She came into the dome and saved me when your energy released. She got me out fine, but...well, she didn't get out fast enough. She's okay, but I'm not sure if I should keep us here. Less than a week and she has lost an eye, a foot, and two fingers. Of course, she is being cavalier about it, but still." She wiped the ghost of a tear away.

Jayce, fighting a scream against the pain, reached out and laid a hand on Erin's. They locked eyes as Jayce again faded to black.

* * *


"Headmaster, we must call off the courses until we can solve this threat. No initiate should be put through this." Jotun's gravelly voice boomed through the office.

Noctharim bounced back and forth as he pecked at a steak.

"This beef that the humans have is quite wonderful. Dear Jotun, I hear you, and I see your concerns, but do you think the humans cannot handle the pressure? For me, it does seem that the group has indeed managed to push past all the tribulations. Even the ones that you and Professor Selvoth were unable to contain." The headmaster chirped. He saw the shadow fall over the troll's face. "Now, now dear friend, that was not meant as a demerit to the two of you, but a high praise of this motley crew," he added quickly.

Jotun grumbled.

"A leviathan, Professor. True, not a fully formed one, but still a challenge that most experienced walkers avoid. Did they win? Sort of. But they won out of misplaced bravery and mild stupidity. Cali is physically falling apart; Leon is bound to die for some unnecessary sacrifice. And my...I mean, Itsy Bitsy has pushed past what should be her limits at her young age. They will break." Jotun ended with a loud clap for emphasis.

Unperturbed Noctharim continued eating, pausing only to say, "We all break, my dear Jotun. Eventually, we all break."

* * *

"Why in the actual heck can this metal *not* take my skin color!?" Cali yelled at her stupid workbench. "Silver, cool. Gold, pretty. Not my foot! Ugh. Zynka, any ideas?"

Zynka, who was balancing a spanner wrench on her nose, froze. Cali laughed.

"Yeah, we have some builders in my species, but we aren't what you would call handy. My greatest creation was bending and tying a tree to another to make some shade," she said as the wrench fell off with a loud bang.

"Noted, need shade, call Z. Handy, really. Especially in Corpus. God, what I wouldn't have done to have you on the beach. Do you like salt water? Maybe we should take a vacation to Port Aransas before I'm all out of skin to tan." Cali poked her arm as she spoke.

Zynka couldn't hold back the trumpet, making Cali grin. She couldn't help but stare at the giant pink elephant and think safety, even though her current circumstances had all happened after meeting her.

"What do you think your species would think seeing me on your beach?"

Cali chewed her lips in thought.

"Probably freak out. Grab torches and pitchforks and try to burn you at the stake," Cali stated matter-of-factly as she continued messing with the silver and gold foot.

Zynka stared at the small girl, a shiver running through her spine. Cali's eyes flicked over to her, and she smiled ferally. She tapped the pen-sized, unshaped eidolon.

"Don't worry, Pinkie. Automo gave me my very own eidolon. Anyone looks at you weird and boom, pink mist," Cali said with no mirth or levity, just a fact. Zynka felt her chest warm.


Azreal's cheek relished the warmth of Leon's chest, her fingers tracing the lines in his abdomen. the mountain around which her small frame was wrapped, though it still worried her.

"Keep rubbing like that, and I'll be inclined to believe you like me." Leon's voice came out ragged but playfully cocky.

Azreal smiled into his chest and gave him a playful smack on the belly. He groaned in an overexaggeration of pain, making her laugh.

"You may be inclined correctly, young Leon," she said teasingly, then her tone grew somber. "I am sorry for using my ability as I did. It is never something I wish to do, even on an enemy." Her voice was quiet, and her eyes grew distant.

Leon laid his hand on her cheek, angling her head towards his own. He smiled at her.

"Darlin, you did nothing I didn't ask for. It's because of what you did that we made it out. Although I'm not one hundred percent sure the kiss added to the compel," he finished with a cheeky smile.

Azreal's golden eyes sparkled.

"Well, that may have been for me." She flashed her predatory smile.

Leon returned it.

"Next time, you don't need to use your power." He winked.

A surge of liquid went into his veins from the tube embedded in his arm. A tingle found its way to his nub and, when it got there, it felt like it was lying on a cloud.

"Damn...I mean, dang, sorry. That is amazing." He looked at his arm. Still angry red and leaking, but painless. "Tell the doctor I'll take another round." He laughed as he lay back on the bed and pulled the elf tighter against him.

Azreal quickly threw a leg over and sat up on top of him. *I have control.* The thought brought a serene feeling over her as she stared down into Leon's eyes. She hesitated for a brief moment before rocketing her mouth to his. He tensed for only a fraction of a second before pulling her in deeper.


Erin looked over her shoulder at Azreal and Leon's violent make-out session.

"Oh my," she said as she hyperfocused away from them.

Jayce's face had cleared up a bit thanks to whatever the liquid in these machines were. The lines of power were all but faded, and it looked like, after a good bit of peeling, she would be back to her gorgeous little goth self.

*Wait. I look like hell. Does she care?*

Her thoughts hit her as she looked up in the mirror.

*Yup. Looks like hell.*

She kissed Jayce on the hand and stood. She took a step and warped, landed in the living room of their cabin, and, after getting past the nausea, walked to her room. The door slid up as she approached, revealing two pink beds, an overstuffed bean bag chair, a bookshelf, and a vanity with a chair. There was a door on the right where she and Cali had added a full bathroom. She entered the bathroom and smiled at the ridiculously oversized shower with six multidirectional heads. She let her uniform melt off and stepped in.

After a few glorious minutes, Erin stepped out of the bathroom, her uniform already melting around her to wipe away the leftover water. She strode to the vanity and sat down. She looked at the pile of makeup on the desk.

"Thank you, Cali and your freaky mind," she said as she sifted through trying to find the right colors.

*What would Jayce like the most?*

Her eyes landed on violet makeup, and she went to work.


Jayce's face didn't hurt near as bad when her eyes opened again.

"E-Erin?" Her throat was still sore, but the words weren't fire anymore.

A familiar weight landed on her chest, and she saw Thought take a seat.

"Good to see you awake, my friend. I should not have doubted your prowess, though if I am honest, I thought our time together was over." The raven's disembodied voice carried a tone of relief.

*Why would he care?*

"It was your master that did this," she internalized.

Thought shook his head.

"No, Jayce. Not my master anymore. I asked to stay with you as the four have become so very boring. At least when they had their schools, we could watch the students, but since the Earth plane was shut off, all there was to watch was the mundane lives of your race."

The words played in Jayce's mind as she digested.

"Their schools? What do you mean?"

"The four each had their own schools. Sure, they all studied here, but they wanted their own 'command'. The chance at putting out walkers with different mindsets."

Jayce moved back against her pillow.

"Why did you want to stay with me? And how does that work?" she asked, not sure how she wouldn't go crazy with a raven only she could see constantly talking to her.

If a raven could smile, Jayce would have sworn Thought did.

"Don't worry, I have been locked in one plane too long. I do not intend to stay and drive you psychotic. I would like to anchor myself to you. That would mean I tether a small amount of our energy together so we may always find and or communicate if we need to. You would be my home base while I go out and spread my wings, as it were," the raven finished with a questioning, almost pleading look.

The sight both warmed and weirded Jayce out. The raven hadn't been aggressive or misleading, but being tied to it, she didn't know.

"Was that you in my dream? At the leviathan?"

Thought nodded vigorously.

"Yes, of course. The trial was too much for my ma—the Wanderer to throw at you and Erin this early. I merely looked to help." He nipped at her stomach as he spoke. Jayce took a breath to stave off a giggle.

"But why tie yourself to me? Why not just be free?"

A wet sound from the bed next to her pulled her attention.

She looked over and saw Leon and Azreal pull their heads away from each other. Leon looked at Jayce sheepishly.

"Sorry, J. Didn't mean to wake you." He gave her a stupid grin.

Jayce laughed and felt the weight from her chest leave with a few final words.

"Untethered, I will die within a time. If you accept my request, simply agree at any time. Goodbye for now." Thought's words faded, and Jayce knew if she purposefully exerted energy, she could join them together.

"Young Jayce, is all well?" Azreal's voice was heavy with the frustration of unfulfilled desire, though she did her best to show concern.

Jayce nodded, not just to agree, but to feel her body move.

"I think I will be okay. Very sore," she added, as a tinge of pain went through her muscles.

Azreal nodded.

"With the amount of energy you used to annihilate the hatchling leviathan, it would be odd if you were not." She finished by gracefully sliding off of Leon, who looked momentarily as if he was going to hold her there, and walked to Jayce. She put her hand on Jayce's forehead. The coolness of Azreal's hand made Jayce shiver.

"You're freezing," Jayce said, not hating the feeling.

"When you are from a species that thrives with no sun, your body adapts." Her words and touch were soothing, driving most of the pain away. They stayed like that for a moment before a voice sounded out.

"My dear initiates, how are we? Hurt? Yes. But alive," Noctharim chirped as he entered the door, followed by Zynka and Cali.

The latter of which was sporting a silver and gold foot, and the ring and pinky finger on her left hand were also in the same shade. Jayce almost looked away, but Cali caught her eye, pointed at her silver pinky, mouthed "flamethrower," and giggled. Jayce couldn't help but laugh and be thankful Cali didn't hate her.

"Sore as all hell, Professor. How are these initiate classes? And what is the survival rate?" Leon asked.

The professor landed on his bed and looked up at him.

"Dear boy, these classes have been interfered with. And normally sixty-two percent." Noctharim hopped as he spoke.

"Interfered wi—sixty-two?!" Jayce stammered. "What are our chances? By whom exactly?"

"Yes, yes, sixty-two. I cannot gauge your chances as I do not know how far they will go. They being what Jotun and I have dubbed The Watchers. Our memories had been adjusted when we thought we had killed Four, otherwise known as the Wanderer. But as we have been diving into the data of your planet, it has brought some true memories back." He gnawed his wing as he let the group digest.

Jayce was on the edge of her seat. The professor was about to continue when Jayce's eyes went wide. Turning around, she saw Erin walk in. Her hair was done up in intricate Norse braids, and she had violet shades smeared under and around her eyes. Jayce noted it was the same way she had done her own makeup the day of their first meeting. She wanted to throw herself out of bed and onto Erin. Instead, she stared open-mouthed as Erin crossed to her, unaware of the effect she had. Jayce's heart only chose to beat when one of Erin's feet hit the floor. The sheer beauty Erin commanded should be illegal, Jayce thought. She closed on Jayce and leaned for a kiss when the mood died.

"Watch out! Got a hottie over here. Whoot, whoot!" Cali laughed. Erin's head dropped to Jayce's shoulder.

"Next time I'll try to be sexy away from the peanut gallery," she whispered to Jayce, who gave her a kiss on the forehead and scooted over so Erin could sit. They interlocked hands and turned their attention back to a confused Noctharim.

The professor looked at the closeness of Cali and Zynka, Azreal and Leon, and Jayce and Erin.

"Is there a dating game happening in my Nexus that I am unaware of?" He shook his own question off. "These Watchers are comprised of four companions. There is the Wanderer, a sculptor. Anansi, a weaver. A huntress who is a seer, and a fourth entity of which we are unsure. Why they are testing you is a very good question, one I cannot answer. But my top assumption is that you all are the first walkers from Earth since before they disconnected the plane." He took flight and hovered above the group. Erin's hand tightened on Jayce's.

"Professor. I don't know if I can keep Cali here. This is all getting too real," Erin said.

Jayce tightened her hand around the other girl's in the hope it would anchor her here. Cali just looked at her sister angrily.

"You think you could get me to leave, Erin?" Cali's words were as much a challenge as the fire behind her eyes. The tone made Erin twitch.

"Cali, look at you. This is the 'training' portion." She looked Cali up and down. "We should think—" Erin started, but was cut off.

"You should think about how my girlfriend is a giant elephant and would crush you if you tried to take me!" Cali yelled.

Zynka lost color in her face as the whole group looked at her. A small smile still threatened her lips at the mention of being a girlfriend. She looked around, hoping something would break the tension, but nothing did.

"Umm. Grrr. Mean elephant smash?" Zynka tried to be funny but only managed slightly above absolute cringe. She covered her eyes with her ears.

The room was silent for a few seconds before Leon let out a pitiful laugh. "Mean elephant smash?" he mimicked her awkwardness and busted out laughing.

The laugh was fake and only meant to break the tension, but that didn't stop Jayce's lizard brain from falling into laughter right after. Erin just shook her head and lay back on Jayce's stomach.

"Whatever," she said.

Cali smiled wide.

"See, look. Everyone is happy. When is the next class, Professor? Stealth and engineering are left, right, Birdo?"

Noctharim nodded and shook his head mid-hover.

"In the morning, you will have a dual class and your initiate solo trip, meaning Automo will not be accompanying your group. I decided I want to see how you all handle the multiverse solo. However, the professor will meet you at your domicile in the morning for a briefing."

You could have heard a feather drop.

*No professor? Why? For what...*

"Rat world, Jotun got knocked out. Marionette world, Antoinette was a psychopath. Underwater world, Selvoth was cool but mostly useless," Leon reasoned. "Not much of a change."

The group nodded collectively in agreement, some tension leaving the air.


Jayce tossed and turned in her comfortable strip bed. She had gotten some sleep, but only enough to make her hungry for more. She had been feeling the disconnected bond with Thought.

*What if it's a trick? What if he can somehow take me over?*

Thoughts like these had been playing in her head for over an hour. She sat up and pulled out her holo. Scrolling through the music page, she picked out some punk and let it flood her room. On the one hand, Thought had kind of saved her. On the other hand, he was the pet of the Wanderer. Though...was the Wanderer a bad guy? Noctharim had said there is no evil. It did seem most of the interference was due to boredom. Did that make it okay? She ran her hands through her hair and went to her mirror. Putting on light makeup, in the style of Erin at her first meeting, she took a step and warped downstairs.

She landed on the neon X Cali had put on the floor and looked at the activity in the dining area. Azreal and Leon were demolishing huge stacks of pancakes. Zynka and Cali were sharing popcorn-flavored ice cream. Erin wasn't there yet, so she went to her door and knocked lightly.

"Come in," Erin said as the door opened.

Jayce stepped in and was again in awe of how good the other woman looked. Erin had her uniform in tight gym shorts and a sports bra. Her toned muscles glistened in a light sweat. Erin had an abdomen so defined that Jayce was going to drool if she didn't look away. Erin winked at her.

"Oh no, you saw me working out and so exposed. I'm sooo embarrassed," Erin said as she walked over and draped her arms over the other girl's shoulders. Without a beat, Jayce put her arms around Erin's waist.

"It's almost like you wanted me to see you like this," Jayce returned the sarcasm. They shared a short kiss.

"Erin, I...You..." She wanted to tell her how beautiful she was, but couldn't find words that explained the depths of it. She hoped Erin would speak to break the awkwardness; she didn't. Erin only looked at her with a playfully hungry grin.

"Thanks for the help, babe," Jayce said in a mock exasperation. "I just wanted you to know that I think...No, I know you are, without a doubt, the most beautiful person I have ever seen. And I hope you know I'm very glad to be here in this absolute madhouse with you." Jayce ended with an enthusiastic kiss, allowing her hands to feel the slick muscles of Erin's back.

"Mmmm." Erin gave a small moan. "I wouldn't want to be anywhere else. But I do have a favor."

Jayce cocked an eyebrow. Erin looked her over, studying her tunic and long skirt combo.

"I know this may be a lot to ask, and feel free to tell me to back off, but have you thought of modernizing your wardrobe?"

Jayce felt relieved; she wasn't sure what the favor could have been, but this wasn't bad. Thinking for a moment, she gave her uniform a command. The silky obsidian fabric shifted and moved, settling on a sundress. She looked away from Erin as her arms and legs below the knee were revealed. The bruises from home were the nasty yellow of almost gone, except the one on her shoulder. Even worse was that her skin was still peeling slightly from the burn. After a long moment of looking away, Jayce looked back at Erin, whose eyes were watering. Not pity, but a weird form of pride. Erin's eyes landed on her freshest bruise.

*Thanks, Richard.*

No judgment, sadness, or disgust crossed her face as she leaned down and gave the bruise a slow kiss.

"Thank you for letting me see you like this," Erin said, looking her over. "You are absolutely beautiful, but are you comfortable in that? Because, no offense, you look like you want to die." She snorted.

Jayce basked in being called beautiful before replying.

"Not even slightly. How do you live in one of these?" Jayce asked as she swayed back and forth. The material shifted into leggings and a three-quarter tee. She welcomed the coverage.

"You get used to it. Kind of. Ready for breakfast?" Erin asked and Jayce nodded in reply.



The moment the table was cleared from breakfast, Automo warped onto the X. He walked over and sat down.

"Greetings, humans, elf, elephant, and Cali."

Cali stuck her tongue out at the professor.

"I would not have adequate taste or nutrition for your body as Selvoth would." Cali rolled her eyes. "I have your contract here. It will be your last before the final exam. The contract is simple. Three of you, Cali, Leon, and Erin, will work with a crew to build a racer. Zynka, Jayce, and Azreal will infiltrate a rival crew's garage and sabotage their racer. Easy? Easy. Do not fail. Details in holo," he said as he tossed a wrench on the table. "Your compass."

And with that, the teacher was gone. The group stared at the wrench for a long stretch. Cali blinked.

"I thought he would never shut up," she joked.

"Well, that was something," Leon said, picking up the wrench. "Ready?"

"The dust plane." Huntress.
"So it would seem." Two.
"Shall we do more?" Anansi.
"Rest for the finale. Observe for now." Wanderer.

# CHAPTER TWENTY-THREE

Jayce breathed in a lung full of dirt as her feet hit the ground, causing a violent coughing fit. She gagged a few times and hocked up a decent ball of phlegm.

"Gross," she said, kicking the yellow dirt over it.

Standing, she saw massive green mountains as far as the swirling dust would allow her to see. Off in one direction was a small town. It had brick buildings, some homes, and some shops with patrons roaming in and out. The citizens were bipedal lizards ranging from her height to past Zynka's. They had different skin tones, some white, some purple, some black, and some grey. They all wore what could only be described as wastelander chic. Leather with welded metal and rebar stuck on randomly. Leon stepped up next to Erin.

"Oh my god. Mel Gibson," was all he said.

Erin laughed and shouldered him playfully.

"You really want to do the uniform, don't you?"

Without missing a beat, Leon pressed the left breast of his tank top. The uniform swirled and twisted before coming to rest. Erin slammed her hand over Cali's eyes as she tried not to hyperventilate. Jayce's eyes grew wide as she covered her mouth. Azreal purred. Standing before them was a very red Leon now clad in a jockstrap that left nothing to the imagination, one black pauldron and a half mask. Azreal stepped between him and the group.

"All mine. No looking. Maybe the kilt here?" she said, not quite ogling.

The uniform was back to normal quickly, though Leon's new skin tone remained. Cali fought out of Erin's grip.

"Hehe, we almost saw your—" she started, but Erin clamped a hand around her sister's mouth.

"We all know." Erin laughed.

Leon kicked at the dirt.

"I just wanted a cool post-apocalyptic outfit. But no, whatever." He sounded truly dismayed.

"You can form it yours—" Jayce started.

"Whatever. I'm over it." Leon cut her off.

"Too bad. I wasn't," Azreal purred.

The girls smiled. Azreal was clearly still interested in the outfit as she made sure air couldn't come between them.

"Worked for me," Zynka said. Her torso was covered in a rebar-looking ribcage and two large, rusted pauldrons.

Leon shook his head in disbelief as he pulled out his holo. He scrolled through until he found the breakdown. The lizards had noticed the students by now but chose to keep their distance.

"Okay, me, Cali, and Erin are supposed to go north to find the Gnashers'—lame—garage. Jayce, Zynka, and Azreal are to integrate into the local town and find the Crushers'—also lame—garage and find out what they have and see if you can sabotage it somehow before the race in.... two days. Neat, timed quest," he ended, putting away the holo.

"How am I supposed to sabotage an engine? I have never even driven," Jayce asked quietly.

Cali perked up. "Big hammer! If it still works, bigger hammer. Simple."

"I guess that could work. Should we get to it?" she asked, looking sadly to Erin.

She knew it was probably clingy and a touch unhealthy to be this attached this soon, but she couldn't help it. She wanted to be in her aura as much as possible. Erin gave her an agreeing smile as she walked over and hugged Jayce. She gave her a kiss on top of the head.

"Don't worry, babe, we got this. It'll be over before you know it."

Jayce went rigid in her arms.

"*It'll be over before you know it*." Belinda's voice sounded in her head as Hector's footsteps drew near.

Erin noticed the freeze and shook Jayce and held her tighter. "You are okay. We are free here. This is real," Erin said.

Jayce relaxed and fell into the embrace.

"Thank you," she said as she pulled back and gave her a quick kiss.

Even these small kisses melted something inside her that she didn't know was frozen. She stepped back and looked around; the other couples were also saying temporary goodbyes.

Azreal and Leon shared a nearly not-safe-for-work kiss. The elf pulled away slightly and purred.

"Do not forget who you belong to." She licked the tip of his nose. Leon smiled and nipped hers in return.

"Yes, ma'am. I will do my utmost best to remember not to fall for a lizard person." He laughed.

Azreal gave him a soft slug on the shoulder and lay her head against his stomach.

Cali and Zynka both looked appalled at the sights. Cali stuck her tongue out and mimed gagging herself while Zynka sucked on her trunk. They looked at each other, gave a quick fist bump, and separated.

"Let's go, you disgusting food hole ruiners!" Cali shouted to break up the gushfest as she walked north.

"See you soon, babe," Erin said with a final kiss before following the shrinking Cali.

"Soon," Jayce whispered after her.

Azreal looked physically pained to pull away from Leon.

"Mine," she said, walking to Jayce.

"Yes, ma'am," Leon replied, turning his back.

Zynka joined Azreal and Jayce as they watched the others fade into dust. Jayce's heart already ached for Erin.

*Jesus. Calm down.*

They watched the other three until they faded into oblivion.

"Let us complete this nonsense and be done with it," Azreal said, walking to the town. Zynka and Jayce fell into step with her.

"Okay, so, our job is to infiltrate the Crushers, lame, and find a way to make them lose the race. I will do the talking, the silent giant will do the sneaking, and the mousy human will follow. Agreed?" Azreal stated more than she asked.

Jayce, finding no reason to argue, nodded. Zynka thought for a moment.

"Let me know when you need me." And with those words, Zynka disappeared into the dust. Both the other girls searched as if they could find her in the thick haze. Jayce shook her head.

"It makes no sense, honestly," she told the elf.

"Thus are the planes,"

They were approached by a tall black lizard in rebar armor as they neared the town.

"It's not often we get visitors from the planes. May I be of service to the young maidens?" The lizard's "s" came out drawn, how Jayce imagined a snake would talk. Azreal took point.

"Thank you, kind sir. We are from the Academy, here to watch the Crushers race in a few days. Where might we find them?" There was a sultry air to her voice as she spoke, and Jayce sensed the tiniest trickle of power loose from the elf.

The lizard began to salivate. "But of course, why else would such a lovely pair grace the unworthy town of Galardo. Please, follow me," the lizard almost gushed.

Jayce looked at the elf, who winked.

"The male brain is so malleable," she whispered to Jayce as they followed the black lizard past shops and houses, all a decently maintained brick.

It wasn't a rich town, but it wasn't poor either. They weaved in between lizards of assorted colors and sizes, all of whom actively ignored them, until they reached a building with massive garage doors. The lizard turned to them.

"Here we are, madams. Is there anything else Salico can help you with?" the supposed Salico said.

Azreal ran a hand down his arm.

"Thank you, Salico, that will be more than enough. I am deeply grateful." The words purred out of the elf.

Salico shuddered, nodded, and scurried off. Jayce just stared wide-eyed as the lizard vanished in the distance.

"Does he know what happened?"

Azreal bobbed her hands in the air.

"Yes, but everything that happened was very sensual to him. He believed, and will for a while, that I wanted to give myself to him. Eventually, he will come to see the truth, but he will be too ashamed to speak of it." Azreal winked at Jayce. Jayce thought for a minute.

"And Leon?" she asked, trying to keep any judgment from her voice.

Azreal laughed and put a hand on Jayce's shoulder.

"It does not work on him." She sounded both pleased and not.

"But the leviathan...Cali told me..." Jayce's words trailed off as she thought about who Leon was. "He didn't need to be compelled."

"No, he did not." Azreal's words were heavy with admiration. "I do not know if he thought he needed help with the pain, or if he just wanted me to feel useful. I did try, only to have my ability fall off of him like rain from an eagle." A touch of desire tinged her last words. "That is why I claim him."

The corner of Jayce's mouth tugged up.

"Is it because you can just be yourself? Not worry about whether he likes you for you?"

*Like Erin.*

Azreal smiled her predatory smile and nodded.

"Now then. Girl talk has been done, let us go meet these

Crushers, lame." Both girls chuckled as they approached the bay doors.

One was open, showing off a massive eight-wheeled vehicle. It was about the size of a dump truck Jayce had seen in a mine near San Antonio. Its cab was the size of a small house with a ladder extending all the way down, hanging just four feet off the ground. It was painted in the most awful pink Jayce had ever seen, with a jackalope with a minigun spray-painted down the side. Jayce's eyes grew wide at the sheer scope of the large vehicle. As they approached within fifty yards, a slim, green lizard in welded plate armor scurried over to them. It stopped within spitting distance and eyed the duo.

"Not lizard. Not from here. Walkers. Why here?" the lizard's feminine voice asked, the S's still slithering out.

Jayce saw Azreal shift uncomfortably.

"Damn," the elf whispered.

The lizard continued eyeing them, mental processes running at full capacity.

"Walkers means contract. We have no contract. Contract from other clan. Sabotage."

The words had barely left its mouth when Jayce felt a shift in the air behind her. Before she could react, a metal collar snapped into place around her neck. Her hands flew to the device as her internal energy flow crawled to a stop. The loss of her newfound power caused her breath to catch in her throat. She dug at the collar, wishing in vain that it would spring free. Desperately, she looked to Azreal, who flailed ferally. It hit Jayce what this meant for the elf, who had been freed so recently. The elf went still on her knees, lips moving with no words accompanying the action. Turning, Jayce saw the assaulters, two large grey lizards in not more than loincloths. They looked pleased with the outcome, and Jayce's skin went cold.

"Not good stealth. Prisoners now. Ransom. Good return," the feminine lizard spoke as she approached Azreal.

Watching her, Jayce noticed the slightest upturn in Azreal's lips as the lizard came within an arm's reach. Before Jayce could comprehend the movement, the elf launched herself, teeth first, at the soft under throat of the lizard. Like a hot knife through butter, her long canines penetrated the soft flesh like a heated knife through butter. The elf ripped away a massive chunk of its throat, leaving a gaping wound that let what would've been a scream escape. Jayce flinched as she watched Azreal swallow before being cracked over the head by one of the grey lizards with a piece of rebar. The elf unceremoniously crumpled to the ground with a wet thud as her blue blood flowed free. That was the last thing Jayce saw before she heard another, much closer, thud, and her vision went black.

"Shit. Did she swallow?" Zynka muttered as she watched her classmates get captured.

Azreal had definitely swallowed the chunk of flesh she took.

"How did we not even factor this as a possibility?" she asked herself.

Zynka had been shadowing the group since the split and had found herself a shady hide on top of one of the automotive stores. Zynka ran scenarios in her head, trying to figure out the best plan of action, but they all ended with the group dead or her captured as well. The two unconscious girls were dragged into the garage, both limp and unresisting.

"Come on, Zynka, think, girl, think!" she quietly chided herself.

She face-palmed with her trunk and pulled out her holo, dialed Cali, and waited.

"Hey, girlfriend!" Cali's cheery voice called out. There was a low rumbling in the background.

"Hey, Cali. Straight to it; Jayce and Azreal just got captured by the Crushers," Zynka replied stoically.

Cali was quiet for a moment; the rumbling from her side was growing louder, and she heard what sounded like popcorn popping rhythmically.

"Bastards!" Cali yelled. "Sorry, how do you feel about a

girlfriend with only six real fingers? I'm sure you don't mind..."
There was a loud explosion that made Zynka swear at her
inability to see or help. "Take that, jerks. So, umm, we are
dealing with some pretty not chill stuff. Leon says watch and
intervene only if it seems life-threatening. Other than that, stay
safe, girlie. Gotta go."

The connection was cut with Zynka staring at the now blank
holo.

"What the hell is going on?"

"Their tactical minds failed them." Huntress.
"So it would seem." Two.
"Tro dem a lifeline?" Anansi.
"Observe for now." Wanderer.

# CHAPTER TWENTY-FOUR

Cali looked over her shoulder as her big, pink elephant faded into nothing. She let out a measured breath and faced forward, having to take quick strides to keep up with Leon and her sister.

"Think they'll be alright?" Erin asked.

Leon nodded as he tried to see through the stifling dust that picked up after they passed a small hill.

"Should be okay. They are a solid group, and if not, they can call us."

Cali coughed on the dust before her uniform formed a dust mask for her. It even filtered the air, which Cali thought was a nice touch.

"Erin, what does it mean to date someone?" Cali tried to sound mature with such a juvenile question.

Erin smiled and thought of the right answer. Leon chuckled.

"Kiddo, it can mean a lot of things. Someone to pass the time with, someone to plan a future with, or someone to have fun with. It really comes down to where *you* see it going. Are they someone you can see forever with?" he ended, with a questioning look down at the girl.

Cali thought for a few seconds, her face screwing up with effort.

"I'm thirteen. Forever means something different to me than it would to Noctharim. So, do I look at it through my eyes or his? Hmm. Because now, for us, forever literally means forever." Cali looked at her silver fingers and foot. "Well, hopefully it does."

Erin stiffened but bit back a response.

*Not right now.*

"Yeah, the 'forever' thing does add a bit more seriousness to forever. Heck, actually, does it make it more or less serious? I mean, shoot, we are all under thirty, and in a thousand years what is thirty?" Leon drawled.

His face took on a tight look except for the line between his eyebrows. He scratched a knot out of his beard.

"Hell, it's wild to think about. I could be around Jayce for billions of years." Erin's voice had a dreamlike quality, and a sparkle made its way to her eye.

Leon and Cali shared a knowing look and grinned.

"Jayce and Erin, sittin' in a tree k-i-s-s—" Cali started.

"Shut up, brat. Can't even let a girl daydream," Erin snapped, but there was no heat in her tone.

The three shared a laugh and continued on.

They walked for thirty minutes before Leon brought up the map on his holo.

"Damn, I didn't realize that it was gonna take so long. We landed nearly twenty miles from our objective. The girls got lucky."

Five minutes later, Leon and Erin stopped to the sound of metal hitting flesh and Cali cursing. They turned and saw her wiping a trickle of blood from her forehead. She smiled at them sheepishly.

"Don't face-palm with metal fingers," She chuckled. "I want us all to agree that for reality explorers, we are dumb."

Leon and Erin shared a look, a shrug, and a nod.

"Yeah, I can admit I'm a few rounds short of a full magazine. Why this time, though, kiddo?"

In response, Cali lifted her hand, showing the ring on her finger. Erin sighed deeply as her shoulders fell.

"For fu—dam—dang," Leon said, making Cali grin.

"You know, at this point I think you can just say f—" Cali started.

"Cali!" Erin exclaimed.

Her sister kicked a small rock.

"I can have body parts melt off, but can't swear. Cool rules, Mother." She stuck out her tongue.

Erin just shook her head and threw her ring on the ground, which instantly reshaped into a board. The other two followed suit.

"Yup, dumb," Leon said, mounting his board.

The others began to mount as well when a rumbling sound caught their attention. Leon's eyes scanned for the source, but the mountains displaced the sound. The ground around them started to shake, small stones being kicked around.

"There." Erin pointed between two large rocky hills.

None of them could make out the shape due to the massive dust cloud being kicked up by whatever it was.

"So...Bye," Cali said, aiming her board away and rocketing off.

Erin was quick to follow, but Leon stayed for a fraction longer to get a glimpse. His eyes went wide, and he shot after the girls, catching up quickly.

"Motorcycles. Lots of 'em. They do not seem friendly. I don't think we can outrun them." His breathing was ragged as his mind spiraled through the possibilities.

"How long?" Erin asked.

As if on cue, the air split close to her ear with a near-deafening whiz. She dropped low on her board and began swerving. Leon fell to the back of the formation and retracted his prosthetic. The snapping and tearing from his nub were barely audible over the cacophony of rapid-fire rifles. He switched his footing so his arm, now a large shield, was behind him. His teeth gritted against the constant pulse of pain from holding the shape. Cali zigzagged, her mechanical eye surveying the oncoming horde. At least twenty beefed-up dirt bikes were hot on them. The green view of her eye made it look like a giant blob of lizards and metal.

"Erin..." Leon started and stopped. His mind flashed back to the last time he was in a firefight; the smell of powder, the screams, the sticky blood on his hands and face. He took a deep breath to bring himself back. "Give me your eidolon!" he shouted as his arm rocked from a round struck on the shield. He bellowed in pain.

Erin, without hesitation, fell back and handed off the eidolon like a baton. As Leon's hand grasped the pen-sized object, it began to form. More rounds impacted his arm, causing him to lose focus. The riders were closing in and becoming more accurate. Erin flew her board right next to Leon and laid a hand on his back, her other extending towards the group. She dug deep for his pain. Finding it, she began the excruciating process of channeling it through her body and out her hand. The pain was like a treble hook being pulled backwards through her veins. Pink energy formed in her hand as she screamed. The ball turned to a beam as, with much effort, she picked a target. The red lizard she chose fell from his bike as the beam made contact, the pain driving any thoughts of its own self-preservation away. It hit the ground and was immediately run over by the nearest bike, causing it to flip as well.

Leon, with his pain lessened by Erin and with his mind clearer, watched as the eidolon formed into a revolver. As soon as the black barrel solidified, he began servicing targets. Blue lizard, head gone. Green lizard, new hole in its neck. Gray lizard, exploded at center mass. His pistol jumped from target to target, sounding like slow-popping popcorn. The bikes from the fallen lizards became obstacles for the trailing riders. Erin's beam swept across the oncoming horde, not as effective as the pistol but still disrupting the flow. Blood flowed from near countless holes on Leon's shield arm, now raw, though the pain was taken from him near instantly. Erin sweat profusely from the agony of her siphon. The riders kept chasing through the valleys.

Cali's mind raced. Her mechanical eye scanned the hills and riders. Her holo vibrated. Cali's eyepatch slid over her mechanical eye as she summoned the holo.

"Hey, girlfriend!" she answered cheerily, seeing it was Zynka calling. A bullet whizzed past her head, taking a chunk of hair with it, a quiet curse escaping her lips.

"Hey, Cali. Straight to it, Jayce and Azreal just got captured by the Crushers," Zynka said stoically. Cali lowered the holo.

"Leon! Jayce and Azreal got got by the Crushers. Ideas?" Cali yelled over the hum of machinery and cacophony of gunfire.

Leon was still shooting when he responded.

"Observe, if it seems like they are just being held, wait. If it gets dicey, intervene." His tone was strained, the exhaustion evident. And the horde just kept coming.

Erin was beginning to wobble on her board.

"Why don't we just fly up?" Erin asked, her soft words were barely audible.

Leon shook his head.

"Right now, only the front rank can shoot effectively. We go up, the whole group could frag us."

Cali was about to return to the call when she felt a sharp burning pain in her right hand. The surprise caused her board to waver. She righted herself and brought up her hand, or what was left of it. Cali had taken a round in between the knuckles of her pointer and middle finger. The middle finger was gone, a bloody crater in its place; her pointer was flopping uselessly on an eight-inch piece of flesh. Tears filled her eyes.

*Even more of a freak. Don't let them see you cry.*

She willed the tears to subside, gripping the pointer finger and pulling it free with a squelch that made her stomach twist.

"Bastards!" she yelled as she returned to the call.

With her free hand, she pulled out her eidolon. As it formed, she spoke.

"Sorry, how do you feel about a girlfriend with only six real fingers? I'm sure you don't mind..." Lowering the holo, she made a decision. "Leon, Erin. Get ready. I'm going to try and block the path," Cali said and waited for confirmation. The other two nodded, and she took aim at one of the rocky hills ahead of them.

"Fire in the hole!" She yelled, loosening a rocket from her eidolon.

The projectile slammed into the hill, kicking rock and dust far and wide. The slope began to collapse into a landslide.

"Take that, jerks! So, umm, we are dealing with some pretty not chill stuff. Leon says watch and only intervene if their lives seem threatened. Other than that, stay safe, girlie. Gotta go," Cali said, cutting the connection and weaving through the falling rocks.

Leon had dismissed his shield and rocketed next to her, holding an unconscious Erin. Cali didn't know where her sister's board was, and Leon just shook his head at her look. Whipping past the last of the falling debris, they heard the rock crushing the metal and flesh of the riders. Not daring to look back, they zigzagged to avoid stray rounds that were no longer coming. Cali slowed to a stop under an overhang of rocks. Leon joined her, hopped off his board, and laid Erin softly on the rocky dirt.

"Did she get hit?" Cali asked.

Leon, kneeling next to her, shook his head.

"Exhaustion. She took so much pain. I can't even count the number of shots I took." He brushed Erin's hair from her face.

Blood pooled over the top of his prosthetic. In turn, he noticed her mangled hand.

"You sure make a boy feel less special about being an amputee," he chuckled darkly and winked.

Cali, with much overexaggeration, clutched her hand to her chest and twirled her metallic foot.

"Sue a girl for wanting to be like her hero." She laughed and gave Leon her best puppy dog eyes.

"I'm just plum flattered, missy." Leon laughed. They both took a seat near Erin's limp form. "You wonder why we stay? At

Aetherion, I mean?" he asked, some semblance of seriousness returning.

Cali chewed her lip and looked at the dust-covered sky.

"You can't close Pandora's Box, I guess. Could you go back to regular life after this? Plus, I don't think Zynka would blend in well in Corpus."

Leon lay back and thought.

"Yeah. I think I could. After the Army, I thought I couldn't go back to real life, but I did."

Cali looked at him.

"Did you?"

After a moment, Leon shook his head.

"You know, for a kid, I think you have too much going on in your head." He chuckled.

"And you've only known her for a week," Erin's ragged and quiet voice spoke. "She can really make you feel dumb if you aren't careful."

Leon and Cali leaned in.

"It still hurt?" Leon asked, looking at her arms. There was no visible damage, but Leon knew she didn't dispel all the pain she took.

Erin started to shake her head, but winced and nodded. "Yeah, who'd have thought getting shot hurt that much?"

Cali and Leon both raised their blood-soaked limbs. Erin, against the agony, shot up and grabbed her sister's wrist, inspecting her ruined hand. Cali tried to pull back but relented when she realized her arm was in a vise. Erin's eyes watered.

"Calm down, Mother. I'm fine," Cali said, showing off the prosthetics on her other hand. "This just means I'm one step closer to being cooler than Professor Automo." She smiled, trying to calm her big sister.

Despite herself, Erin laughed.

"You're so dumb, Cali." Erin continued the strained laugh.

Seeing Cali's remaining fingers go pale, Leon rested his hand on Erin's until she relented.

"Thanks, bro. Freaking tourniquet hands over here," Cali

said, shaking her hand, inadvertently spraying blood over the group. She laughed a full-bellied laugh at Erin's hurry to use her uniform to clean her face. "My bad."

Erin finished wiping off her face with her uniform.

"Back to business," Leon said. "It seems like we are about ten miles from our target location. I think maybe you and Cali should head there, and I'll head back to help the others. I'd like to take your eidolon, if that's cool?" Leon spoke to both but looked at Erin, who nodded. "Also, I will get my own back at school. Seems not having one is an issue."

"Please do. Don't let Jayce get hurt anymore." There was pleading in Erin's voice. Leon nodded solemnly.

"I promised her she'd be okay and I intend to keep that promise." He spoke softly, but his voice still held the gravity of what he told Jayce. "Are y'all going to be okay? If so, I'm gonna head out."

The girls nodded, and he moved to step on his board but stopped at a light metallic tap on his shoulder. He turned and looked down at Cali, whose eyes were round. It looked like she wanted to speak, but instead she threw her arms around his midsection. Leon wrapped both arms lightly around her head, pulling her into his stomach.

"Be safe, Da—I mean, Leon." Her face buried in his gut muffled the words, but to Leon they were the most clearly spoken he had ever heard. His eyes watered as he squeezed her tighter.

"I will, kiddo," he said, leaning down and kissing the top of her head. "Love you, kiddo," he said, straightening up.

Cali released him and looked up, her eyes screaming in reciprocation. Leon turned and mounted his board, shooting off before the first tear fell.

After a few minutes staring in the direction Leon left in, Cali turned to Erin.

"Think you can ride?"

Erin stretched her arms and flinched.

"As long as I don't have to do anything, I should be good." After a pause, she asked, "Wanna talk about it?"

Cali shook her head and got on the board. She held out her less-injured hand and pulled Erin up. Once they got somewhat comfortable, Cali lifted them off. Briskly, they began the last stretch of the journey, weaving between hills and over dried riverbeds.

Thankfully, the rest of the flight was uneventful. Twenty minutes later, they crested a hill and saw a small, not even a village, community. There were several small stone huts, a larger building that reminded Cali of a poor man's H-E-B, and a massive garage with its roller doors down. In the middle was a flagpole with a light blue flag depicting strange looking demon eating a lizard. Coming to a stop, they surveyed the locals. All of them were different shades of blue, ranging in height from three to ten feet. It was a snapshot of suburbia. The residents swept their dusty lawns to no avail, watered dead plants, and made small talk as they passed each other.

"It's weird, isn't it? We are realities away from home, but it's nearly identical to home. Minus the dirt lawns and lizard people," Erin said.

Cali agreed and descended the hill. As they got close to the bottom, one of the larger sky-blue lizards in a suit of armor made of rebar approached.

"Hail, travelers. I assume you come from Aetherion?" the lizard hissed.

"Yes, I am Erin, and this is my sister Cali. We were given this contract to help the Gnashers. Is that you?" Erin inquired. The lizard's tongue flicked and tasted the air.

"Gnashers are us, yes. I am Fred."

Cali and Erin gave each other a quick, quizzical look.

"Fred?" Cali mouthed. Erin shrugged.

*Honestly, not the weirdest part of today.*

"We are here to help with a vehicle for a race?" Erin questioned.

The lizard nodded fervently.

"Yes. Our clan has a race against the Crushers. Last race we lost and were left with this." Fred outstretched his arm and swept it over the village. "The winner gets the town until the next race. So we are stuck here."

"What kind of race is it? Track? Distance?" Cali asked, getting kind of excited thinking about the racing games she used to play.

"Demolition. Last man standing. The Crushers have an advantage in this race as they have the town's garage and resources. They have a massive truck with all the bells and whistles as well." Fred spat in the dirt. Cali almost vibrated with excitement behind Erin.

"Can we go see your garage?" Cali asked enthusiastically.

Fred nodded and turned, leading them into the small village. Lizards smiled and waved at the girls as they passed on their board. Some small, obviously children, lizards ran behind the board before getting distracted. They stopped in front of the large garage. Fred went up and flung the rolling door up until it stopped with a metallic clang. Light flooded into the garage, showing three sedan-sized dirt buggies. The excitement that had swelled in Cali's chest crashed.

*A bulldozer? Sweet. Massive truck with machine guns? Even better. Freaking dune buggies? Lame.*

"This is what we have left over. It is not much, hence us contacting Noctharim." Fred's hiss was apologetic; he seemed to notice Cali's disappointment. "However, we have scavenged some rather interesting materials and parts," he continued as he walked to a corner of the garage near a large tarp. With no ceremony, he ripped the tarp down, and what it revealed had Cali cackling.

"The race should be fun." Huntress.
"So it would seem." Two.
"Dis be wort watchin'." Anansi.
"Indeed, it is." Wanderer.

# CHAPTER TWENTY-FIVE

"Urgh," Jayce moaned as she came around.

The bright lights battered her injured brain. She had to blink away the pain and sensory overload. When it was only slight torture to look around, she tried to get her bearing. She was in a cage in the garage, the massive truck giving that away. Lots of metal scraps and smaller buggies were scattered throughout the place. Some of the lizards, all different shades of green, scurried about doing one form of mechanical work or the other. Jayce breathed in the heavy scent of oil tinged with the iron of dried blood on her face. She tried to wipe her face, but heavy iron cuffs on her wrists and ankles held her back.

*You're to be used again. You still deserve it.*

Her thoughts hammered against her already pounding head. Before she could panic, Jayce heard a whimper from her side. Looking over, she saw Azreal as flat against the corner of the cage as she could get. The elf's silver hair and pale face were drenched in the sickly dark blue of her blood. Her yellow eyes were wide and darted about the room, and she was quietly muttering.

"Not again. Please, Gods, not again. Not again." The mantra was quiet but rapid and repetitive. Sweat mixed with the blue blood on her face, rehydrating it and causing it to run.

Jayce moved closer to Azreal, who tried to flatten herself further. She raised a hand towards the elf but stopped when Azreal flinched.

*I know. I know.*

Jayce didn't voice her thoughts, deciding to lower her hand instead.

"Azreal. It's Jayce. We go to school at Aetherion together." Jayce spoke slowly and clearly in hopes of reaching past the elf's obvious PTSD. Azreal's mantra slowed but didn't stop. Jayce moved the smallest amount possible closer.

"Talio and The Baron are dead. And..." Jayce looked around at the barely clad workers. There was no sign of reproductive organs. "I don't think we have to relive *that* part of our past today." Jayce didn't want to say the words that could break both Azreal and herself, the words that most feared in captivity.

Azreal's eyes slowed, and her breathing, while not steady, calmed.

"Yes. It seems that issue may be avoided this day." Azreal's normally angelic voice came out cold with a small hint of relief. "Dying is not unlikely, though preferable as it is."

Jayce motioned that she wanted to come closer, and at Azreal's assent, she moved shoulder to shoulder. As much as she abhorred touch, Jayce felt the closeness was needed for them both.

"Can we just call the others?" Jayce asked.

"No. Our energy is being restricted. No holo. Nothing," Azreal replied.

Jayce felt for her energy, but it was almost completely blocked. There was a quiet tug, though there was nothing she could think to do with it.

"I had prayed to never be locked up by another man...Well, maybe Leon," Azreal said with a weak wink.

Jayce returned a weaker smile.

"How long can these collars hold back our power?"

Azreal shrugged noncommittally.

"Mine never failed on the marionette plane. So, for a long

time. I believe we will have to rely on the others, unfortunately. Hopefully, the elephant has a plan."

They leaned back against the cage in silence. The tug of energy in Jayce's chest pulled harder; it was hers, but it wasn't at the same time. Jayce's eyes went wide in realization. Immediately, she tried to pour everything she was into the small opening. She felt a small line of power shoot from her chest; she couldn't see it, but knew it traveled at speeds a fighter pilot would blanche at. In what felt like an instant, she felt a familiar weight on her left shoulder.

"I cannot express how grateful I am with your acceptance, dear Jayce." Thought's soothing voice replaced her fear with hope. He looked over the collar and sighed. "You should have minimal energy flow now that you have linked with me. Consider me a battery pack of sorts. However, I do not believe it is enough to nullify the collar," he ended, concentrating.

Azreal noticed Jayce staring at nothing on her shoulder.

"Jayce, are you well?"

Jayce had forgotten that, to the outside world, there was nothing on her.

"Is there a way for her to see you?"

"But of course, master. Anything is possible. Simply allow me to be seen, and I will be."

Jayce recoiled at his words.

"I-I allow it." She shuddered at saying allow. "But I am not your master."

"I have no mast—" Azreal started to reply, thinking that it was directed to her, but froze as a swirl of black mist made a small cyclone on the other girl's shoulder.

It spun and spun, not making wind, only emitting a low whizzing sound. A few seconds later, a quiet pop sounded, and Thought materialized on Jayce's shoulder.

"What the hell?" The phrase felt foreign on Azreal's tongue, but gave her a fleeting warmth as it reminded her of her warrior.

"Good afternoon, Lady Azreal. It has been some time." Thought bobbed his head in greeting.

Azreal stared, half-shocked, half-disbelieving. Her mouth was slightly open, her sharp canines glistening, her yellow eyes fixed on the bird's obsidian ones. Jayce didn't know you could actually smell tension until that moment.

"Huginn? Why are you here? What game is your master playing?" The momentary shock was replaced with anger.

The raven simply idly pecked Jayce's ear. She couldn't help but giggle at the feeling before going stoic just as quickly.

"My master is who you see before you. What games she chooses to play are her prerogative, not mine."

Azreal seethed.

"You know well what I am asking. What is Odin's plan? Why send you?" The words were spat.

*Odin? I know that name. But from where?*

Jayce scanned her brain, trying to place the name. She thought of movies that she would hide in the hallway to watch quietly at Hector's. Her eyes went wide as she thought of a superhero movie. That character was based on a god.

"Odin is no longer my master. He set me free so I may join Jayce here on her journey. His stories were no longer being written, while Jayce has an empty book."

"Odin? Like the god?" Jayce whispered. Azreal and Thought scoffed and laughed simultaneously. Confused, Jayce asked, "What?"

"Sorry, my dear. It is simply funny how mortals deify the unknown. He is no god. Nor are his companions. Well, Two I am not sure of, to be honest," Thought replied. "Odin, or Four, or the Wanderer as you know him, is indeed a very powerful sculptor. And when he interacted with humans, they did see him as a god, but he can die the same as the rest of us."

Jayce looked at Azreal.

"Why do you hate him?" she asked the elf.

Azreal stared daggers into Thought. "We have other issues," she replied, pointing to her collar and then to a large green lizard making a beeline for the cage.

Thought disappeared with a few words.

"I will be here for you, mas—friend."


The wind whipped Leon's long hair and beard behind him as he rocketed his board back towards Zynka's location. He weaved the massive dusty rock hills at breakneck speeds. Though he was furious at the capture of his friend and...girlfriend? ...he couldn't help but smile at the thought of surfing on the wind. It was the most stressful feeling of relaxation he had ever felt. He was free, yet on a mission. He called up his holo and looked at the map.

*Twenty minutes.*

He pulled up the phone app and called Zynka, who answered quietly.

"Hey, they are being moved. There's a metal structure towards the south side of the town. Lots of dark stains on the sand," she whispered.

Leon couldn't help but smile stupidly, then caught himself.

"It uh, it's not shaped like a dome, is it?"

"Uh, yeah, I guess, kinda."

Leon almost vibrated on his board.

"I'll be there in fifteen minutes. See ya." He ended the connection, let out a "Yee Haw!" and shot towards Zynka.

Fifteen minutes later, he landed on the rooftop with the elephant, who watched Jayce and Azreal being led through a gate made of what looked like an old tin roof.

"I think it is an arena," she said as she heard him approach.

Leon looked out. It was a good three-quarter mile away, so he flowed some energy into his eyes to help see. Sure enough, there were the two girls. The gate shut behind them, and the massive green lizard threw in two pieces of rebar, about thirty inches long, through the cage.

"Weapons," Leon stated absently.

On the other side of the cage was a very malnourished white lizard that seemed uncomfortable in the sunlight. It kept chasing the moving shade.

"More than likely, that lizard is not meant or hasn't been able to live on the surface in a long time."

Zynka nodded in agreement but stayed silent as the most massive forest-green lizard in a metal loincloth walked up a raised dais outside the cage, a cone-shaped object in his hand. Reaching the top, he put the cone to his mouth.

"Brothers and sisters! Welcome one and all to the death cage!" The lizard stopped for the cheers from the packed, raised bleachers surrounding the cage.

Leon groaned.

"Crushers, Gnashers, Death cage. It's like they are being paid to make this lame for me," he complained. Zynka snorted.

"Today's first match is between the albino, who was found guilty of stealing eggs from the nursery...*to eat*!" The speaker ended on a yell to emphasize. The boos, even from this distance, were deafening. "I know. I know! And on the other side are two walkers from the Aetherion Academy. Accused of conspiracy to commit sabotage on our racing vehicles."

Surprisingly, the boos were almost louder than the egg stealers were.

"They take their cars seriously," Zynka noted.

"As for the rules, there are two; one, the walkers will be collared so no abilities; two, the match ends in death." The cheers erupted, echoing for as far as the ears could hear.

Leon flinched. Knowing that was going to be the case and hearing it were two separate things. He watched Jayce and Azreal hesitantly pick up their weapons and take a more or less defensive posture. Leon looked at the crowd and saw the obvious signs of gambling, which made him smile.

"I have an idea. Go disable their vehicles; I got this," he said, remounting his board and shooting off towards the dais.

Zynka blinked.

"Okay, bye. Good luck, I guess," she mumbled to his shrinking image.

The speaker lizard noticed the board approaching and called a stop to the match, to the boos of the crowd. He took up a fighting stance as Leon landed next to him and de-summoned his board, placing the ring back on his finger.

"Who are you?" the speaker asked.

Leon grinned.

"I'm a gambler with a wager."

The speaker, though hesitant, was very obviously interested.

"You are a walker, yes?"

Leon nodded. He tried sending energy to his throat to amplify his voice; surprisingly, it worked.

"I am. I am also a trained boxer. I want to offer the crowd a real match between me and whoever you see fit. I win, me and mine leave. You win...well, do what you want with us. I will let you collar me to make it fair," he stated so the whole crowd could hear.

There was a deafening cheer. The speaker looked around, fidgeting. He then steeled himself and let out a hissing laugh.

"Or I could kill you now and be—"

Before the speaker could finish, Leon had his eidolon revolver in the large lizard's face. "Or I could kill you now and get what I want? Was that what you wanted to say?"

The lizard swallowed.

"Of course not," the lizard backtracked. He raised his megaphone. "Would my people like to see this?" The positive roar from the crowd seemed to deflate the speaker. "Very well, remove the prisoners and fetch Braulio." He lowered the speaker and whispered to Leon. "Making a fool of me was your last mistake."

Leon shrugged and placed the eidolon in one of his kilt pockets. "Don't promise me something you can't deliver," Leon said coldly.

The lizard glared at Leon's back as he hopped off the dais and headed to the gate. A bright green lizard opened it and put the cuffs back on Jayce and Azreal as they exited. The elf walked up to Leon and, with hands behind her back, stood on tiptoes for a kiss. Leon grabbed her face and kissed her. They let it linger for a moment before the lizard cleared his throat. Azreal shot him a quick look.

"Fight well, my hero," she said before walking back to Jayce.

Jayce gave Leon a thankful smile, and he returned it with a nod. A new lizard approached Leon with a collar, which he took and placed on himself. He immediately felt his energy slow to a stop. His prosthetic lost functionality as well.

*Shit. Didn't plan on that.*

Sighing, he made his way into the arena. He paced the perimeter twice to gauge the distance. It was about forty feet in diameter. He posted up on the far side of the ring and shadow boxed, trying to get a feel for his dead hand. He could still get some power behind it, and he figured the metal impact would hurt like hell for his opponent. The crowd roared as the gate opened, revealing a light tan figure that resembled a horny toad more than anything. Its body was covered in spike-like scales with two deadly-looking horns on its head. Red, beady eyes scanned him thoroughly. It stepped in and threw its hands up with a deep guttural growl. The metal bars of the cage vibrated with the noise. The crowd went wild. The speaker cleared his throat into the megaphone.

"Ladies and gentlemen. Once again, I thank you all for your patience and would like to introduce our contestants. Fighting from the gate side is the Death Cage Champion, Terror of the Wastelands, and Batterer of the Broken...*Braulio*!"

The crowd went absolutely feral. Cheers, hisses, hoots, and hollers. Leon had to fight the urge to cover his ears. It took a few minutes for order to be restored, and Leon was pretty sure there was a lot of the lizard equivalent of flashing from the stands, punctuated by Braulio winking at each of them.

"And fighting on the other side is that asshole," the speaker said flatly.

*All the cool that could be in this plane sucks.*

Leon sighed again.

"To the death. No weapons. *Fight*!" the speaker boomed to another cheer.

Braulio made the first move; he had taken a boxer's stance, orthodox, but moved to his right, crossing his own feet. Leon watched curiously. A trained fighter should have the knowledge not to do that.

*Oh well.*

Leon took a southpaw position, moving slightly left to meet the threat.

"How does it feel to know today is the day you die?" Braulio asked as they entered range.

Leon replied with a right jab to gauge distance. It landed square on his opponent's snout, whose head rocked back from the light impact.

*He's tense.*

That meant Braulio was taking the full impact rather than letting his body roll with the punches. Leon nodded and smiled. The lizard continued circling the wrong way, which moved him right into a hard left hook with the prosthetic, Leon couldn't make the arm function, but it made one hell of a club. Braulio staggered, clearly dazed as he went on the back foot. From years of fighting, Leon knew he was going to win unless he got caught unaware; so, rather than pressing, he stood his ground. The lizard recovered from the daze and charged, throwing a right hand from the hayfields. Leon lazily pivoted, causing Braulio's momentum to send him to the dirt. The crowd booed.

"I will rip you to shreds!" the lizard yelled, rising back to his feet.

Quicker than Leon anticipated, the lizard charged, grabbing him by the tank top and slamming him into the wall. He sent a scaly headbutt that connected on the bridge of Leon's nose, causing him to see white momentarily. Then another headbutt and another. Leon's nose broke, and his cheek ripped open on one of the horns. Despite the pain, remained tranquil. There was an opening to be had—he just had to find it. Braulio took one hand off Leon's shirt and raised it in a pre-victory celebration. Leon heard Azreal screech.

*Guess I can't let myself die yet; she'd kill me.*

He chuckled at the thought. That enraged Braulio, who asked, "Any last words?" he growled. His right arm was still raised in victory.

Leon smiled.

"Welcome to the Thunder Dome, bitch." He punctuated his quip with a hard left uppercut into the lizard's unprotected jaw.

Braulio dropped the human who came again with an overhand left, connecting with the lizard's temple. Braulio staggered back, now obviously unaware of his surroundings. Leon didn't let up; he hit three quick right jabs, his knuckles bleeding from the scales. A right-left combination put the lizard on his back. Following him to the ground, Leon brought his left hand down in a flying hammer fist, denting Braulio's skull. The lizard was out. Leon looked to the dais for a stoppage, but the speaker just shook his head.

He looked at the unconscious lizard and sighed. He slammed home four of the heaviest hammer fists he had ever swung, turning Braulio's skull into a green and tan clumpy paste. He rolled off the lizard and lay on his back, removing the collar before the speaker got any ideas.

"The...The winner is...him," the speaker choked out. "Exit the arena, collect your prize, and leave." His voice was pained. This was obviously a fighter he cared for.

Leon stood and walked to the opening gate, holding his nose. Jayce and Erin were freed from their bonds without question. Azreal rushed to Leon and moved his hand, the red blood running freely from his nose, cheek, and fist. She looked at him hungrily for only a second before pulling his face down and licking his blood-soaked lips. She almost purred as she moved her tongue over his cheek, continuing to lick away the blood. Leon wanted to say something, but he learned at that moment that he really enjoyed whatever the hell was happening.

"I fear this group is not very wise." Huntress.
"So it would seem." Two
"Dey ar' eider lucky or good." Anansi.
"Strong too." Odin.

# CHAPTER TWENTY-SIX

Twenty minutes after the fight, Azreal, Jayce, and Leon found themselves on top of a hill waiting for Zynka. Leon cradled Azreal's head while sitting on his board.

"Did she say how long she would be?" Jayce asked.

"She has no idea how to sabotage a vehicle, so a while, I reckon," Leon replied.

Azreal had cleaned the blood from his face and was currently picking at the dried blood of his fist. Jayce made a face.

"Are you like a vampire?" She tried to keep judgment out of her voice.

Azreal rolled her head to look at the other girl. She bobbed her head back and forth.

"If the translation is working correctly, yes and no. My species doesn't require blood to survive, but we do have a taste for it. Kind of like a fancy dinner you only have on special occasions."

Leon laughed.

"Not gonna be so rare 'round here," he said, thinking of all they had been through in a week. "Speaking of which, I forgot to mention, the gremlin lost two more fingers. And Erin is a little woozy from an attack on the way to the other village." He saw Jayce's concern and quickly added. "She's okay, just jammed up a bit. Took a lot of pain from me." He retracted his prosthetic to show the raw meat of his stump.

Azreal licked her lips, and Jayce decided to walk to the other side of the hill to make a call.

"Hey, babe," Erin answered cheerily, though there was an obvious tiredness to her tone.

"Hey, Erin. Leon just gave us Cliff Notes on the attack. Are you okay?"

"Yup, all good here. What about you? Cali made it seem like you got captured?" Erin's worry was evident.

"Yeah, head hurts pretty bad...But I have something I need to tell you. The rest of the group, too. Before I do, though, I want you to know that I didn't keep it from y'all for any reason other than the only thing we can do is worry about it," Jayce said quickly.

The other end was quiet for a bit.

"Do you have another girlfriend?" Erin asked teasingly. "Kidding, if you thought that was worth keeping, I get it."

Jayce felt relieved at the tone of Erin's voice. She walked to Leon and Azreal, who, unsurprisingly was working her mouth on Leon's nub. He grinned sheepishly up at her and pulled the elf's head away, with much protest. Jayce sat down with them and told them everything she knew. Azreal added what she knew as well. When they finished, the group was silent. Leon looked at his vegvisir, eyes searching.

"Odin is real. You own one of his ravens, and these four 'not gods' are watching and dicking with us, sums it up?" he asked Jayce, who replied with a noncommittal shrug. Thinking, Jayce summoned Huginn. He, shortly thereafter, materialized in the middle of the group.

"Greetings, friends of friends, and Azreal."

The elf hissed at him. Leon visibly shook with excitement.

"You are Huginn? Thought? One of Odin's ravens?" he asked. The raven nodded. "So, the myths aren't myths?"

"Not all of them. Valhalla is a place, but the einherjar are not brought there, just students. Or anywhere we can figure. Death is death unless we just haven't found that plane. Thor, Loki, Freya, all real but not deities," Huginn replied. Leon looked deflated. "What is it?"

"Back in the war, we convinced ourselves if we died in battle, we would see Odin's Great Hall. I know they died, but we always hoped it was real, ya know?" Leon said, crestfallen.

Huginn nodded.

"Humans, well, mortals in general, tend to try and find comfort in the afterlife. Whether there is one or not, I find it debilitating. Why look forward to a possible life when you have the real thing in front of you?"

Jayce thought, then said, "Well, you said you didn't know. None of us do, which means anyone could technically be right, right?"

Huginn nodded again.

"My thoughts are absolutely my own, of course. Simply gathered from what I have seen. What I have not seen is great, though...also, to go back to the myths. Odin used to walk among the mortals of Earth. He was a storyteller for a long time. Those stories became revered and then deified. It has also happened with Anansi and Artemis, Huntress."

Jayce and Leon locked eyes. Artemis, Jayce knew immediately. She had done drawings of her for school before. Her head spun.

*What else is real? What isn't?*

"Wait," Erin's voice chimed in. "Why is it they are messing with us?"

Huginn looked at the holo for a moment, then answered.

"Why not?" he returned her question simply. "On Earth, when you are bored, do you not watch others' lives on your screens?" Leon and Jayce shared a look. "And, have you never wished to influence the story? They watch because they are bored. They interfere because they can. As I have told Jayce, they are not going to put anything in front of you that there isn't a way to overcome. If they did, the show would end. Simple."

There was a pregnant silence.

"So, what do we do about it?" Leon asked.

The raven looked at him.

"Survive."

"*Erin*! I did it!" Cali's excited voice came over the holo. "These buggies are gonna kick some tail pipe!"

"Hey, I need to tell—" Erin started.

"Yeah, yeah, yeah. Some god, not gods, are being dicks. Whatever. This race is gonna rock!" Cali cut her sister off. "Sending Leon and Zynka coordinates for a hill we can watch from. Let's go, Erin. Love y'all, bye!" Cali's voice rang out as the holo went dead.

"That child is not a normal human, yes?" Huginn asked.

Despite all their surroundings and situations, Leon, Jayce, and Azreal shared a true laugh.

That evening, the whole group was back together on the hilltop Cali had designated. They caught Zynka up, who was, as usual, unbothered by the situation.

"Life throws weird stuff at you. We just know where it's coming from now," was all she said.

So, they had decided to finally relax and wait for the next morning. The night had brought a chill to the air, so Azreal used some kind of power to start a small fire. The three couples sat separated around it. Cali and Zynka were chattering on about their mechanical day. Azreal was busy giving Leon chapped lips. Jayce and Erin found themselves on the outer rim of the fire's heat, Jayce's head resting comfortably on Erin's shoulder.

"Be honest. In your wildest dreams, could you have imagined any of this?" Erin asked, staring wonderingly at the elf, the elephant, and around the alien environment.

Jayce nuzzled her shoulder.

"To be real, my wildest dreams only included being away from foster care. So no, all of this is a blessing or a curse. I guess we got to wait to figure that out." Her eyes watered.

Erin wrapped her arm around Jayce's shoulder.

"Well, you are safe now, right?"

"I think I might be more unsafe now than I have ever been.

But at least now, I have made the choice. And let's be real. This stuff is scary but cool as hell. And I have y'all," Jayce ended with a note of ease.

Erin kissed her on the top of the head.

"You do have us. A warrior, a creepy ass elf, a silent tank of an elephant, a girlfriend, and...whatever the hell Cali is now." She laughed. Jayce shared in a chuckle.

They sat just enjoying each other's presence and the warmth of the fire. After about an hour of just existing, Erin let out an overly loud Dad-yawn that made all the group stare. She went bright red.

"Sorry. That wasn't meant to make a noise." She laughed. "I think I need to hit the...I was gonna say sack, but I guess hit the rocks?" She looked around as if she waited for a mattress to materialize. Jayce bolted up.

"I think I can fix it. I can try to sculpt a few mattresses." Her eyes gleamed. She was excited to use her power; despite the headache she knew was going to obliterate her.

The group shrugged simultaneously. Jayce let her mind replay her time with Richard. The fear, the pain, and the helplessness sending her energy into overdrive. Then, sound, movement, wind, everything stopped. The beating of her heart was the only active thing in her frozen world.

*Okay, Jayce. You have changed things, but never created any. You got this, or you don't.*

She focused like she would when she painted. Using her hand, she drew a rectangle in the air; it formed in purple energy. Then she painted in the lines and turned the flat rectangle sideways. She painted the side and the back. Once the painting was done, she thought "mattress". The large three-dimensional purple cuboid solidified and sat itself on the ground as an ordinary-looking mattress. She repeated the process five more times before she released her hold on time. Every sensation hit like a truck. The greasy, dusty-smelling air. Five "wow"s sounded out together. Erin quickly leapt on the nearest.

"Oh my god. This is the greatest mattress ever! Come here," Erin said, extending a hand to Jayce.

Jayce stared at the mattress and the woman she was falling for, but couldn't move. She wanted to join her, but being with someone on a mattress? She wasn't ready. Jayce shivered as Erin lowered her hand and stood up. She took a step towards Jayce, who, breaking Erin's heart, flinched.

"Babe, it's okay," she whispered. "You don't have to do what anybody says anymore. If you aren't ready to share a bed, I get it. I'm here for you. I see you."

Despite herself, Jayce threw her arms around Erin and sobbed quietly as Erin rubbed her back and made shushing noises. Azreal and Leon, not wanting to eavesdrop, hopped on a bed, and the elf lay on his chest. Her hand was wandering.

"Stop it!" Leon laughed. "There are kids here." He moved her hand gently but firmly to the other side of his chest.

Azreal hissed disapprovingly but didn't resist. Cali and Zynka both stuck their tongues out.

"Not kids, kilt man," Zynka said before returning to her conversation with Cali.

Erin broke up their hug and guided Jayce to a separate mattress. She helped lay her down. Gave her a deep kiss, then went back to her own bed.


The sound of engines revving woke Jayce in the mid-morning. She sat up slowly and wiped away an eye booger. The promised fallout headache was present, but not nearly as intense as she would have imagined. Looking around, she saw she was the last to wake up. She scrambled to her feet and went to the edge of the hill next to Erin, where everyone watched the cars line up. Erin grasped her hand when she stopped next to her. The interlocking of fingers still sent electricity through Jayce's body.

"Looks like the race is gonna start soon," Erin told her.

Jayce nodded, and they watched. The large dump truck-like vehicle lined up about three hundred yards from the small buggies of the Gnashers. Pure numbers were in favor of the Crushers; they had the dump truck, six buggies, and nine motorcycles. The Gnashers, on the other hand, only had three buggies and four bikes.

"No wonder they hired us to help. What did you say you did to sabotage them, Z?" Leon asked.

Zynka grinned at Cali, then looked at Leon.

"I simply did what Cali told me to," she said cheekily.

Leon looked skeptically at Cali, the chaos gremlin, then smiled.

"Ba ba boom?"

"Ba ba boom," Cali replied.

A grey lizard moved a hundred meters in front of the vehicles, carrying a large green flag. He waved it twice, then swung it downwards hard. All the vehicles took off like mini rockets. Cali looked at Zynka and nodded. Zynka pulled out her holo and pressed a button. All the Crushers' vehicles detonated simultaneously in actinic black fire. Each melted in less than five minutes.

"What in the world was that?" Erin asked, shocked at the sudden chaos.

Cali grinned ferally.

"Had Z go grab some of the fridge generators and make a bundle of bombs and boom, baby!" Cali cackled.

"Okay, great, explosions. However, is it not a slightly lackluster end?" Azreal asked.

"Exactly," Cali replied.

"Home?" Leon asked.

"Home," they all replied.

"That...wasn't as exciting as I had hoped." Artemis.
"They chose not to entertain." Two.
"Me tink dey grew tired." Anansi.
"Then we make it impossible for them not to put on a show."
Odin.

# CHAPTER TWENTY-SEVEN

Hours later, the group found themselves scarfing down another dinner at their tiered table. Jayce watched Leon and Azreal's not-so-subtle flirting with a weird mix of admiration and jealousy. Not for Leon, but for Azreal being able to be intimate so quickly after being rescued. Why couldn't she take that step with Erin? She cared for the redhead and trusted her. Still, there was a wall that she couldn't see or dismantle yet. Pulling her eyes away, she kept picking at her steak.

"So, what do we think happens next?" Cali asked.

Leon looked over at the young girl.

"I messaged Noctharim when we got back. He said he and Jotun would be by in the morning to brief us on the entrance exam."

"I do not believe I shall partake," Azreal said lazily. She seemed surprised at the five faces, who now looked confused. "Well, it is not like we are required to. And I see no point. I have been a walker longer than you all have been a species. I plan to talk to the headmaster and ask him about a teaching role." She shrugged, then smiled deliciously at Leon. "Don't worry, fraternization is not frowned upon here." She ended with a wink.

Leon went a light pink in the face, and the elf giggled.

"Wait, so none of us have to take it?" Jayce asked, confused still.

Azreal bobbed her head. "Well, no, technically. But you can only remain in the Nexus as a teacher or a student. So, to stay here, yes, you do. If you don't care to stay, then you don't. And no one will force the issue either way. Not like the school in Asgard," Azreal said flippantly.

She looked around at the gawking faces and sighed. She took a long pull off her Lone Star, which she had become extremely fond of.

"Story time. Gather around, children. As Huginn said, Valhalla is where students are taken. Emphasis on the taken portion. Back in his days as the headmaster, Odin would scour the planes for students with outstanding potential." She took another swig. The group was locked in on her, but if it made her uncomfortable, it didn't show.

"So, I was one such student. And I want to tell you how lucky you are to have walked here and not there. The consent rule is nonexistent. You do not have a personal domicile, nor do you have the right to refuse contracts. Where Noctharim teaches almost by not teaching, Odin taught by force. Mind you, he had been gone a long time when I arrived, but his replacement kept the spirit alive." She concluded by draining her beer and retrieving another, cheering up as she continued. "I will now accept questions."

Cali leapt at the chance to talk.

"What did they teach? How long did you go there? Do you think learning is better here or there?" She bounced with each question.

Azreal smiled sweetly at her.

"Young Cali, always with more than one question at a time. Love the inquisitiveness. They taught the same specializations as here. I was enrolled for about two to two and a half thousand years. And I like the way you asked the last question. The teaching here, I would guess, is better on the level of being able to come and go and feel homey. There you learned, or you died.

So, the overall learning puts out more fierce walkers, but not compassionate ones," she said, absently tracing lines on Leon's hand.

Jayce could see he got the same tingly feeling she got when Erin touched her. He noticed her looking and smiled in a way she imagined a brother would. Jayce looked at Erin's hands resting on the table and considered mimicking the elf, but decided against it.

"How did you get away? Seems like they wouldn't want you to get out," Zynka said skeptically.

Jayce realized Zynka was still heated about Azreal snapping at Cali. The elf narrowed her eyes at Zynka.

"If you must know, I accepted a contract back to my home plane. I had assumed I could hide with my family, and we all know where that ended for me, don't we, pachyderm?" Azreal spat.

The two stared at each other for a moment before a pigtailed blonde head appeared between them.

"So, if we could just not be assholes to each other, that'd be great," She said jokingly, but eyed both Zynka and Azreal with a look Jayce couldn't quite place. Leon busted out laughing and looked at Erin.

"You let her watch that?"

Erin smiled around her glass of whiskey cola.

"Never said I was a good guardian."

"We watched all the classics! Monday was classic movie Monday," Cali said happily. "Oh, should we do a movie night tonight?" she asked, forgetting about anything else. "I bet the old guy knows some good ones," Cali said, pointing at Leon.

"Old?" he said with mock indignation.

Azreal laughed as well.

"You are all pups. But yes, Miss Cali, I would love to relax with a movie," Azreal answered.

The rest of the group agreed.

"We should watch *Mean Girls*!" Cali squealed.

"I will literally gouge my own eyes out if I have to watch that movie one more time. What about *Grind?*" Erin asked. To Jayce's look, she said, "A million times is enough." Jayce giggled.

"*Braveheart* is a classic," Leon suggested.

"You know how historically inaccurate that was?" Cali chided.

"Still a good movie."

"What about *The Matrix?*" Cali offered.

Leon and Erin looked at each other, then at Azreal and Zynka.

"I don't have the energy or the words to explain that to them," Leon said, pointing to the two non-humans who watched silently.

Cali was about to roll her eyes, but she stopped, thought, and nodded in agreement.

"*Saving Private Ryan?*" Erin suggested.

Leon shook his head quickly, his hair and beard hitting Azreal.

"Sorry, darlin'. But hard pass on any modern-ish war movies, please."

"Shoot, sorry. Didn't think of that."

Jayce opened her mouth, then closed it, hoping no one saw.

"Jayce has an idea," Cali blurted.

Jayce went red at the five gazes on her.

"I uh...haven't really watched many movies. But I heard some of one that sounded interesting. *The 8th Warrior*, or something like that." She smiled nervously at Erin, who looked in thought.

"*The 13th Warrior*. Fantastic movie. I'd say it's probably Antonio Banderas' best. I'm down," Leon said.

"Despite the fact that you are completely disregarding *Shrek 2*, I'm also down. Excellent choice, babe." Erin smiled at her.

"I guess I haven't seen that one yet. I'm in," Cali agreed.

Zynka looked at Cali, then Jayce, and nodded.

They all got up and grabbed some popcorn from the fridge and hopped over the couch, settling in. Leon flew through his holo, trying to find the movie.

"There is literally every movie ever made on Earth here." He kept scrolling. "And from everywhere else, it seems." He found what he was looking for after finding the search bar and cast the movie onto the large screen on the wall.

"Can I put my arm around you?" Erin asked Jayce softly.

Jayce looked up into her eyes and scooted closer. She gave Erin a kiss on the cheek and lay her head on her shoulder. Erin's arm softly yet possessively wrapped around her. The opening credits played as Jayce fought back a happy tear. She was warm, she was here, and she was safe.


About halfway through the movie, Jayce woke up to Leon giggling.

"Stop it, girl," he laughed as Jayce heard the sound of one hand swatting another. She tried not to move much as she looked over at the couple. Leon was having a hard time wrestling Azreal's head away from his neck. "It's not even a sexy movie," He laughed again.

Jayce felt that pang of odd jealousy again and blurted out before she could stop herself.

"Can I ask you something?" she asked.

Azreal, aware that the question was to her, answered. "Of course," she replied, again trying to kiss Leon's neck.

"In private?" Jayce asked again. Azreal groaned.

"But of course." She got to her feet with much hesitation.

Erin looked at Jayce, who just gave her a kiss and an apologetic look. They got over the couch, and Jayce followed the elf to her room. At the entrance, Azreal set the permission to temporarily allow Jayce in. When they walked in, the door shut, and low blue lights came on. The sight froze Jayce in her spot. Around the room, there was a suspended swing made of softened black leather. The four-poster bed had blue satin sheets with more of the leather coming out of the ornately carved headboard, and there was a wall with...exotic items mounted on it. Noticing Jayce's shock, Azreal smiled.

"What? A girl cannot have a hobby?" She laughed as Jayce went pink.

Shaking herself, Jayce looked her in the glittering yellow eyes, the blue lights dancing off of her snow-white skin. Jayce cleared her throat.

"I actually...I kind of wanted to talk to you about this," she said, waving around the room.

Azreal's eyes rounded slightly.

"Oh, my dear. I am quite flattered; however, I do believe Leon and I will be exclusive," Azreal said carefully.

Jayce's eyes bulged.

"Wha-no-I-what?" Jayce sputtered. This is not at all what she planned. "I-I just wanted to know how you do it?"

Azreal cocked an eyebrow.

"Sex? It's really quite sim—" the elf started.

"No!" Jayce half shouted, causing Azreal to jump slightly. "Sorry. What I meant was, after what you went through, how can you be so open with Leon?"

Her questioning look was followed by a knowing one.

"What has happened to me..." Azreal started but stopped and truly saw Jayce. "My apologies. What has happened to us is a scar, not a physical one, but a mental one that will follow us for a literal eternity. What has been done to us has always been done to us and will always have happened to us." Azreal sighed. "But look at Leon. Would he ever do anything to me that I didn't want him to?"

Jayce didn't even have to think before shaking her head. Leon would kill, and more than likely die, to protect any of the group, and that is one week of knowing him. Confidently, she shook her head again.

"Exactly. He is a dangerously safe man. As a fiery redhead is also a dangerously safe woman," Azreal said and winked. "They would both never do anything they knew would harm us. Well, that is the best hope, at least. Though even if it wasn't Leon, my sensuality or sexuality, whichever you prefer, is mine to freely give. Just because it has been taken before, that doesn't mean it has to be taken forever."

Jayce took in a breath along with the information. There were not a lot of words, but the way they hit her was baffling. Jayce nodded slowly.

"So...to get it back, I need to take it?" she asked, unsurely.

In her head, she thought about and shivered about going out and pouncing on Erin. She shuddered at the thought. Azreal grabbed both of her shoulders and shook her slightly while making the fiercest eye contact Jayce had ever seen.

"No. I must repeat no. That is my way of reclaiming myself, not a damn road map. If you were me, then yes, it might be the right choice. But you are not," Azreal snapped seriously.

Jayce flinched at her tone and instinctively looked at the ground. The elf lightly raised Jayce's chin with her hand.

"Sorry, love. It is just that I know my path is a risky one. One day, I may be in bed with Leon and try to strangle him during a flashback. So, I do not know which path will bring you closer to right. Seeing how Miss Erin is with you, though, I feel you have the time to find the right way for you," Azreal said softer.

Jayce's face brightened, and she stepped towards the elf.

"Hug me, and I will tear your throat out," Azreal said in a light voice, though there was a hint of a threat.

"Sorry. Thank you," Jayce said and slowly backed out of the room, nodding in thanks. She made her way back and hopped over the couch between Erin and Leon.

"You are very lucky, Leon," Jayce said with a smile.

Leon returned it.

"Lucky or gonna be murdered in my sleep. Either way, I like her," Leon laughed.

"Both are indeed possible," Azreal purred in Leon's ear as she approached. He turned and his eyes went wide. Azreal's uniform, normally in the shape of a robe, was now barely more than a bikini revealing her curves. She let him ogle her for a moment before purring.

"Could you tuck me in?" She swayed towards her bedroom without an answer.

Leon took less than a heartbeat to vault the couch and rush after her. He scooped the elf up and disappeared into her room. Erin and Jayce stared after them until the door whizzed down. They looked at each other and blushed, Jayce finding the hem of her sleeves very fascinating.

"Imma hit the sack. I set up my own room, so we don't have to share one. Love y'all. Goodnight," Cali said, leaving the room.

Zynka, enthralled by the action in the movie, watched silently as she ate the popcorn from the other initiates' now vacant bowls.

"I'm sorry I'm not there," Jayce said so quietly that Erin barely heard.

She wrapped an arm around Jayce's shoulder.

"You are here, though. And that's all that matters. Will we get there? Maybe, but only when you're ready. We have an eternity, literally," Erin whispered back. Jayce looked up quickly. "That...um...that wasn't meant to be me saying..." Erin floundered.

"I like the sound of that," Jayce said, resting her head on Erin's chest. She could feel Erin's rapid heart. It soothed her to know that at least she wasn't the only one truly nervous.


Jayce woke up to the sound of Jotun's gravelly laugh. Immediate warmth shot through her even before her eyes opened. She rolled her head, her pillow not as conforming as usual. She gave it a slight headbutt to soften it.

"Ouch. Not a pillow, babe," Erin said with a smile as Jayce set up.

She realized she had fallen asleep on the couch with her head on Erin's stomach. Red flooded her face.

"My bad."

She looked around. Jotun, Noctharim, and the rest of the

group were already at the table. Wiping the sleep from their eyes, Jayce and Erin made their way to their seats.

"Good morning, Itsy Bitsy." Jotun's deep voice boomed happily. "It is a pleasure to see you."

"You, too, Mr. Jotun. How has everything been going for you?" Jayce asked, smiling.

"The headmaster and I have made a discovery we feel is necessary to share."

"Is it about the bored not-gods screwing with us?" Cali asked around a mouthful of cereal.

Noctharim looked at her quizzically. "Well, yes, my dear. We have come to realize our memories have been tampered with and have recently remembered the identi—"

"Odin," Leon cut him off.

"Artemis," Erin added.

"Anansi and an unknown," Jayce finished.

Jotun and Noctharim blinked.

"Well, yes," Noctharim replied, nonplussed. "How..."

Jayce sent a mental invitation to Huginn. A fraction of a second later, a small black cyclone materialized and shortly gave way to a sleek, black Huginn.

"Good morning, my old friend," Huginn said to Noctharim. "War Master, I hope all is well."

The two professors only stared.

"Yeah, we kinda just know stuff," Zynka said, sucking up Cali's cereal with her trunk and transferring it to her mouth.

Cali gave a fake scowl, then giggled when Zynka sprayed some of the milk at her. Noctharim didn't take his eyes off the raven.

"It has been many years, Huginn. Why has your master sent —" Noctharim again started.

"The raven has left his previous post as Odin's eyes to follow Jayce as he finds her more interesting," Azreal cut in.

Jotun sucked on his lips to stifle a chuckle at Noctharim's bafflement. The headmaster looked at everyone around the table in turn.

"Before I am cut off again, how do you all feel about the circumstance?"

There was a collective shrug.

"Life throws weird shit your way, we just happen to know who's doing the throwing," Erin said with a shrug in her voice. "We can't do anything about it anyway, right?"

"Very true. You humans, and pachyderm, and elf, are a very odd group. I love it," Noctharim said happily. "Shall we speak of your entrance exams?"

"Professor. I would like to withdraw from the initiate program and instead ask for a position as an energy instructor," Azreal stated plainly.

Noctharim looked at her, then the rest of the group.

"I can offer a trial teaching position. Speak with me after the exams. The rest of you do plan to take the test, yes?" The remaining five looked at each other and nodded. "Splendid. The exam will start in the room across from my office. You will step through a void. It reads your abilities and aptitudes. Then, it walks you into a simulated reality it deems most likely to propel you forward as a student." He paused and looked at the group.

"Can we assume there will be interference?" Zynka asked.

"Most assuredly. That is why, if you choose not to participate, it will not be frowned upon," Jotun said, looking almost pleadingly at Jayce.

"I-I think I will be fine, Jotun," Jayce said, trying to give a reassuring smile.

Jotun seemed to want to protest, but didn't, instead sinking in his chair slightly.

"These tests, even without Odin's interference, are trying. It will be difficult, but remember, once you pass, and you will, you will be part of the finest institute of walker instruction," Noctharim said.

"If you have finished, Headmaster," Huginn started. "I would like to speak with you in your office."

"But of course. Good luck, young ones. Jotun will take you all to the room when ready." With that, Noctharim and Huginn disappeared. Jotun let out a huge belly laugh.

"In billions of years, I have not seen him speechless or behind the curve," he boomed through his laugh.

Leon cocked his head before asking, "Jotun, on Earth, the Norse myths have Odin's son Thor fighting giants in Jotunheim. Does that have something to do with you?"

Jotun, still smiling, nodded.

"Yes, brave one. Though it is not as depicted in your plane. Thor and I were great friends long ago. We wrestled and fought constantly. I believe Odin embellished those stories in your plane." Jotun had a nostalgic smile.

"Are the exams solo?" Jayce asked.

Jotun bobbled his hands.

"Could be. Could be a group. The void usually decides. Though I would guess your watchers will play a hand in the sorting."

Jayce's breath caught, but she nodded through it.

"No time like the present," Leon said, slapping his knee and standing.

The rest of the group stood, pushed in their chairs, and nodded at the professor.

"I will see *y'all* there." Jotun tried to drawl the "y'all" as he warped away.

One by one, the room was emptied until Jayce was alone.

"Shit," she muttered, as she doubled over and vomited. Her hands shook, and her breath came too fast. "Shit, shit, shit." She wiped the forming tears from her eyes.

Walking to the fridge, she pulled out a bottle of mouthwash and took a swig, swirling it around her mouth and spitting it on the floor. The floor quickly cleaned it and released the calming vanilla bean and gasoline scent. She took a few deep breaths and warped as well.

Jayce landed near Cali, staring at a large void opening.

"Only the ones taking the exam may pass through," Jotun

said. He laid an engulfing hand on Jayce's shoulder. "Try and be safe, Bitsy."

"I will, sir. Thank you for being kind to me," she finished in a small voice.

The giant troll restrained himself from scooping the small girl up and running her safely away. Instead, he gave a weak smile to the group and walked to Noctharim's office, the door closing quickly behind him. A wet sound drew Jayce's attention; Azreal again was wrapped around Leon, giving him deep kisses.

"Be well, my love," she said, prying herself off him.

Leon kissed her head and stepped through the void, followed by Zynka and Cali.

"Ready for this?" Jayce asked. Erin pulled her into an enthusiastic kiss, her hands claiming purchase on Jayce's face. Jayce, in turn, put her hand around the back of Erin's head. They stood there tasting each other for what felt like an eternity, but when they broke apart, the time felt painfully insignificant.

"I-I think I love you, Jayce," Erin whispered.

Every internal organ Jayce possessed seemed to freeze. Her brain heard the words but didn't want to accept them.

*No one loves you.*

It screamed at her. Her heart moved too slowly, but it was too loud to be real. Ice in her veins stopped her movement, her hand still around Erin's head. When Jayce looked up into her eyes, they were full of intent, desire, and what Jayce could only guess was...love. The look in those eyes melted the ice. It made her heart beat so rapidly she thought it would spring free of her chest. She felt the voice in her head, for the first time, losing out to another.

"I know I love you...babe," Jayce said with a quivering voice. They shared another kiss, a long embrace, and stepped into the void together.

"I will take Cali." Artemis.
"Leon will do." Two.
"I be takin da red one." Nansi.
"Jayce shall come to me." Odin.

# CHAPTER TWENTY-EIGHT

Zynka found herself on a plain of azure grass blown this way and that by a playful wind. It felt like home in a different shade. Instinctively, she reached down and picked a trunkful of grass and shoved it into her mouth. She savored the flavor as she let the sights and smells come to her. There was a touch of salt and sulfur in the air; her trunk wrinkled. On the outskirts of the plain were large trees resembling what Cali called "Christmas trees" in a beautiful shade of light pink. With no direction, Zynka walked towards the trees, picking up and munching on grass as she went.

"I wonder which watcher is going to interfere with me?" she thought aloud with a bite of grass to punctuate her own question. "Artemis would be cool. Anansi seems like a wild card. Odin...no thank you. The other?" She shrugged.

When she made it to the tree line, she spotted a familiar birdlike creature.

"Headmaster?" She raised her eyebrows.

"A version, yes. The real one, no. I am simply an avatar of this exam," the not-Noctharim stated.

Zynka shrugged again.

"Where are the others? Did we all get individuals?"

The professor gnawed his wing in thought. "According to

speculation and the fact they are not present, leads me to believe they have been hijacked by the watchers."

"Oh...but not this exam?" Her shoulders fell slightly.

Noctharim took flight. He flew high, circled twice, and landed back on his tree.

"It would seem we are alone."

Zynka couldn't help but cast her eyes to the ground.

"Gotcha," she said quietly. She sniffed through her trunk. "Whatever. What is the test?"

Noctharim analyzed her.

"You wished to be examined by a watcher?"

Zynka rocked her head from side to side.

"I mean...I just feel like a side character to Jayce and the others. Like, I'm always there, but am I?" She sniffled again. "Like, am I just a novelty? Big, pink elephant, oh, cool. But then what?" She blew air violently from her trunk in a frustrated trumpet.

"Is that what you see? When you look at yourself?" the headmaster inquired.

"I guess, kind of. I don't know what to think, really. How could they see me as a member of theirs? My whole thing is not being seen." She kicked at a non-existent rock.

"Not seen? I have seen you. The real me, I mean. You are not an experienced walker, yet he put you in charge of showing around a, until then, uncontacted species," the fake Noctharim advised.

Zynka shrugged and got another trunkful of grass and shoved it in her mouth. There was a stretch of digestible silence before she spoke.

"I don't wanna sound, I don't know, like a kid—" she started, but the headmaster cut her off with a tutting noise.

"You are a child, Zynka. Barely thirteen. It is okay to sound like a child. I, and the real me, love the childlike barbarity you bring to the group."

Zynka, despite her turmoil, let the edges of her mouth lift.

"Growing up with fourteen brothers and sisters, you kind of

have to learn to fight if you want to eat more than scraps. But that is also what it feels like in the group, sometimes. Like I'm the forgotten youngest child." She exhaled deeply as she finished.

"Did I ever tell you?" Noctharim's eyes went blank for a split second. When they refocused, he continued. "No, I have not. I myself was the youngest of my conspiracy. I was born seven hundred and sixty-fourth," he said without considering the number further. Zynka's already round eyes went rounder.

"Seven hundred and sixty-fourth..." she muttered, her face revealing that she was trying to place herself in that lineup.

"Yes, yes, yes. My parents adored each other. But the point I am trying to make is that an overwhelming family can make you feel less-than, but you are not. I, or me, have seen in you great things, and your group does, too. However, miscommunication is the detriment to most things, so seeing as this could be a fracture, speak with Jayce and the others. A more receptive group I have not seen for a millennium."

Zynka, regaining her resolve, nodded and smiled at the professor. "Thank you, Headmaster. Now, we have an exam, do we not?" she said with a grin so feral it would have made Cali proud.


A few minutes later, fake Noctharim and Zynka stood in the middle of the clearing.

"Okay, my girl. We have five trials. Engineering, Stealth, Mysticism, Energy, and Combat. Please take the time and pick one to—"

"Combat." Zynka interrupted.

Noctharim rolled his black eyes.

"I truly adore when so much thought is put into a decision," he said with a smile and much sarcasm. "The combat trial will be as follows. One-on-one combat with a young version of the War Master. Eidolons are an accepted means of weaponry. Any questions?"

Zynka shook her head and drew her eidolon. As it formed into her large black war hammer, Noctharim flourished a wing. A cloud of smoke appeared a dozen yards ahead. When Zynka's weapon was fully formed, a large azure-skinned troll rushed out of the smoke. He carried a large mace and tower shield and was clad in dented black plate armor.

"Let's go, ya blue bastard!" Zynka roared as she charged, war hammer held firmly in her trunk.

When they closed, she had to dodge under a powerful horizontal mace swing, but she was caught in the side of the head by a quick push of Jotun's shield. She fell back, shaking away the white light that flashed in her eyes. Jotun pressed his advantage and took a large kick at her midsection. Zynka swung the hammer and connected with his shin. The sound of metal on metal rang through the plain. The impact seemed to knock the troll off balance, but instead, he used the momentum to throw the edge of his shield into Zynka's gut. She hit a knee and tried to swiftly catch her breath. Jotun gave her no time as he sent a large overhand swing with his mace down at her. She raised her hammer at the last second, blocking some of the force and redirecting the blow to her shoulder. There was a loud pop, and Zynka cursed as she rolled backwards to avoid a follow-up.

"What a dick."

She tried and failed to roll her left shoulder. Wincing, she again stood and stared down Jotun. The troll moved his club in a figure eight pattern as he approached.

"You may always yield, pachyderm," he said frigidly.

Zynka cast her eyes about.

*I can't win straight up. Cheat.*

She noted the azure grass went up to her mid-thigh. She smiled wide as the War Master got in range. Without warning, she sent a forceful kick right into Jotun's groin. Caught off guard by the quick action and the sudden hammering pain in his stomach, Jotun fell to his knee. Zynka took the pause to throw herself into the tall grass. She utilized a part of her ability that was never really relevant, and the grass, rather than being flattened by her bulk, grew around her, erasing her imprint. The War Master bellowed and began slamming his mace randomly, using his shield to scythe the grass.

*Sneaking, sneaking, just keep sneaking.*

Zynka snaked around the rampaging troll.

"You dirty, filthy cheater!" Jotun kept yelling as he tried to erase the grass from existence.

Zynka was trying extremely hard not to laugh at his rage. She kept worming around him until his swings became softer and more pushed by gravity than muscle. On one last swing, the War Master was spent; no longer could he raise the mace. Zynka took that moment to silently rise up behind him and, with full extension of her trunk, slammed the war hammer into the back of Jotun's head. He disappeared in a mist of black smoke.

"Very good, very good," the fake headmaster cheered. "Highly entertaining. Also, I got a message from the real me. Jotun is none too pleased about the low blow, but commends the win. As I said, very good." Zynka smiled, and smiled wider when the pain in her shoulder disappeared.

"I do believe we call that a pass on Stealth and Combat. Yes, both were commendable," Noctharim said with cheer as he did lazy barrel rolls. "Now how about we move into Energy?"

Zynka shook her head immediately, Noctharim cocked his head curiously.

"Yeah, I don't do the whole energy thing. Not really in my bag of tricks," she said dismissively with a small shrug.

"Well...I actually do not know how to respond to that." He did a few quick rolls and landed deftly on a tall blade of grass. "I suppose it is not technically a requirement."

"There are requirements?"

"Hmm. Well, I mean, yes...and no, really. As you know, everything at Aetherion is based on consent, so if there is something you don't want to do, you don't have to. Hmm." The fake professor's eyes went blank for a few long moments.

Zynka took this opportunity to munch another trunkful of

grass. In the calm, she noticed that the grass slightly resembled the mixture of sweet and salty popcorn she had grown to love.

"Hmph. The 'real' me is quite unhelpful. I inquired about my next steps, and he found it very humorous. Apparently, 'this group has provided more entertainment and new situations, and I love it,' was his, oh so helpful, response." The fake headmaster gnawed on his wing. His eyes went blank again for a moment.

"I bet those pines taste good," Zynka said, walking to the edge of the clearing.

She plucked a few of the needle-like leaves. Tossing them in her mouth, she salivated instantly. It tasted like a mix of steak and potatoes Jayce had let her try. "Yum!"

The sound of beating wings drew her attention to Noctharim. He landed on her delicious tree.

"So, Noctharim, the real one, has made a call. If you do not wish to participate in the Energy test, that is fine; however, that will mean you cannot participate in the classes for that subject."

"Works," Zynka said, unbothered.

The fake headmaster sighed.

"Very well. Would it be acceptable to you if we moved into Mysticism?" he asked in a ruffled manner.

Zynka gave an overexaggerated and gracious bow.

"Very well. The trial is to reach a platform. The way, however, is not how one would expect. I shall send you, and you may begin." With a flourish of a wing, Zynka felt herself lifted and pushed through a claustrophobic abyss.

When the world materialized around her, she stood in a large chasm. She looked ahead and saw a platform half a mile away. The path was unobstructed. She looked around and saw nothing but a rock face on either side of her. She again looked at the platform and took a step forward. As her foot landed, she felt herself pushed back to exactly where she started.

"The hell?" she muttered as she took another step.

Again, she felt herself pushed back. She tried jumping forward, a difficult task given her size, but again, as her feet hit the ground, she was back where she started.

"Hmm. So, I can't go straight."

She looked at the rocky walls, then took a step towards them, making sure not to go farther forward than her starting point. She grinned at not being pushed back. Following her don't-move-forward-motif, she made it to the wall. It was smoother than she had originally assumed. No real hand holds. She sucked on her trunk and stared at the surface.

"Brute force it is."

She grabbed her eidolon with her trunk. When it formed, she took a massive swing, the impact threw crushed rock and dust into the air. What remained was a large crater she could fit her hand in. She took another swing and made another. With a satisfied grin, she lifted herself with both hands.

"Okay, I might need to start working out," she said as she felt gravity fighting her. With both hands in the craters, she swung her hammer and created another one.

She repeated the process unperturbed by the setback loop for twenty minutes. By the time she was within ten yards, her shoulders burned, and the hammer's impact was severely lessened. Still, she struggled through it. The last few yards felt like they took as long as the last half mile did. When she finally dropped to the platform, she collapsed. She tried to take deep breaths through her trunk to steady herself.

"Well. That was not the way the test was supposed to be done," the fake Headmaster said, landing on her heaving chest.

"H...h..." Zynka panted.

Noctharim summoned a blue syringe of pure energy.

"May I revitalize?"

Zynka nodded, and the syringe melted into her ear canal. Her breathing instantly slowed, and her fatigue faded away.

"Thank you, sir. How was it supposed to be done?"

"You didn't look behind you," he said admonishingly. With that, Zynka was pushed back the half mile and landed at the starting position. She turned around, and her face dropped.

"Damn it," she said as she stared at the platform, not forty yards behind her.

"The lesson? Sometimes it is okay to move backwards...you know what? Whatever. Engineering." With his words, they were whisked back to the azure grass plain. The only difference from the time they had left was that there was a small altar with something metallic on it.

"Disable the bomb," the fake headmaster said shortly.

"Did I pass the last—"

"Yes. Bomb," the fake Noctharim replied briskly.

Zynka shoved her trunk in her mouth to stifle a laugh. Striding to the altar, she examined the bomb. It had a timer that read three minutes and was counting down. It had red, blue, green, and yellow wires going from the triggering device to the presumed explosive.

"Okay, the red wire goes there. Blue to that thingy. Yellow loops back to itself. Green goes to that cannister?" she mumbled as she traced the wires. Two minutes.

"What would Cali do?" Zynka questioned and heard a feral voice in her head.

"Hit it with a hammer." She smiled at the gremlin's voice playing in her skull.

Without any more thinking, Zynka pulled her eidolon. It formed as the timer reached one minute. With a swift horizontal swing, the triggering device was broke free from the explosive. She flinched and squinted against what she thought was an explosion, but was just a green smoke that formed the words:

*Congratulations to Aetherion Academy's newest student. The step from initiate to student is no small feat. Be proud of what you have accomplished.*

"At this point, I don't even know why the real me put me here. Good job and all that," the fake professor said, clearly perturbed.

Zynka let out an amused trumpet and couldn't stop her shoulders from shaking.

"Thank you, Pro—"

"Enjoy school."

Then the world went black.

"It is our time to play." Artemis.
"Let us direct." Two.
"Dis gon' be good." Anansi.
"Enjoy." Odin

# CHAPTER TWENTY-NINE

Cali, once through the void, found herself suspended midair at the intersection of Staples and South Padre Island Drive in Corpus Christi.

"What the hell?" she asked when she tried to move, but couldn't.

She looked around, noticing it must be rush hour as the traffic was at a standstill. The car horns blew loudly and mixed with the sound of passing gulls, which didn't seem to notice her. She breathed in the salt air and, despite her situation, sighed happily.

"Salty wind is a blessing, is it not?" a voice said next to her.

Cali snapped her head around and saw a gorgeous woman with chestnut hair tied in braids. Her sharp facial features were flawless. She wore browned hunting leathers, a pair of sturdy leather boots, a quiver hanging from her belt, and a large recurve bow around her shoulder.

"Artemis?" Cali asked, trying not to let her voice waver.

*That is a freaking not-god!*

The figure nodded.

"I am known by that here. The Greeks gave me that name, and I do adore it. I have watched this city before, but have never been here myself. It is lovely, is it not?" Artemis asked, taking in the view.

Cali, despite herself, looked around and smiled.

"It is home. Where is home for you?" Cali couldn't think of a reason not to talk to the not-god.

"Troy, not the one in Turkey. They stole that one."

"Like the movie with Brad Pitt?"

The not-god chuckled.

"More or less. I rather enjoyed that film. The abdominal muscles," Artemis purred.

Cali giggled, then stopped, realizing the absurdity of the situation.

"Why are you here?" Cali asked.

"I wanted to be the one to do your exam. I see such potential in you, but I also see what is holding you back. While we are here, I will show you what I see and, in turn, how you may correct it to be a better you," Artemis said seriously, then added. "What is going to happen here is not going to be fun for you. It will hurt more than anything you have been through."

Artemis nodded at Cali's two prosthetic fingers and foot and the place where her ring and middle finger should have been. Cali looked down.

"Damn it all. Got busy watching a movie and I forgot to build new fingers," she sighed.

Artemis laughed sympathetically.

"Don't worry, love. There will be no need for them here. I will say, watching your little team is quite funny. The face-palm in the wasteland had me howling."

Cali was about to retort before remembering what was happening, then did it anyway.

"Oh, shut up. Like you never did anything dumb. I didn't have to go into hiding for billions of years."

Artemis only chuckled louder.

"We were not in hiding. We were merely done walking ourselves, and Odin asked me to be the 'director' of his show. If you can see anything, why would you ever leave?"

"Well...wouldn't that kind of be like sitting in a living room watching TV and waiting to die?"

"In a different sense, yes. However, being immortal, you really do have the time to laze about," Artemis countered.

Cali bit her bottom lip in thought. "Fair," was all she could come up with.

Artemis looked around and nodded.

"Know that I don't do this for pleasure. I really do see potential. But it is time."

With Artemis' last words, Cali felt that she could no longer speak. Opening her mouth to try, only air escaped. Her eyes went wild, shooting a piercing glare at Artemis.

"Young woman. This is a time to use your eyes and your ears. Let us go." With that, Artemis clutched Cali's arm softly and flew her to the entrance of the La Palmera Mall. They landed in front of the sliding doors and walked in. The A/C was a godsend that both women basked in momentarily. Then Cali's blood froze. A tear fell from beneath her eyepatch.

"Dad, please! Please, please, please! I swear I will do all my chores now and forever! Kayley has one, and we could play together without you having to drive us." A small, blonde pig-tailed child pestered her tall, red-haired father as the short, beautiful blonde mother held the daughter's hand.

"Kiddo, I just don't know if you are old enough for a tablet. Call me old-fashioned, but there is plenty to do outside. You could skate with your sister," the father said with no real conviction.

Cali stared at the group, tears running freely. She mouthed "You don't need it."

"Oh, come on, honey. It ain't the 90s anymore. This is how kids connect. Plus, I heard from Brenda that you can put locks and limits on them." The mother looked at her small child and winked.

The father gave a fake sigh and headed into the electronics store with his family.

"Here is the first instance you blame yourself, yes?" Artemis asked.

Cali nodded, tears still streaking her face.

"I wanted you to see this because you are wrong with your assumption of guilt. Your father brought you here to get you the tablet. You convinced him of nothing."

Cali could only sniffle. Time sped up, and Artemis and Cali found themselves in the back of a minivan, the blonde girl in a booster, her parents up front.

"Can we open it now? If we do, I can have it set up before we get home. There is a painting app. It shows it here on the box... see?" Young Cali shoved the box into her father's lap.

He pulled out a knife and removed the plastic film. He pulled the tablet out and handed it to her.

"Does it use a USB-C?" he asked her.

"Umm." Young Cali hummed as she turned the tablet this way and that. "Ovalish."

"Don't plug it in!" Cali wanted to scream, but was still unable. She reached for the tablet, but her hand phased through it.

"This isn't for changing. This is for healing," Artemis said. "You did not make him plug it in. That was his choice alone." Cali heard the words, but they rolled off like water off a duck.

"Here ya go, kiddo," the father said, handing a long charging cord. Young Cali grabbed it, inserted it, and smashed the power button. A chime sounded as the manufacturer's logo populated the screen. Young Cali squealed.

"Thank you, thank you, thank you, Daddy."

"Chopped liver over here, I guess," the mother said in a mock offense.

"Sorry, love you, Momma," Young Cali said happily.

The grown Cali felt her heart break as her father put the car in reverse and left the parking space. To Cali, it felt there was nowhere near enough air to survive in the van. She began sweating as her father merged onto South Padre Island Drive.

"The art app is kick-ass...I mean... really cool," Cali quickly corrected.

"Damn it, Erin," her father laughed. "You get a freebie on that one. I'm glad you like it...learn to drive, dickhead!" he shouted as he was cut off.

"Yeah, blame Erin," her mother laughed.

The grown Cali laughed. It was a physically painful laugh as the pain of knowing the outcome versus the joy of seeing her parents smiling waged a war inside her that could have no winner. Her father sped up to get around a fender bender.

"I swear this town has the worst drivers," the mother said, shaking her head. Cali forced herself to keep her eyes open.

"Dad, look," the young Cali said, shoving her tablet forward.

"I can't, baby, I'm driving," her father said, changing lanes.

"He can see it when we get home," Cali said, wordlessly. A pleading aura surrounded the car.

"But I drew a really cool dog, maybe like one we could get." Young Cali said, pushing the tablet farther forward.

Cali closed her eyes and then opened them. Her father turned to look as her mother screamed. At 55 miles per hour, their minivan slammed into a semi that had just been in a wreck. The trailer compacted the front of the van. The windshield shattered, sending bullet-like glass shards through the vehicle. The real Cali felt the glass rip through her younger self. She saw her father's head bounce off the steering wheel with a dull thud and a crack. Her mother was thrown headfirst into the trailer and landed on the mangled hood, her head lying at an unnatural angle. Young Cali's arm snapped as she threw it up to brace on the seat in front of her, and the world for the young Cali went dark.


"Here is the point where you truly blame yourself. This is where your potential falters. Your father did not have to look. Your mother could have worn her seat belt. The driver of the semi didn't have to fall asleep. There are so many variables that could have been different, and none of them have to do with a nine-year-old girl," Artemis said with finality.

Cali heard the words but could not look away from the devastation that was her old family car and her parents. Now it was just mangled metal and two bloody heaps that she loved so much. Cali tried to speak, but still didn't have access to words.

"I am again very sorry, Cali. We are not done," Artemis said as time sped past.

Cali saw her interaction with Erin at the hospital. In court, where Erin fought and won custody of her. The cost of the court was extravagant. Erin had to sell almost everything they owned, minus their parents' mortgaged house, but she won. Time went by and then stopped abruptly.

Young Cali was almost eleven and sat at the table waiting for Erin to get home. It was past midnight when her sister walked through the door.

"Cali, what are you doing up?" Erin asked, tiredly setting down her purse and taking off her club nametag.

Cali looked at her sister, run down and ragged. She had picked up a waitress job after dropping out, and when that wasn't enough, had taken to being a server at a local strip joint. The money was good, but Cali knew it ate at Erin; well, now she did.

"I wanted to see if you wanted to eat dinner. I made ramen with an egg like you like," Young Cali said, making a gagging sound.

Erin smiled and got the bowl out of the microwave.

"What about you?" she asked, taking a bite of slightly warm, slightly crunchy noodles.

Cali smiled.

"I fried up some Spam. I'm good," Cali replied cheerily.

Erin returned the gag. They sat there as Erin crunched through her food. Erin knew Cali wanted to ask something, but was holding back. Knowing it was Cali's birthday on Saturday, she knew the young girl wanted a birthday party.

"Hey, if you could do anything for your birthday, what would it be?" Erin asked, trying to sound hopeful.

Young Cali looked anywhere but at Erin.

"Don't leave her. This is where you break her." Cali fought every bit of magic, trying to be heard. She shook furiously as though that would express her point.

"I-I uh, just wanted to make you dinner. Night, Sis," Young Cali said as she got up, kissed Erin's head, and walked to her room, eyes full of tears.

Erin dropped the spoon in the bowl.

"Shit," Erin muttered.

Cali knew then and now that Erin had done everything possible to keep a semblance of normalcy, but she wasn't ready to be a mother. Cali stared at her sister as her familiar hidden tears dropped into her cooling soup.

"This birthday is gonna be a good one," Erin whispered, resignation in her voice.

Cali again felt her heart break.

Time sped up to the next night; this time, though, they watched Erin, and not the young Cali. Erin walked through the seedy strip club with two beers in her hands. The dancers spun lazily for the Wednesday night "crowd", which consisted of a fat, bearded trucker putting quarters on the table and a man in a suit with slicked-back hair. She set the first beer with the suit-man and walked to the trucker.

"That'll be four fifty, sir," Erin said with her best smile. The trucker looked up and smiled a smile with not as many teeth as a person should have. He handed her a ten.

"Sit a spell?" he asked genuinely. Erin looked around for an excuse. Not finding one, she sat and smiled. "What's a pretty girl like you doing serving beers in a shit hole like this to dirtbags like us?" He gestured to himself and the sleezy-looking businessman.

"It's a job, and I have a mortgage," Erin replied, all smiles.

"I'm Earl." He extended a grease-covered hand.

"Erin," she replied, returning the surprisingly sweet handshake.

"Not a dancer?"

"Oh god no. I have fallen watching the girls dance." She laughed.

"Hey, beer girl! Need another," the sleezy man called.

"She's got a name, asshole," Earl hollered.

"It's fine. Thank you for not being a jerk," Erin told him as she stood and went to the bar. She returned to the table with the beer.

"About time. Thought I'd die of thirst before you got here," he said, placing a five in her hand. He pulled out a twenty and added it to her hand before releasing her.

"Thank you, sir." She smiled politely and turned to leave.

"Having to pay a mortgage at your age must be difficult." The sleezy guy said. Erin froze.

*Here comes another proposition.*

Cali watched in shock at the next scene.

"I get by," Erin said, willing her feet to move, but she was rooted.

The man got up and walked right behind her.

"Pretty girl like you could make a lot of money here doing... extracurriculars."

"Get out. Run!" Cali again fought the binding magic. The futility of it caused her body to go limp.

"How much?" Erin asked, stone-faced, still looking away.

"Hundred and fifty for some head."

A tear fell down Erin's face. The man put his arm around Erin's shoulder and guided her towards the men's room. Cali started thrashing against nothing. Her silent screams falling into oblivion. The door closed behind them, and time sped up again. Cali caught a quick glimpse of Erin leaving the bathroom in tears, wiping at her lips. Cali's fury reached a crescendo.

"Enough!"

Her words not only shattered her verbal bonds but also the memory itself. The fractured scene fell to a solid white abyss.

The only thing remaining was a furious Cali and a dumbstruck Artemis. Cali spun on the not-god and shoved her hard. The surprise knocked Artemis back more than the force. She put her arms up to stop another shove.

"Cali, I showed you that not to hurt you or to think less of Erin—" Artemis started. Anger raged in Cali's blue eye.

"Think less? You think that would make me think less of her? That woman gave everything to me!" Cali snarled.

Artemis smiled.

"Yes. Erin *gave* everything to you," Artemis said hotly. "Never once did you take. That is what I am trying to show you. You think what you did, what you said, or what you didn't say led to any outcome for anyone. It didn't. Shitty choices made in shittier situations. That is what happened. You didn't cause it." The not-god breathed in, then ended softly. "You didn't cause any of it."

Cali cried harder than she had ever let herself, her shoulders shaking and snot freely flowing.

"You have seen what you needed to see. If you ever need anything, Troy's gates will open for you," Artemis said, placing a hand on Cali's head.

And the world went black.

## CHAPTER THIRTY

"Urgh," Leon groaned as he rolled over. His eyes shot open as he realized he floated in a white void.

"What the hell?" he questioned, trying to see anything in the blinding abyss.

He rubbed his face to rouse himself and stopped dead. Both of his hands were flesh. He blinked rapidly as he flexed his unfamiliar left hand. "Weird." Looking over his arm, he realized he wasn't wearing his normal silky black tank top. Instead, he was in his old digicam uniform. He looked down at his chest and saw the three chevrons and a rocker of a staff sergeant.

"Never made it that far," he muttered, shaking his head.

"What rank did you achieve?" a disembodied voice bounced around the void.

Leon snapped into a ready stance, made difficult by the fact that there was no ground. He remained silent, listening for movement that didn't come.

"What rank did you achieve?" the voice repeated. Leon, still seeing nothing, also saw no reason not to answer.

"I was a corporal." He tried to calm his breathing.

*Fire fights, fine. Explosions suck, but sure. Disembodied voice from hell? I'm out.*

Leon waited for a response. There was a grunt.

"A man-at-arms. More or less. Trusted to lead a few. Barred from leading many." The voice seemed to explain it to himself. "Tell me, soldier, what was your occupation?"

"Infantry," Leon replied proudly.

"Hmmm. A foot soldier. A 'door kicker' as you might say. I, too, started as an 'infantryman.' Oh, how I do miss the days of responsibility being on others' shoulders." The voice was almost nostalgic.

"Yeah, show up on time in the right uniform, and you're set. Now who are you?" Leon's question had a mild frustration tinged with fear.

"I am known by your group as Two. Ridiculous. Not even a real name. For now, just know I am the dragon's head and will be conducting a combat trial," the dragon's head replied.

"Why? And why am I a staff sergeant?"

"Because should the time ever arise where we find each other on a battlefield, likely thanks to Odin, I want you to be able to hold a fight worthy of legend," the voice boomed. "You are wearing that rank as your first test will be on a raid. You will be the senior field soldier. I will give you the mission, and it will be up to your discretion to accomplish it. Very simple. You will have your old squad."

*Follow orders, easy enough.*

"I can do that; doubt I really have a choice."

He shook his shoulders to get loose.

"There is always a choice to be made," the voice said as a room quickly formed around Leon.

He found himself standing in a briefing room. One large, round, white plastic table with ten chairs, nine of which were filled; paper was strewn across it. A large screen with a map of a small compound was on a wall. The rest of the dark room was bare.

"Hey, Sarge. What's good?" a black man around Leon's age asked. His name tag read Childers, and his rank was corporal.

"I don't know. What do we got?" he asked the soldier.

Childers rifled through some papers until he found what he

was looking for. "Small compound. Intel says eight to ten tangos. Light arms. Maybe explosives—"

"Maybe? What kind of intel is that?" Leon snapped, his soldiering coming back into him.

Childers shrugged.

"Hey, Sarge, this is what M.I. gave me. Not a lot to go on, but it's what we got. Oh"—he flipped a few pages—"looks like we have hostages. Four. Zynka, Jayce Torres, Erin, and Cali Walker."

Leon's heart caught in his chest.

*Are they simulations? The real ones? Treat it as real. You are not allowed to lose again.*

His face lost its normal softness, replacing it was hard facial lines. "Who's demo?" he asked.

"Yo." A slightly overweight, mid-aged white man with a fiery mustache raised his hand. Specialist Donahue.

"Thoughts on entry?"

"Dump some boom on the front door and go kaboom?" the specialist questioned.

Leon chuckled; demo guys were some of the smartest he knew, but damn, could they be thick.

"What do you need from draw?" Leon continued.

"P equals plenty. Don't worry about it, I'll get what I need and steal what I want," Donahue said and leaned back.

Leon loved this man.

"Next. We got overwatch?"

"PFC Villanueva, Sergeant," a slight Mexican teen said. "I got you." There was a cold hint in his voice that made Leon feel warm.

Smiling, Leon continued.

"Commo?"

"Private Johnston, Sergeant," a small, weathered man said. Leon looked him over with instant recognition.

"Not your first time being a private?"

Johnston chuckled.

"Or the second," the soldier replied.

Leon nodded. The thing he learned about his time in the

military was that busted down soldiers fell into two camps: competent as hell but couldn't play the game, or epic dirtbags. He got the feeling that the first was more accurate.

"Weapons?" he moved on.

"We have Specialist Stone on the two-forty." Childers nodded to the largest black man Leon had ever seen.

*Rashad...*

Leon fought back a tear seeing his old best friend.

Stone gave a large smile, then returned to playing with what would be a machete to a normal man.

"Private Greenly runs the two-four-nine," Childers continued pointing to a medium-build white man with a heavy, blonde five o'clock shadow. Greenly waved excitedly, went red, and looked away.

"First time going outside the wire, Private?"

"Yes, sir. Shit. I mean, Sergeant," the soldier replied, twitching.

"You have one task. If we all are aiming one way, do the same. Got it? Also, don't worry about "sir." Sergeant is correct, but in here, as long as you don't call me asshole, we're good," Leon said with a smile.

Greenly let out a forced laugh.

"Roger, Sergeant."

A low alarm went off, the team stood quickly and, with practiced precision, fell out of the room. When Leon exited the door, the heat from the Middle Eastern summer hit him like a Mack truck. Sweating in an instant, Leon remembered one of his least favorite parts of his deployment. The squad gathered around two Humvees.

"Gather round. Quick safety brief," Leon ordered. The squad quickly formed a semi-circle around him.

"Our intel is shit. So going in, we gotta stay loose, boys. They have hostages, so let's stay black as long as we can. ROE states —" Leon was cut off.

"That it isn't a war crime the first time?" Stone said in a serious baritone.

Despite the interruption, Leon chuckled. The rest of the squad joined in except for Greenly.

"Hell, y'all know the rules. Don't shoot civies. If you shoot anyone, they better have had a gun or a really mean look in their eyes. If we get separated, don't die. Seriously, the rally point will be fifty meters west of the front gate. If you get bogged down, hunker, call for fire, and Johnston will call the gods in, yeah?"

"Gods, angels, demons, hell, the devil himself. Call out, and I got ya," Johnston stated.

"Villanueva—" Leon started.

"Heard, Sergeant," the soldier replied. Leon nodded satisfactorily. Without another command, the group condensed into a tight huddle.

"Til Valhalla, brothers," Childers said.

"Til Valhalla," the squad replied.

Leon also said it, though now he knew or was pretty sure those words didn't hold the meaning they once did. The squad broke up into teams and went to the trucks. Leon rode as TC for the front truck. Childers drove, Villanueva on the turret-mounted fifty. Donahue and Stone in the rear.

"Thirty out," called Childers over the squad freq as they pulled out the main gate.

Leon leaned over and nudged him.

"Shit, I forgot to ask. Route clearance?"

"All good. Swept yesterday," Childers responded. Leon sat back and breathed a sigh of relief.

*That could've sucked. Tighten up, asshole.*

A low piano began to play from the backseat, the opening to the original Bad Company. Leon turned and saw Donahue holding a portable speaker. The soldier gave Leon a grin.

"Got a nerve calming playlist, good?"

"Good," Leon replied and let the song wash over him.

Over the course of the drive, the playlist was banger after banger to Leon. After the first song, it went into "Don't Fear the Reaper," followed by Nazareth's "Hair of the Dog," then "Freebird." Leon made Donahue throw in "That's Texas" by

Cody Johnson. They were trying to decide the final song when they hit the five-minute mark. They had decided to park a few miles out so as not to give away the mission that easily. The actual argument fell into mother jokes, manhood comparisons and bodily insults between Leon, Donahue, and Childers. Four minutes out, and Stone quietly wrenched the MP3 player from Donahue's hand. A minute later, the drum beat and pipes known to all of them started, and their focus on the task to come returned. "March of Cambreadth" by Heather Alexander was near sacred to Leon. Before every mission in the real world, he would play it as a reminder not to quit.

"Good choice," Leon said, trying not to show he was on the verge of choking up. He hadn't listened to that song since the day of his last mission. He unconsciously flexed his left hand.

As the song faded out, Childers pulled off the dirt road and parked behind a small rocky hill. Villanueva grabbed a long black case and headed off into the heat without a word. The rest dismounted and met by the front of the bumper. Greenly was in full twitch at this point.

"Private, I am going to need you to tone back them nerves by like ten," Leon ordered, half joking, half serious.

"Hooah, Sergeant," Greenly replied, zero nerve change.

Johnston busted out with a laugh.

"Hooah, Sergeant? Fuckin' boot," he said, getting a chuckle from the group.

Leon shared the laugh. After a moment, his face went hard.

"Lock it up. It's game time. Stone, Donahue, and Johnston with me. Childers, you have the rest. We are gonna take this slow. My team will take the east gate. You and yours take the north. We will avoid the main gate. Keep the squad freq free and clear. Team chatter to a minimum. Command freq for any mission-related questions. Questions, comments, concerns?"

The group had shifted from joking young men to stone-faced killers. There were no questions.

"Grab your rucks. Weapons on yellow. Let's do the dance, boys."

Weapons yellow referred to having a round in the chamber but the rifle on safety; this prevented accidental discharge during the march. Leon, putting actions to words, went to the rear of the truck and grabbed a large ruck sack full of ammo, food, and miscellaneous gear. He then pulled out an M4, slotted a magazine in it, and jacked a round. After assuring it was on "safe", he wrapped the carry strap around his elbow and took a position, waiting for the team. Donahue was the first to join him. The soldier was even more weighted down than Leon.

"Light infantry, my left nut," Donahue complained. He wasn't wrong either; "light" infantry would regularly carry rucksacks of seventy to a hundred-and-twenty pounds.

"Good training."

The rest of his team gathered, and he split them into an offset wedge. Against normal conventions, he took point. Stone with the 240 on the left; Johnston, then Donahue on the right.

"Regulators. Let's ride," he called out as he set a brisk pace to the east.

The march took about twenty minutes until they got their first glimpse at the compound. The map had not done it justice. There was a building on each of the four corners and a central building that resembled a small mansion.

"Childers," Leon sub-vocalized through the mic.

"Yeah. I see it. What do we think?" the soldier responded.

"Hostages are more than likely in the central building. Sun is going down. Hunker down. Wait for true dark."

"Check, rog," Childers signed off.

"V?" Leon called over the radio.

"In position."

"Keep me updated on rotations."

There were two clicks on the mic as a response. He had his team spread out and staying low.

When the sun fell below the horizon, Leon roused his team. Donahue had fallen asleep. The response to anxiety came in many forms and, while not excited, Leon understood this one.

"Wake up, fat ass," he said as he lightly kicked Donahue's gut.

The larger soldier rolled, let out a slight groan, and got to his feet.

"I was in a mountain cabin with Christina Ricci. Could've given me a few minutes," the soldier mock complained.

"A few minutes? You like to cuddle?" Stone's baritone said quietly. Donahue gave him the finger.

"Game faces," Leon said stoically. He formed them up again before reaching out to Childers.

"Ready?"

"Approaching. Callout for ready," the reply came.

Leon nodded to his guys, and they began an agonizingly slow march to the western gate. When they were within three hundred meters, he ordered them into a low crawl. The pace was slowed significantly as they drug themselves across the rough ground. They arrived at the small wooden gate and lined up around it. Leon, then Stone on the left; Donahue, then Johnston on the right.

"In position," he said quietly into the radio.

"We have some movement outside the gate. Looks like one tango—" Childers started as the sound of a 249 firing went off. "Shit. Greenly got froggy," a hurried response came; with it the sky brightened with the flash of multiple rifles firing. The cacophony of shooting was deafening.

"Breach it!" Leon yelled unnecessarily at Donahue, who was already planting a shape charge. They took a dozen steps back.

"Fire in the hole!" Donahue called as he detonated it.

The force of the charge splintered the wooden gate inward, the layout of the explosive minimizing the back blast. Without needing orders, Donahue charged in, skirting the left wall. Then Leon went in, skirting the right. Johnston followed Donahue, and Stone followed Leon.

Leon followed the wall and stopped when he reached the first building and scanned the central plaza. He saw a man with a rifle in the window of the central building firing north. A quick burst from Stone silenced him.

"Greenly down," Villanueva said.

Leon noted it and continued his move to the building. He was at its door now. Stone, not waiting for an order, booted the door and Leon entered left, scanning the wall, then turning inward. He saw a shooter stick his head out of a side door and ended him with two rounds. Stone was about to take a shot at another target, but held back when he saw it was an unarmed woman. Time slowed as Leon saw the seemingly grateful woman run open-armed to Stone. He noticed too late that the tears in her eyes were not thankful. She wrapped her arms around Stone, and Leon's world went white.

He awoke a minute later, his ears ringing so loud that it disoriented his thoughts. The wall with the door now had a clear opening to the outside. The room itself was a violent shade of crimson.

"Shit," he groaned as he got back to his feet, looking much like a freshly birthed giraffe.

Muffled pops could be heard, but he couldn't determine the direction. He slowly wiped the blood from his eyes, not knowing if it was his, Stone's, or the woman's. Before he could regain any semblance of bearing, he felt his arms being wrenched behind his back. He was spun around and had a brief glimpse of a rifle's buttstock before it collided with his nose, sending another episode of white haze. The sound it made, more than the feeling, told him his nose was obliterated. He slumped to his knees, still restrained. Unconsciously, he moved his tongue around to dislodge the two front teeth that had been knocked loose and spat them along with a goblet of blood onto the ruined floor. He tried opening his eyes but shut them against the intense pain the small amount of light caused. Leon felt himself being dragged forward but had no power to resist. He was shoved onto his knees, and his head was pulled back by his hair.

"Leon," a small, familiar voice called out.

Embracing the suck, Leon opened his eyes and wished he

hadn't. Behind eight bloodied uniformed bodies were Jayce, Erin, Cali, and Zynka; all on their knees with a rifleman behind each of them. His tears burned like magma.

"I'm sorry," he croaked. The riflemen all chambered a round and put their rifles to the back of each of the girls' heads. Cali looked at him; her eyes touched with fear. With a bang, the world went white again.

"That did not go well for you," the dragon's head said as Leon was returned to the void.

The pain was gone, but the horror of the situation clung to Leon. He was hyperventilating. He tried and failed to control himself. The look on Cali's face would haunt him for his eternity.

"What could you have done differently? What would you do now that you didn't?" the voice asked in the void.

Leon couldn't answer. His hands shook with such ferocity that he was concerned they would come off. He tried to steady his breathing, but failed.

*You lost. Again.*

"Were—were they—simulations?" he choked out.

"Naturally. The show ends when the cast dies. I asked what you would do differently." The voice's voice was tinged with frustration. "I forget what death means to the young."

"Greenly. He should have been on my team or left off the mission. We could have dropped the rules of engagement. That would have saved Stone," Leon said shakily.

"Why did you not gather intelligence? The information given to you was incomplete."

"We had...to complete the mission?" Leon half asked.

"You did, yes. But there was no timeline. The only mission was the hostages."

Leon dropped his head. He had complained about that exact issue countless times, about the mission that cost him everything.

"I made the same mistake as my old commanders..." His eyes locked in on nothing in the distance.

"You did. It is a mistake many leaders make. The good ones

only make it once. Intelligence will win a battle every time. Be glad you made your mistake in a false scenario..." The voice trailed off. "Not all of us are as lucky."

Leon locked away the feeling of empathy for the disembodied voice. A red and black mist blinked quickly before coalescing into a large figure in front of Leon. Before him floated a nightmare. A being standing over a dozen feet tall, clad in thick black plate armor, with a large crown of gleaming daggers. The armor had scenes of battles inscribed over every inch. Its unarmored hands had talonlike fingers, sharp and deadly. Leathery red wings jutted wide out of his back. Finally, Leon made it to the creature's face. Dead, black eyes stared at him; sunken deep into a scaled, crimson face.

"Learn and learn well, young soldier. One day, we shall meet in battle. May a legend be born that day," the creature said and slowly turned.

The ice in Leon's veins tried to stop him from calling out.

"Who the hell are you?" he yelled, pain still evident in his words.

The creature spun and closed on Leon, its scaly nose scraping Leon's. "I am Alaric. Patriarch of Pendragon blood. Mark my name. Etch my face in your memory."

And the world went black.

# CHAPTER THIRTY-ONE

Dee-dee, deedle-dee-dee, dee-dee. The circus music roused Erin and she felt her face on a sticky pavement. The smell of funnel cakes and popcorn overwhelmed her senses. Shaking the grogginess from her head, she rose to her knees and looked around. The sight of a large red and white tent in front of her caused a double take.

"A circus?"

She looked around but outside of the tent there was only a void and a ticket stand. Without any other option, she hesitantly approached the booth. Her first glimpse inside made the hair on the back of her neck stand up. A large coiled green python in a barber pole vest was stationed inside. Its red eyes watched her hungrily. Finding movement impossible, Erin only stared.

"Come, Red One. Tickets are cheap to the Cirque L'échec Perpetuel, this evening," the python coaxed.

Erin's body felt heavy with the words, upset and grateful she had taken French in high school.

*Circus of perpetual failure?*

The python's eyes narrowed at her lack of movement.

"The show will happen whether you have a ticket or not," the creature snapped.

The distance between Erin and the booth closed in a

disorienting blur. Standing face-to-face with the snake, Erin found it even harder to concentrate. Snakes had never been creatures she had much cared for; *Anaconda* still gave her nightmares. Now being in front of a python that rivaled that one was petrifying. The snake's head went below the counter and came up with a four-by-six ticket that simply read "Admit One." It laid it on the counter and hissed.

"Enjoy the show."

With those words, the python and the booth vanished, and Erin found herself holding the ticket, staring at the closed flap of the big top tent. Her palms sweat as the flap slowly opened into darkness. There was a pull on her internal energies into the tent, like her power was being drawn inside. She shook herself, her black and pink sundress flowing with the movement. She took a deep, steadying breath and stepped in.

The lights blinded Erin as the room materialized around her. The roar of a crowd deafened her, and the scent of sweat and unwashed bodies threatened to cut off her sense of smell.

"Welcome to me Cirque, red one. Me are glad to be havin ya," a playful voice called out with a heavy patois accent.

Erin blinked away the light and saw the speaker in the middle of the main ring. His skin was almost obsidian; his hair was in thick, heavy dreads to his waist, and it was capped by an overly large top hat. The most eye-catching thing was that his red, with gold-tassels, ringleader's coat had six arms coming out of it. He looked like a grotesque man-tarantula hybrid. His face had eight humanoid eyes seemingly placed randomly on his face. His mouth was bordered by two pincer-like fangs. The image drove the breath out of her harder than any time she had biffed it on her skateboard. The creature relished her reaction.

"Yes girl, me be da big scary spider man. Dough I may not be the ting that troubles yu da most dis day."

Erin tried to speak, but even the air in her lungs was too afraid to exit. The creature smiled, its pincers clacking happily.

"Me been watching yu, girly. Yu tink yu can be savin da

world. Dat all de weight be on you. Good. Dat is wat me want to see t'day." There was a hint of playful malice.

"For dos dat don't be knowin me, I be da masta of ceremonies today, da keepa o' da stories, da weaver of de tales, de one, de only, Anansi."

The cheers from the unrealized crowd boomed so ferociously that it almost took Erin off her feet. The unsettling speaker sauntered to her. His slow, unbothered demeanor only heightened her sense of foreboding. When he was just feet in front of her, his height hit her. He stood just over eight feet tall. Anansi had to look down to meet her eyes, which only amplified the feeling of being dominated. One of his hands reached out and lifted her chin to make her focus on his face. Erin's eyes jumped all around his face, not knowing how to make eye contact.

"Come on me girl. Focus on de nose or we be spendin de whole time here," Anansi stated with mock frustration.

She did as she was told and focused on the small nose surrounded by three eyes; one blue, one green, and the other a deep brown. The figure nodded.

"T'day we be seein how ya do when ya can't save da world. For one test"—he gestured to one of the three rings on the ground—"we have da test o' mirras. Tru dat one be da lovely Cali, waitin' on her sista."

Erin went rigid at the mention of her sister. Anansi's smile grew, pincers again clacking with cheer.

"Tru de second ring, we have de trial o' de lost. Tru der be da warrior, Leon. Tru de main ring" —he pointed each arm that wasn't holding Erin's chin to the center ring—"true der be da lova, in der, we have da trial of da truth. Now I know what ya be tinkin, 'I be doin all da trials., But no, no, no mi fren. We ave but a small time togedda. Pick two and de tird be lost. Yu can pick wat ya want." Anansi walked back to the center ring, not looking back once.

Erin was crippled by choice. The sweat that had started in

her hands spread across her body like a wildfire. She was unbelievably hot, yet she couldn't shake the chill.

"Why-Why can't I do all three?" She thought she yelled, but the words barely left her lips.

Anansi smiled wider still.

"Ya want to be savin all? Den we have a deal to be made. I be given you all de time to do de two, but if ya want de tree, I be given you a timer. Tree hours. That is wat ya be avin." The spider had set the web, and Erin had walked into it. Erin shuddered; she knew she had made a wrong choice; she just didn't know how.

"Wen ya start da first test we be startin da time. So, girly, which be ya first?" The question was punctuated by the clack of pincers.

"Cali," Erin said with no hesitation.

"Den step right up, Red. One hour to complete da mirrors."

Erin, on shaky legs, approached the ring indicated. When she stood right on the precipice, the ring changed. A large structure shot out of the ground. It was completely made of highly reflective mirrors, with only a small door she would have to crawl through. She took another long, steadying breath and got on all fours. As her head breached the opening, Anansi called out.

"De time be startin!"

As the last bit of herself entered the house of mirrors, the atmosphere changed; Anansi's presence was gone, but the air was much more dense and oppressive. She crawled through the narrow passageway.

"That's a good girl. Crawl for Daddy," a familiar voice rang out in her head. She looked into the mirror and saw herself crawling to a man in a hotel chair.

*The first time.*

She watched herself slowly make her way across the floor. As she reached the man, the real Erin shook herself and pushed forward. Her body felt heavier as she continued.

"I don't really need it," Erin heard Cali's voice.

Looking at another mirror, Erin saw her and Cali at Wal-

Mart. Cali had picked up one of the model cars she loved. Erin remembered this. It was just shy of Cali's eleventh birthday. The car wasn't expensive by any means, but Erin had run thin this month due to her hours being cut at the restaurant she waitressed at. She remembered the shame of going into the strip club for an application.

"Really. I don't need it," Cali said to that version of Erin. Her voice was chipper, though Erin knew all too well how it hurt Cali to be the only one of her friends to go without.

There was never any resentment from the small child, but Erin remembered how it broke her own heart to ever have to say no to an unasked wish. The real Erin looked at her reflection and saw the shameful determination on her own face that led to the previous scene. She closed her eyes, a small watery droplet falling onto the mirror she crawled on.

"Yo E.Z., they saw the tape. They want us to come do some lines at their HQ. It's Friday, we goin'?" Erin heard the voice of Josh, her ex, and a member of her old skating crew.

She looked at that mirror and saw him at her front door. There he was, in baggy jeans and a black tee. And there she was, a floral-patterned sundress.

"They're coming to do a check on Friday. I've gotta make sure shit is perfect here if I wanna keep Cali," she replied.

"But, Miss Mom! This is our chance. We can't do it without you. That set you hit before ya biffed it is what got us in the door," Josh pleaded.

Erin saw her own internal struggle.

"Look, man, I think that part of my life is over. If I get hurt, I can't work. Cali needs someone to be an adult," Erin heard herself say, and then saw in the mirror something she never saw before. Behind her, peaking out of the hallway, was a nine-year-old Cali with tears in her eyes.

"No..." the real Erin muttered.

Cali was never supposed to know why she had quit her passion. And the fact that Cali just nodded to the lie of "I just didn't care for it that much," hurt more than Erin imagined it could have.

She forced herself to keep going until she could finally stand.

"The conditions here are less than satisfactory," she heard the CPS man say. Erin breathed heavily as soon as she heard the voice.

"No. Not this," she pleaded to nobody.

Instead of looking, she ran. Trying to get away, she ran straight into a mirror that knocked her down. The mirrored ground seemed to hold her there as the memory played.

"The refrigerator is damn near empty. The child has almost no toys. Why do you try to keep her when she could be so much happier elsewhere?" the man continued.

She saw herself, older and slightly ragged. This was maybe six months before Aetherion existed to her. She had been fighting back the government the best she could, but it was hard to hide her lack of a decent income.

"She's my sister. I will be the one to raise her, not some country club asshole with a savior fetish," her reflection stated hotly.

The man slightly recoiled.

"What have you been able to do for her? Since your parents died, it shows that Cali has not been affiliated with any after-school activity. No sports or clubs. And it also states you work at a restaurant six days a week and"—the man looked at his clipboard and scoffed—"a strip club six nights a week? Who is watching her?" the man asked pointedly.

Her reflection's face faltered before catching a subtle heat.

"There is no set age that states at what age she can be left alone. And you already asked her; she wants to stay."

The man got a greasy smile and a look in his eye that Erin had come to hate in men.

"Look, if I go back with my report as is, there is little chance the kid stays with you. However..." The man looked at her as no more than meat on a deli counter.

She saw her reflection making one of the dirtiest choices she had made. Yes, for rent, she had. For food, also yes. But as a tic-for-tat, she never understood why that hurt worse. The man advanced on her, pushing her into the small kitchen island. The real Erin fought the hold the ground had on her and sprang up. Before she ran, she again saw Cali watching from a hallway.

"No...Please, God, no."

The images in all the mirrors changed to an enraged Cali.

"I didn't know that I was being parented by a whore."

Erin's heart and the mirrored walls around her shattered into a million pieces.

Anansi looked at the ring where the house of mirrors had just disintegrated and saw Erin sobbing in the middle of it.

"Your hour be up on dat one."

Erin barely heard the spider's words over her sobs. Her shoulders shook so violently that it was agonizing. Years of the fear of being seen had just crashed into her with the violence of a stampeding bull.

"De time for da second trial be startin. Who be next?"

"L-Leon." The words caught her and Anansi off guard.

"Da warrior? Why not de lova next?" Anansi asked with the first real interest he had shown.

"Out of all of us, Jayce is the strongest. She doesn't know it, but she is." The conviction in her own words reassured her that she made the right decision.

The spider nodded and pointed to the other, smaller ring. Erin walked over to it and stepped in. The world disappeared.

The next moment, Erin felt sand between her bare toes. The sound of waves lapping the shore filled her ears. As she opened her eyes, she saw the slowly being reconstructed Bob Hall pier. She was back in what was once her happy place, North Padre Island. She looked around; the beach was empty, save for a motionless figure a dozen yards away, surrounded by beer cans and a cooler. After letting the salt air kiss her skin for a fleeting moment, she approached the figure. A large, tanned, and tattooed man lay with a towel over his face. By the thick muscles and missing arm, she knew it was Leon.

"L-Leon?" she asked unnecessarily.

The figure moved, his abs tensing in an altogether not unpleasant way. He moved the towel, revealing Leon's big, messy beard and untidy hair. But the eyes were different. Blood shot like the first day they met with none of the warmth they had acquired.

"What?" Leon snapped.

The tone made her recoil. He eyed her as though her mere presence offended him.

"It's me...Erin," she spoke in a soothing voice.

"Don't know her," Leon answered, reaching his nub to the cooler. "Damn it all!" he shouted and pulled a beer out with his good hand. He popped the top, drained it, tossed it, and grabbed another.

"What happened?" was all she could say or think.

This wasn't Leon. Not her Leon. Not the Leon that Cali loved.

"War happened," he said plainly. "What the hell do you want?" he barked at a now shaking Erin.

She opened her mouth, nothing came out, and she closed it.

*What the hell am I supposed to do here?*

Leon drained another beer and tossed the can with the other dozen or so. Grabbing another, he looked at the pity on her face.

"Oh, I get it. 'Oh, gotta help the cripple'. Get out of here with that bullshit."

"We can talk about it?" she half-whispered.

Leon let out a malicious laugh.

"Yeah, I came to the beach to tell a stranger shit I don't talk about with my therapists. Sounds like a grand ol' time," he spat.

*How do I help someone like this?*

Leon took another swig from his beer.

"You could very easily, and I really hope you do, leave me alone now," he said between sips.

Erin was at a loss. She knew this wasn't the real Leon, but she knew it was who he might have become without the group. The thought made her ache for him and this version of him. Biting her lip, she racked her brain for something, anything to do. She decided to sit next to him. He looked at her dismissively out of the corner of his eye.

"Sit with the freak? How noble," he spat again.

Erin held back a sharp retort and took a breath.

"You aren't a freak, Leon." The words came out softly, yet firm. He snorted into a fresh beer.

"Original. Let me guess. You've got a complex where you have to help someone to feel better about your own shit?" he called her out.

Erin wanted to reply to fight the accusation, but she couldn't disagree with any shred of honesty. So, she sat staring at the low rolling waves.

"Besides the savior complex next to me, this is a damn fine day," Leon said, eyes glinting.

"This was always my favorite place," Erin said, though she knew it would no longer be the case.

The waves no longer held the promise of hope they had. The sand could no longer scrub away the dead skin. So, for this last time, she let the atmosphere engulf her. The two sat silently.

Thirty minutes later, Leon pulled out the last of his twenty-four packs and popped the top.

"I appreciate what you wanted to do. But I think sometimes you are gonna find that you can't save everyone. And I think that's okay. Learn to live with that, and you'll be alright." He reached into the cooler. There was a metallic click, and this version of Leon looked at her.

"You're not gonna want to be here for this."

The world faded back into the ring at the Cirque D'Echec Perpetuel. Erin sat on the dirt floor and stared at Anansi's feet.

"Da hour ran out der too." His voice held compassion for the quivering woman.

Erin just stared. Her body shook, but didn't move.

"Was there a way I could have saved him?" she whispered.

"No, me girl. Some tings be out of ya hands."

His face was questioning if he pushed too hard. Erin nodded

slightly and shakily got to her feet. After a moment of steadying herself and wiping fresh and stale tears away, she stepped towards the center ring. Her footsteps were labored as she approached. Another failed attempt at a calming breath, and she stepped forward. Two large black hands grasped her left arm and spun her in place. She was face-to-chest with Anansi.

"Wat yu be doin, girl? Been tru enough, ave ya not?" His voice carried slight concern for the initiate.

She sniffled in return and looked over her shoulder at the ring. Anansi shook her.

"There...there's another trial."

"Ay, Red. Der always be anudda trial. No matta wat we do, der will always be anudda. Der neva be more den one of us." He again raised her chin to face him. "Be learnin to protect yaself, girly."

The weight of release played on her chest.

*Can I be someone that just stops? Is that me?*

She stared at the three-eye-surrounded nose. The pressure of years of unasked for responsibility came off of her as she gave the not-god a gentle nod.

And the world went black.

---

# CHAPTER THIRTY-TWO

---

Jayce's eyes opened to an oppressive white void with a lone figure a few yards ahead of her. The figure was clad in a cloak of white fur with a wide-brimmed grey hat. He held a large spear in one hand and there was a dark grey raven with milky eyes on his shoulder.

"Odin?" she asked cautiously. Her heart sped up in her chest. The figure nodded. "Why?"

Odin seemed to ponder her question.

"Why not, would be the answer I would give from the hip. However, I do believe my real answer should be that I am curious about another sculptor." He nodded to his own assessment. "It has been some time since another sculptor was brought to my attention."

Jayce fought against a flinch from his gaze. It felt like when Cali looked at her with her mechanical eye.

"You have great potential. Dangerous, but great." His tone held no malice, but an odd endearment.

"Are you going to kidnap me?" she let out before she could stop herself.

Odin looked amused.

"You know, many, many years ago, the answer would definitely have been yes. The stories on earth of me taking the worthy dead weren't truly false. I would indeed 'kidnap' walkers I deemed worthy. Some came willingly, others, not so much. I do believe my interim headmaster has continued that tradition; though, when I return, that may change. Willing students do make the best walkers."

Jayce looked at the not-god skeptically.

"So why come here? Why hijack my exam?" Her electric violet eyes returned his scan.

Again, Odin pondered.

"Have you received any actual training on sculpting? I will answer that myself; you have not. So that is why I am here. I want to see what your level of ability is," he said matter-of-factly.

Ice tried to creep into her veins. She sent a small course of energy through herself to clear it.

"Then why try to kill me?" she snapped.

"Kill you?" Confusion etched his wrinkled face.

"The Murdenex, the leviathan."

Odin chuckled.

"Those were never meant to kill you; though, there was the potential. But there is always a potential for death in the planes. Did the Murdenex not teach you to use your gift? Did the leviathan not teach you to take control of your past?" His gaze grew heavier on her.

She didn't reply, just stared back. For a long moment, they just stared at one another. Odin, a mentor's gaze; Jayce, a mixture of hate, fear, and, against her will, curiosity.

"We can either debate on the ins and outs of my methods, or we can use our short time to teach you your gift."

No question was asked, though an answer was demanded. With more hesitation than at any other time in her life, Jayce nodded slowly. Odin smiled and floated to her side.

"A basic thing to know about being one of us is that if time stops for one of us to sculpt, the other will not be frozen like non-sculptors would be." Putting action to words, Jayce felt the oppressive stillness and deafening heartbeat; only this time, there were two of them.

"We can start small," Odin said, raising his spear and drawing out a large throne-like chair. When the chair was roughly formed, time continued, and the jagged outline became a beautiful three-pointed throne with claw feet and felt armrests. Odin floated to it and sat down.

"A chair?"

Odin shrugged.

"I said we would start small. Would you like a better example of what we can do?"

"Yes," she replied with a hunger playing in her eyes.

"Very well."

From his seated position, he again raised his spear. Everything stopped once more. Odin drew a large sphere that felt like thousands of miles away. He spun the sphere, adding greens and blues to the outside of it. Jayce watched intently, sending energy to her eyes to amplify her vision. With one final spin, time resumed. The green and blue ball had become a slowly rotating sphere. Jayce looked at Odin, confused. When she saw his face, she flinched. Blood nearly gushed from under his eye patch and nose, though he looked unbothered by the situation.

"You never get over the fallout. You only get used to it," he said, his voice only slightly ragged.

She turned her attention back to the sphere, and her mouth dropped. With her energy-enhanced eyes, she saw it was not a sphere, but an oddly Earth-looking planet spinning in the void.

"How..." She didn't know how to end her sentence. Odin grinned, showing bloody teeth.

"It is wonderous when you first see it. I remember the awe when I was shown, and an even greater awe the first time I did it," he said with a heavy lacing of nostalgia.

Jayce just stared, even more dumbstruck when he said the first time.

"How many?" was all she could force out.

Again, Odin thought.

"Millions? More? I have not really kept track, and my memory" —he gestured towards the sickly raven—"is not what it used to be." With his words, he reached up and petted the pitiful bird, who seemed completely detached from any reality.

"Millions..." Again, she felt an overwhelming oppressive presence. "Earth?"

Odin waved his hand.

"No, that was there when we arrived. Though it was not nearly as developed, naturally. Enough with the shock, I am not here to flex my power, but to gauge and guide yours. Show me something." His words were soft, yet again Jayce felt the demand.

*Next to a planet, you have nothing.*

The voice in her head cried. She really couldn't even argue. What could she do that would impress him?

*Why do I want to impress him?*

Deciding she couldn't match him at all, she focused on what she thought she could do. Raising her hand, time stopped. Pressure closed in around her as she again made a mattress.

"No. I have seen this before," Odin chided.

Despite only starting the creation, Jayce's head began to throb dully. Thinking quickly, she dismantled the bed and began pushing her energy into a small floating sphere, nowhere near the scope of Odin's. Hers, though, was solid blue and about a yard in diameter. As she released time, she felt the trickle of blood fall from her ear. In front of her and the not-god floated a perfect sphere of condensed water. Odin clapped.

"Very impressive, Jayce," he boomed. Despite herself, Jayce warmed at the praise and the sound of her name. "You do not realize why that is impressive, do you?" he asked with a knowing smirk. Jayce looked at the water and shrugged. "Young lady. You have just created a living element. You created a place where beings could survive. Try and create a creature to live in there."

Again, she focused. Raising her hand, the oppressive time-stop hit her. She took a moment to decide what she wanted to do, letting the pressure envelope her. Then she focused on the inside of the sphere and began. A violet, three-dimensional S-shape formed. Going into minute details, she textured the shape with a scale-like exterior. She worked on the face and added small fins to its side before letting time resume. Her creation manifested into a violet seahorse-looking creature. It moved around the small blue sphere gracefully. The beauty of the creature was marred only by the piranha-like teeth at the end of its snout; it chomped hungrily.

"Very..." Odin started but stopped as Jayce again raised her hand.

The pressure returned as quickly as it had fled. She quickly sculpted a few small shrimps and released her hold on time again. At once, her seahorse lunged and caught one of the shrimps. It shook it like a shark until the shrimp stopped moving, then proceeded to chomp and swallow it, nearly whole.

"Impressive, again."

Jayce felt her face warm; she thought at the praise, but when she touched her face, she pulled back a crimson hand. Blood had begun coming from her eyes and nose, and now that she was past the thrill of creation, she felt the throbbing presence of a migraine. She rubbed her temples hard to drive away the pain.

"Shit..." she muttered as the pain seemed to triple.

Odin watched her, again, with his knowing smile.

"You have created a minuscule world with a small ecosystem. You should feel immense pride," he said, rising out of his throne.

Jayce felt the awe in herself that she felt when she saw Odin create a planet.

"I feel pain," Jayce said through gritted teeth. The pain in her head made her want to vomit.

Odin floated to her, and once she saw him, he made a slow move to touch her shoulder. She watched his hand wearily and, to her credit, avoided flinching.

"A sculptor's existence is pain, Jayce. Life in general, I guess, is pain with brief moments of relief. What we must do is become used to it." Jayce looked him in his one blue eye. "Power demands a toll. Only those willing to pay it can defy infinity."

Jayce remembered Noctharim saying that exact line.

"I heard that before."

Odin nodded.

"I saw. But also, I would know anyway. That is one of Noctharim's favorite lines for initiates."

"You and him... what happened?" She tried to distract herself from the agony in her head.

Odin got a tinge of sadness in his one eye.

"That is a long story. I can, however, in our time together, give you the abridged version." He took a deep breath. "Noctharim, Anansi, Jotun, and I were close at one time. We were young and had grand dreams of starting an academy. The issue arose in my youthful desire for power. I wanted to take the most powerful walkers, by force, if necessary, and I did. Anansi, to be fair, I am not sure how he recruited; he has always been a bit cryptic, even for me. Noctharim and Jotun wanted to create a beacon that drew in walkers on their first walk. That is how you and the others ended up there." He paused and gave Jayce time to catch up.

Jayce still looked up at him, something she realized bothered her. She floated up to be eye-level with the not-god, who smiled at the gesture.

"So, we started our own schools as we could not come to an accord. For a few million years, everything was neutral for us. Then I made a grave mistake." His eye grew misty, and he took a slow breath. "I *recruited* Noctharim's son."

"You kidnapped the headmaster's son?" Her eyes were wide with a mixture of awe and fear.

"Yes, that would be the situation. I had planned on teaching him as I want to teach you—"

"He was a sculptor?"

She realized she knew nothing about the professor at that moment.

"Indeed, he was. A gifted one, too. No offense, but he had a much higher initial potential than you."

Jayce felt an unwelcome sting in her chest. Her stare turned into a slight glare.

"Come now, that is not to say you cannot be greater than him or me. But he was raised by a walker. You were not."

"Yeah, no kidding." Jayce felt the snark in her tone.

"Yes, well, I made a very large, even larger than kidnapping him, mistake. I pushed him. I pushed him extremely hard. Moreso than just testing limits, to be honest. I tried to get him to create a planet too early. His heart couldn't...couldn't take it." He choked out the last three words. Jayce didn't know if she should feel pity or appalled. So, she went with both.

"What happened after that?" Jayce asked, trying to keep her voice neutral.

"The rest was a blur. Noctharim sent a walker to kill my darling wife, Frigg. I deleted his home reality. We fought but were too evenly matched for a victor to emerge, and when Jotun joined, I knew I would lose. Anansi erased our identities and created a filler character, and we left."

The information, though Odin said it was a blur, made Jayce open and close her mouth.

*Noctharim killed his wife?*

The thought didn't sit right with her.

"He did?"

"A wife for a son," he said solemnly, shaking his head. "I would like to return to the intended task." His tone left no room for questions or discussions, so she nodded in ascent. "You have shown aptitude for creation. But there are two sides to our gift."

Odin extended his spear, and the pressure mounted again. The constant on and off wore at Jayce's psyche. He pointed his spear to the planet, and with a short thrust, the sphere blinked out of the void. When time returned, Jayce's entire body remained frozen. The sheer level of power, not only to create a planet, but to destroy one as well, was petrifying.

"Destruction," he said quietly. "Now you." Again, trying to leave no room for discussion.

Movement returned to Jayce in the form of shivers. Twitching, she looked from Odin to her creation, eating another shrimp, and back.

"No," she replied in barely a whisper.

Odin's relaxed face became harder.

"Delete the creature," he ordered, with more ice in his voice. Jayce, despite her trembling, met Odin's eye.

"No," she said louder. A small fire lit in Odin's eye.

"I said to destroy it." His voice had become a snarl. Jayce felt the supposed mentor start to turn.

*He's going to hurt you, Jayce. You are going to deserve...*

"I do not deserve it!" Jayce yelled, all semblance of fear leaving her. Electricity shot through her violet eyes as she stared at Odin.

"You want to hurt me? Like every other piece of shit in my life. Try it." She glared with a confidence she had never known.

The smirk Odin gave her in return enraged her.

"If I wanted to hurt you, there is nothing you could do—" Odin started, but was cut off when he had to dodge a violet beam of energy.

He stared bewilderedly at Jayce, who drew back her hand to send another. This time, Odin let it approach. As it was about to hit, time froze, and a hastily constructed wall was built. As time continued, the beam shattered the wall but left Odin unharmed. He raised his spear and sent a thin violet beam of his own. Jayce, in turn, froze time and created an angled piece of metal that deflected the beam as time restarted.

"Argh," Jayce groaned as the fallout hit harder from extended use. She gagged, and a small bit of blood and saliva rolled out of her mouth.

"The toll will always win," Odin said. He put up a hand to forestall Jayce's next attack. "Now is not the time for us. I had not realized you would be so petulant about a creature that hardly exists." He gave her a wide smile and a tip of his hat. "We shall meet again when you mature. But I shall leave you with a test of destruction." With that, Odin flew at Jayce, grabbed her, and took a step.

The hurricane between planes was stronger than ever. Jayce couldn't tell if it was the distance or the vice-like grip dragging her through. Being unready for the walk had made her scream, and as she found out, not having air in her lungs made it painful and even more suffocating than usual.

When her feet hit the ground, she collapsed to her hands and knees, gasping for air.

"This should be a good one. Just know, little Jayce, the all-father is always watching." With Odin's words, she felt his presence leave.

Her eyes blurred with pain, and the migraine threatened to split her skull. The smell, though. The smell was very familiar. Something intimate but foreign. The mixture was rotten eggs and stale laundry. Her body went rigid as her brain placed the smell. And she prayed to whatever would listen that her ears deceived her.

"Ay, Bel, is that you?" The distinct accent of Hector drilled into her skull.

She hyperventilated at the sound of footsteps approaching the room. She furiously rubbed her eyes to clear them. As the door opened, she looked over her shoulder. Her heart stopped. Standing there in boxers and a stained white tank top was Hector. The new and even more familiar smell of tequila and old cigarette smoke assaulted her nostrils. Hector was clearly drunk and had a hard time comprehending what was happening. Jayce wished she could move from this vulnerable position, on all fours in front of this "man".

"Jayce?" Hector asked. "Didn't you leave for college or some bullshit?" His lips twitched. "You missed Daddy, didn't you? Even in a skirt." He licked his lips as he took a slow step forward.

She willed her body to move, tried to send energy to her muscles, but couldn't even muster a twitch. He took another step.

"Daddy did miss you, baby girl." The tone was filled with intent. "Bel doesn't care much for the rough stuff like you did," he finished, standing over her.

"N-No..." she barely mumbled.

Hector's face screwed up.

"You know that word isn't allowed in this room." Before she could understand what was happening, a large hand impacted her cheek, driving her to the ground. A burning white light replaced her vision. She felt a hand wrap around the back of her neck and lift her deftly. She was held in the air for a mere moment before she landed on a familiar mattress.

*No, no, no, no.*

The voice in her head was already screaming in pain. Her brain started to drift into pleasant memories, but another slap fought them away.

"Stop," she said feebly as one of her knees was pinned.

Another slap caused her to fade in and out. Hector's strength and the repeated use of her ability had her nearly motionless. Blinking rapidly to regain vision used all the conscious energy she had. The bed sagged between her legs.

"No harm will come to you while I am around," Jotun's voice called in her head.

"I'm okay..." Jayce heard herself say.

"You will be," Leon replied.

Tears came to Jayce's eyes at the internal words. The sag in the bed grew nearer.

"Damn, bestie." Zynka laughed.

"If you hurt her, I'd have to stab you." Cali's playful voice called out, even in her head, it sounded like a threat.

"I-I think I love you, Jayce." Erin's whisper kissed her ears.

"I know I love you...babe," she heard herself say.

She gave a faint smile at the memories as Hector pulled up her skirt.

"Tell Daddy how much you missed me," he said, his greedy lust taking over completely.

"Fuck you!" Her words were barely audible. Her vision came back vividly as she drank in the rage of this asshole.

"What did you say, you little bitch?"

Fury took over lust.

She had never dared to speak out even slightly before, and his face was glorious for her.

"Fuck you!" she yelled as a surge of energy expelled itself from her, throwing him against the far wall with a thud.

He rolled onto the ground and started to get up. Still slightly groggy, Jayce rolled from the bed, landing on her feet. She wavered as the exhaustion from the day threatened to fully take over.

"I'm gonna kill you, bitch," Hector snarled as he got to his feet.

"No, you aren't. Nobody will. What you are gonna do is regret." With those words, Jayce raised her hand and once more time stopped.

"Feel what you made me and all the others feel," she said, and time resumed.

Hector took a step forward but stopped dead as his eyes bulged. His dark skin took on the yellow-purple of fresh and fading bruises. He choked as a large red handprint appeared on his throat. Jayce looked on with a smile as she tried to stay standing. He clutched at the invisible choking hand and turned. Hearing a whip crack that wasn't there, dozens of slashes and welts blossomed on Hector's back, ripping his tank top.

"This, this is what you did to me," Jayce spat. Hector fell to his knees, and blood poured out of the leg of his boxers. "How does it feel, you piece of dog shit?" Jayce yelled, taking a hesitant step towards him.

A struggling cry left his mouth. A cry she had cried on so many nights.

"Please...make it stop," Hector pleaded as he fell and rolled to his back, staring up at her.

"How many times? How many times did I beg you to stop?"

When he didn't answer, she sent a small violet beam that burned a hole in his kneecap and all the way out the back of his leg. His scream was earth-shattering. It hit something inside her. Something that was fighting to be heard.

*Stop. You're better than this.*

"He deserves it!" Jayce yelled, enraged by her own voice.

*But you don't.*

Three words. Three words she had needed to hear.

She looked at Hector, raised her hand, and stopped time one last time.

"Just die already."

The last thing Jayce felt before she fell in a heap onto Hector's corpse was a tug of energy at her chest.

And the world went black.

# CHAPTER THIRTY-THREE

J ayce could sense but not feel. See, but only nothingness. The sound of her heart hammering like a slow rhythmic drumbeat was the only noise. There was no smell, no taste, just a vast emptiness.

*If this is death, it is peaceful.*

Though she might be dead, an overwhelming sense of relief spread through her consciousness. Floating through an abyss that both existed and didn't was more comfortable than she could have ever believed. She was sorry that she wouldn't see the group again, but that was more of a fleeting thought. Instinctively, she knew pain did not exist here. No emotion either. Just being.

*You did good. I'm proud of me.*

Erin lay on the infirmary bed holding her little gothic love. Huginn had brought Jayce back to the Academy more dead than alive. Her heart had stopped when she killed Hector, Huginn had said. She watched as the raven had held his small head against hers, watched as some of his black feathers faded into grey. The heart monitor beeped slowly five times before the rhythm became steady. Now the same raven was curled up on Jayce's other side.

"I'm sorry, babe. I know you said you didn't want to share a bed," Erin choked out as she squeezed her. Not even a twitch came from Jayce.

"I-I will not be able to save her like this many times. That is how my brother ended up in the fate he now has," he said in a strained and raspy voice.

Erin looked at him through tear-filled eyes.

"Thank you...thank you," she replied, scratching his head, which elicited a coo.

Erin didn't know a raven could look embarrassed, but this one definitely did. She smiled again.


"Fingers, fingers, making more fingers," Cali caroled as she melted some metal together. She looked at the plain cybernetic fingers she had made.

"Boring." She shredded the metal with her green energy and thought. "Let's see. Left pinky is a flame thrower. Left ring finger has mace; I don't know why, whatever. Oh!" She got her feral grin. "Pistol, pistol, index finger's a pistol," she sing songed. Putting together the right components, she shoved the screw-like base into her hand with a yelp. "Freaking stupid, dadgum pain is bullmess!" she hollered, trying to stay PG like Erin had wanted.

Finding out what Erin had gone through was even more painful than the guilt of causing her parents' deaths. So, she had decided to be a little less of a punk; a little, like a very small amount, less. Cackling as she decided on her middle finger, she began working again.

Her holo vibrated. She checked it, smiled, and screwed in the middle finger. Cursed. Then warped.

"I don't think it was malicious at all, really," Leon said to Azreal, who had her head on his chest. She rolled to where her chin was on his pec and blew the hair out of her face.

"Malicious or not, he did challenge you. From what I know of Alaric, he is not one to be trifled with," she said seriously, her yellow eyes boring into his. Leon could see worry, but it was mixed with something unreadable to him.

"Well, at least he's giving me time to train, yeah?" He tried to disarm her with what he hoped was a dazzling smile. She gave him a knowing look, but a slight purr undercut any false perturbations.

"You know, that smile would work so much better without that bushy beard and mustache blocking it," she said as she pushed some of her siren ability into him.

He just smiled.

"Oh, I shall fall on bended knee and remove it at once, my one and only." He laughed but stopped when he saw her eyes shimmer. "Hey, what's up?" He rubbed a thumb over her porcelain white skin.

"Will...*Can* I be your one and only? For now, or as long as you would like?" The normal coolness was replaced by a near plea. His only answer was pulling her head deeper onto his chest.

His holo buzzed a few moments later.

"It's time."


"Father, I have passed the initiate exam and will be a fully-fledged student!" Zynka said into her holo.

"Very good, Zema. Your mother Hilda and I are quite proud. Sorry, I must get off... lots to do." The connection was cut before she could respond.

"Hilda was your first wife," Zynka said, lying back on her bed and staring at a picture of her and Cali from the lake. Erin had taken it when Leon and Cali were playing king of the hill, and she was the reluctant hill.

"That guy sounds like a dick," Cali's exuberant voice called out. Without looking at her, Zynka smiled.

"Lots of kids, ya know?" Zynka tried to sound unbothered. She let out a small trumpet of shock as Cali landed on her chest.

"I will one hundred percent kill them all for you," Cali said with a grin that said, "I'm playing, but I totally will."

Zynka adored that face. She gave Cali a light bump on the head with her trunk.

"Nah, it's alright. Can't let it get you down," Zynka said softly and then saw Cali's face take on a screwed-up, introspective expression.

"You know we see you, right? I know things have been crazy, but you have been a freaking bastion for all of us. Once us goofy, squishy humans get our feet on the ground, I think it'll be easier to see." Cali gave Zynka one of the softest smiles she had ever seen on that little face.

"Shoot!" Cali yelped. Zynka involuntarily trumpeted. "It's time."


Still floating in an empty abyss, Jayce had given up on thought and decided just to be. She had relaxed every sense that she still had control of. Drifting without being. Calm without feeling.

"It does not have to be over," a voice called through her consciousness. "It is your choice. But I must know what to tell Noctharim, as I am the only one able to consent for you." Huginn's voice came in like it was underwater, hundreds of yards away. Thinking it might just be a glitch, she continued to just be.

"I understand the appeal here. No pain. No worry. No emotion. But that is a double-edged sword. With no pain, there is no pleasure. With no worry, there is no relief. With no emotion, there is no love. And love is something you have in spades on the outside."

"Erin." The thought more than the word travelled through her mind.

"Yes, Erin. The others as well. But staying in here is your choice. It would be a peaceful eternity."

Images flashed through the abyss. The horror of the Murdenex. The joy of Erin's first forehead kiss. The sickly, gaudy mansion of Baron Kingsley. Erin holding her for the first time. The fight with the elves. Her first true kiss. The memories kept playing. The good outfighting the bad in each scenario.

"Yes," she thought.


"What happened?" Erin asked as Huginn's body reanimated.

Instead of answering her, he turned to Noctharim.

"Do it. She is ready to come back," he told the headmaster.

"Know that when I rouse her, pain will hit her," the headmaster said as he concentrated on summoning a large violet syringe.

"I know. I'm here for her," Erin replied.

She placed a hand on Jayce's small shoulder and searched for where the pain would be. The syringe melted into her temple with a squelch. Erin found the pain as soon as the syringe was gone. It was in her head, and there was a lot of it. She took it into herself. It went from a dull ache to a headache, to the beginnings of a migraine when a hand lay on hers.

"H-Hey...That's mine," Jayce croaked. "Thank you," she finished, squeezing Erin's hand.

Her head still throbbed, but it wasn't as overwhelming as it could have been. She looked around the room with squinted eyes. Leon gave her a goofy smile. Azreal nodded. Zynka and Cali gave four thumbs-ups together. Jotun was in the back, towering over the group; he gave her his lopsided grin, his ground-down canine still showing off. Noctharim was doing slow laps around the room, and Huginn was nuzzled into her free hand.

"Thank you. Thank all of you. Y'all saved me." She tried to smile, but pain reminded her to lie still.

"I would say that is a successful initiate week, wouldn't you, my dear Jotun?" Noctharim chirped. The troll grunted in what was either amusement or exasperation.

"Well now, are you all ready to see infinity?"

## EPILOGUE

Anansi stared at his old school from a distance and smiled. Much had changed since he departed all those years ago. What was once a few hundred large stick huts was now a sprawling mega city. The warm, red sun sparkled off the windows like glistening diamonds. He walked down a paved road towards the city, whistling "Three Little Birds"; his pincers only slightly distorting his smile. He passed shops and bakeries. He paused as he saw a patron in one of the shops exchanging coins for the bread.

"Wat be dis now?" he asked, moving closer to the window.

As the patron, a ram-headed man in a hooded sweatshirt that read "Osebo University" turned to leave, Anansi stopped him.

"Mi sorey mi fren, wat be on da coins des days?" he asked; the ram looked at him, and his eyes went wide. The former patron dropped to all fours and bolted away. "De ell was dat? Mi don't tink me smell," he said, sniffing one of his six armpits. "Okay, it not be great."

Bending down, he picked up one of the coins; on the back was the image of the old Academy; on the other side he saw what at first glance looked plain and flat, but as he focused, all eight of his eyes looked at what was an unrealistically beautiful woman. He dropped the coin.

"Moatia," he said with a hiss, his pincers clacking.

It had been over a billion years since he checked on his old place. Things like this got lost in eternity, but Moatia being on a coin, when she should still be held under lock and key, pissed him off.

"I told Osebo not to be trustin' her," he muttered.

He continued towards where the old school had been. The citizens of his old world were mainly humanoid animals. He passed chickens and laughed at a cartoon he enjoyed on Earth.

"Boy, I say, boy." He laughed as the chicken strut across the road.

"So, he be crossin' due to da Anansi." Anansi laughed.

He passed a rhino in a vaguely policeman-looking uniform talking to the ram that had run from him. The ram pointed directly at him, and the rhino walked his way.

"Wat be da problem?" Anansi asked.

"Anansi? *The* Anansi?" the rhino asked gruffly.

Every part of Anansi told him to lie, except the part controlling his mouth.

"I be de one, de only Anansi, yes." As he said it, he felt his ability to plane walk get blocked.

His eyes flashed with the fear of a caged animal for an instant before the rhino shoved a needle in his chest.

"Dis can't...dis can...dis..." he mumbled as he faded out.

"I told you he was too stupid or arrogant to stay away," a harsh voice hissed.

Anansi came to on the ground, with chains locking his six arms together, a chain holding each foot to the ground, and, to his sheer terror, a collar around his neck. He thrashed on the floor, the chains digging into his slightly armored flesh.

"Stop moving, Nansi. You won't break them. Much like I couldn't break the palm branch," a voice hissed.

Anansi stopped struggling at hearing the voice.

"Onini? Mi jus saw you in mi trial."

A large green and brown, molted skin, python slithered in front of him.

"I will assume I was doing your bidding?" Onini hissed.

"Well...ya okay, dat be tru," Anansi admitted. "So, wat be dis?"

"Wat be dis? Dis be retribution," a small, feminine voice answered.

Anansi's blood ran cold.

"Ah, quite a recognizable voice, no?" The voice came from a figure stepping out of the shadows in front of Anansi. The tall male figure was a bipedal leopard in a tan, linen-like suit.

"Osebo. I should hav known not to be leavin' ya in charge." Anansi spat at the leopard's feet. "Yu be da backstabbin' kind."

"Backstabbing?" Osebo roared with laughter. "I would have stabbed you in the face from the moment you dangled me from a tree."

"So, we got de Onini, de Osebo, and de...udder one. Where be da wasp man?"

For the briefest moment, Anansi caught a glimpse of a gorgeous woman's face. Her eyes were such a deep brown, they were almost black; her skin was like polished ebony under the kiss of moonlight. Her sharp features faded as quickly as they arrived.

*Moatia...*

"Now that you are back, you can take us to Mmboro," she said.


Artemis had returned to Mars to watch the other trials before returning to Troy. Seeing Alaric's trial, she knew there would be a war in the future and she would have to decide if she would have Achilles pick a side or not. Watching Anansi's trial, she had to smile. The trickster was an asshole, but if he cared for something, he would do what was right. The only problem was that what he cared for was a moving target.

"You rat bastard," was all she could say as Jayce's trial finale came up.

She knew Odin was a man of questionable character. Hell,

she had seen him delete universes. But this was personal; intimate in a way that made her skin crawl. She was about to go to Aetherion to check on the poor girl when she got a ping. Long ago, she had put tracers on the other three watchers in case they ever ran into problems and she couldn't see them quickly enough. The ping meant the power had run out. Which was a huge problem as it ran on the occupant's energy.

"Anansi." Flooding energy to her eyes, her vision pierced through the void. She saw Anansi laying on a floor in chains.

"Now that you are back, you can take us to Mmboro," a feminine voice said.

"Shit."




*IS IT EVER TRULY*
**THE END?**